THE ___ ___ A HUNGRY GHOST

Life, Listening and a Headful of Music

Duncan Marshall

@iamselfpub
www.iamselfpublishing.com

In Buddhism and traditional religions across south-east Asia, there are restless spirits that wander the earth, consumed by cravings they can never satisfy: hungry ghosts.

Just after 2000, the German post-rock/electronic trio To Rococo Rot released an album called *Music Is A Hungry Ghost*.

The title of this book offers another take on that idea: it's actually the ear that is a hungry ghost, consumed by constant craving and a boundless appetite for sound, speech and music.

CONTENTS

INTRODUCTION
ONCE IN A LIFETIME

I've got a headful of music. It's taken a lifetime to accumulate, and I suppose it always will.

As a period in which to achieve something, anything, or even nothing, a lifetime used to seem like a long time. However, I've come to realise it's not as long as I thought, and being more than halfway through my own, I can't help thinking how strange it feels to be me, here, now, with this headful of music that keeps on expanding.

Over the years, I feel I've absorbed music like an enchanted sponge that's constantly grown, soaking up more and more of the stuff until it contains a whole ocean. And still there's more out there for my curious, greedy, promiscuous ears to take in. It started accumulating drop by drop in the early 1960s, swelling from puddle to pool to lake to sea throughout the 1970s and beyond, with the jaunty insistence of 'Run Rabbit Run' by Flanagan and Allen somewhere near the very beginning, emerging from a dark wooden sideboard thing known as a radiogram and sounding sort of giddy and exciting. The Beatles were there somewhere at the start as well, along with Rolf Harris and the Dave Clarke Five.

But a headful of music is more than just an accumulation of tunes, and more than just a very long list – even one that, if unscrolled, would reach the horizon. It's also a private world – my story so far and its great big messy soundtrack hidden away between my ears. And if you're someone like me there's a lot of pleasure to be had in such a vast, immersive soundworld, diving and drifting; collecting, comparing and cataloguing; creating some kind of meaningful compilation that might make sense of it all, and of me, an ocean in a glass. Whatever I decide on will involve more music than I have

1

now, because a headful of music isn't the same as a head full: there's always room for more songs, more albums, more bands, more musicians, more music.

Having accumulated a headful of tunes, I suppose I'm now setting out on an aquatic voyage of discovery that's also a holiday, to explore and enjoy some of what's out there, or in here. What this book is *not* is a definitive, all-encompassing, objective or fair-minded account of anything. After all, it's my voyage, it's my ocean, my soundworld, and my headful of music. I'm the one who's spent a lifetime creating and inhabiting it, accumulating and absorbing, accruing and accreting in states of mind ranging from despair to euphoria, also taking in excitement, glee, yearning, a need to belong, a need to be different, disappointment, shock, contempt and an occasional glow of smugness.

Even at my most desperate, pretending I don't have a headful of music never worked, because that's like trying to deal with something by not thinking about it: don't think about polar bears; don't think about sex; don't think about music. So you do. It's like trying to ignore an itch – sooner or later you know you'll end up scratching it, because that's what itches are for. It sometimes feels good and it sometimes doesn't, but either way what you get is a brief, comforting rush of relief that's just enough to keep you scratching, and itching.

My headful of music is part of me. I can't not think about it, like I can't help itching and scratching; like I can't help nipping into charity shops 'just to see what's there'; or spontaneously hitting '*buy now* with Amazon 1-Click" last thing at night while turning the computer off. Much of the time, I live immersed in music. Maybe you do too. I wear headphones when I'm on the bus or the train. While cooking or washing up, I slide in a CD, turn the radio on, get the i-Pod going or, more recently, hit Spotify.[1] It's the same when I'm driving, especially on a long journey: maybe a long

---

1 Spotify is a streaming service. Streaming sounds sedate, almost manageable like an irrigation system or turning on a tap: it *actually* feels more like a flood, torrent, tidal wave, downpour or tsunami.

journey like life, because every journey needs a soundtrack and so does every life.

You don't always need an external music source: at the moment, the song playing inside my cranium is 'Once In A Lifetime' by Talking Heads. If you've never heard it before, go and listen to it a few dozen times on the playlist at the end of this chapter, watch the video, then carry on reading.

The words of this song aren't sung – they're declaimed like a sermon, as much rhetoric as they are music or poetry, almost biblical in tone. Quoted in full or laid out on the inner sleeve of the record cover, they resemble a strange new translation of a psalm.

The song opens with a formulaic list of speculations: *And you may find yourself…* repeated four times, evoking a wide range of possibilities and leading inevitably to the fifth line, which asks the climactic question, the one we may all ask ourselves, the one we *must* ask ourselves. After the flourish of a *Well…* and a brief pause for dramatic effect, up it jumps: *how did I get here?*

That's what I ask my self, anyway; perhaps you do something similar, perhaps you don't. I'm not complaining about my situation, just wondering. Because you may end up in a shotgun shack;[2] or far from home; or nomadic and rootless; or living the dream – but you have to ask yourself: *how did I get here?*

Part of one possible answer is in the song's refrain: *letting the days go by* – the passing of time, the unpredictable unfolding of events, the unforeseen consequences of the choices you've made, or the implacable autopilot you find yourself ceding control to. Maybe these things, rather than your plans or dreams or sense of entitlement might be enough to explain it all: your childhood, adolescence, adulthood; family, education, work, relationships, pleasure, joy and sadness.

---

2   For years, I never knew what a shotgun shack was. It's a small narrow house, often built from wood, and latterly used to indicate poverty. One suggested derivation of the name is that such houses are small enough for a shotgun blast fired through the front door to pass cleanly through the house and out of the back door.

All through 'Once In A Lifetime' runs water, oceans and rivers of it. Wherever you strike out for, wherever you wash up; whether you go with the flow, or swim against the tide; whether you let the water hold you up or down, still the days go by, and time passes, same as it ever was.

In the video for the song, singer David Byrne harangues us in his white suit, his funny glasses and his funny haircut. As he gestures frantically, we succumb in a daze to this gorgeous non-tune and urgent non-song, borne on its ecstatic wake to suddenly realise with a jolt something profound, maybe something disturbing. As the repetitions pile up in each verse, it seems like all possible lives are being channelled by this crazed ecstatic with his manic shamanic preaching and his repertoire of tics. From time to time, formulaic questions and insights arise like moments of clarity or confusion on awaking from a dream, beginning with the bewildered 'How did I get here?' and culminating with the anguished 'My God, what have I done?'

Part of one possible answer is, of course, contained in the refrain. Time passes; things change; life can numb you or overwhelm you or pass you by and suddenly, well, here you are. And for as long as the song is playing, wherever, whenever, whoever you might be, its euphoria prevails and the water holds you, same as it ever was.

'Once In A lifetime' was released as a single in 1981 along with its clever, strange video. I'd never heard or seen anything like it, because there hadn't been anything like it. It came from the band's fourth album, *Remain In Light*, co-produced and co-composed by Brian Eno. On first hearing it at Brock's house on his massive stereo, I was stupefied. Brock was a friend who played me some amazing music though a stack of hi-fi components the size of briefcases, connected to speakers the size of suitcases.

Appropriately, we connected through water. After leaving school in 1978, I would regularly walk the half hour or so to Woodchurch Swimming Pool, and while I ploughed up and down doing the breaststroke because it was all I knew, the same blond, long-haired attendant would stroll nonchalantly round the poolside, hands in pockets, seemingly in a world of his own. A few years later at university I got a regular holiday job as an attendant at another swimming pool, and met the same long-haired, nonchalant pool attendant who had worked at Woodchurch. This was Brock. We worked together and became friends; doing late shifts on summer evenings we would climb out of an upstairs window and sit on the flat roof, the better to enjoy our shared sense of humour and Chinese takeaways. It turned out he lived just round the corner from me and his parents were working in Saudi Arabia, so he and his stereo had the house to themselves. This was where I heard *Remain In Light*. At around the same time, three other albums also stupefied me. One was Brock's copy of *The Catherine Wheel* by David Byrne, unearthly music commissioned for a dance project. Another was his *Here Come The Warm Jets*, Brian Eno's first solo work after leaving Roxy Music, an LP that's still strange after all these years. Another was *My Life In The Bush Of Ghosts* by Byrne and Eno, which I took round to Brock's because I took it to the house of everyone I knew who had a record player.

This kind of music was something new and alien, a Byrne-Eno soundworld in which music emerged from layers of swirling, pulsing loops and built into songs and tunes, or 'songs' and 'tunes': a lot of the tracks weren't really songs at all, or consisted of rhythms rather than actual tunes. And over it all were voices that hectored and murmured and chanted about nothing and everything. This music used sampling before samplers, as if calling the technology into existence, assembled by painstakingly slicing and splicing lengths of tape into dozens of continuous loops. Also in there were 'found sounds': recordings off the radio and off obscure LPs. And 'found objects' used as percussion. This all seemed extraordinary to me, and still does.[3]

---

3 For the complete early 80s experience, search online for the extraordinary Channel 4 concert documentary *Once In A Lifetime*. This was when *Remain In Light* and *The Catherine Wheel* were new, TV remotes were new, and rapid channel surfing felt like a psychedelic experience, especially while listening to these LPs with the TV muted.

Looking back, it represented all kinds of change. There was the musical change from the 70s to the 80s as recording techniques, production values and musical style mutated and evolved. There was the transition from analogue to digital, a bridge we have now crossed and that lies in ruins behind us. There was the incursion of music and voices from other cultures, sounds from a different present or near future, stuff I had heard next to nothing of, because it was before what became World Music.

So, how did I get here? In part, by listening to Talking Heads and Brian Eno. Letting the days go by – that happened as well. Largely, I think I got here by listening to, thinking about, talking about, dreaming about, painting pictures of, writing poems about, reading about, collecting and sharing music – in this case, the music of David Byrne, Brian Eno and Robert Fripp, another eccentric futurologist whose own experiments with looped music he called Frippertronics. It was Eno who nudged David Bowie towards what became *Low* and *"Heroes"* and *Lodger*, the so-called Berlin trilogy; it was Eno who produced Talking Heads then worked with David Byrne; Eno who collaborated with Robert Fripp on an extraordinary series of ambient works before ambient had even become a thing. But at the centre of this web of influences, experiments and connections, sensing the vibrations, pulling the strings, and himself pulled about by them, there was Bowie, the Space Oddity, the Spider From Mars, Ziggy Sane, Diamond Dog, Thin White Supercreep, Hunky Lodger, the Man Who Sold The World, the Man Who Fell To Earth.

Looking back at Bowie looking forwards, being the age I am now, I realise that what I'm looking back into is an imagined future that came about because of him. And it feels as though that particular future made of pasts, that past made of futures, is a huge part of our *zeitgeist*, the spirit of our age, especially now that we are unable or unwilling to look forwards any more into the actual future because so many of the things we see there seem too scary or too painful to contemplate.

The first month of the year is named after Janus, the Roman threshold god of transitions, gates, doorways and passages. The Latin for door, *ianua*, is taken from his name, and also gives us the word *janitor*. Janus, the Janitor of the Gods, is traditionally shown with two faces, one looking forward and one looking back. The question is, does he use one face, one pair of eyes, more than the other? Does he spend most of his time looking forward or looking back? And, more importantly, does he have two pairs of ears so he can listen to the future as well as the past? And which does he prefer?

It's now possible to think about all this, in fact it's become necessary, being here, being now. I can look back and at the same time I can look forward; at my parents, and at my children; at Mum and Dad, and at my wife the mum, and at me the dad, and also at my siblings. Somewhere in between, at the gate, in the doorway, on the threshold, there's me, husband, father, brother and son, through everything a collector, collator, cataloguer, curator, and complier of my ongoing oceanic soundtrack. The music is a way of defining myself, of measuring out my life and making sense of it, by compiling a soundtrack for the story I have lived. Not just me as a middle-aged middle-class white heterosexual English male with particular roles and relationships, but as a thinking, feeling, sponge-like entity that is a repository of music – a fan, a collector, a member of the audience, a consumer, a face in the crowd, a listener, a pair of ears.

Considering all of this, it makes perfect sense for 'Once In A Lifetime' to be playing in my head – although it's not just about making sense, is it. When you reflect on your life as you have lived it, you may ask yourself all kinds of questions about the what-ifs; you may feel jolts of insight, surges of joy or regret, and maybe in amongst everything else there's a sense of acceptance. Things might have been different, but they are what they are. As far as I can gather, many of the boys I went to school with seem to have become officers, pilots, scientists, bankers, barristers, doctors and captains of industry. Some of them are dead. Me? I'm a part-time library assistant. I've not had a permanent, full-time job in thirty years, but when I look back, I realise with some surprise that I have at various times done things that include lexicography, adult literacy, pottery, writing, editing and proofreading, FE lecturing, deafblind guiding and communication, metadata creation, van driving and child rearing. And what's more, having spent time as a volunteer in a charity shop that sold books, videos, LPs, CDs, 45s, 78s and cassettes, I can also say I've worked in a record shop.

So here I am. What do I do now? Part of me wants to try and make sense of my life based on a headful of music, and latterly this has come to sound increasingly like a plan. So with this rather vague ambition in mind, a few years ago I did something I'd not done for a while – sent my three siblings Christmas presents. They cost very little and were all the same. I wasn't being mean – we'd previously agreed to withdraw from the joyless tit-for-tat of an annual nine-gift festive exchange (not including partners, offspring and pets). But this was different: although I wanted to give something festive, it was more about sharing than shopping. I wanted to offering a gift of time, because if you're fortunate enough to have the choice, time is more precious than money.

So, with my headful of music and the festive season, I bought and sent my three identical cheap Christmas presents. With each one was an explanatory yuletide message – in summary:

- *This 12-CD case is empty*
- *In the coming year you'll receive a CD a month to fill it*
- *Merry Christmas and Happy New Year.*

After that, I was committed. It might not sound like much but it was quite an undertaking. To complete these gifts, throughout the year I sent out a CD a month in triplicate. By the end of the year I had sent out 12 CDs three times, three lots of 219 songs, or 14 hours of music times three.

It was from my headful of music; it was the gift of time; it was commitment, and maybe it was obsession. But it was also Random: not random – Random. I didn't compile the CDs myself, not completely, because I had Random to help me. Random is my friend, and the more I listen to music now, the more he's my friend (my Random's a he, but yours might not be).

With around 23,000 songs on my i-Pod, Random and I spent that year listening only on shuffle: walking to work at the library; getting the bus home; wandering about the kitchen cooking, drinking and listening on the docking station. Whenever Random played me something I liked, I saved it. Every month from what I'd saved I put together a CD's worth of music. To avoid decisions about sequencing, which can be interesting but also stressful, the songs were ordered alphabetically by title. The average for each CD was 18 songs lasting 70 minutes, though November's CD consisted of a single 60-minute track: 'E2 – E4', an electronic piece by the German musician Manuel Göttsching.

At the end of the year as the project reached its conclusion, my wife thought it would be a nice idea to send an end-of-year CD with some of the Christmas cards. So I looked through what Random and I had collected over the year, and distilled the 12 CDs, 219 songs and 14 hours of music down to a single CD of 23 songs that lasted 75 minutes.

What I now had was a one-disc compilation, based on a twelve-disc compilation, assembled from my music offered up by Random and then chosen by me. It was called *It's All Too Beautiful* and I hoped it was the kind of music people would like, because as well as being about sharing, time, obsession and Random, music is also about the enjoyment of surprise, and the surprise of enjoyment. As it turned out, we got a bit carried away – or maybe it was just me, I'm not sure. Either way, we eventually sent out around 50 copies.

These were the songs that became the essence of that year, as compiled on *It's All Too Beautiful*. The only thing I would change is the first track, which should have been 'Airwaves' by Kraftwerk, from the album *Radio-Activity*:

Playlist 0 – It's All Too Beautiful		
1.	Across The Universe/Airwaves	The Beatles/Kraftwerk	3:48
2.	Another Girl, Another Planet	The Only Ones	3:02
3.	Bohemian Like You	The Dandy Warhols	3:31
4.	Chimes Of Freedom	The Byrds	3:52
5.	City Of New Orleans	Willie Nelson	4:53
6.	Down The Road Apiece	Amos Milburn	2:57
7.	Dreadlocks In Moonlight	Lee Perry	3:47
8.	Hitsville UK	The Clash	4:22
9.	If I Were A Carpenter	Johnny Cash	3:01
10.	Itchycoo Park	The Small Faces	2:51
11.	A Little Bitty Tear	Burl Ives	2:05
12.	Low Rider	War	3:09
13.	Me And Bobby McGee	Grateful Dead	5:42
14.	Mean Woman Blues	Jerry Lee Lewis	2:27
15.	Mystery Train	Elvis Presley	2:29
16.	The Oppressed Song	Bunny Wailer	3:21
17.	Paris, Texas	Ry Cooder	2:54
18.	Ride A White Swan	Marc Bolan and T Rex	2:15
19.	Rocket 88	Jackie Brenston	2:52
20.	Twin Peaks Theme	Angelo Badalamenti	5:07
21.	When We Were Young	The Residents	1:02
22.	Within You Without You	Easy Star All Stars	5:14
23.	Your Cheatin' Heart	Van Morrison	2:32

And you may ask yourself – what kind of person would do this? That, amongst other things, is what this book is about.

Playlist 1 - Once In A Lifetime		
Once In A Lifetime	Talking Heads	*Remain In Light*
The Red House	David Byrne	*The Catherine Wheel*
Needles In The Camel's Eye	Brian Eno	*Here Come the Warm Jets*
The Jezebel Spirit	David Byrne and Brian Eno	*My Life In The Bush Of Ghosts*
Kurt's Rejoinder	Brian Eno	*Before And After Science*
Subterraneans	David Bowie	*Low*
Moss Garden	David Bowie	*"Heroes"*
Fantastic Voyage / Boys Keep Swinging (two versions of the same chord sequence, so in effect just one song)	David Bowie	*Lodger*
"Heroes"	David Bowie	*"Heroes"*
21st Century Schizoid Man	King Crimson	*Radical Action To Unseat The Hold Of Monkey Mind (Live)*

To listen to a playlist, visit Spotify via the QR link, or go to the website www.hungry-ghost.info.

In addition to Spotify links, the website offers photographs, notes and archive material to enhance the reading/listening experience - like a great big gatefold LP cover, only better.

1

THE SOUNDS OF EARTH

On 20 August 1977, something amazing happened. Then, on 5 September, it happened again. On both occasions, a space probe the size of a small car and weighing around 800 kg was propelled into space by a Titan-Centaur rocket. The probes were both called Voyager.

First to go was Voyager 2, then a fortnight later it was the turn of Voyager 1. Between 1979 and 1986, borne on a series of audacious and meticulously planned slingshot trajectories, they swung by the giant planets of the outer solar system – Jupiter, Saturn, Uranus and Neptune, along with their 48 moons. On the way they took a lot of photographs, made a lot of measurements and sent back massive amounts of data, after which they kept on going – and going, and going, and going.

They're still going now, and the distances involved are hard to grasp: by 2012 Voyager 2 had travelled about 15 billion km – 100 times the distance from the Earth to the Sun. Voyager 1 had travelled even further: around 18 billion km or 120 solar journeys. Even so, it's only recently that they have actually left our solar system and passed beyond the vast magnetic field and solar winds of the Sun's influence to enter interstellar space. That's if you consider the Heliopause to be the edge of the solar system: if you think the edge is defined by the limits of the Oort Cloud instead, then there's still another 50,000 sun journeys to go, which is about a light year. The distance covered so far is around 15 light hours.

In a few years, around 2020, after more than four decades of service their batteries will run down and the Voyager twins will become inert 35,000 kmph pieces of space junk. It will be about another 40,000 years before either of them gets within a light year or so of any nearby star, and therefore any nearby planet.

Even if all we were doing with the Voyagers was hurling them out of our solar system into interstellar space to drift forever, that would be quite a feat in itself. Analogists and clarifiers have worked hard on statistics to reinforce this: 65,000 individual parts in each probe, many made up of thousands of smaller components; tape heads that have played back the equivalent of a long movie a day for around 40 years, the tapes travelling the equivalent of coast to coast across America; the accuracy required to contact a Voyager the equivalent of a successful 3,000 km golf putt; its electrical signal reaching Earth billions of times weaker than that in a digital watch.

But there's more to it than that: as well being ingenious, intricate and highly successful machines, the Voyagers are the most distant artefacts from our planet and, by default, messages from humanity to the cosmos. But what kind of message are they? Maybe all they say on our behalf is something as simple as:

Hi.

And perhaps some or all of the following:

We are

- *Earthlings*
- *scientifically minded*
- *the kind of beings you might want to know*
- *reaching out to the cosmos in peace and friendship*
- *primitive compared to you*
- *too big for our boots*
- *unable to look after our own rubbish.*

Whichever of these messages a Voyager would embody just by being there and being found, assuming it ever was found, you might wonder whether or not some other, more explicit message might be sent on our behalf. And the answer is yes – in a strange, beautiful, moving and perhaps ultimately futile kind of way. Because the answer takes the form of an LP; a golden LP; a cosmically-minded Concept Album. Attached to the side of each Voyager is a gold-plated aluminium cover, inside which is a 16 ⅔ rpm gold-plated copper LP called *The Sounds Of Earth*, along with a metal stylus arm and cartridge to play it, because otherwise how would aliens be able to listen to it.[1]

The LP weighs about 800 g, and the cover and stylus arm together weigh about the same. A standard vinyl LP weighs around 130 g,[2] and a recent LP I bought, *Lucifer In Dub* by Peaking Lights, feels heavy at an audiophile 180 g, though its weight is still less than a quarter of *The Sounds Of Earth*.

As well as being a strange, beautiful, moving and perhaps ultimately futile gesture, sending two complimentary copies of *The Sounds Of Earth* into interstellar space was a hopelessly inefficient way of distributing them to their potential audience, as any record company accountant will tell you. Because in order to be heard, or even potentially heard, each copy of this promotional album has required a postage, packaging and distribution outlay that includes a Voyager, weighing about 1,300 times more than a single golden LP, carried on a Titan-Centaur, weighing about 1.1 million times more.

You might wonder what kind of a species would perform such a whimsical task, and the answer to a large extent is a species that has included the one known as Carl Sagan: variously a scientist, writer, broadcaster, humanist, careerist,

---

1 The questions are many. There's a stylus arm, but no turntable, cables, amplifier or speakers. Perhaps extraterrestrial beings will be able to infer the need for these from the presence of the stylus arm, along with the need for a power supply. Or maybe they'll build a mechanical phonograph, with a crank handle and an amplifying horn. Or maybe they don't have ears.

2 Based on the average weight of three different space-themed LPs: *Doremi Fasol Latido* (Hawkwind); *Motivation Radio* (Steve Hillage); *Apollo: Atmospheres And Soundtracks* (Brian Eno) .

exobiologist,[3] and marijuana enthusiast. Employed as an advisor to NASA, Sagan was associated with the US space programme from its early days. His first message on our behalf was a six-inch by nine-inch gold-coated aluminium plaque attached to the Pioneer 10 space probe in 1972. It showed

- a naked male and female drawn to scale alongside an image of Pioneer 10
- diagrams of a hydrogen atom, intended as a base unit of time and length for those in the know
- a map of 14 local pulsars, intended to show our location
- a diagram of the planets of our solar system all lined up in a row like they never are, with an arrow pointing at Earth as Pioneer's planet of origin.

This was the first intentional, physical message from humanity to be sent Out There, and an identical copy was included with Pioneer 11 in 1973. The hydrogen atom, the pulsar map and the planet images were later reproduced on the Voyagers.[4]

When illustrations of the Pioneer plaque appeared in American newspapers, the human figures had their genitalia blanked out and a debate ensued about the desirability of NASA sending smut into space – and the word 'smut' was actually used. There was also controversy about the relative sizes and postures of the male and female figures, and their apparent racial characteristics. What this suggests is that we were as a species spending a lot of time looking downwards

---

3 A term he coined to refer to the study of life but not as we know it.
4 This might have been the first intentional, physical message, but unintentional messages from TV and radio broadcasts have been radiating outwards from our planet in a massive expanding electromagnetic bubble for decades at the speed of light. In Sagan's 1985 novel *Contact*, the first extraterrestrial message we pick up includes a return transmission of the first terrestrial TV signal considered powerful enough to pass through the ionosphere and enter space: Hitler's opening speech at the 1936 Berlin Olympics.

rather than upwards, or inwards rather than outwards, or into the mirror rather than through any telescopes. The inclusion of the plaque in the first place reinforces this suggestion: Sagan, a passionate believer in the space programme and its scientific and social symbolism, was also a great populariser of science with a canny eye for big gestures. He was given to sweeping statements that could capture the public imagination and keep the space programme lodged in the collective consciousness, which of course also helped validate NASA's budget. Sagan was ideal for such a role, being articulate, media-savvy, telegenic, and soon to become a regular on astronomy enthusiast Johnny Carson's show, as well as producing his own TV series, modestly entitled *Cosmos*.[5]

Following on from Pioneer, Voyager became the next project to require a public-friendly, alien-friendly message, for which NASA approached Sagan at the end of 1976. Upgrading from a plaque to an LP was the idea of Sagan's colleague Frank Drake, who had helped design the Pioneer plaque and was one of the originators of the SETI (Search For Extraterrestrial Intelligence) project. Drake had also headed a team at the Arecibo radio telescope, Puerto Rico, that had in 1974 beamed out the first intentional radio message from us to whoever, aimed at the relatively nearby globular star cluster M13.[6] Drake's other claim to fame is the Drake Equation, formulated to stimulate debate about the likely number of detectable civilisations in the Milky Way. Unhelpfully, its solution can vary from zero to tens of millions.

---

5 Currently 30-odd light years from Earth, though repeats will not have got as far as this.

6 'Relatively nearby' means about 25,000 light years away. 'Message' means a sequence 1,679 binary digits that could in theory be assembled by the recipient into a crude seven-part graphic, assuming they had the necessary technology, could understand the relevant maths and were willing or able to join in with the relevant mind games. Which is quite a set of assumptions.

Once the LP idea had been approved, a core team of six individuals was assembled, along with specialists who could be called on as required. The idea of a small team probably suited NASA as there was next to no funding available, and it probably suited Sagan because the principal four were himself, his wife Linda and two of his friends. One friend was science writer and *Rolling Stone* editor Timothy Ferris and the other was Ferris's wife Anne Druyan. The other two were Frank Drake and another Sagan collaborator, the artist John Lomberg. It was Ferris and Druyan who chose most of the music. Ferris apparently wanted to get John Lennon involved: Lennon was interested but unable to help because, as a tax exile, he needed to stay outside the US. Had it been otherwise, who knows what might have happened. And if you think having only four people involved in the core team would keep things simple, you might like to know that over the course of the project, Sagan and Anne Druyan fell in love, subsequently left their partners and ended up getting married, a bond that lasted until Sagan's death in 1996.

The LP might have been Drake's idea but it was Sagan, the populist, who gave it a cultural context, describing how at the age of five in 1939 he had visited the optimistic, futuristic New York World's Fair, where a time capsule had been buried for recovery 5,000 years later in the year 6939. Along with a wide range of everyday objects and materials, newsreels and microfilm were stored, together with instructions on how to construct a microfilm viewer and movie projector. Sagan was fond of alluding to Assyrian kings such as Ashurbanipal, who in the seventh century BCE accumulated and stored written records to tell future generations of himself and his achievements, in much the same way that other beings might learn of us through Voyager.[7]

---

7 A more cynical or perhaps grounded observer, one who was a kind of AntiSagan, rather than evoking the nostalgic futurism of the World's Fair or the ambitions of Assyrian kings, might shrug their shoulders and direct us to Shelley's difficult, unsettling poem 'Ozymandias' (see appendix one).

So what was on this LP, this 12-inch gold-plated copper disc called *The Sounds Of Earth*? The track listing, if there had been one on the cover, would have included

- 118 photographs and diagrams
- greetings from the US President, Jimmy Carter
- a photographed list of US congressmen
- greetings from the UN Secretary General, Kurt Waldheim[8]
- greetings in 55 different languages, some extinct
- greetings from UN officials[9]
- a minute of whale song
- a 12 ½ minute collage/essay of Earth sounds, natural and human
- 90 minutes of music.

The playback speed of 16 ⅔ rpm – half that of a standard LP – allowed a lot of information to be encoded, including colour images as well as sound, though there was a trade-off in terms of fidelity. But whatever the level of fidelity, a record is no use without a record player, which is why the stylus arm and cartridge were provided. Although there was no track listing on the cover to identify the various sections as music, sound, speech or images, there were diagrammatic operating instructions on the cover. There was no mention of the possible means of operation and amplification, though two of the copied Pioneer images did show where the LP had been made. And electroplated onto the cover was information about when – a two-centimetre area of uranium 238, with a half life of around 4 ½ billion years, whose rate of decay was meant to reveal the length of time since Voyager had been launched into space.

---

8 Another can of worms.
9 Probably the most tellingly anthropocentric spoken message on the disc is from Wallace RT Macaulay on behalf of Nigeria: 'My dear friends in outer space, as you probably know, my country is situated on the west coast of the continent of Africa, a land mass more or less in the shape of a question mark...'

Although it was all assembled by Sagan and his team, NASA retained the final say on what was included. One of the images was to have been a black-and-white photograph of a man and a pregnant woman holding hands, both white, both naked. This was disallowed and so, confusingly, a silhouette of the couple was included instead. There were no penises, breasts or vaginas anywhere in the pictures, and no conflict, disease, pollution, violence, poverty or death because we didn't want to bring our future alien friends down, freak them out or show ourselves in a bad light. And there was no overtly religious material of any kind because of problems over which religions to include and/or omit; and there were no images of artworks because the selection process would have been too fraught given the six-week time period available.[10]

And it very nearly didn't make it. To add a human touch Tim Ferris, inspired by the *Sergeant Pepper* album, had an impromptu message scratched on the run-out area of the record: TO THE MAKERS OF MUSIC – ALL WORLDS, ALL TIMES. When the NASA quality control officer checked the specifications and found that this brief handwritten message was not included, there was much consternation, and a blank disc was nearly sent instead of the non-compliant artefact.

But what did it all mean? Was this ultimate limited-edition cosmic concept album a compromised work, summarising humanity for the benefit of unknown and probably unknowable, possibly non-existent, extraterrestrial beings – but without sex, conflict, disease, pollution, violence, poverty, death, art or religion? Or were the discs a soft-focus compilation, copiously but selectively illustrated and put together by a committee of well-meaning white middle-class liberals just to make humanity feel good about itself?

---

10 However, image 89 does show a bearded man sitting on a tall stool working on a landscape painting while a woman gazes thoughtfully into an open fire. John Lomberg considered sending only images of works of art, but in the end decided to take a more literal approach. It could have been so different.

Did it mean that we, or the NASA committee, had made the LP for whoever or whatever might eventually listen to it, or was it for us, here, now, a naïve, slightly pompous, rather too flattering piece of PR, a self-portrait with all the wrinkles, scars and blemishes photoshopped out, a vanity project, a golden selfie? The question was addressed early on by one of the consultants, BM Oliver of Hewlett-Packard: 'There is only an infinitesimal chance that the plaque [as it was at that time] will ever be seen by a single extraterrestrial, but it will certainly be seen by billions of terrestrials. Its real function, therefore, is to appeal to and expand the human spirit, and to make contact with extraterrestrial intelligence a welcome expectation of mankind.'

It's a gift to the cosmos, and it's also a gift to ourselves; it's a hugely ambitious piece of conceptual art; a dizzying 'what if?' thought experiment; a Big Idea. If you had been involved, how would *you* have summarised human existence on an LP for Them and also for us? And although a project to make and send out a gold-plated space LP with a title like *The Sounds Of Earth* may be derided, thinking about what makes us human and what unites us rather than divides us is an important thing to do. Especially once you've seen images of Earth from space, reminding us how small and fragile we seem from a bit further away, however big and powerful we may think we are in close-up.

What's more, on a personal level I find the music enthusiast in me inevitably drawn to such a noble project, like I was once drawn to the idea of compiling cassettes – for myself, for people I knew and even for people I didn't know. Because deep down in me there is a combination of unseemly (or passionate) enthusiasm for music, together with an extensive (or obsessive) capacity for gathering, categorising and cross-referencing, all of which is unchanging and unchangeable. It's part of who I am and what I am, to the extent that my first proper job was working on a dictionary and now I work in a library.

I used to compile cassettes, and now I compile CDs, like *It's All Too Beautiful*. Compilation is about focus, about liberation through limitation, doing what you can with what you have. The constraints of space and time focus the mind, distilling preferences down to priorities, making sure every piece of music counts: it's in the selection and, just as importantly, it's in the sequencing. Do you go for an arc, a plateau, or segued peaks and troughs?

A CD lasts about seventy-five minutes. Ninety minutes was the limit of a standard cassette, and it was the limit for *Sounds Of Earth*, making this particular LP a sort of uber-C90 compiled for people you didn't know and never would, to be played on a player they had to build themselves. If you're someone like me, what's not to like?

I have no idea how I would have summarised human existence on an LP in 1977, and I'm not sure how I would do it now, but it's something to think about. 1977 was the year of my A-Levels: English Literature, General Studies, French and Spanish. At that time I was also immersed in, and euphorically conflicted by, the breadth and intensity of my musical tastes, which ranged from prog to punk, with the latter generally foregrounded for dramatic effect. As a result of this foregrounding, my personal sounds of Earth would have been from LPs like *Never Mind the Bollocks, Lust For Life, Leave Home, Two Sevens Clash, Low, "Heroes", The Clash, Trans Europe Express, Suicide,* and *Pink Flag.*[11] And something from Hawkwind and Abba – there was always Hawkwind and Abba, and there always will be.

1977 was a time of looking forward, and also of looking back. Looking forward, there were still seven years to go until we found ourselves up against *Nineteen Eighty-four* and could finally measure ourselves against it, something we had been doing ever since the book's publication cast its shadow into the future from 1948. It's clear that political and social upheavals, along with a sense of disillusion, frustration and discontent that punk articulated, convinced

---

11 By the Sex Pistols, Iggy Pop, the Ramones, Culture, David Bowie, David Bowie, the Clash, Kraftwerk, Suicide, and Wire.

a significant minority that it felt like 1984 already, and the future sucked.

And so did the past, because as well as being seven years before 1984, 1977 was also ten years after 1967, a decade on from the Summer Of Love. It seemed the right time for an anniversary, time for a reassessment, time for it all to be weighed in the balance and found wanting. Because how could 1967 not be found wanting? How could people not feel let down, embarrassed or bitter ten years on? Only two years after 1967 came the hopeless infantilism of Woodstock, the mayhem and darkness of Altamont, the darkness and mayhem of the Manson killings, and then the Beatles split up and the sixties were done.[12]

And in 1977 the Stones were still touring, Saturday night fever had become a pandemic, and punks were wearing DESTROY T-shirts which they hadn't even made themselves, so the present sucked as well.

Back then, a decade seemed a long time, and therefore a good reason to examine 1967 from the vantage point of 1977. Especially if you wrote for or read the New Musical Express and wanted to reflect on punks versus hippies, old versus new, and everything else relating to the symbolically loaded transition from sixties LOVE AND PEACE to seventies HATE AND WAR.[13] In fact, those ten years from 1967 to 1977 seemed like a long time because they *were* a long time – about half of rock and roll's lifespan. In those ten years, so much had happened, maybe more than would ever happen musically in any other ten years – it was the journey from *Sergeant Pepper* to *Never Mind The Bollocks*;

---

12 Mind you, that year there was also the first Stooges album, so things weren't all bad.

13 The latter was painted onto their second-hand clothing by the Clash, along with slogans like STEN GUNS IN KNIGHTSBRIDGE, UNDER HEAVY MANNERS and WHITE RIOT, together with dribbles and splatters that may or may not have been a homage to Jackson Pollock. 'Hate And War' was also a track on their first album, as was 'White Riot', which was also their first single. Pithy slogans, catchy titles.

from 'Strawberry Fields' to 'Pretty Vacant'; from 'All You Need Is Love' to 'Anarchy in the UK'.

I'm not sure how I would summarise humanity on an LP then or now, but what Tim Ferris and Anne Druyan went for, with advice, was:

1	Bach's Brandenburg Concerto No 2, first movement	4:40
2	'Puspawarna' (Kinds Of Flowers): Javanese gamelan	4:43
3	'Cengunmé': percussion and flute music from Benin	2:08
4	Mbuti ('pygmy') song from Democratic Republic of Congo	0:56
5	'Barnumbirr' (Morning Star) and 'Moikoi Song': Aboriginal songs from Arnhem Land, Australia	1:26
6	'El Cascabel' (The Rattlesnake): Mexican mariachi	3:14
7	'Johnny B Goode' by Chuck Berry	2:38
8	Men's house song from Papua New Guinea	1:20
9	'Tsuru No Sugomori' (Crane's Nest): Japanese flute music	4:51
10	Bach's Partita No 3 in E Major for Violin	2:55
11	'Queen Of The Night': aria from Mozart's opera 'The Magic Flute'	2:55
12	'Tchakrulo': Georgian choral folk song	2:18
13	Roncadora pipe and drum music from Peru	0:52
14	'Melancholy Blues' by Louis Armstrong and his Hot Seven	3:05
15	'Mugam': Azerbaijan bagpipes	2:30
16	'Sacrificial Dance' from Stravinsky's 'The Rite Of Spring'	4:35
17	Bach's 'The Well-tempered Clavier', Book 2, Prelude and Fugue No 1 in C major	4:48
18	Beethoven's Fifth Symphony, first movement	7:20
19	'Izlel Je Delyo Hagdutin': Bulgarian traditional song	4:59
20	Navajo night chant	0:57

Continued

21	'The Fairie Round': early English music	1:17
22	Panpipe music from the Solomon Islands	1:12
23	Wedding song from Peru	0:38
24	'Liu Shui' (Flowing Streams): Chinese guqin (zither) music	7:37
25	'Jaat Kahan Ho': Indian classical vocal music	3:30
26	'Dark Was The Night, Cold Was The Ground' by Blind Willie Johnson	3:15
27	Cavatina from Beethoven's String Quartet No 13 in B flat	6:37

Twenty-seven tracks. Ninety minutes of music.[14] Two criteria. Firstly, the inclusion of a wide range of cultures. Secondly, only music that had an emotional as well as an intellectual justification. Consultants argued passionately for the pieces they submitted, some of which they had also recorded. One piece, the second track ('Kinds Of Flowers'), was recorded by Voyager music consultant Robert E Brown, who had set up and taught on a ground-breaking World Music Program at Wesleyan University, Connecticut, from 1961, a long time before the term became more widely known. More significantly, over half (fifteen pieces) were submitted by Alan Lomax,[15] who would eventually spend around fifty years documenting folk music around the world, beginning in the American South, working his way outwards in all directions and culminating in the online Global Jukebox project at www.culturalequity.org.[16]

So how are we meant to make sense of this list, these twenty-seven pieces of music, the sounds of Earth? There are three by Bach, two by Beethoven, one by Mozart and one by

---

14 See appendix two for full details.
15 3, 4, 5, 6, 7, 8, 12, 13, 14, 15, 19, 20, 22, 23, 26.
16 Lomax went global in another, unexpected way after recordings from the *Sounds Of The South* CD box set were extensively sampled on Moby's album *Play*.

25

Stravinsky – a total of seven (about a quarter) representing the Western European classical tradition.

Three are by African Americans, all commercial releases; there is one by Native Americans, and none by white Americans (though a country song was originally proposed to represent America, NASA and the folk who actually assembled Voyager). Together with the seven classical pieces and an English instrumental, this leaves just fifteen for anywhere that isn't Western Europe or North America.

There are five from Germany/Austria and four from Eastern Europe, making nine, a third of the total. There are no female composers, and only four identifiable female performances. There are seven pieces from the Americas; three from Australasia; two from Africa. There are six by black people. There are ten by white people. There are – oh, what does it matter: at the end of the day and the end of the galaxy it's still all MOTO (Music Of Terrestrial Origin) – is there any other kind?[17] That might sound simplistic, but perhaps *The Sounds Of Earth* was simplistic as well, and perhaps it needed to be; and anyway the whole point was *not* to include things just because Congressman X or Y liked it or thought it ought to be there. There was no Jewish or Irish music, which upset a number of people; and there was no country music; and on it goes.

Carl Sagan was of the strong opinion that Bach and Beethoven represented the best of the West. He didn't like pop or rock music, but was apparently fond of Bobs Dylan and Marley, although neither made it onto the LP.

---

17 Well, there's MOBO, with its spuriously purist yet at the same time spuriously multi-cultural awards for 'Music Of Black Origin'. MOBO is popular music's most extensive ghetto, containing within its boundaries almost everything apart from perhaps MOIO (Music Of Indie Origin) or maybe MOPO (Music Of Punk Origin) or MOMO (Music Of Metal Origin), in other words the kind of music that's not allowed to be called things like MOWO (…White…) or MOYO (…Yellow…) (or paradoxically MOBO, as in 'Music Of Brown Origin'). However well-meaning, this all takes us back to 'race records' and segregation.

Jefferson Starship made their recorded works available, and were declined. In the end, despite objections from some, a single pop song was allowed, something by the Beatles, the favourite briefly being 'Here Comes The Sun'. However the band's publishing company had a history of making things difficult and time was short, so 'Johnny B Goode' was used instead, which Alan Lomax dismissed as 'adolescent'. And although there was only one rock and roll song, at least it was the essence. Just read the lyrics if you want to know how to tell a story in a loose yet tight string of brilliantly observed details without wasting a word. And while you're reading the lyrics, make sure you listen to the music – it's Chuck Berry's entire career in one song, and most of the Rolling Stones' as well, not to mention all the others.

After the Voyager launch, a joke on the TV show *Saturday Night Live* suggested that sometime in the future a message from space would arrive, and when translated it would read SEND MORE CHUCK BERRY. On the other hand, the biologist Lewis Thomas suggested that the complete works of JS Bach would suffice, though this might be considered boastful. This may or may not be the case, but why was there so much classical music? And why three by Bach and two by Beethoven? This was apparently meant to anticipate the possibility of the record being found by beings without ears, or those whose sense of hearing was different from ours, or who had no idea of music. According to Tim Ferris, such beings could make sense of it using mathematics, 'the universal language that music is sometimes said to be'. He goes on to explain, 'they'd look for symmetries – repetitions, inversions, mirror images, and other self-similarities – within or between compositions. We sought to facilitate the process by proffering Bach, whose works are full of symmetry, and Beethoven, who championed Bach's music and borrowed from it.'

Although I knew nothing about the Voyager project in 1977, my head was still out there in space. I couldn't get enough science fiction – books, TV, movies, comics, posters, music. I had bookshelves of paperbacks, scores of Michael Moorcock interspersed with JG Ballard, Frank Herbert, Philip K Dick, Robert Heinlein and other random pulp sci-fi. There I was, taking my A-Levels, my hobbies after music being swotting, sneering and science fiction, which fed back into the music again, via the likes of Gong and Hawkwind. I might have foregrounded other music for effect in 1977, but I loved these two, who were actually quite similar bands: Gong have been described as a more feminine Hawkwind, which makes sense. They were a jazzy space-rock psychedelic coalition of freaks, and included guitarist Steve Hillage and his partner Miquette Giraudy, remarkable not just for being a female band member, rare enough back then,[18] but also because she played synthesisers. Not only that, she played them without using a keyboard. The trancey, spacey burbling and bubbling and whooshing in Gong music came from synthesisers activated by the twiddling of knobs rather than the tickling of ivories, and the same is true of Hawkwind, the other cosmically minded band of the early seventies that colonised my consciousness with their bleepy, swooshy, outer-space strangeness and sci-fi white noise thrash.

This was cosmic music, space music, sci-fi music made by knob twiddlers rather than ivory ticklers. Knob twiddlers don't need to actually twiddle knobs, they just need to be more interested in knobs than notes, in experiment rather than exhibition, in messing about and making noises as opposed to all the virtuosic ego-jamming, soloing and posturing that characterises ivory ticklers. Gong twiddled knobs, Hawkwind twiddled knobs, Tangerine Dream twiddled knobs. Tangerine Dream may have had lots of keyboards, but the sounds that made them famous were really the sounds of knobs being twiddled, buttons being pushed and switches being flicked. They were one of the first bands to use sequencers on their early Virgin albums *Phaedra* and

---

18 How many pre-punk females can you think of who weren't rock-chick singers, fey singer-songwriters or decorative backing vocalists?

Rubycon, before which they had been travelling the galaxy visiting desolate space stations and swirling interstellar gas clouds on albums like *Zeit* and *Atem*.

That was a time when synthesisers and sequencers were huge, exotic, esoteric and also a bit unpredictable, just like the music. So the sound of an ascending scale you hear at one point on *Phaedra* is actually the sound of the synth unit being tuned during recording, which was left in rather than being expensively and time-consumingly overdubbed. That type of chance event could never have informed works by progmeisters like Keith Emerson or Rick Wakeman, the two ivory ticklers I most admired in my early teens. Proper Musicians. They could solo and noodle and gurn and show off their glittery outfits and split-level open-plan keyboards for hours, and did, but they still always sounded like keyboard players or orchestras rather than, say, neutron stars collapsing or the wind singing through a deserted alien metropolis or crystalline space ships slowly smashing into one another. To sound like a universe coming into being or disintegrating, Tangerine Dream played deep, reverberant, evocative sounds that slowly expanded and evolved to fill the room, the house, the planet, and everywhere beyond. And when knob twiddlers do go fast, they don't sound jazzy, rocky, classical or virtuosic, they sound trancey or minimal or just static, repeating the same thing over and over or varying it slightly. Or they sometimes just wig out and sound like exploding robot orchestras in an obsidian cathedral.

I read books about flying saucers, witchcraft, mythology, pyramids, ley lines, Nazi occultists and extraterrestrials, wanting some or any it to be true, knowing deep down that it probably wasn't. Books like *Chariots Of The Gods?* and *Flying Saucers Have Landed* filled me with yearning, but Voyager's irresistible fusion of cosmic ambition and music, of compilation LP and noble space mission, passed me by – and continued to do so for centuries. I first learned about it through events that took place 294 years after 1977, in the year 2271. This is when the starship *Enterprise* returns from its original five-year mission[19] and undergoes a re-fit. In that same year, a powerful alien force in the form of a massive energy cloud is detected heading towards Earth, destroying everything in its path. Sent to investigate, the *Enterprise* manages to enter the cloud and establish communication, after which it becomes apparent that the cloud is in fact a sentient being, referring to itself as V'ger. Travelling to the cloud's centre, our heroes find V'ger is in fact the space probe Voyager 6. It turns out that after its mysterious disappearance at the end of the 20th century, a badly damaged Voyager 6 had been found and repaired by a race of living machines that had misinterpreted Voyager's original purpose (to gather information and return to Earth). Endowed with almost god-like powers and despatched to search for 'the creator', on its journey home V'ger had gathered so much knowledge that it achieved consciousness. Spock, realising after a mind-meld that what V'ger lacks is human awareness, persuades it to merge with a willing member of the *Enterprise* crew, after which V'ger and the crew member dematerialise into a higher realm of being, Earth is saved and sequels are more or less assured.

These future events reached me in 1979 via *Star Trek: The Motion Picture*. Directed by Robert Wise[20] and appearing a mere two years after the launch of Voyagers 1 and 2 mission, the movie was a brilliantly simple nugget of story encased in a bloated, shapeless mass of over-production, a bit like Voyager 6 in its vast alien cloud. The nugget was derived from the pilot episode for the follow-up TV series *Star Trek: Phase II*, which was abandoned in favour of a movie once the suits had noticed how successful *Star Wars* and *Close Encounters* were. The pilot episode was called *In Thy Image*

---

19 'To seek out new life and new civilisations; to explore strange new worlds; to boldly go where no man has gone before.' 'No man' duly became 'no one', which was more inclusive but for some reason less resounding.

20 *The Day The Earth Stood Still, West Side Story, The Sound Of Music, The Andromeda Strain.*

and the tortuous, labyrinthine process whereby various TV and film projects developed, intertwined and then unravelled over several years also mirrored the complex but ultimately hollow vastness of V'ger with, at its nucleus, a grain of something overworked, confused and in search of meaning.

Despite or even because of all this, the irony of our own space probe Voyager 6, a piece of us sent back in mutated form through a simple yet huge misunderstanding and almost destroying us, seems far cleverer and stranger than any tale of a direct encounter with an alien race. And when we get the Voyager 6 reveal after the interminable journey into the cloud (big green glowing stuff intercut with stilted reaction shots, repeated, with bad sound effects) there's a real thrill at the cleverness of the idea. Unfortunately, what follows once Kirk approaches the probe to rub at the name-plate and reveal V'GER as VOYAGER, is a profound sense of disappointment: it's just a tacky model with a few wires inside, the kind of thing you would have seen in the original TV series. Even worse, the metal plaque glimpsed as Kirk inspects the probe was actually off the LAGEOS geostationary satellite launched in 1974 to measure continental drift. Also designed by Carl Sagan, it's intended to be read 8 million years from now by our future selves and shows the imagined configuration of the continents in our distant past, the way they look now, and their projected layout in the distant future. So what's it doing on Voyager 6? Or is it just me?

Despite such a let-down, the V'ger idea was inspired. So, deciding to find out more I did some research, only to learn there wasn't any more. In fact, there was less: no Voyager 6, apart from in the movie; no Voyager 5 either, and no 4, or 3 – just Voyagers 2 and 1, the identical twins. It was then that I learned about the Golden Disc.

There was another disappointment: in the movie there's no Golden Disc or any equivalent artefact attached to Voyager 6. We are (or I am) left wondering what music from the late 20th century would or should have been included on the next volume of *Now That's What I Call MOTO*. Which begs the question, what would the alien race that found Voyager 6 have made of *MOTO*, and how might the returning V'ger have differed as a result?

You would expect that a selection of music as important as *The Sounds Of Earth* – music that could in theory be heard by entire alien civilisations – might be available on Earth. And if it was free to anyone or anything out there and there's no © or ® or ™ anywhere to stop Them copying it and sharing it, shouldn't we be entitled to the same privileges? After all, whoever happens to own it all in a narrow legalistic sense, it's still *our* music, everyone's, The People's Music, Music Of Terrestrial Origin. Especially when you look upwards rather than downwards and outwards rather than inwards, taking in the bigger picture; and especially if you think of us all down here on this tiny blue dot as a single species, whose music was compiled and shipped out on an LP without our being consulted.[21]

In fact, not even Carl Sagan got a copy of the LP: extra copies were made, but they were distributed to NASA facilities, with one also going to the President. Sagan wrote requesting a copy as a keepsake, but was turned down because of 'concern about the matter of highly valuable mementoes being given to individuals'.

The more I found out about this LP and how rare it was, the more I realised I had to hear it. What NASA's website said at the time was:

> The definitive work about the Voyager record is 'Murmurs Of Earth' ... this book is the story behind the creation of the record ... published in 1978

---

21 Characteristically, Carl Sagan campaigned for years to get a 'family portrait' of our solar system taken by Voyager 1 before it went on its way: NASA didn't see the point, though Sagan's persistence eventually paid off, and thank goodness. Taken in 1990, the 60-image mosaic was the last photographic data received from the Voyagers. It includes the 'Pale Blue Dot' image of a barely visible Earth-pixel, our azure speck of a planet as seen from a distance of 6 bn km. Compare and contrast this with the earlier image of the big blue Earth captured close up during the early Moon missions.

> … reissued in 1992 by Warner News Media with a CD-ROM that replicates the Voyager record. Unfortunately, this book is now out of print, but it is worth the effort to try and find a used copy or browse through a library copy.

So there's the answer, or one answer. Warner Multimedia was somehow able to cut through the corporate copyright issues to obtain all the original images, sounds and songs for the CD-ROM that accompanied its 1992 re-release of the original book, but that was a one-off, and apart from that it had never been available for you, me or anyone else here on Earth. It proved easy to order a second-hand copy of the *Murmurs Of Earth* book for a few dollars. Dating from 1978, it had previously been owned by someone whose name looked like BE Zelley, which I assumed I had misread, but a brief Google check and 28,600 hits for 'Zelley' proved me wrong. NASA describes the book as 'definitive', and it really is, because there's almost nothing else.[22]

The CD-ROM was a lot harder to find. In fact it proved impossible, even after I registered my interest on eBay. You know what it's like. You hear, or maybe just hear about, a song or an album or a book, and you think, I've got to have that, then you discover it's unavailable, incredibly rare or ridiculously expensive. If you know what it's like, you also know how frustrating and time-consuming this kind of activity can become. I spent over a year fiddling about on eBay in search of the Warner CD-ROM, and in that time I ended up buying

- an official NASA Voyager mission sew-on patch
- a series of 60 beautiful 'Saturn Encounter' 35mm slide images from Voyager 2, with printed commentary, manufactured by Finley Holiday Films

---

22 There's a Haynes manual. Related volumes currently include manuals for the USS Enterprise, the Death Star, the Millennium Falcon, the NASA Space Shuttle, the Moon, the International Space Station and Alien Invasions.

- a small plastic self-assembly Voyager model, as sold with the Japanese confectionery company Furuta's 2003 space range of 'Choco-Eggs'
- a full-size replica of the Golden Record cover, laser-etched onto a brass disc, which I later had mounted and framed.

In the meantime, I got even more fed up than I had previously been of the *Star Trek: Voyager* TV series, which was named after the space probe. I also got sick of the sight of smug, prissy Katherine Hepburn clone Captain Janeway.[23] I learned about the Chrysler Voyager MPV (multi-purpose vehicle), and discovered that Voyager Recruitment Software was a leading provider of innovative solutions for the recruitment and employment industry. But still no CD. Then, finally, after about fifteen months I saw a copy on eBay, got all in a sweat and, full of adrenalin, bought it right away for $101 including postage. Well, what else could I do.

I've played it over and over again driving, sitting, lying on the floor, in the kitchen, in the attic, in the car, in the sitting room, sober, drunk. What does it sound like? Strange. Like no compilation I have heard before. Like the ultimate limited-edition cosmic concept album. Like MOTO. Like world music. Like the sounds of Earth.

It opens with an uplifting piece by Bach and closes with one that is almost unbearably sad by Beethoven, and in between are 25 others. The first transition, from Bach's German orchestral music [1] to a Javanese gamelan piece by Mangkunegara IV [2], is very peculiar to my Western Earthling ears. The perhaps too-familiar dizzying precision and dynamism of Bach lets you think you know where you are at all times, though you might not know how you got there or where you're going. On the other hand, the less familiar gamelan (a tuned, usually metal, percussion orchestra), immerses you in a fuzzy, euphoric bath of

---

23 If you were cynical, you might think that she and the rest of the multi-ethnic multi-gender multi-species happy-clappy Voyager crew are an analogue of the LP – nothing too controversial or chal-lenging, just everyone being brave and nice and hoping for the best.

microtonal harmonies that don't sound like harmonies at all, until you've got your ears round them, after which they sound exquisite. This juxtaposition of musics is of course as heard from my personal perspective (there is no aural equivalent of 'perspective') and that of the compilers, part of a musical world view (there is no aural equivalent) that has assumed dominance and become 'normal' and 'natural' on the part of the planet where I live.

This sense of the contrast between West and East is something I still find striking. It was the starting point for the idiosyncratic 1995 book *Ocean Of Sound* by David Toop, the subtitle of which is 'aether talk, ambient sound and imaginary worlds'. One of the beginnings for Toop's meandering story is the occasion on which French composer Claude Debussy first heard Javanese gamelan music at the Paris Exposition Universelle of 1889, after which he began working on a new kind of immersive, nonlinear, impressionistic music. Appropriately, there is a 32-track double CD to accompany Toop's book, which takes in dub, ambient, classical, pop, jazz, improvised and experimental music as well as field recordings.[24] Like the Voyager CD, it's strange: like no compilation I have heard before; like the ultimate limited-edition cosmic concept album. And like the Voyager CD, it's no longer available.

If Debussy's reaction to gamelan changed his ears and his music, and if that's my reaction to the juxtaposition of these opening pieces as a Western European Earthling, what would extraterrestrials think? Without a track listing or sleeve notes, or even with one, it's not certain they would know that there are 27 different pieces of music here. Would they even be able to tell the speeches from the sound essay from the tunes? Maybe they would just like the whale song, like the aliens in the fourth Star Trek movie. These questions ask themselves throughout the LP, to all the musics and the programmed continuities and juxtapositions as piece succeeds piece on this flat, circular, gold-plated thought

---

24 See appendix three.

experiment. And on the disc itself, Debussy was squeezed out by the anonymous Azerbaijanis and Peruvians championed by Alan Lomax.

After these two rather formal pieces there are three short recordings from Benin [3], the Democratic Republic of Congo [4] and Australia [5], to give these 'countries' (invisible from space) their most recent English names. If they weren't on *The Sounds Of Earth*, these pieces would perhaps have been considered anthropological documents or 'field recordings' rather than music as such. If you wanted to buy these recordings in a shop or online, where would you have looked? World Music? Surely everything is 'world music': maybe in the groundbreaking Robert E Brown sense, or in the more recent sense that came from eighties marketing, or maybe just in the sense that it's all music of this world, all MOTO. It might not be a good category, but what else can you do with all the music in the world:

- include everyone and everything in one huge alphabetical list from A to Z, organised by name so you'd find someone like the Malian musician Ali Farka Touré by browsing the A section (or maybe the F section, or the T section)?
- organise by country from Afghanistan to Zimbabwe, so you'd find Ali Farka Touré under M for Mali, and dub, ska or ragga under J for Jamaica? And then there are the continents: an *African* or *Indian* section?
- organise by genres or styles, assuming you can identify them and tell your soukous from your samba from your soca?

'World Music' is separated from 'Our Music' for reasons that happen to suit us rather than anyone else. This all might seem a bit obscure, a bit academic, but it matters because it's how we ultimately make sense of music and all the other *stuff* out there in the world: by ordering and classifying, though some of us might spend more time and thought on it than others.

After these three 'ethnic' recordings there's 'El Cascabel' [6] an exhilarating high-speed train-ride of mariachi, followed by 'Johnny B Goode' [7], a pairing that to terrestrial ears is hard to beat, a double A-side single. These two belong together.

Then there are two Pacific solo flute pieces. One is an earthy New Guinea field recording [8], the other is an airy piece played on a shakuhachi [9].

The *shakuhachi* is a Japanese bamboo flute that is played by blowing across the end while being held upright like a recorder. It's made from the lower stem of a species of giant bamboo, and can take a year or so to cure and shape before it's ready to play. The name refers to its traditional length, 1.8 *shaku* (54.54 cm). It has only five holes and is tuned to the minor pentatonic scale.[25]

The instrument was played by the medieval Fuke sect of wandering Zen monks, known as *komuso* (priests of nothingness, monks of emptiness) who used it for practising *suizen* (breathing meditation), each musical phrase being based around a single breath. The monks would often wear a *tengai*, or woven basket that covered the entire head. This headgear and the flute characterised the Fuke sect, and their anonymity sometimes led to the Shogun sending out spies disguised as monks. In response, a few particularly difficult pieces of music developed, and in territory hostile to the Shogun those unable to play these pieces might be considered spies and unmasked, perhaps even killed. Does shakuhachi music sound different if you know this? (East is East, West is West, Earth is Earth, Space is Space. Or, is it more about principles of acoustics?)

Flutes and panpipes are considered to be the earliest and most widespread instruments after voice and percussion, and they feature strongly in this compilation. Although the

---

25 A melancholy five-note scale that can be played using only black piano keys. Pentatonic music was included because it shows an understanding of certain fundamental principles of acoustics.

Bach solo piece [10] is played on the violin, it seems to follow on naturally from the flutes.

Following the orchestral/vocal pyrotechnics of the Magic Flute aria [11] comes a contrasting male choral piece from Russia [12], then panpipes and drum [13], and a Louis Armstrong instrumental [14]. After this there's a drone piece played on bagpipes [15]. The contrast between bagpipe drone and Louis Armstrong is remarkable. The bagpipe is modal – its restless, wandering notes are lodged in a single key, with a drone underpinning it, whereas Louis Armstrong struts and strolls about from key to key, all over the place, playfully bending and stretching the tune in a similar way to Bach.

The contrast between this and the next piece, from 'The Rite of Spring' [16], is remarkable, as is the next transition to the wanderful and wonderful piano of Bach's 'Well-Tempered Clavier' [17], which seems to travel anywhere and everywhere before returning to the start, without ever actually leaving it in the first place.

Aliens wouldn't know, but this is an important piece of music in the Western European canon, because the way it's composed makes it the opposite of the modal bagpipe music. Modal music is often played with a drone accompaniment: everything in one key using a single scale, staying the same even when it changes, which is where its beauty and power lies. You can't deviate too much from the central note because you might move into another key, which would wreck everything, so the drone is there to remind you where you are and where you should stay. If you changed the drone to a different note, the whole mood (or mode) would change, and you'd have a completely different piece of music.

That doesn't happen in 'The Well-Tempered Clavier'. A clavier (keyboard) that's well-tempered is one that has been tempered or tuned in such a way that it's possible to use any note at all as the starting point and then wander up and down the keyboard more or less at will, rather than being confined to a particular mode. To achieve this dynamism, this freedom to roam, a well-tempered keyboard is tuned so that some or all the notes are slightly out of tune which, paradoxically, makes everything sound as though it's more or less in tune. This is a musical equivalent of an optical illusion. Like perspective in painting, it only appears once you've adjusted to it: to ears that aren't used to it, and there are still many in the world, it just sounds wrong. Although keyboards are now tuned in this way and we don't even notice, when first introduced this was a revolutionary idea, one that Bach's 'Well-Tempered Clavier' celebrates in a series of 24 pieces, one for each of the standard major and minor keys.

By contrast, the Stravinsky is the only modernist piece to be included, and feels like the opposite direction to the one Debussy went at around the same time. Modernism was taken to its logical cul-de-sac of a conclusion by the likes of Arnold Schoenberg: the equal tempering and scales we had spent centuries getting used to were stretched and twisted by the challenge of dissonance, recognising no one key and giving equal emphasis to all the notes in the twelve-tone scale (every black and every white key in an octave, rather than the usual eight). 'The Rite Of Spring' is easy listening in comparison to Schoenberg, but it still caused scuffles when first performed in Paris in 1913. And while the audience for Schoenberg might appreciate his intellectual daring, few outside this small group would call it music in the broad sense that most people understand the word: it's perhaps what you might refer to as 'art music' rather than 'folk music'.

There are many systems of tuning, different scales, different ways of measuring the notes between the octaves. The technical details are less important than the fact that other beings might not recognise equally tempered music or modal music; or eight-note octaves, microtonal scales, pentatonic scales or twelve-tone scales or dissonance or any other system we take for granted: it might all sound like squeaky doors, breaking glass and road drills sound to us, rather than being revealing or compelling or moving.

However aliens may perceive unfamiliar configurations of sound, we sometimes have the opposite problem, with being deafened (the aural equivalent of 'blinded') by the familiarity of a piece like Beethoven's Fifth Symphony [18]. The originally daring opening has been used as a morse code signal ('V' for victory) during World War II; incorporated into 'Roll Over Beethoven' by the Electric Light Orchestra (1973);[26] and adapted into 'A Fifth Of Beethoven' by Walter Murphy (1977).[27] Within its opening, you can hear the same note-patterning games that Bach played earlier and Schoenberg played later.

Throughout this listening experience you find yourself constantly flexing your mental listening muscles as you move from the familiar to the unfamiliar. Beethoven is followed by three high-pitched pieces that, although diverse, all run together: Bulgarian choral [19]; falsetto Navajo chant [20]; reedy Elizabethan instrumental [21]; then there are more panpipes [22] that seem to grow out of what came before.

After this, a short unaccompanied wedding chorus sung by a young Peruvian girl, the shortest piece of all [23]. Then a graceful, flowing, shimmering Chinese guqin (zither) solo piece [24], the longest of all. It's longer than the first movement of Beethoven's Fifth or his Cavatina (the only two other pieces longer than five minutes).

The guiqin is a long fretless seven-stringed instrument played across the lap. It's another instrument that uses a pentatonic or five-note scale. The instrument is not loud, and was made to be played in private: usually alone, though sometimes a small number of people might be present either in a quiet room or outdoors in a place of natural beauty. Playing techniques include plucked notes, bent notes, scraped notes and plucked harmonics – this is the only time such sounds are heard on the LP. The techniques used have names such as 'the fading sound of a temple bell', 'dragonflies alighting on water', 'fallen blossom floating downstream' and 'cold ravens picking at snow'. Some include manipulation of

---

26 Originally a hit for Chuck Berry in 1956, but without any actual Beethoven.

27 A disco version.

the strings after notes have faded, in order to incorporate silence and emptiness within the music. 'Flowing Streams' is almost certainly the LP's only example of programmatic music: the title is 'Flowing Streams' and that's what it's meant to sound like, just as Vivaldi's *Four Seasons* is meant to evoke spring, summer, autumn and winter.

The final three pieces fit together as a trio. The sad, haunting vocal raga [25] with tabla and harmonium was apparently one of the few pieces that virtually everyone who was consulted during the compilation process agreed on. After this comes one of the most spooky pieces of music I've ever heard, which seems to emerge from the previous one. It's a wordless slide-guitar blues moan [26], the one used by Ry Cooder in the *Paris, Texas* movie soundtrack that, like Beethoven's fifth symphony, has become so familiar we know it rather than recognise it.

It all ends with another piece by Beethoven [27], the third of three melancholy pieces, and one you can listen to as you picture the Voyagers travelling silently through space, their power supplies getting lower and lower, the amount of information they transmit getting less and less, the instruments gradually shutting down until they stop transmitting altogether, their power supplies fade and die, and they continue unpowered and uncontrolled into the depths of space.

Having written about *Murmurs Of Earth* while listening to it from start to finish time and again, the sequencing has begun to make a kind of sense; pieces seem to merge into and emerge from one another in ways I hadn't originally noticed. Sagan himself said the intention was to avoid establishing any kind of 'Western European ghetto' on the record, so music from different cultures was deliberately juxtaposed. Pieces were also paired because of 'emotional and tone contrast' or 'common solo virtuosity on quite different instruments' or 'similarity of instruments or rhythmic and melodic styles between seemingly disparate cultures.'

Four years after the launch of the Voyagers, on 18 July 1981, Carl Sagan was Roy Plomley's guest on the radio programme *Desert Island Discs*. His eight choices of music were

1	Vangelis
	Symphony To The Powers B
2	Johann Pachelbel
	Canon in D
3	Roy Buchanan
	Fly, Night Bird
4	Dmitri Shostakovich
	Symphony No 11 in G Minor 'The Year 1905'
5	Goro Yamaguchi
	Cranes In Their Nests
6	Vangelis
	Alpha
7	JS Bach
	Partita for Solo Violin No 3 in E Minor
8	Valya Balkanska
	Iziel Je Delyo Hajdutin

Choices 5, 7 and 8 were from the Voyager LP. His favourite piece was 7, the Bach. His chosen book was *The Boy Scout Handbook*, as used by the Boy Scouts of America and a descendant of Baden-Powell's original Scouting for Boys. His luxury item was a reflecting telescope. Sagan clearly believed in the LP: much of it was also used in his *Cosmos* TV series, keeping it in circulation on planet Earth even though most people had no idea about its existence.

Since Carl Sagan was washed up on his desert island and I bought my Warner CDs, it's finally become possible to hear all the Voyager sounds and music and see all the images online, at goldenrecord.org and probably elsewhere. And, unbelievably (or perhaps completely believably), in 2017 on the fortieth anniversary of the Voyagers' launch it became possible to listen to everything on LP for the first time: a triple cosmic concept album on golden yellow vinyl, issued by Ozma Records[28] and comprising

- three translucent gold 140 g vinyl LPs in poly-lined paper sleeves
- three heavyweight record jackets, gold ink on black
- a full-colour 96-page softcover book containing all the images included on the original Voyager golden record; a gallery of images transmitted back from the Voyager probes; and a new essay by Timothy Ferris, producer of the original golden record
- a gold foil print of the Voyager golden record cover, archival paper, 12" x 12"
- a turntable slipmat showing the Voyager trajectories, gold ink on black felt
- a full-colour plastic digital download card for all audio of the Voyager Golden Record (MP3 or FLAC formats)
- a deluxe record box with pull-ribbon, gold ink on black
- a pin badge of the Voyager golden record cover, gold on black.

You might think this is a good way to end the story, with the people's music being shared with the people, and with the music that went into space also going into cyberspace, as well as coming home again on vinyl. It isn't the end, though, because the music we sent out isn't all there is: there's also the music we got back – the music of the cosmos, cosmic music, space music, the music of the spheres.

Although the Voyagers didn't have microphones on board, they did have a number of devices for investigating magnetic fields, charged particles, plasma waves and cosmic rays. We think of space as a vacuum, but that doesn't mean

---

28 Project Ozma was the first SETI experiment, set up by Frank Drake in 1960. Its name is derived from that of Princess Ozma, the ruler of the land of Oz. She appears in all fourteen of L Frank Baum's Oz books apart from the first, which is the one everyone knows from the movie.

there's no sound: in space, sound exists not acoustically but as electromagnetic vibrations, which can be picked up by scientific equipment. The Voyager instruments detected and recorded these vibrations, caused by the interactions of charged particles. Travelling through the solar system, the Voyagers have revealed that every planet and moon has its own distinctive electromagnetic-acoustic signature, and recordings of these acoustic signatures are available in two CD box sets.

Having bought the Voyager badge, slides, toy, LP cover, book, CD-ROMs and LPs, I had to buy the box sets as well. The first one was *Symphonies Of The Planets*, a five-CD set of 'NASA Voyager Recordings', issued by Delta Music and costing a few pounds on e-Bay. The second was *NASA Space Sounds*, issued by the Center For Neuroacoustic Research, and it cost about the same as the original Golden Record CD-ROMs. The Center for Neuroacoustic Research is run by Dr Jeffrey Thompson, a specialist in the therapeutic and healing use of sound.

I don't know what I was expecting – buzzing, crackling, humming, static, whistles and bangs perhaps, but what listening to the *Symphonies Of The Planets* and *NASA Space Sounds* CDs actually did was take me back to the original idea of cosmic music, back to Tangerine Dream and the other German knob twiddlers because, I can't help it, that's what the interactions of charged electromagnetic particles in space sound like: rich, slow, deep, immersive oceanic drones, washes and hums; drifting and ringing and singing; rising and falling, harmonies that blend together in an immense amniotic ocean of music from the cosmos; it's the music of the spheres, because that's where it comes from.

I emailed Jeffrey Thompson via his website (www. neuroacoustic.com) to ask him about these recordings, where they had come from and what he thought they meant. He told me his involvement began in 1989 when he was contacted by the head of science and technology at a US government contractor to NASA and the Jet Propulsion Laboratory (JPL), whom he referred to as 'Raymond'. The contractor was responsible for handling the space sound recordings, which for many years required top secret clearance to access. These sounds from Jupiter, Saturn, Uranus and Neptune were apparently having strange effects on those that listened to them – what Dr Thompson refers to as 'out of body experiences, precognitive dreams, personal epiphanies, spiritual-type experiences.' Once a portion of the sounds had been declassified, 'Raymond' eventually obtained copies of the recordings, which was when he contacted Jeffrey Thompson.

These are some of the questions I asked Dr Thompson, and the answers he gave me.

What was its effect on you?

> The effect of these sounds has been profound both with me and with my patients. In a nutshell: my work with 'primordial sounds' showed that a scientifically accurate reconstruction of the womb's sound environment had deep subconscious visceral responses in patients: deep peace, relaxation, safety and surrender. Many of these [space] sounds had a remarkable similarity to some nature sounds: wind, ocean, etc.

> Recordings of human vocal statements played at different speed showed a ...remarkable property: speeded up three times they sounded like birds, by eight times like crickets and by sixteen times like dolphin chirps. That led me to experiment with nature sounds at different speeds: crickets slowed down sounded like birds, birds slowed down sounded like dolphins and dolphins slowed down sounded like people singing.

> A week before 'Raymond' ...came to my office with these recordings, I had been experimenting with playing Tibetan bowl recordings at different speeds

as well. A 6" bowl slowed to half speed sounds like a bowl twice the diameter (a 12" bowl). Continued halving of the speed gives you the sound of a 2 foot diameter bowl, a 4 foot bowl, 8 foot bowl, 16 foot bowl, 32 foot bowl, etc. The 32 foot bowl harmonics are now slowed to a point where new ones become audible, and these sound a lot like monks chanting.

All of these human voice sounds, nature sounds and bowl sounds sound remarkably similar to the recordings from the Voyager I & II spacecraft of the outer planets: ocean, wind, breathy choirs, monks chanting, crickets, birds, dolphins and whales.

What, if any, are the differences between the 'Symphonies of the Planets' CD set, and your own ' NASA Space Sounds' series?

In 1989 I produced the first five tapes of some of these *NASA Space Sounds*… and a year later five more. Each [was] devoted to sounds from a single planet, moon or rings. The next year, I was contacted by the Laserlite/Delta Music label (that normally produces classical music CDs), who wanted me to make five space sound CDs for their catalog, to be sold in mainstream stores. That became the *Symphonies of the Planets* 5-CD set. These were different insofar as I mixed together some of the sounds I had from various planets and moons to form the series of 'Symphony' pieces.

In what ways, if any, is the material on the various CDs treated, filtered, edited or enhanced to improve the sound quality? Are the recordings in real time, or do they consist of various sound events combined sequentially, layered or whatever?

The sounds on the original series of *NASA Space Sounds* CDs have been pieced together from shorter clips as I got them from NASA. Some sections were as short as 20 seconds long and some, 20 minutes. In addition, in some sections you [could originally] hear the attitude rockets firing to keep Voyager pointed to Earth – these were removed. In addition, I used a new system at the time (the BASE audio 3-D enhancement system) to spatially expand the sounds in 3-D for a more realistic effect.

What do you think is the significance of this material as a whole?

These sounds, to me, seem to be a deeper extension of what I have observed over time with patients (and myself) with the use of womb sound recordings and the voice/nature sound recordings at different speeds. Vocal recordings at different speeds sound like nature sounds. Nature sounds at different speeds cause fantastic results ... and all these sounds sound like the sounds from space: crickets, birds, dolphins, whales, choirs and Tibetan Bowls, etc. It aligns with my view of Carl Jung's idea of the 'Collective Unconscious' where my body knows how to grow me out of two cells and ... is deeply affected by sounds ... [that are] deeply recognizable at an unconscious level. Do the nature sounds disguised awaken a deeper level of the larger unconscious mind recognition ... that designed the planetary eco-system that my body grows out of? And what about these space sounds? Do they tap a solar system level of the larger unconscious mind that knows how to 'grow' a solar system, that earth grows out of that my body grows out of ... and is all deeply familiar at various collective unconscious levels?

To what extent is this material music?

Sound: single frequencies of a certain [number of] cycles per second – or combinations of these frequencies forming harmonics and overtones that give a sound its 'timbre'.

Music: a combining of different notes either together in chords (mathematical relationships that seem pleasing to the ear) and/or as strings of notes played in relation to one another to form a melody.

What music would you personally submit for inclusion on a future Voyager mission?

I would include the classics of the greatest composers (as the Golden Disc already did) and update the list with the most loved newer composers and popular music musicians from around the world – including, perhaps the sounds from space collected from the Voyager missions.

Cosmic music. Space music. The music of the cosmos. That's what our brains tell us it is, so that's what it is.

Playlist 2 - The Sounds Of Earth		
The Passenger	Iggy Pop	*Lust For Life*
Glad To See You Go	Ramones	*Leave Home*
Calling Rasta Far I	Culture	*Two Sevens Clash*
Summer Night City	Abba	
Silver Machine	Hawkwind	
Ghost Rider	Suicide	*Suicide*
Ex Lion Tamer	Wire	*Pink Flag*
El Cascabel	Antonio Maciel and Los Aguilillas with El Mariachi México de Pepe Villa	*The Sounds Of Earth*
Johnny B Goode	Chuck Berry	*The Sounds Of Earth*
Dark Was The Night	Blind Willie Johnson	*The Sounds Of Earth*

To listen to the playlists, visit Spotify using the QR links provided.

Links to every playlist are also at www.hungry-ghost.info, along with photographs and archive material to supplement each chapter and enhance the reading/listening experience, just like a great big gatefold album cover.

2

IN THE WARDROBE OF MY HEAD

In 2002, twenty-five years after the Voyagers had departed, one afternoon I found myself rooting about in a large, shoddy fitted bedroom wardrobe that felt a bit like a box room in the Tardis and a bit like a landfill site on the edge of Narnia.

It started as a way of keeping myself and my two unruly children busy indoors one winter afternoon. For some reason I thought they might be interested in helping me pull out piles of dusty boxes and rummage through remnants of my earlier life. Most of it had been deposited a decade earlier when we moved from Manchester to Glasgow. It was all still there, piled on sagging shelves around and beneath the clothes; scrupulously ignored, and on occasions sneakily augmented.

Opening boxes, what I found included

- a box of reel-to-reel tapes on which were sounds recorded almost 20 years previously: the tearing of aluminium foil, the dropping of marbles into large bottles and so on, accumulated as raw material after attending an evening course on experimental music
- boxes of paperwork going back almost 20 years, accumulated from editing work on various dictionary and thesaurus projects
- boxes of photographs and negatives going back almost 20 years: basically, everything not in the photo albums downstairs

- a large sweet jar full of regimental badges, music badges, brass buttons, keys, coins, chains, motorcycle parts, bullet cartridges and other items including several of my own teeth, going back about 30 years
- boxes of postcards, collected over about 30 years.

When we moved to Glasgow we brought 26 boxes of books with us, and got rid of six before we started to fill our 72 feet of specially made bookshelves. Most of the books were mine, many bought back in the seventies when I was a student, mostly old science fiction or cult/occult paperbacks, mainly bought from K Law's precarious mountain range of a bookstall in the corner of Birkenhead market. K Law's was manned by an agreeably cantankerous old bloke with a bulbous red nose, a small silver Parachute Regiment badge pinned to his cardigan, and a cheery greeting of 'Oh bloody hell, it's you again'. I never found out whether or not he really was K Law but we, Radar and I, named him Klaw. Radar was quite small, quite scruffy and wore glasses. He was known as Radar because everyone watched the TV show *MASH* in which there was a character called Radar O'Reilly who was quite small, quite scruffy and wore glasses. Radar was, I suppose, my friend and musical soul mate, though I would never have dreamed of saying anything like that, because you didn't, and I'm a bit surprised at myself even now. He and his brother had albums by everyone from Kraftwerk, Neu! and Can to Parliament, Tamla Motown, Leon Redbone, the New York Dolls and Captain Beefheart, along with all the usual prog and rock and punk, and a lot of non-usual stuff as well. Between them they had the largest, most eclectic record collection of anyone I knew. Both of them were unkempt and brainy, and lived in a large detached house next to the war memorial along with their sister, whom they hardly ever spoke to, and their parents, whom they hardly ever spoke to. The house was so big and old that in the kitchen was a set of bells designed for summoning the servants, and an Aga, something I had never seen before. A serving hatch allowed tea and coffee to be passed through from the kitchen to the only room we ever used. It looked out over a decaying tennis court and there was a snooker table in the middle; a stereo surrounded by cardboard boxes on a chest of drawers in one corner, and shabby armchairs around the walls. Nobody ever played snooker because the table was always covered in records and record covers that every so often would get matched up and put back in the cardboard boxes next to the record player, allowing the process of entropy to begin all over again.

When I first started going to Klaw's in my early teens I was an avid, precocious and promiscuous reader, and the books were 3p as new, 2p otherwise. Prices did go up in later years, all the way to 10p and 5p. I think the book I most regret not buying is *The Velvet Underground* by Michael Leigh. This was an exposé of the New York sex industry and the book from which the band got their name, apparently after someone found a copy in the street. On the cover were pictures of a whip, a key, a mask, and a lace-up boot with a heel so high it made the wearer's foot look like a pig's trotter. Despite considering myself quite worldly, I was baffled by this apparel. But I did know from a literary point of view that the terms 'masochism' and 'sadism' came from the surnames of noted pervs Leopold von Sacher-Masoch and the Marquis de Sade, respective authors of *Venus In Furs* and *120 Days Of Sodom*. I had read neither, though I did get a copy of *Venus In Furs* from Klaw's which I soon abandoned, finding it baffling and unreadable. This was around the time I was first getting to know the Velvet Underground at Radar's, but before I realised that their music was among the greatest of the twentieth century.

A book I did buy was *Generation X*, which had the byline *today's generation talking about itself, talking about Education, Marriage, Money, Pops, Politics, Parents, Drugs, God, Sex, Class, Colour, Kinks, and Living for Kicks*. 'Today's generation' was young people in the early sixties: the book was published in 1964, the year of Beatlemania and now over half a century ago.

It was a racy, quite shocking and still contemporary mixture of British journalism, newspaper articles and interviews. Like *The Velvet Underground*, it was a book that a band got their name from, apparently after Tony James found a copy in Mrs Broad's bookcase. Tony James was Generation X's guitarist, and Mrs Broad was singer Billy Idol's mum. He had previously been William Michael Albert Broad, but probably wouldn't have become as famous if he'd kept this name. I know it's not much of a band/book comparison, *The Velvet Underground* and *Generation X*, but it's the best I can do.

For a number of years, every time I bought a book I would write my name in the front, followed by the date, and from this I know that I bought *Generation X* on Thursday 7 June 1979, probably after signing on. Unlike *The Velvet Underground* and the Velvet Underground, the book is much more interesting than the band. It came about because a Woman's Own journalist called Jane Deverson was sent out to speak to the youth of Britain and write a feature on why the nation should be proud of them. When she handed in the finished piece, her editor refused to print it because it said teenagers slept together before they got married, didn't believe in God, didn't like the Queen and didn't respect their parents. Deverson subsequently met up with Charles Hamblett, a Hollywood-based journalist who had written about Marlon Brando and James Dean and was an admirer of Beat culture; he came up with the name 'Generation X' and together they turned the material into a book. The 'X' was meant to suggest an unknown quantity, as well as something shocking or forbidden. It was an early piece of pop sociology, and became a huge hit; Mick Jagger said he liked it and John Lennon said he wanted to turn it into a musical. You can see why, and goodness knows what he would have done with it.

It's a bizarre and in places compelling read about disaffected, alienated youth, and clashes of culture and morality: in one way, nothing's really changed – since 1979, or since 1964 when the book was published. In the foreword is a passage about the problems faced by the young:

> Thanks to post-war developments in mass-communications … these problems have become more concentrated, are more universally shared and more rapidly absorbed. Things, people, ideas get used up more quickly – yet are cast aside with the same old primal ruthlessness.

It goes on to say:

> This is one of the problems the young must face and conquer: the problem of social and scientific acceleration at the expense of biological time.

That was in 1964, the year the book was published; the year the Beatles went to America; when they were still a real band living in more or less the same world as the rest of us, rather than getting stoned while watching the telly with the sound turned down and the record player turned up. The changes the band and their fans were going through are tellingly revealed during a rambling pseudo-hipster monologue by a 23-year-old David Frost, supposedly typed from the roof of his house in the Canary Islands. Most telling is the divide he perceives between his own insider/London sense of superiority and the outsider/provincial naivety of everyone else, noting that

> …communication between the founder members of Generation X was comparatively difficult at the beginning of the sixties. A group in the south could be completely foreign in dress, language, manners, and crazes to a group in the north.

As evidence of this he offers his 'discovery' of the Beatles in the pre-Cavern days of 1960:

> These lads were so green at the time it just wasn't true. I was embarrassed at using sayings which were

hip on the London scene because if I did I'd have to explain patiently what they meant. And their clothes!

However, he reassures us that

> ...they were more of the bohemian ilk than most young northerners at the time, and their pleasant eccentricity made them acceptable.

At the centre of the book, ideologically as well as from a stationery perspective are four full-page photographs labelled SAVOY, MARGATE, HARROW and YOUTH CLUB. The middle two images juxtapose a ruck of grimacing mods kicking at an unseen body on the beach (MARGATE) with a group of young men in boaters and blazers, complete with pocket handkerchiefs and carnation buttonholes, looking rather pleased with themselves (HARROW).

Although I bought the book fifteen years after it came out, there were uncanny, not to say uncomfortable, parallels with my own situation at the time. Talk about a culture clash. Talk about alienation. Talk about disaffected youth. In the months before I bought *Generation X*, I accepted a place at St John's College, Oxford, to *read* (or *study*, or *do* – they use all three on University Challenge now) English Literature. After years of being told at school that this would be the zenith of my education, here I was, so the only way was down. The trajectory had begun at Oxton College seven years earlier when I passed the entrance exams, thereby obtaining a free place and state support to attend this Victorian single-sex private school; or maybe it was a public school, I'm still not sure. Either way, my conflicted attitudes had me regarding it simultaneously as a kind of fascist mini-state and a secure, even benign environment that allowed sensitive, intellectually precocious and socially awkward adolescents like myself to flourish. It felt at times like a filmic mixture of Harry Potter and Lindsay Anderson's *If...* In the first year, at the age of eleven, all ninety-odd new boys were considered equal and placed randomly in three classes: I Greeks, I Romans and I Trojans. I was in I Trojans. There used to be a I Spartans for boarders until numbers dwindled; by the time I attended there were only thirty or so in the whole school. By the end of the first year, ten boys from each class had been selected on the basis of academic performance in monthly 'mark orders' to enter the elite II Greeks, with everyone going into II Trojans and II Romans. Selected for II Greeks, I duly proceeded onward and upward through Junior School and Big School, O-Levels, A-Levels and Schols.

Radar and I hated Oxford from the start, me from before I even got there. We both left after a term, as did our new-found pals Furb and Sten. When I started at Oxton College I felt horribly out of my depth, a feeling that was amplified massively at Oxford. Shortly after arriving there I got talking to someone called Charlie at a sherry-fuelled do of some kind: actually, it was the kind where you get drunk and talk bollocks to people you don't know and are quite intimidated by, in the hope that if you talk enough bollocks you won't get found out. Suddenly, here we were, being referred to as 'men' in all the official bumf – quite a shock after seven years at a school where you were your surname, and the dress code included hair above ears and shirt collar until the day you left. Hair mattered back then.

I hung around with Charlie for a while out of desperation. He was confidently quiet, he was quietly confident – everything I wasn't. He had floppy blond hair and wore an Indian scarf wound several times around his neck, a collarless granddad shirt, loose linen trousers, leather sandals and no socks. On the walls of his room were large pieces of Asian fabric and there were kidney beans soaking in his sink.

Before coming to Oxford he had worked as a waiter in Paris, then gone to Indonesia. I had worked in a cornflake factory, then hitch-hiked to the Reading Festival and back. I wore a pair of clumpy black work boots that were still encrusted with fragments of cornflake beneath the polish. I had ill-fitting narrow-legged jeans. I had a black British

Rail three-button, double-vented jacket, though because I didn't like the vents I stitched them up. And because the sleeves were too long and the cuffs were edged with leather, I folded them back and fixed them in place with studs. This was my uniform, my non-conformist's security blanket. The walls of my room were covered with posters and flyers and magazine pages, and a selection of photographs from inside *Quadrophenia*, even though I didn't like mods. There was a page from the News of the World about Keith Richards: DRUGGED AND NAKED ON A BED OF FLAMES. There were two posters for the local paper, stolen from newsagent displays: WOMAN HURT AS SINK FALLS OFF LORRY and BABY SAVAGED TO DEATH BY FERRETS. I had a sink in my room but used it for washing my face, occasional shaving and frequent peeing.

When Charlie told me about his travels in the same understated way he spoke about everything, a way that filled me simultaneously with contempt, rage and envy, we were sitting outside a pub and were for some reason sharing our table with a loud dark-haired girl in a hessian poncho and a lot of wooden jewellery. My response to Charlie was probably quite muted. Hers was a shrieky '*Oh riiiight – I just loooove Indonesia*' at which point I clenched my teeth so hard I more or less bit through my beer glass. An alternative way of illustrating my discomfort in this social milieu would be to reveal that when I first met Charlie at the sherry do, after I had been talking bollocks for a few minutes he asked me where I came from and because I didn't think he would have heard of Birkenhead, I said Liverpool, to which he replied, 'Oh, I *love* the northern accent'. I don't think I was quite ready for Oxford: the next year I went to Sheffield to try again, and Radar went to Manchester. This time we both stayed.

ANYWAY there we were, the children and me, clambering about in the Tardis landfill wardrobe, humping boxes back and forth, with me curious and them initially curious then bored then irritable as I persisted with my adventure. In amongst everything else, I uncovered a dusty grey box file that had lain untouched for so long I literally had to blow the dust off it before lifting the lid. Inside was a tiny hoard of vaguely remembered artefacts, accumulated as a teenager by someone who was me and yet not me. These included

- a Royal Mint commemorative edition of pre-decimal coinage in a vacuum-sealed plastic case
- several first-day-cover issues of commemorative stamps
- school photographs, as old as primary school, as recent as sixth form
- psychedelic drawings and obscene photocopy collages from school and university
- a signed copy of a poem about Sid Vicious, as read out by 'punk poet' Patrik Fitzgerald (and written down by me) sometime in late 1978 at the Oranges and Lemons, our favourite pub in Oxford, haunt of local punks, skinheads, hippies and the like. I can't remember how I accomplished this feat of transcription, but I know I got Patrik to sign his name in a notebook, after which I copied out the poem onto the signed page.

> goodbye Sidney Vee
> cos I know they're going to get you now
> he's been a silly boy
> one too many times this time
> and now he's in the papers
> on the tips of all the tongues
> known by all the pensioners
> and all the stupid old bags
> who talk to themselves on the bus
> and I'm the same as them
> I don't know the facts
> but I think it's very sad
> because I think I see what happens next
> all the scars across his chest
> and all the men from Glitterbest
> and all the freaks and all the clowns
> they do not look good

down town at the station
and there the boys in blue
or whatever they call them over there
are waiting for somebody like Sidney Vee
and a hero he ain't
and a martyr he ain't
and Jesus Christ he ain't
but he's liable to get crucified
all strung up and they will say
the boy committed suicide
oh yeah
I've heard that one before
I don't know if he killed her
but they all say he did
and that's very very very easy
with a mixed up wreck like Sid

- front pages and accompanying features from the Saturday 3 February 1979 editions of

  - the Daily Star SID VICIOUS FOUND DEAD
  - the Daily Mirror SID VICIOUS DRUGS DEATH
  - the Daily Mail DRUGS KILL PUNK STAR SID VICIOUS
  - the Daily Express SID VICIOUS DEAD

  These were bought at Liverpool Lime Street Station as we were setting off on a trip to Birmingham. The Sid headlines were mainly ironic, on the basis that everyone hating him made him an icon. It wasn't like he was talented or interesting, just a sad, confused cartoon character caught up in a series of lurid incidents that became lurid headlines, releasing a few awful singles before his brief car crash of a life ended with two sad deaths.

'We' were myself, Radar, Radar's brother, my cousin and perhaps some others. We were going to Birmingham to visit someone who was only ever known as Holmes. It was in the second month after dropping out from Oxford and Radar and I were still feeling quite pleased with ourselves for being so daring. We all started drinking Newcastle Brown Ale at 10 am, and by the time we got to Birmingham New Street we were steaming drunk, so we headed for the pub, drank more beer, got a carryout, and headed for our destination: Holmes's university flat. Once we got there we carried on drinking, played loud music, shouted a lot, set fire to his waste paper bin, then headed for the pub again. Later on, after we had lost all sense and all feeling, Radar's brother and I had a competition to see who could hold a succession of lighted matches to our skin for longest, and I'm not sure who won. When I got home, on my forearm was a smallish patch of glistening mess, so I told my mum I'd fallen asleep leaning against a radiator. She didn't believe me, though having been a nurse she did supply the correct dressings. I wouldn't have believed me either, but I know that on this occasion the truth probably wouldn't have helped. I've still got an area of pale wrinkled skin that commemorates this act of tomfoolery.

- concert programmes, mostly with ticket stubs still inside
  - Genesis (18 April 1975)
  - Tangerine Dream (16 October 1975)
  - Dr Feelgood (22 January 1976)
  - Camel (2 April 1976)
  - Rick Wakeman (30 April 1976)
  - Steve Hillage (18 October 1977)
  - Reading Rock '78.

As I rifled through this dusty box of scraps with cries of amazement, for a while my children were in intrigued. Then as more emerged they rapidly lost interest, but not before seizing the chance to laugh uproariously at black-and-white photographs of various teenage mes in various school rugby B-teams, resplendent in navy shorts, pale spindly legs, grim expression and shocking haircut. Then off they went to watch Captain Planet on the Cartoon Network, leaving me to reflect on this moment, and put everything away again.

Most amazingly of all, in the box I found a couple of lists, neatly handwritten in small capitals. One documented every band I saw throughout the seventies, and the other was a list of every LP bought during the same period.[1]

There were 224 bands on the concert list. It included support bands and main acts, details of whether I had bought a badge (marked B) or a programme (P). If this notation is correct, and I have no reason to doubt it, I am missing printed material from

- the Zones/Iggy Pop
- China Street/Wilko Johnson
- Orchestral Manoeuvres in the Dark
- the Clash
- the Psychedelic Furs

and a badge from

- Poison Girls/Crass.

On the album list were 190 LPs, including albums I had bought and subsequently sold (crossed out, or with the original black ink overwritten in blue). To avoid confusion and untidiness, I recall that I had on occasions copied the list out again.

These two lists, of teenage concerts and LPs, are the cartography on which a strange, meandering odyssey

---

1 See appendix four.

through the seventies is plotted – mine. You might have your own map somewhere, either on paper or in your head. If not of the seventies, then of an equivalent time. On my lists or map or odyssey, the first entries were in 1973 when I was thirteen. The final entries were in 1980 when I was 20, was at university for the second time and found my disposable income and my social life expanding to such an extent that cataloguing LPs and gigs became unfeasible. It was also getting to seem like the kind of thing a crazy young bohemian didn't do, so after the 1980 Futurama 2 festival in Leeds it all stopped.

One list begins with *Piledriver* by Status Quo, and ends with *Closer* by Joy Division. The other begins with Emerson, Lake and Palmer, and ends with Gary Glitter. I have seen all four acts live, and still own records by them. However, to be truthful the Emerson, Lake and Palmer list actually begins with Back Door, because they were supporting ELP on their 1974 tour and were therefore the first live band I ever saw.

As long as you don't include Cain and Collinson. In 1973 a boy in my class called Collinson invited virtually all of us, his class, III Lang,[2] to his large detached house for a party one Saturday evening, with free beer and everything (everything apart from girls, that is). After we had all quaffed a few half-pint cans with no idea about how to drink beer, but erring on the side of too quickly and therefore feeling a bit giddy, he and Cain got out their electric guitars, their denim waistcoats and their fuzz boxes, turned everything up loud and treated everyone to a selection of instrumental rock songs including 'Paper Plane' by Status Quo, which remains a personal favourite. It was pretty damned exciting, and I believe this particular experience of being pummelled by loud guitar music with flashing lights in someone's spacious through-room after a few drinks was my introduction to live rock and roll.[3] And then, as if that wasn't enough, things

---

2 Junior School's II Greeks became III Lang in Big School; II Romans and II Trojans became III Ling and III Science.

3 As long as you don't include Mr Oxton. In 1969-70, about three years before this when I was in the 48-strong Class 3 at Prenton

moved up a gear when Cain started soloing, more and more often, more and more exuberantly, with his eyes closed. He even played the guitar behind his head just like Jimi Hendrix, and was on occasions given to thrusting his pelvis and therefore his guitar about, so when the strobe kicked in things took off to another, even further out dimension. For a few moments, time was suspended as he flashed and flickered about wildly in a thrilling, twitching barrage of fuzzed-out noise.

I don't know how long it all lasted, but my reaction to this cocktail of electricity, testosterone, adrenalin and alcohol was one of slack-jawed amazement. Such proficiency, such daring, such confidence. A couple of years later Collinson loaned me his cream-coloured Jedson Telecaster copy, the one on which he had played 'Paper Plane,' so I could teach myself to play guitar, which I did in a self-effacing, half-hearted kind of way (barre chords, in my bedroom, not very well, mostly without an amplifier). I kept the instrument for years even though it had a bendy neck, and it eventually ended up in a skip along with piles of junk when we moved to Glasgow. I didn't set fire to it or pretend it was my willy, though I did trash it – in a similar self-effacing, half-hearted, private kind of way to the one in which I'd played it: standing in the street in my slippers, hoping nobody would see me as I held it by the neck, raised it above my head and whacked it smartly against the side of the skip. With an apologetic crack, it broke in half disappointingly easily.

So, Back Door were the first live band I saw if you don't count Cain and Collinson appearing as Status Hendrix or Jimi Quo; or Mr Oxton. And paunchy, silver, bewigged

---

Primary School, our teacher Mr Oxton accompanied us singing folk songs on what I now think was a dark wood Fender Telecaster with white scratch plate, played through a practice amp that was turned up quite loud. It was thrilling. Mr Oxton was so rock and roll he had a beard, wore a brown corduroy jacket and drove a pale turquoise Beetle. Everyone loved Mr Oxton. He was kind, patient, enthusiastic and knowledgeable, and so up to date he taught us French using a tape recorder.

paedophile Gary Glitter was the final act at Futurama 2, which kind of summed the whole event up.

Status Quo

The first two LPs I bought were *Piledriver* and *Hello*, thanks to Moir's dad, who worked in Rumbelow's and could get a discount. I bought them in 1973, and that was all I bought. The cover of *Hello* was black, mysterious and austere. The cover of *Unknown Pleasures* by Joy Division was also black, mysterious and austere: in one of these cases the blackness, mystery and austerity seem a bit misguided, though it was perfect for Joy Division. *Piledriver* looks a bit mysterious, but not all black or austere. On the front cover is a colour photo, the use of flash showing up the shabbiness of the gig experience when deprived of its coloured lights, in much the same way that flashlight photos taken at an amazing party tend to make it look seedy and ridiculous. But Status Quo don't look seedy or ridiculous. All you can really see is three anonymous hairy flarey guitarists in trainers, jeans and T-shirts on a scuffed black stage, frozen in full boogie, heads down, hair so long it hangs over their faces and their guitars. Perfection, despite them being hemmed in by the garish graphics. I was irresistibly drawn to Status Quo's denim scruffiness, and the relentless monotony (in a good way) of their sound. I also loved the flailing abundance of their hair, something I was denied while at school and by the time I left I no longer wanted. While listening to *Piledriver* I would stare at that image, willing my hair to grow, in the same way that I would stare at other LP covers, holding them close or at arm's length, either willing things to happen or retreating into some inner world. It's easy to do this kind of thing gazing at a square foot of cardboard, 144 square inches. Squinting at 144 square centimetres of paper or thin card held behind a sheet of perspex by four tiny studs, it just seems ridiculous.

When I first heard *Piledriver* I think I was a bit disappointed because all the songs didn't sound exactly the same. For example there was a slow, sad, sensitive, soaring song called 'A Year' that brought a lump to my throat the first few times I heard it. And there was what struck me even then as a quite un-Quo song called 'Roadhouse Blues', the only cover version on the album, by Morrison/Densmore/Krieger/Manzarek, whoever they were. And there was a fairly rude song called 'Big Fat Mama'. And there was 'Paper Plane'.

I suppose in later years the sense of disappointment engendered by needless variety was remedied by the Ramones, who were a particular kind of noisier stripped-down turbocharged Status Quo machine without all the flappy, irrelevant superstructure like ultra-long hair, flares, twin guitars, chugging boogie and soloing. Instead, you got martial discipline, relentless speed, short bursts of streamlined pop noise, brutal comic-book poetry, and street-punk cartoon iconography. The Ramones all dressed the same, even more so than Status Quo, and they all looked great, even more so than Status Quo. They all had the same surname, so it was the band not the almost interchangeable members that mattered most (though it was Tommy, Johnny, Joey and Dee Dee who were *really* the Ramones). The songs said what they had to say and then just stopped, and because they didn't have a lot to say they never lasted very long. The first few LPs were nothing short of miraculous; fourteen two-minute tracks, seven on each side. Each album was only half an hour long because any longer would have been too long. When they played live the songs were even shorter, and the live double LP was pure piledriver white-noise adrenalin, with a demented, thrilling, perfunctory, yelping bark of *waadaadraafaa* (too fast for spaces, or even hyphens) at the start of *every* song, the syllables barely recognisable.

Apart from that, one song ('Today Your Love, Tomorrow The World') had an *eins-zwei-drei-vier* in it. Another song ('Now I Wanna Sniff Some Glue') had a *one-two-three-four-five-six-seven-eight* in the middle and only one line, 'now

I wanna sniff some glue, all the kids want something to do', repeated over and over again, sometimes with a slight variation.[4] In another song ('Judy Is A Punk') you got a verse that started 'second verse, same as the first' and then one that started 'third verse different from the first'. *And all that was on the first album*, which was perhaps all you needed, though the first three (*Ramones*, *Leave Home*, *Rocket to Russia*) and then the live double (*It's Alive*) were all more or less perfect. Was this smart or was this dumb, and because you couldn't tell the difference or didn't care, did it matter?

The first Quo single that sent me ape-crazy was 'Paper Plane', which was the reason I bought *Piledriver*. I felt the same about 'Mean Girl', 'Caroline', 'Down Down' (especially seeing Pan's People sexing off to it energetically when it got to number one) and 'Mystery Song', which was so good John Peel featured as a Peel's Big Forty-five in 1976. These singles were the real thing, unlike many of the other ninety-odd songs of theirs that chugged into the hit parade and gave them more chart hits than any other band, ever, in the history of rock.

By the time I actually got to see The Quo, it was a few years too late for me, and for them. In 1978 I went to the Reading festival, and they headlined on Saturday night after the Speedometers, the Business, Jenny Darren, Next, Greg Kihn, Nutz, Gruppo Sportivo, Lindisfarne, Spirit and the Motors. The first few bands of the day were completely forgettable, though I do recall badges being handed out that said JENNY DARREN'S GOT BALLS. Next were from Birkenhead and were a bit like Genesis in pantomime mode. Gruppo Sportivo were Dutch and quirky and likeable and won the audience over. Lindisfarne were Geordie and beardy and boring and one big singalong, none of which I knew or liked. Spirit

---

4 'All the kids wanna sniff some glue, all the kids want something to do.' When this song was banned, it was replaced by 'Carbona Not Glue', Carbona being a cleaning fluid. The replacement song was subsequently deleted to avoid a lawsuit over unauthorised use of the trade name. Carbona Not Glue later became the name of a long-running Ramones tribute band.

were good, the Motors were good, but the day and the night belonged to Status Quo – not because they were the best, but because from about eleven in the morning, even before the very first band played, right until The Quo appeared almost twelve hours later, denim and banners started gathering at the front of the crowd, and there arose an unending chant of 'Quo-ooo-ooo-ooooo-o', which swelled with the massing ranks of denim and the swaying banners, and grew and grew and never stopped, during songs, between songs, hour after hour until you almost didn't hear it any more. By the time The Quo finally came on and launched into 'Caroline' there was near-universal denim dementia. 'Caroline' is a great song and it was great to hear it live for the first couple of minutes, after which the soloing began and the novelty rapidly wore off. The same was disappointingly yet predictably true of every other song they played. In fact, while they were playing the ominously titled 'Forty-five Hundred Times', I needed a pee and stumbled off into the dark through the boogie hordes in search of the toilets. Having made a long detour to avoid the expanse of acrid squelch next to the urinals, I joined the queue, had a pee, made my way back through the crowd again, and The Quo were still playing 'Forty-five Hundred Times', which was relentless monotony, but not in a good way any more. I mean, even on the album this song was almost ten minutes long.

The Ramones at the Manchester Apollo in 1980 were even more disappointing. The Apollo was a big seated venue policed by a small army of large ugly bouncers in evening suits who gestured threateningly at anyone who stood up or looked like they might. At a Ramones gig. I couldn't believe it. By the time a determined knot of fans did eventually make a rush for the edge of stage to cluster nervously along one side of the orchestra pit, it was too late. It had always been too late. At the end of their perfunctory performance and perfunctory encore, Dee Dee threw a handful of bass plectrums into the crowd and I got one. I felt even more let down when the word RAMONES that was printed on it smudged and dissolved as I rubbed it with my thumb. Shortly after this I foolishly went back for more at the Sheffield Top Rank: another efficient but soulless show, which I suppose is what you should expect from a band that toured for 22 years and played over 2,200 concerts. The black T-shirt with white logo that I bought that night looked great but was too small: why did I even buy it? Thirty-three years later I was with my son looking for a belt to hold up the trousers of his suit before we went to my father-in-law's funeral, and we got distracted by corporate band tee-shirts, so he got a Rolling Stones one and I got a Ramones one. In Matalan.

Joy Division

I don't think I've ever forgiven New Order for not being Joy Division, even though they've been New Order for more than ten times longer and are probably at least a thousand times as successful. I'm not sure what I ever wanted New Order to be, apart from Not Joy Division, and on that level they didn't disappoint. The name 'New Order' sounds a bit pompous, but it was better than other options such as 'Witchdoctors of Zimbabwe' and 'Khmer Rouge'. Whatever they decided to call themselves, I suppose all they ever really were to me was Ian Curtis's backing band in the way that Talking Heads were David Byrne's backing band or the Pixies were Black Francis's backing band or the Fall were Mark E Smith's backing band. I guess I thought that whatever alchemy or synergy or chemistry the musicians generated in their various ways, when the kids had killed the man, or the man had killed himself, they should have broken up the band because that was that. But what do I know.

I bought 'Blue Monday' when it first came out as a 12" single that looked like a great big floppy disc. I loved it, and I loved the story about the sleeve being so expensive to manufacture that every copy that was sold lost money, so the more copies were sold, the more money was lost – it seemed like such a perverse, clueless thing to do with one of the best selling singles ever, but that was Factory for you. If it was true, it must have annoyed the hell out of New Order. If it wasn't, it ought to have been, which is presumably why people keep telling the story. I've bought and sold quite a few of their albums over the years, trying to find something I really liked. The only one I succeeded with was *Get Ready*, which came out in 2001 and was their first album for eight years, which means the gap between it and the previous album was more than twice as long as the career of Joy Division.

I bought *Get Ready* and kept it because it sounded so towering and monumental and, surprisingly, it was a rock album. Most of the time I can't get past the weedy vocals and the banal lyrics, the pedestrian rhythms and the tinny melodies, but democracy proves me wrong. When *Low Life* came out in 1985 I was living in Manchester, and instantly disliked it for all those reasons, slagging it off to everyone around me, which was unfortunate because they all loved it. They sort of pitied me for not getting it. It might be hard to argue about tuneless vocals and pedestrian rhythms and tinny melodies convincingly in a book, but when you see them on the page the lyrics look even worse than they sound. I know that's not always fair, because words that move people to tears when set to music can look stupid in print, but in this case I know I'm right.

So in 'Perfect Kiss' the protagonist states he has been in an ongoing state of indecision (always thought about) regarding the optimal use of his leisure time (staying in or going out). He concludes that on this occasion a domestic context would have been more conducive to his wellbeing (should have stayed at home), allowing as it did an opportunity to indulge in an unspecified act of gratification (playing with my pleasure zone). We've all been there.

And in 'Sooner Than You Think', the singer suggests that our country is a wonderful place and pales his England into disgrace. Consequently, in order to buy a drink that is so much more reasonable, he intends to go there when it gets seasonal. I mean, you don't have to be Shakespeare or Oscar Wilde or Cole Porter or Bob Dylan to write lyrics, all you have to do is come up with words that fit the music, sound right and don't read like 'The Perfect Kiss', or 'Sooner Than You Think'.

On the other hand, take a look at or a listen to the lyrics for a song like

'Strawberry Fields Forever' by the Beatles
or Elvis's 'Heartbreak Hotel' (even though he didn't write it)
or '54-46 (That's my Number)' by Toots and the Maytals
or 'Johnny B Goode' by Chuck Berry
or 'I'm So Lonesome I Could Cry' by Hank Williams
or 'Now I Wanna Sniff Some Glue' by the Ramones
or 'Stan' by Eminem
or 'Young Savage' by Ultravox!
or 'Surfin' Bird' by the Trashmen
or 'Kurt's Rejoinder' by Eno
or 'The Passenger' by Iggy Pop
or 'I Think I'm In Love' by Spiritualised
or 'Suffragette City' by Bowie
or '12XU' by Wire
or 'Rape Me' by Nirvana
or 'I'm Losing My Edge" by LCD Soundsystem
or 'Subterranean Homesick Blues' by Dylan
or 'Shaved Women' by Crass
or 'Orange Claw Hammer' by Captain Beefheart
or 'You Suffer' by Napalm Death
or 'I Zimbra' by Talking Heads

Or 'Let's Dance to Joy Division' by the Wombats, in which we're invited to dance to Joy Division while celebrating the irony that, despite everything going wrong, we're so happy.

The idea of dancing to Joy Division because you're happy, especially if you lived through their brief, beautiful, anguished existence, makes me shiver, even now, because the last album on my LP list is their album *Closer* (meaning either 'more close than before' or 'a means of closure'. Perhaps both).

I saw Joy Division four times, three times more than was necessary to realise that they were brilliant, and also doomed, or Ian Curtis was. He was gloomily charismatic, pale and other-worldly, he had a weirdly deep, deeply weird voice, and he looked like a ghost even when he was at his most animated, especially when he was at his most animated, staring blankly into the lights or into the dark, arms and legs flailing as if he was trying to keep death at bay, like maybe he thought wouldn't die if he danced fast enough for long enough, but at the same time realised that he couldn't keep moving for ever, that one day he would have to stop, and that it wouldn't be long until that day came. It's impossible to know to what extent Joy Division's brief, intense career was the way it was and became what it became because of being so starkly illuminated by Ian Curtis's roman candle life and death, because now that's the only way to see it.

After the tweeness and mellowness and virtuosity and pomposity of the early seventies, then the amateurism, confrontation and racket of what became known as punk, the music on *Unknown Pleasures* was shocking, sparse and coldly exotic. So was the front cover, a plain black square with a small central area of thin wavy white lines that grabbed my attention and held it in a way that was the complete opposite of something like *Never Mind the Bollocks*. What the small square showed was 100 successive pulses from the first pulsar to be discovered, CP 1919. A pulsar is a collapsed dying star that rotates emitting a beam of energy, a bit like a lighthouse, which is why it is detected as a series of pulses. When first picked up in 1967, its regularity convinced some astronomers that it was a signal from an extra-terrestrial life form.

But I knew none of this, all I knew was that it was utterly strange and utterly different. I was fascinated, and also a bit annoyed, by the fact that there was no side one or side two, just an 'outside' and an 'inside', and there were no track listings on the labels, just a positive and a negative image of those same jagged lines on the cover. In fact there was virtually no information at all anywhere, almost like whoever had made it didn't care if you bought it or not if you weren't curious enough to wonder what it sounded like.

Closer was also shocking. The music was shocking because it was such a beautiful, lush, yet bleak experience –

it actually sounded like poems sung by a dead man. The cover was shocking because it was so white after the black of *Unknown Pleasures*, so shockingly right even without connecting the cover image with Ian Curtis, a depressed, exhausted epileptic in a failing marriage, who may or may not have been a good bloke (or a complete twat) but definitely wasn't a saint or a monochrome Christ, despite what the sick-making monochrome video for 'Atmosphere' with its monks and its Ian Curtis banner might suggest – though Joy Division did always seem to exist in monochrome, even when they were in colour. The abrupt track titles of *Closer* said it all, one or two words at a time – 'Atrocity Exhibition', 'Isolation', 'Passover', 'Colony', '24 Hours', 'The Eternal', 'Decades'. I know the music from both albums so well I hardly need to listen to it even now, and I can still hardly bear to hear it, even when all I'm doing is imagining I'm hearing it. Not because of the myth, but because of the music itself, although it's hard to avoid the fact that the myth has become music and the music has become myth, combining with almost unbearable perfection to become the most beautifully presented atrocity exhibition ever.

In addition to Ian Curtis, Peter Hook, Steve Morris and Bernard Sumner, the other member of Joy Division was Martin Hannett, the producer who made them sound like Joy Division could be their name rather than Warsaw; who made them sound like a band named after the female concentration camp inmates kept for the entertainment of German staff in a paperback called *The House of Dolls* by someone called Ka-Terni 135663. And even though Martin Hannett made them sound like Joy Division could be their name, they did also sound like a sparse instrumental track called 'Warzsawa' on the second side of David Bowie's *Low*. In fact, a sparse instrumental track off a Bowie album made perfect sense as a place for them to get their name, and as something to sound like. You could even imagine that the Bowie track started off being called 'Warsaw', after which for some reason he decided to re-record it, have it remixed by a madman called Martin Hannett, then re-named it

'Joy Division'. My eye was once caught by the lurid green cover of *House of Dolls* at Klaw's, but I didn't buy it because I hadn't heard of Joy Division, because they were still in the future. I did buy *The Atrocity Exhibition* on Tuesday 2 October 1979, though, and had read more or less everything else of JG Ballard's by that time. Joy Division also sounded like a weird, shocking, disjointed 'novel' by JG Ballard, only beautiful as well. They didn't sound like Stiff Kittens.

Joy Division were lean and anguished, they played so few notes and they had such fragile or limited expertise. There was so much space in their haunting, haunted sound that Martin Hannett could easily expand it, rarefying and interweaving the music with vast tracts of emptiness that implied the dark, booming, whispering interiors of oil tankers, cathedrals, abattoirs and crypts, huge desolate spaces in which strange, disturbing things happened but only the echoes and reverberations were ever heard, never the sounds themselves. That's how Martin Hannett made Joy Division sound, and I'd never heard anything like it. And between *Unknown Pleasures* and *Closer* he introduced synthesisers, something that would have been unthinkable a few years before, helping to reclaim keyboard music and make it something new and amazing, like what Mike Thorne did with Wire on *Chairs Missing* and *154* after the 21 tracks in 35 minutes of art attack that was *Pink Flag*, an LP that made the Ramones sound like Kiss, and the Sex Pistols sound like Led Zeppelin, and the Clash sound like Fleetwood Mac, and Pink Floyd sound like Pink Floyd. In fact, Joy Division sounded like Joy Division with Martin Hannett, and New Order sounded like New Order without him.

Apart from not being Joy Division, the only other thing I've never forgiven New Order for is playing a bouncy summery serotonin-drenched version of 'Love Will Tear Us Apart' at some televised festival or other, with the audience jumping up and down and punching the air, on the silver anniversary of Ian Curtis's death, or if that's too po-faced, about twenty-five years after Joy Division split up. Unfortunately, when Hooky yelled out 'Yeah! C'mon!'

before launching into the chorus, it suddenly became clear that everybody was dancing to Joy Division, but nobody was celebrating the irony.[5]

The only other thing to say about Joy Division is that the final track on the Talking Heads album *Remain In Light* is called 'The Overload' and was meant to sound like Talking Heads imagined Joy Division might sound, but without ever having heard them. Which is a silly yet brilliant thing to do.

Emerson, Lake and Palmer

Eee Ell Pee were my first name-on-rucksack band: the *Brain Salad Surgery* album logo in black marker pen. The second band I saw live. For a couple of years I thought they were The Greatest – such Serious Musicians they needed a lorry each for their equipment, a lorry each with a surname in capital letters on the roof, presumably to impress the likes of parachutists, helicopter pilots and people in tall buildings who were looking out of windows as the lorries rumbled past. I imagined that the EMERSON lorry would be crammed with keyboards, and the PALMER lorry would be full of percussion, whereas the LAKE lorry only contained a few guitars and his Persian rug, so to even things out they'd probably put all the amplifiers and speakers in there as well. All the gear told you that this was Serious Music, played by Serious Musicians, virtuosos. You also knew that was what they were because they played so fast, and for so long, one at a time. It was self evident that the better they were, the more gear they had and the longer their solos were, and the more expensive Greg Lake's Persian rug had to be.

There may have been an Eee, an Ell and a Pee, but the man who mattered was Eee, wild maestro of rock Keith Emerson. He had a huge throbbing organ that he would grab

---

5 And since Hooky and New Order parted company, he's been performing New Order covers *and* Joy Division covers to ecstatic crowds.

hold of and yank about whenever the opportunity presented itself, pouting and gurning as he gave it what for. Organ? Sounds a bit rude. And it *was* a bit rude, because it absolutely *was* a dick thing, just like it was with guitars – I mean, he had something called a ribbon moog, a gizmo roughly the size and shape of a guitar neck, and he would grab this and prance about the stage with it, spanking his plank and rubbing it in intimate ways to produce screeching howling electronic orgasm noises. And he would jam knives between the keys of his organ to hold them down while he soloed furiously, manhandling it, knocking it over and humping it and bumping it to make it groan and whine like his bitch, which it clearly was.[6] And he would throw his knives at it just to show it who was boss, Hitler Youth knives that he said he got from Lemmy while Lemmy was a roadie for the Nice. And he played a grand piano that rose into the air and then tipped forward and went round and round, over and over, which is nothing if not memorable. So memorable that when Keith Emerson met Duke Ellington, he said that's what Duke remembered – not his talent or his technique or his feel for the instrument, just the fact that it went round and round while he played it, which Emerson seemed thrilled to bits with.

Such was the extent of our teenage clique's admiration for Keith Emerson and his antics while I was in the third year at school, we would humorously manhandle our desks around the classroom in imitation and homage. For a time we even abandoned air guitars in favour of air keyboards, played at parties when tipsy. After a few more drinks, we would tussle ostentatiously over whose turn it was to take their place at the mantelpiece and play along to selections from the improbably titled *Welcome Back My Friends To The Show That Never Ends (– Ladies And Gentlemen, Emerson, Lake And Palmer)*. Which was, of course, a live triple album.

---

6 To be fair, jamming knives in between the keys also creates a drone to solo over, and bumping the organ about is a way to produce distortion and feedback, and both of these techniques were highly innovative. Even so…

These guys were so good that they knew classical music. The first LP, *Emerson, Lake And Palmer*, included versions of music by Bach, Janáček, and Bartók. And it had a Greg Lake ballad.[7] The second LP, *Tarkus*,[8] included a side-long suite, called 'Tarkus'. It didn't have a Greg Lake ballad, but it did have him singing a jaunty, crude number called 'Jeremy Bender'. The third, *Pictures At An Exhibition*,[9] was a prog version of Mussorgsky, and had a Greg Lake ballad. The fourth, *Trilogy*,[10] included a rousing version of 'Hoedown' by Aaron Copeland, and a Greg Lake ballad. The fifth, *Brain Salad Surgery*,[11] included a rendition of the fourth movement of Alberto Ginastera's first piano concerto; it included a side-and-a-half-long suite called 'Karn Evil 9'; it had a Greg Lake ballad, *and* a jaunty, crude number called 'Benny the Bouncer' as well.

The sixth album was called *Welcome Back My Friends To The Show That Never Ends (– Ladies And Gentlemen, Emerson, Lake And Palmer)*. After that, they didn't manage another album until 1977, by which time it was too late, much too late.[12] It had been too late for some time.

Back in the day, the first, second, third, fourth and fifth albums rocked me to bits: classical references signified that rock was progressing and becoming art; was evolving into upper-case Progressive Rock, and therefore upper-case Art. Progressive Rock was LPs not singles, and therefore way beyond the lowbrow lightweight pap that was pop, the kind of music smartly dressed youngsters danced to in discotheques. Knowing about classical music proved that Progressive Rock could be every bit as clever and ambitious as classical music, rock musicians could be every bit as skilled and talented as classical musicians, and dancing in discos didn't count. The lyrics were serious, clever, introspective and intense, just

---

7 It was my eighth album.
8 My twelfth album.
9 My fourth album.
10 My sixth album.
11 My third album.
12 I never bought this.

like poetry. Progressive Rock was total art; it was just like Wagner's *Gesamtkunstwerk*, wasn't it, because Wagner used to describe his operas as *Gesamtkunstwerken*, which means 'total artworks', a fusion of all the arts, just like Genesis or Yes or ELP (or Bowie or Pink Floyd[13]). Live, as well as the music and the words there were the costumes, the lighting, the choreography, the props, the stage sets and sometimes films and slide projections. At home there was the music and the lyrics, and there was the artwork – the LP cover, a new art form the size of a small painting, often with gatefold extendability as well as inner sleeve and lyric sheets which you could read and pore over. And as further evidence of *Gesamtkunstwerk* (or maybe it was the optimisation of corporate identity via a multi-media marketing strategy) there were logos that appeared on the stage backdrop and the LP cover, and also on badges, concert programmes, patches, posters and T-shirts. There were no sports logos then, but there were music logos, and we were their willing billboards. If there were no logos to buy, we would copy them by hand onto exercise books, rucksacks, denim jackets, toilet walls and desks.

I was for a while in awe of Progressive Rock's cleverness and seriousness and ambition, its desire to evolve and grow up. This was a paradox, because although I wanted adults to respect this music rather than ridicule it, I didn't really want them to like it too much, because it was mine not theirs. The Who made 'rock operas' like *Tommy* and *Quadrophenia*. I never liked Deep Purple, but they'd played with a symphony orchestra, hadn't they. There were concept pieces like *Aqualung* and *Dark Side Of The Moon* and *Tubular Bells* and *The Lamb Lies Down On Broadway*. There was difficult music and there were song suites and there were tracks that filled a whole side and tracks that filled a whole album, then there were double albums by bands like Yes and sometimes there were triple albums by bands like Yes. Their keyboard player Rick Wakeman made an album about

---

13 Bowie was progressive but not Progressive. Despite what people might say, Pink Floyd were neither.

the six wives of Henry VIII, one track per wife and lots of different keyboards per track. Then he made an album with an orchestra and a narrator, based on Jules Verne's *Journey To The Centre Of The Earth*, and then one about King Arthur that was performed on ice (by ice skaters; the musicians wisely stayed away). I listened enthralled to jazz critic Derek Jewell pontificating about all this clever, interesting music on Radio Three's *Sounds Interesting*, and he pointed me in all kinds of clever, interesting directions. It was Serious Art and I took it seriously.

ELP played at the Liverpool Empire, though the first band on was Back Door, a trio of bass, drums and saxophone, after which, from about as far back and high up as it was possible to be while still remaining in the building, I and three of my pals saw ELP. They opened, as they always did, with 'Hoedown'. From my distant seat I took in three small and very loud luminescent blobs, the loudest thing I had ever experienced, and so far away I definitely needed the binoculars that Uncle Les from church had thoughtfully lent me. Peering through these I could make out in blurry detail Keith's every scowl and grimace as he slapped, prodded and tickled his multiple ivories, several of which belonged to a huge synthesiser that looked like an telephone exchange and was about as state of the art as you could get. And Carl Palmer's huge stainless steel drum set revolved during his interminable or 'expansive' drum solo, and he had drum synthesisers that made all kinds of screeching, popping, splatting, farting noises, and his huge gongs had red dragons on the back of them, and there were strobes, and he rang a big bell by pulling on a rope with his teeth, and as he played his drum kit revolved... and ... you may be a gifted percussionist, you may not be, but a drum solo, really? And Greg Lake sang his latest ballad, called 'Still... You Turn Me On', apparently dedicated to all the female members of the audience. The atmosphere was spoiled a bit by the fact that he wasn't always in tune; and a bit more by someone in the audience yelling FOOOKIN BRILLIAAAAAAAAANT during one of the quietest bits; and by the fact that the lyrics quite blatantly included the observation that things were getting progressively sadder and madder, after which he asked someone to get him a ladder.

The album they were promoting was *Brain Salad Surgery*. It's a strange name for an album and it had a strange fold-out cover that looked wonderful but was easily damaged, and was therefore too clever for its own good. The outer image was of a pitted metal clamp holding a skull in place, and through an opening in the centre of the clamp you could see a pair of pouting female lips where the mouth of the skull would have been. When you opened the cover up, you saw not just the mouth but the whole female head: swollen mouth parts, closed eyes, metallic palsied skin, snakelike coils of metallic hair held in place by a headband. It was an eerie, beautiful image in a sci-fi, pervy kind of way, which is appropriate because it was painted by a sci-fi, pervy kind of guy called HR Giger, the Swiss artist who a few years later would design the alien in *Alien*.

With or without Giger, 'Brain Salad Surgery' was a strange name for an album. It's a term for fellatio and came from a song by Dr John called 'Right Place, Wrong Time'. The previous title was apparently 'Whip Some Skull On Ya', also a strange title for an album, and also a term for fellatio. In the artwork for the outer sleeve you can make out the end of an erect penis rising towards the woman's mouth, the lower part of the organ visually implied by the vertical shaft that comprised the bottom part of the metal clamp, an ELP logo wrapped around the shaft like some kind of over-engineered cock ring. In effect the woman's head is being held in place while ELP symbolically fuck her in the mouth. It's very HR Giger: his work often portrays women being restrained and penetrated orally, vaginally or anally by machines or 'biomechanoids'. When the original artwork was turned down by the record company, the penis was airbrushed out, but you can still make out the top of the shaft on some versions of the image, the shiny glans visible just below the woman's swollen mouthparts. I knew nothing of this at the time, and would have been mortified if I had known. I found sex difficult enough to deal with, without Great Artists displaying the aroused male member on their LP covers. And when I saw a TV documentary about ELP in which they all dropped their pants and mooned the audience at one of their shows, I nearly died of shame – firstly because they were Proper Musicians so how could they do such a thing, and secondly because my mum was sitting next to me after I had urged her to watch the programme so she could learn what Great Artists and Proper Musicians ELP were.

It's easy to mock ELP now, a band that John Peel once called 'a waste of talent and electricity'. It was probably easy then as well, though not for me – not for a few years, anyway. I wanted so much more from music than you could get from straightforwardly vivacious pop, the stuff enjoyed by fashionably dressed kids who knew how to dance and were confident enough to talk to girls. My music was intellectual rather than physical, I could listen to it carefully and ponder over it and lose myself in its seriousness and expansiveness, rather than having to get up and shake my thing, or whatever it was that young people did when they went to discotheques. Anyway, you couldn't dance to ELP even if you wanted to because it was art, and girls didn't understand it, nor did a lot of other people who weren't clever enough or intense enough or middle class enough to be like me.

Gary Glitter

How do you deal with Gary Glitter when you're old enough to

- remember how great some of the singles were?
- know that 'Johnny B Goode' is a work of genius, though if you're still singing 'Sweet Little Sixteen' in your seventies there's something wrong, especially if you've been sued in a class action by more than 50 women because you installed video cameras in the ladies' toilets of a couple of restaurants that you own?

- remember listening to *Tommy* at a time when Uncle Ernie fiddling about was just a Keith Moon joke?
- remember being creeped out by the talentless, inexplicably successful Jimmy Saville?
- recall your amazement at Rolf Harris's way with paintbrushes and rollers?
- picture the old (which is to say young) version of Michael Jackson in your mind's eye?
- have children of your own?

One of the first singles I remember hearing when I started listening to Radio One was 'Rock and Roll Part 2'. Whoompa Whacka Whoompa Whacka Whoompa Whacka Whoompa Whacka drums, accompanied by absurdly simple chords on a ridiculously tinny fuzzed-up guitar, and no voices apart from the odd grunt and a few 'Heeeeey-hey's. There were no vocals on 'Rock and Roll Part 2' because it was the B-side, basically the A-side without the vocals – what in reggae is referred to as a version and everywhere else as lazy or a rip-off. But it worked – it was minimal, it was moronic and it was utterly brilliant, it was better than the A-side, and quite rightly got all the airplay.

It made a deep impression on me, though the only reason I noticed it at first was because it didn't sound like a proper song, because it wasn't a proper song, it was just whoompa-whacking drums, distorted guitar and some grunting. It must have made an impression on other people as well, because Bowie stole it for Iggy Pop's album *The Idiot*, twisting it and mangling it until it turned into 'Nightclubbing', a darker, sleazier version of 'Rock and Roll' that was perfect for Iggy, who at that time seemed a lot darker and sleazier than Gary Glitter. And later I was amazed and delighted when I saw the Human League, way before the girls joined, doing 'Rock and Roll' with rumbling, roiling synths and a whoompa whacka drum machine accompanying Phil Oakey, and slide projections of Captain Scarlet, Scott Tracy and Joe 90. And the Human League's version morphed knowingly into 'Nightclubbing', and that was wonderful too.

I remember hearing 'Rock and Roll Part 2' on a tinny, fuzzy transistor radio at my granddad's house when I was twelve. This made the song even tinnier and even fuzzier, and made him shake his head and tut-tut and go 'good gracious' in sorrowful disbelief at the kind of music that young people were listening to. And he hadn't even heard the one about the leader of the gang that also became a football chant, or the one about it being good to be back, or the one about touching me there (oh yeah) that annoyed Mary Whitehouse. He had a point, my granddad, and so did Mary Whitehouse, because although it was a great song and they were all great songs, and still are, they are now tainted by what we found out about Paul Gadd when he took his computer to PC World to be repaired and carelessly left 4,000 or so images of kiddie porn on it.

I'd gone off him way before that. In September 1980, only eight years after 'Rock and Roll Part 2', Gary Glitter was already on the nostalgia/irony circuit, and he headlined at Futurama 2, a dismal weekend 'festival' in a grotty old market hall in Leeds city centre. Inside, it was dark and noisy and stinking and crammed, then when you went out to buy food or drink you walked straight out into the unforgiving glare of Saturday afternoon, crowds of people milling about doing their Saturday shopping and trying not to stare at all the bleary-eyed punks and goths stumbling about looking for places to buy cigarettes and Rizlas and beer and pies.

All kinds of bands played, though I don't remember much, apart from Bono's stupid mullet and his stupid tie-dye top and trousers and his stupid dancing, and Siouxsie Sioux's amazing white fringed jacket, white mini skirt and green lasers. And Gary Glitter, marching onstage to a rumbling, throbbing version of 'Rock and Roll' played on keyboards so it didn't sound right, not like when the Human League did it; and neither did the next number or the one after that or the one after that as he churned and gurned his way through hit after hit in his silver boots and his silver suit and his ridiculous wig, camper than camp, handing out red roses to the audience during a maudlin 'Oh Yes! You're

Beautiful', or was it 'I Love You Love Me Love', breaking down in tears like a podgy bacofoil Liberace as he told the audience between sobs how much he loved each and every one of them.

In case you're wondering who else played, on the Saturday it was I'm So Hollow, Altered Images, Acrobats of Desire, Modern English, Clock Dva, Blah Blah Blah, Wasted Youth, U2, Echo and the Bunnymen, Siouxsie and the Banshees.

On the Sunday it was Household Name, Naked Lunch, Vice Versa, Artery, the Frantic Elevators, Boots for Dancing, the Flowers, Brian Brain, the Not Sensibles, Classix Nouveaux, Tribesman, Blurt, the Soft Boys, Durutti Column, Young Marble Giants, 4 Be 2, Hazel O'Connor, Psychedelic Furs, Gary Glitter.

Those are the beginnings and the ends of my LP and gig lists, in chronological order. In alphabetical order, the first and last acts I saw would be Acrobats of Desire and Tapper Zukie, though if you don't follow the surname-first convention, the last act would be Young Marble Giants. I used to always go surname first, but now I've got iTunes I'm not so sure.

The first and last LP artists would be the Adverts and either Neil Young or Yes. These things are important. I don't know, maybe I'm a bit obsessive, but what else would you expect. A few years ago, I spent twelve months or so volunteering in a charity shop. It was partly my social conscience, and partly the fact that they had a lot of vinyl, CDs and cassettes that needed sorting, and I figured this might be my only chance to work in a record shop. So I volunteered, and I made some notes.

Notes from the attic

Here I am in a dim, dusty attic that's damp and freezing in the winter, hot and airless in the summer. A lot of the time is spent arranging hundreds and hundreds of LPs into rough categories of my own that have emerged during the sorting process:

- 70s pop and rock
- 80s pop and rock
- pop and rock compilations
- classical
- country and western
- easy listening
- Scottish.

Scottish might not be immediately obvious as a separate category, but this is Inverness, capital of the Highlands, so Scottish music is common enough to get its own category. As well as LPs there are also 7" singles and 12" singles, and a few 78s.

It feels strange being in such a huge room full of other people's records. I have no idea how many collections or people are represented in the rows and rows, piles and piles or boxes and boxes of often unplayable LPs – old records that have presumably lain in cupboards, attics or other forgotten spaces for years before either being ousted by shiny, convenient, iridescent compact discs, or dumped because they were in the way after someone had died, moved house or de-cluttered.

I am surrounded by images of grinning, leering, pouting, smirking pop and rock nobodies who were once somebodies, in absurdly outdated leisurewear and fashionwear, on the covers of eighties pop and rock albums. Discarded pop and rock is now mainly eighties; there's hardly anything from the seventies and even less from the sixties. Collectively they tell a story about the transitory nature of fame, a story repeated on hundreds of squares of scuffed cardboard containing hundreds of scratched discs in hundreds of paper sleeves in dozens of plastic crates in a dim, dusty attic. The only form of salvation for any of these nobodies and somebodies will be via nostalgia, irony or occasionally sampling.

I found a compilation LP on the Alternative Tentacles label run by Jello Biafra, formerly of the Dead Kennedys. There was no cover, just an A5 insert and the record in a clear plastic sleeve. On the insert was a track listing and a stark xeroxy logo that parodied the US seal of state – instead of an eagle clutching arrows and an olive branch there's a scowling bat clutching a broken US missile in one claw, a broken cross with a dollar sign on in the other (not as good as the Ramones logo). It made me remember that in the late seventies a friend brought me back a copy of the shouty anthemic Dead Kennedys single 'California Über Alles' from America. The cover included crudely Xeroxed Nuremberg and death camp images as part of an attack on liberal governor Jerry Brown and his 'suede denim secret police', who it was claimed would by 1984 would be exterminating uncool people using organic gas, then making their skin into lampshades. The band's confrontational tastelessness reached a wider audience in 1985 with the release of the album *Franken Christ*. Free with every copy was a poster of an HR Geiger image known as 'Penis Landscape' that depicts penises entering vaginas as seen from beneath (Picture nine copulating couples sitting on a rectangular sheet of glass in a tight three-by-three formation with their feet in the air. The middle couple on the top row are using a condom.). The obscenity trial that ensued resulted in acquittal, though Alternative Tentacles was almost bankrupted. At some stage I saw the Dead Kennedys in Sheffield, and wasn't too impressed. It was still light, and there was a lot of thrashing about but no atmosphere. Jell-O Biafra twisted and yelled operatically and, strangely, seemed to spend a lot of time and effort trying to put a length of imaginary thread through the eye of an imaginary needle. I have no idea why.

Stuck up here surrounded by the past, I feel like I've lost touch with the music of today. My son has bought an Arctic Monkeys album – it's noisy, eclectic, smart, catchy and very English. I also keep hearing him play the Ramones because they feature on the imaginary in-car radio station in one of his drive-by mayhem video games. Where else would you expect to hear them now.

A man came upstairs from the shop and rooted about for a while, looking for anything 60s, 70s, Krautrock or psychedelic. Definitely an anorak's anorak, I decided, after realising I had never heard of most of the bands he was enthusing about. I found him a copy of Fripp and Eno's monumental 1973 *No Pussyfooting* and he was quite pleased with it, though it wasn't the original gatefold sleeve. He said he had some LP or other that was worth a thousand pounds. Would like to see his record collection.

What was treasured is now trash. Obsolete formats pile up – VHS, Bet Amax, 45 rpm, 33⅓ rpm, 78 rpm, 7" single, 12" LP, 12" single, cassette album, cassette single, cassette computer game. Only books stand the test of time, it seems.

A man came upstairs from the shop in search of Elvis, in particular the Reader's Digest LP box set. Most of the Elvis LPs are in a terrible condition and a lot of the sleeves are empty, but he still bought a couple of albums. He said he had an expensive hi-fi system and preferred vinyl to CDs, even with his digital-to-analogue converter. I'm not sure how much of this I believe.

Before the 90s, before the 80s, before the 70s, there was Easy Listening. Perry Como, Johnny Mathis, Liberace, Val Doonican, Nana Mouskouri, Max Bygraves, Des O'Connor, Harry Secombe, Ken Dodd, Jim Reeves, Bing Crosby, Acker Bilk. Of all the categories this is by far the largest: it's the people's music. At least it was, but now it's impossible to get rid of.

A man came upstairs from the shop, a shaven-headed, weatherbeaten chap with tattooed knuckles and an enormous rucksack. I first saw him riffling through a box of LPs I had just set out downstairs, picking out one after another to set aside. We got talking and he showed me some photos that he had on his phone of his record collection, which seemed to fill an entire room from floor to ceiling. I invited him to come and have a browse in the attic, because he seemed to have a pretty clear idea what he was looking for, which seemed to be almost anything. We chatted and he chose and he chose and we chatted, and every so often I would carry his selections downstairs, then we would chat and he would choose some more. In the end there were 69 12" singles and 74 LPs, which came to £210. Because he had no money, he went off to find a cash machine and returned with £100, about half the full amount, and because he had a large rucksack he managed to take about half his records away with him. To do so he removed a sealed bulk pack of about 40 white toilet rolls from the rucksack then crammed it with vinyl, and when he put it on his back he could hardly stand. Then off he went, staggering under the weight of 100 records with an armful of toilet rolls. The rest of the records were never paid for or collected, and I never saw him again

There are original copies of two Bob Dylan albums, *Bringing It All Back Home* and *Highway 61 Revisited*. Both look as if they have been kept in sleeves lined with sandpaper. Whatever they sound like, they're originals, with their history written onto them, forty-odd years of it, just like Dylan's history is written on his face and etched into his vocal cords. Neither album is on my 70s LP list because the only Dylan album I bought back then was *More Bob Dylan Greatest Hits*, which I hardly ever played, because at the time I didn't think I liked Dylan. This was partly because everyone else thought he was so great, which meant I was sick of the sight of *The Basement Tapes* before I heard anything off it. When I did get to hear it I still wasn't convinced, though I now consider him a genius and own the complete six-CD box set. Ironically designated 'The Bootleg Series, Vol 11', it comes lavishly packaged with faux worn cardboard covers and crinkled paper sleeves, et cetera et cetera.

Today while clearing some bookshelf space upstairs I found a box of unfamiliar-looking LPs in amongst the crumbling paperbacks and outdated dictionaries. When I asked why they were up there I was told nobody knew what to do with them, and they were going to be binned. I excitedly explained what they were, which made no difference to the decision to throw them out, so I got to keep them: 52 albums of library music issued by the likes of KPM, de Wolfe and Sonoton. Titles like *Industrial Prestige & Scenic Magnificence*, *Codex Antiquus*, *Journey Into Space*, *Light and Bright*.

This morning I found an original copy of the first Rolling Stones album on which the grooves had more or less disappeared beneath the surface scratches (Why is an aged Bob Dylan or Neil Young okay, but the ancient Rolling Stones merely sad and ridiculous, whatever anyone might pretend?) There are boxes and boxes of 78s, mostly folky Scottish quaintness along with boxed sets of classical pieces chopped into impossibly short segments that would drive people mad nowadays. Amongst everything else I came across a copy of 'Rock Around The Clock' by Bill Haley and the Comets. About a tenner on eBay, though in other ways absolutely priceless.

Because it seemed strange to be sorting through thousands of LPs without hearing any of them, today I managed to get a hi-fi upstairs. I listened to *The Real Donovan* from sometime in the sixties. It sounded OK, but not memorable, not now. I listened to *The Yes Album*, which reminded me why I used to like Yes. Recently, Stuart Maconie played selections from *Relayer* on the radio, which reminded me why I went off them. I also listened to a selection of John Foxx 12" singles that I hadn't heard before and that I really liked, so I ended up keeping them, then bought a cheap CD compilation of all his singles called *Modern Art*, which reminded me why I used to like Ultravox, then the thought of Midge Ure reminded me why I went off them. Next time I was in, the hi-fi had disappeared and it was back to silence or the muted sound of some rubbish or other rising through the floorboards from the shop downstairs.

The categories that have emerged from sorting, the ones that make the most sense in terms of what's actually there, are

- 70s pop and rock
- 80s pop and rock
- easy listening

- folk/jazz/blues/world
- classical
- religious
- compilations
- children's
- TV/film/theatre/musicals
- Scottish
- country
- 12" singles
- spoken word
- solo singers and instrumentalists

Compilations is probably the strangest category, along with easy listening. *The Rock Machine Turns You On*? Issued in 1968, it was the first bargain sampler of its kind, and is now therefore Iconic: so much so that a certain music magazine gave away a pastiche *The MOJO Machine Turns You On 2018* CD with a recent issue.[14] There are compilations of compilations, compilations of compilations of compilations, the same fifties or sixties or seventies or eighties or romantic or country or instrumental numbers being recombined in different configuration over and over again. *NOW 27*, *NOW 28*, *NOW 29*, half of *NOW 35*. Going further back, all the albums of Top 30 cover versions. Photos of pouty women with tousled hair in tight, unbuttoned or wet shirts, nipples the size of grapes. Chas and Dave, Henry Cooper, Mrs Mills, Motown Chartbusters. Boxed sets of disco classics. Classical chill out. Country greats. Orchestral Dylan, orchestral Beatles.

Piles and piles more LPs to go through, especially easy listening– the Carpenters, Dean Martin, James Last. How many records did James Last make? We must have them all here. Loads of Cliff Richards, loads of James Galway, loads of Shakin' Stevens, loads of Simply Red, loads of Lionel Ritchie. Pop and rock and pop-and-rock easy listening, mostly from the time that vinyl started to disappear in the

---

14 See appendix five.

eighties, pictures of interchangeable guys and girls looking sparkly, slick or foppish; big hair, melodramatic clownlike make-up. This is popular taste in popular music, but it's no longer popular: it's not classic or retro-classic or out-there or ahead-of-its-time or knowingly ironic; it's just middle of the road and out of date. A kind of musical vox pop from voices that are now silent.

I am a sort of musical archaeologist / archivist / historian, and around me is a dispiritingly democratic selection of what people have been listening to over the past 30 years or so, probably starting during my teenage years and continuing until records became obsolete. Most of it is crap. Maybe this is just what's been discarded, and every time someone dies or moves house all the bad records end up here and the good ones are kept or sold on. Either way, I am rooting through a kind of musical scrap yard, a rubbish tip, a landfill site, a great big ditch.

When I started secondary school we had a history teacher called Jock Austin. He was old-school, even at my school, with his slicked back grey hair, old-fashioned glasses, tweed jacket, brown leather briefcase, nicotine-stained toothbrush moustache and long-range tobacco stench that took your breath away. To him teaching history consisted of filling the blackboard with closely-written notes, which he then read aloud, then we copied them down, then he wiped them away – over and over again. I can't remember any of it. What I do remember is my astonishment when he said in an offhand remark that archaeologists preferred rubbish tips to temples and palaces. Back then, at the time when I was in awe of a stamp being issued on the 50th anniversary of Tutankhamun's tomb being found, it turned my idea of history upside down. Now I get it, and here I am, rooting around in a kind of musical rubbish tip, bringing some order to the chaos of the past as best I can.

Playlist 3 - In The Wardrobe Of My Head		
Going Back Home	Dr Feelgood	*Malpractice*
The Salmon Song	Steve Hillage	*Fish Rising*
Paper Plane	Status Quo	*Piledriver*
New Dawn Fades	Joy Division	*Unknown Pleasures*
Young Savage	Ultravox	
I Think I'm In Love	Spiritualised	*Ladies And Gentlemen, We Are Floating In Space*
Losing My Edge	LCD Soundsystem	*LCD Soundsystem*
Hoedown	Emerson, Lake and Palmer	*Trilogy*
Nightclubbing	Iggy Pop	*The Idiot*
Starship Trooper	Yes	*The Yes Album*

To listen to the playlists, visit Spotify using the QR links provided.

Links to every playlist are also at www.hungry-ghost.info, along with photographs and archive material to supplement each chapter and enhance the reading/listening experience, just like a great big gatefold album cover.

3

46 29 50

I was at my cousins' house the night I first saw the Beatles the Famous Beatles, black and white in suits and moptop haircuts. They were barely audible over the screaming, the thin sound of the song itself lost behind a wall of noise that seemed to clog the air, harsh and metallic, almost solid, like jets landing, or thousand of frantic birds in an aircraft hangar, or thousands of frantic Beatles fans in a theatre. Hearing it felt exciting, especially when the band shook their hair about and went 'ooooooooooooh', after which the screaming got even louder. Some time after this sensory assault my dad arrived to take me home in our grey split-windscreen Morris Minor with its red leather seats and orange flip-up indicators. Mildly intoxicated by Beatlemania, as soon as I got though the front door I launched into an impromptu rendition of she-luvs-yew-yeeeeh-yeeeh-yeeeeh, shaking my head vigorously for extra effect, but my mum just went '*Duncan!*' and looked scandalised.

The song was released in August 1963, so when I saw the Beatles I would have been three or four years old, though it's hard to remember that far back. My earliest memories of music exist only as bits of an incomplete soundtrack to an incomplete movie; a series of fragments emerging and receding through mental static. Some bits are blurred, some bits are quite vivid. There's very little connecting narrative between the few slivers of early film that have been sellotaped together and projected onto the inside of my skull as the bit of me that I call myself, and who lives there, sits in his armchair and watches. As he does so, pieces of music on crumpled, spliced-together audio tape rumble over the playback head of an ancient tape machine, and he, the little man in the armchair, comes up with ways of matching the images with the sounds to make a story. Sometimes, gaps of days or weeks or even months are compressed to brief black flickers as fragment succeeds fragment.

From these rumblings and fragments and flickers the homunculus in the dome of my head has assembled my story of me. It tells of a carefree childhood watched over by loving but strict Christian parents in a modest semi in a town called Birkenhead, along with two brothers and, later, a sister. Odd bursts of theme tunes and pop music become more frequent and more important as time passes. To start with, there was no TV set, and when we eventually did get one, it stayed off on Sundays.

We all make up these stories, our homunculi sitting and watching and listening in their bony little caves, making movies and compiling soundtracks; editing and splicing and segueing; closing the gaps, making patterns from the fragments of our remembered and reconstructed lives. It's hard to know now how much of each story is really real, how much of it was ever real.

I remember 'Sun Arise' by Disgraced National Treasure Rolf Harris, released in 1962 when I was just three. I remember it as a sparse, insidious, rhythmic drone that made my hair stand on end. At the time I had no idea that it was meant to sound like aboriginal music, nor that it was produced by George Martin and engineered by Geoff Emerick: I just felt it burrowing its way into my skull, where it has stayed ever since. And I had no idea that it would later be covered by Alice Cooper on his album *Love It To Death*, because 1971 hadn't happened yet. Nor had 1993's *Welcome to Our Nightmare: A Tribute to Alice Cooper*, on which 'Sun Arise' was performed by the Flaming Lips as a tribute to Alice's tribute to Rolf's tribute to …

What, exactly? The story goes that Rolf co-wrote 'Sun Arise' with a naturalist called Harry Butler after Butler had played him a field recording of aboriginal music. There's no actual didgeridoo in 'Sun Arise', just some double basses made to sound like one. There are no other instruments either, just a bit of banging, and some woodblocks or sticks or something, and presumably the rest is just tape multi-tracked and overdubbed into something unreal and, at the time, for me, mesmerising. Although he wasn't playing one on 'Sun Arise', Rolf did eventually learn the didgeridoo, and two decades later ended up playing on the title track of Kate Bush's album *The Dreaming*, which, strangely, or maybe not strangely at all, had been inspired by the original aboriginal imitation that was 'Sun Arise'.

As well as producing 'Sun Arise', George Martin also produced Rolf Harris's previous hit 'Tie Me Kangaroo Down, Sport', another song I remember.[1] The song is a bleak, jokey calypso-based novelty item about a dying Australian stockman disposing of his property, livestock and 'abos'; this last item was removed from the re-released 1962 version, and Rolf subsequently apologised. After he was dropped by George Martin, for a while he worked as MC on early Beatles shows.

Everything comes back to the Beatles one way or another, and back then Liverpool was Beatletown. And Beatletown was just a ferry trip away from Birkenhead, as Gerry and the Pacemakers never tired of reminding everyone. In fact, when I made the crossing a few years ago, Gerry and his cardiac regulators were still at it, using speakers thoughtfully provided by Mersey Ferries, as part of their Ferry 'Cross The Mersey Experience. And this year (it doesn't really matter which year it is: time passes so quickly now) a leaflet I picked up in my local library tells me that The Solid Silver 60s show is in its 23rd year and will be at a theatre near me soon, featuring Gerry and the Pacemakers performing 'How Do You Do It?', 'You'll Never Walk Alone', 'I Like It' and of

---

1 I also remember the weird sound of Rolf's wobble board, originally a painted sheet of hardboard he was trying to cool down after leaving it drying too close to a heater. The National Museum of Australia had one in its collection right until 2013, around the time Rolf's smiley mask slipped.

course 'Ferry 'Cross the Mersey'.[2] And whatever year it is, it's more than 50 years since 'Ferry 'Cross the Mersey' got to number 8 in 1964. Which means it's more than 30 years since it reached number 1 by default in 1984, covered by Frankie Goes to Hollywood on the B-side of 'Relax'.

Liverpool might have been Beatletown, but once I heard T Rex the Beatles were wiped off the map. If I had expressed my thoughts about the Beatles after hearing 'Get It On', assuming I had any, I might have said they didn't matter any more, with their stupid suits, stupid haircuts, stupid singalong tunes and stupid Scouse banter. Either that or I might have said they were just boring hairy old men who were always in the news. I might have said some or all of that, or I might have just forgotten about them. Then, if I had expressed my thoughts a few years later, assuming I had any, I might have damned them for being so popular – everybody liked them apart from me, and what was the point of liking a band everybody liked, even mums and dads and old people.

Then, after all the years of not liking the Beatles and of everyone else thinking they were great, and after it seemed like the whole Beatles thing had died down and everyone was finally over them and they really didn't matter any more, there came the news that John Lennon had been shot. I heard it on the radio at teatime while my student flatmates were cooking student chips in our student kitchen full of mouldy student milk bottles. And after that, millions of people around the world lit candles, built shrines, cried, and sang Beatles songs, and 'Imagine' was on the radio all the time, along with almost every other song John Lennon had written or co-written. Ten years after splitting up, the Beatles had followed me from Beatletown all the way over the Pennines

---

2 Also in The Solid Silver 60s show are Swinging Blue Jeans. I'm sure I remember 'Hippy Hippy Shake'. I had no idea what a hippy hippy shake was, but it sounded like a riot, a screaming, hairy, sexy riot. And there's Dave Berry – Never heard of him. And Dave Dee, Dozy, Beaky, Mick and Tich. I definitely remember 'Bend It!' though I could never work out how many there were in the band or where the commas were meant to go.

to Sheffield University. There was no escape. Imagine there's no Beatles. Sorry, I tried really hard, but I can't.

I sort of remember hearing Beatles songs all the time when I was little. I'm not sure which ones, despite singing them with everyone else in the playground at primary school – or pretending to because I didn't know the words. I would mumble away, not wanting to feel left out because everyone apart from me knew what to sing, and had a television, and was allowed to play out on Sunday, and was allowed to wear jeans. I think there was 'Close Your Eyes And I'll Kiss Yew' and 'Can't Buy Me Love' and 'It's Bin a Hard Day's Night' and 'A Wanna Hold Your Hand'. A few years later my brothers and I sang incessantly about living in a yellow submarine, to the eventual irritation of our parents. This song had a strangely infectious tune, or maybe it was infectiously strange: peculiar harmonies, and weird background sounds of distorted voices shouting things over tannoys, and a brass band, and a peculiar drum sound that pounded away insistently and got inside my head.

All of this obviously made an impression, because here I am writing about it now, not having heard 'Yellow Submarine' for years until, after my ferry 'cross the Mersey, I went and bought a copy of *Revolver* from Skeleton Records in Birkenhead. I bought a copy of *Sergeant Pepper* as well because, not liking the Beatles, I had never listened to either album.

I was a child of the sixties. Not in the Beatlemania or even the hippy sense; more in the 'that's when I went to primary school' sense. I was born at the end of the fifties: twenty years after John Peel; nineteen years after John Lennon; three years after John Lydon. In the Beatlemania/ hippy sense, I was actually a child of the seventies, a child of glam rock, prog rock, krautrock, disco, dub, pub rock and punk rock, my teenage years and the years of that decade coinciding for around three-quarters of the time. I was 13 for three-quarters of 1973, 14 for three-quarters of 1974 and so on, with my teenage years and the seventies ending together, give or take a month or two, in October 1979. As the chimes of midnight rang out from the Sheffield University clock tower announcing my twentieth birthday and the day I would get my ear pierced, I found myself peeing against a stone wall after emerging hurriedly from a late showing of Sam Peckinpah's Third Reich spaghetti movie *Cross of Iron* with an over-full bladder. But that's still in the future.

When I was a primary-school child of the sixties my dad was a teacher and my mum was a housewife who had previously been a nurse. Neither of them went in for pop music and so for a few years neither did I. However, Dorothy Clark did. She was a teenager who lived in the house on the corner opposite ours in Edinburgh Drive. I remember standing fascinated and a bit shocked in the doorway of her front room, watching her enthusiastically doing the twist in her bare feet on a cream-coloured carpet to the tinny overamplified dansette sound of songs like 'Bits and Pieces' by the Dave Clark Five. Whatever songs she played, she played them one after the other without going near the record player, because it had an auto-changer. I stared, amazed as the records dropped down onto the turntable by themselves, one after another as if by magic. After a song finished, there would be a loud frying-bacon sound as the pickup arm worked its way to the centre of the disc, then an explosive silence as arm and vinyl separated. Then there was a whirr, a plop as the next disc dropped, a bang as the stylus hit the record, another prelude of crackles, and we were off again, or at any rate Dorothy was. Magic. Technology. What's the difference when there's loud pop music playing, you're very small and you're watching a teenager do the twist in her bare feet.

We didn't have a dansette – we had a radiogram. It looked a bit like a teak veneer drinks cabinet on legs, though my parents didn't drink. We didn't have any Beatles records, so I must have heard them on the radio. We had some classical LPs, including *Peter and the Wolf*, which I liked a lot, and the Brandenburg Concertos, which I don't remember, though I got my dad to buy me a CD version for my 40th birthday. Although most of the LP covers were very sombre, with black-and-white photos on the sleeves, a colour photo adorned the sleeve of *The Four & Only Seekers*. I liked harmonious Australian folkies the Seekers a lot. On the gospel track 'We're Moving On', they really rocked and I would play this over and over again, thrilling to its raucous edginess. For some reason the radiogram speaker was on the underside, so sometimes I would lie on the floor between its legs with my head underneath to obtain maximum benefit. The adrenalin flowed less freely on their second gospel offering, 'Kumbaya', and the third, 'This Little Light Of Mine', lay somewhere in between. 'Morningtown Ride' sounded babyish so I pretended not to like it.

At some stage my dad took me with him tramping round Liverpool to various record shops to buy a copy of Schubert's piano quintet in A major, better known as *The Trout*. Lots of shops back then had listening booths, so we would stand or sit in these little compartments with their magnolia coloured pegboard walls, me mostly in grumpy silence and my dad mostly immersed in a private world of Trouts. If it was a headphones shop he would let me put them on for a while so I could hear the tinkly, noodly piano and strings that I suppose sounded quite like quickly moving water. I've no idea which version Dad wanted or which version he ended up buying, but I do know that I love this piece of music. Amongst the shops we visited would have been Nems, the shop where Brian Epstein had once worked as manager.

Everything comes back to the Beatles, I suppose, though by the time I was old enough to decide, I knew I didn't like them. Before that, during the four years when they were famous as a proper band and then the four years after that when they disappeared into the recording studio, I was a small child growing up in Birkenhead just opposite Beatletown, and of course I liked the Beatles, everyone did. Things didn't change much until I started acquiring my own opinions about music, which was around the time I got to hear 'Get It On'. Before that, I remember songs like 'She Loves You' and 'Bits and Pieces' and 'Sun Arise'. I remember living in Edinburgh Drive, then I remember living in Waterpark

Road, just round the corner, where we moved when I was about five because it was bigger and so was our family by that time. I remember the Dave Clark Five and Rolf Harris, and I remember the Beatles.

Paul McCartney remembered Penny Lane, which runs between Allerton Road and Greenbank Road in the Mossley Hill area of Liverpool, but one of the differences between what I remember and what he remembered is that he went and wrote a song about what he remembered. Another difference is that he was a Beatle, so millions of people soaked up this version of his impressions and memories like sponges, absorbing it and making it part of their own memories and impressions. John Lennon remembered a Salvation Army orphanage in Woolton where he used to play as a child, and he wrote a song about that. Paul and John used their fragments, their impressions and memories of these places to create two of the Beatles' best-loved songs, released together in February 1967 and occasionally voted the greatest single of all time. You can go on a Magical Mystery Tour bus journey around Liverpool, and see the places mentioned in 'Strawberry Fields Forever' and 'Penny Lane' and other Beatles songs. What you see on this Beatles pilgrimage are Beatles places, and what you hear is Beatles songs because they play them on the bus, so you can join everything together and create your own personal or shared Beatles story.

What you don't get to experience is what went on inside John Lennon and Paul McCartney's bony little headcaves, not the actual snatches and fragments, memories and impressions, real or otherwise, that made them write the songs in the first place, though you can marvel at how it all came about and you can enjoy listening to them in Beatletown. On the Beatles bus listening to Beatles songs visiting Beatles places, what you end up doing is constructing a Beatles story, the story of your life set to Beatles music, using bits of your idea of their ideas of their story, set to your memories of their music. That's the real magical mystery, the fusion of the power of music and the power of memory that takes place inside your head and my head and everyone else's head, in each head a homunculus gazing at pictures on a wall, listening to music and coming up with a story that joins it all together.

At the end of the Magical Mystery Tour you get to visit the world-famous re-excavated, refurbished, repurposed Cavern Club on Mathew Street to maybe buy some souvenirs and enjoy a refreshing drink or two. There's a range of beers, and there's Beatles merchandise on view in glass cases. In fact, there's beer and Beatles merchandise everywhere around the Cavern Club, in the area that your free Beatles map refers to as 'Beatle Village' or 'the Cavern Quarter'. On a recent visit I spent a few hours wandering up and down Mathew Street in a state of bemusement, carrying my free map like a tourist, which is what I was. At one end of the street was a bronze statue of an early period John Lennon. He, or it, was standing on the cobbles outside the Cavern Pub, which is nothing to do with the Cavern Club, though in another way it's everything to do with it, like everything else around there. He, or it, was leaning against a wall like Lennon himself in the photo on the cover of the *Rock 'n' Roll* album, in which he has short pre-moptop hair and wears a pre-suit leather jacket. I suppose the bronze statue looked a bit like him, but it had a moptop rather than a quiff, and the head was too big, so it also looked a bit like a Thunderbirds puppet. As you might be expected to imagine, Japanese tourists were taking photos of one another all around.

Up above the statue and the tourists, on a wall where you would expect to see the sign for Mathew Street is one that says BEATLE STREET, beneath which is a small sculpture of a lady-madonna figure holding three babies, beneath which it says FOUR LADS WHO SHOOK THE WORLD. There were originally four baby-lads, but apparently one disappeared and was replaced by a sign saying PAUL HAS TAKEN WINGS AND FLOWN, while Paul was in Wings. On the wall to the left is another baby, holding a guitar and with a halo bearing the words LENNON LIVES. This appeared a few years later, at a time when the statement wasn't true but everyone wished it was.

All of which shows how real the Beatles still are, or how unreal they are, it's hard to tell. Millions of people regard them as friends, as heroes, as idols and icons, as extensions of themselves. Some of these people grew up with them, and many grew up before them or after them. Even saying people grew up with the Beatles makes it sound like they were their neighbours or their brothers or their mates, but what people really did was pass into and through their adolescence and maybe on into adulthood while listening to the music of the Beatles, maybe growing and changing at the same time that the music grew and changed and the Beatles grew and changed and the world grew and changed. Me, I was too late, I couldn't see what all the fuss was about; I don't remember much apart from early songs that saturated the air like the steam from Monday washing, as the washing machine gurgled, the spin-drier whined and the radio played somewhere in the background. The Beatles never shook my world, but there I was years later, a tourist in what had once been Mathew Street, unsure of what to think now that it was Beatle Street instead.

Last time I had walked along Mathew Street it had been old and grey and run down, a murky canyon between tall decaying buildings, with a few small, strange, interesting places to visit, like the Armadillo Tea Rooms with its bust of Jung leaning out of the wall, and LIVERPOOL IS THE POOL OF LIFE carved underneath, whatever that means; and there was Probe Records, and the Grapes pub, and a club called Eric's. What is there to say about Eric's? It was a place that felt like the best club in the world with the best music in the world, because for a few years at the tail end of the seventies (October 1976 to March 1980), that's what it was. It was a noisy sweaty black-walled cellar opposite the Cavern, where the nearest thing to Beatlemania happened for me and a few hundred or a few thousand other children of the seventies. It happened and, just like Woodstock, it's carried on happening ever since in our heads, enveloping the middle-aged offspring of Eric's, whoever they are, wherever they are, in a warm mood-altering cloud of intense emotion, strange haircuts, amazing music, and also some not so amazing music.

It was at Eric's between April 1978 and March 1980 that I saw Slaughter and the Dogs, then Steve Hillage, and then

- Sham 69
- the Germs / Penetration
- Wire
- Magazine
- the Specials / the Clash
- Tanz Der Youth
- Cygnus / Tapper Zukie
- Gang Of Four
- Stiff Little Fingers / Essential Logic
- Wire / Prag Vec
- the Undertones
- Those Naughty Lumps / SPG
- the Skids
- Patrik Fitzgerald
- the Pretenders
- Jean Jacques Burnel
- Iggy Pop / the Zones
- Penetration
- the Undertones
- the Pop Group
- the Human League
- the Teardrop Explodes
- the Mekons
- the Cramps / Pink Military
- the Fall / Echo and the Bunnymen
- Wire / Nightmare In Wax
- Activity Minimal
- the Merton Parkas
- Joy Divison / Swell Maps
- the Not Sensibles
- Crass / the Poison Girls

- the Damned
- Orchestral Manoeuvres In The Dark
- the Psychedelic Furs.

And just as the music from Eric's seemed to briefly eclipse the Beatles, so in Mathew Street in the 21st century the Beatles have in turn eclipsed Eric's, like my Cavern was never there, almost like it never happened.

In one way Mathew Street had always been Beatle Street: the sculpture on the wall had always been there, though in the seventies that's about all there was. Back then, the city seemed ashamed of the four lads who shook the world, and talk of honouring them with statues and monuments was met with indifference or derision. In the years since then, Mathew Street has truly become Beatle Street, and the Beatle virus has grown, replicated and mutated exponentially, colonising the whole area, sucking in visitors and pilgrims and tourists from all around the world, creating a benign environment in which they can spend their time and, more importantly, their money. And any old tat is fine as long as it's Beatles tat; you only have to take a look around the Cavern Quarter to realise that.

There's lots of Beatles tat on Mathew Street, but nothing about Eric's, not even a plaque.[3] I asked someone in a Beatles shop, and they said that if I went halfway down a flight of stairs in a place that wasn't open at the time there was something or other about Eric's there, near the toilets. As if to make the point even more starkly, whatever the point might have been, further along the street I caught sight of a 'boutique emporium' called Cavern Walks, which was situated above the Cavern. Feeling compelled to enter, I numbly climbed the stairs and found From Me To You, a Beatles and rock memorabilia shop, maybe *the* Beatles and rock memorabilia shop. If you're into music and bizarre knick-knacks it would be hard to come away from here without buying something,

---

3 Although there was *Eric's the Musical* at the Everyman Theatre in 2008.

even if it wasn't the Insane Clown Posse 'Fuck The World' ashtray. What I bought was a set of Sex Pistols drinks coasters.

I also got into a conversation with the man behind the counter, who had caught sight of me making notes about all the Beatles products that were on sale. We began by talking about the Yellow Submarine children's pyjamas, and ended up talking about an LP I remembered called *Jukebox at Eric's*. The man behind the counter said he thought he knew someone who had a copy and might be able to get a CD burned for me. He gave me his email address and I tried emailing him, but my message got bounced back. I've since bought a copy of the LP, and the track listing is:

	Side 1	
1	The Lion	Duke Mitchell
2	Elevator Operator	The Rays
3	Jim Dandy Handyman	Shelby R Smith
4	Jungle Fever	The Playboys
5	Do It Bop	Billy Prager
6	Georgia Slop	Big Al Downing
7	Underwater	The Frogmen
8	F - Olding Money	Tommy Blake
	Side 2	
1	Rocket Trip	Jackie Lowell
2	50 Megatons	Sonny Russell
3	The Catalina Push	Catalinas
4	3 Young Rebs From Georgia	Bobby Day
5	The Fugitive	Lamar Morris
6	Shanghaied	The Wailers
7	New Dance In France	Bobby Lee Trammell
8	Monkey's Uncle.	Ray Sharpe

It's not music from the jukebox at Eric's; instead it's the first and only volume issued by Eric's Records from a projected 'Twentieth Century Jukebox' series of ten – 'Vol 1: Rock 'n' Roll'. The man behind LP, the label, the club and the actual jukebox at Eric's was Roger Eagle, a quiet giant of a man both physically and in terms of his contribution to popular culture. As a DJ, promoter, mentor and music enthusiast he probably deserves the same level of recognition as someone like John Peel, but Eagle never achieved widespread recognition, never lived a settled life and never enjoyed a secure tenure of any kind. When he died in 1999 at the age of 57, the master tapes for *Jukebox At Eric's* were buried with him. One of his most valuable pieces of advice to local musicians was 'never listen to the Beatles'.[4]

As I left Cavern Walks, downstairs beyond the plastic potted topiary chained to the railings there was a themed restaurant called Lucy In The Sky With Diamonds. Outside was a plaque that claimed the restaurant was *built on the site of the world famous Cavern stage* which, bizarrely, implied that the stage in the nearby Cavern Club wasn't in the right place. So, where is the real Cavern Club stage? It depends on your point of view. When the Cavern closed in 1973 and the warehouse above it was demolished to make way for a railway ventilation shaft, the Cavern cellar got filled with rubble, which is the way it stayed until the early eighties. Then, when the Beatles refurbishment project began it was discovered that the proposed Cavern Walks boutique emporium couldn't be built on top of the Cavern cellar because the cellar couldn't bear the weight. So the cellar was filled in and Cavern Walks was built, after which a replica Cavern was constructed nearby incorporating 15,000 of the bricks from the original cellar. The new replica Cavern occupies most of the original site but is slightly to the right, slightly deeper underground and faces a different direction. And the ventilation shaft was never built. When the original

---

4   The oral account *Sit Down! Listen To This!* compiled by Bill Sykes is the only book you can buy about Roger Eagle. Try and find a copy.

Cavern closed, owner Roy Adams used the compensation money to set up another club on Mathew Street called the New Cavern. It didn't do well, and was later split into two separate premises. The ground floor became Gatsby's. The basement of the New Cavern was taken over by Ken Testi, Pete Fulwell and Roger Eagle, and became Eric's.

Near the Cavern plaque outside Lucy In The Sky With Diamonds was a bronze sculpture of four young men who didn't look anything like the Beatles, with another plaque that said *This plaque is to commemorate the charitable work undertaken by 'Father Tom McKenzie', compere to the Beatles, with thanks from Beatles fans worldwide.*

By then it felt like time to leave, so I retired to the Grapes for a swift Guinness before meeting my mum and dad at the Walker Art Gallery for lunch. The pub was pretty much how I remembered it. The only difference was that the jukebox was now playing the likes of the Pretenders, Dire Straits, Blondie, Brotherhood of Man and Dave Edmunds. And on a wall near the back there was a grainy framed photo of four young men who looked very like Beatles, sitting in the seat directly beneath where the photo of them was mounted. After lunch at the Walker I visited the gallery shop and the man who served me was Norman, a small, balding, bespectacled man who used to work in Probe Records at the end of Mathew Street. He also on occasions manned the turntables at Eric's, and I had numerous yelled conversations with him in the style of

Me: WHAT WAS THAT YOU JUST PLAYED?
Norman: WHAT?
Me: WHAT – WAS – THAT – YOU – JUST – PLAYED?
Norman: NO BONES FOR THE DOGS
Me: WHAT?
Norman: NO – BONES – FOR – THE – DOGS
Me: WHO'S IT BY?
Norman: WHAT?
Me: WHO'S – IT – BY?
Norman: JOE GIBBS

Me: WHAT?
Norman: JOE – GIBBS.

The same thing happened when I first heard 'Back To Nature' by Fad Gadget, for example.

I felt like I'd had enough of the Beatles by then, but maybe you want more, perhaps something a bit more real, a bit closer to the Beatles than all the touristy cultural heritage tat. A lot of people must feel the same way, and that's maybe why they go on Magical Mystery bus tours to get closer to the Beatles, or their idea of the Beatles, or someone else's idea of them. Over the years so many fans have stolen the street sign from Penny Lane that the council stopped replacing it and painted the name on the wall instead. Nobody has yet stolen the wall, but someone once stole the wrought iron gates from the Strawberry Field Salvation Army orphanage in Woolton. And 5,000 bricks from the original Cavern were sold in 1983, ten years after it closed and a year before it re-opened. And 150 bricks from the house where John Lennon grew up on Menlove Avenue in Woolton were supposedly auctioned off after a wall was demolished to make room for cameras while a TV movie about him was being filmed there.

Even so, none of that matters, because none of it is real. Only the songs are real. Places can be closed down, filled in, excavated, re-located, re-built, re-named, or sold off brick by brick, but the songs go on for ever – on vinyl, on tape, on CD, on iPods, on phones, on bus tours and in people's heads. Or maybe the places are real because of the songs. It's hard to tell, because it was never just about the music, it was also about the times and places, the feelings and everything else as well. Penny Lane is a real place, but Strawberry Fields isn't; at least it isn't a Salvation Army orphanage in Woolton. The place in Liverpool is called Strawberry Field, without the –s at the end. There never was a place called Strawberry Fields, not while John Lennon was still alive.

But.

Imagine there's a garden. Imagine it's shaped like a teardrop and it's in Central Park, just opposite the New York apartment block where John Lennon lived, and where he died on December 8, 1980. Imagine the garden was named 'Strawberry Fields' the following year, and was dedicated by Yoko Ono on October 9 1985, which would have been John's 45th birthday. Imagine that on the pathway near the entrance is a reproduction of a mosaic from Pompeii, made by Italian craftsmen as a gift and including the single word IMAGINE – rather than FINGE, which is what it might have said if it really had come from Pompeii.

Imagine Strawberry Fields wasn't a real place, but now it is: I know this for myself, because I've been there. It was a strange experience, and utterly Beatles. There were signs designating the area A Quiet Zone, which meant 'no amplified sound or musical instruments'. Did this mean musical instruments were forbidden, or just amplified musical instruments? Either way, an elderly gent with a grey ponytail was sitting on a park bench playing 'Hey Jude' on his guitar and people were quietly singing along. There was a gentle scrum of photograph-takers around the IMAGINE mosaic, and flowers had been laid along with a framed photo of the mosaic itself, bought from one of the nearby vendors. It was all relaxed and low-key, but busy – the first decent weather in months, apparently – so I didn't stay long. As I was leaving I heard a disturbance, and went to investigate. The ponytail gent was engaged in an eyeball-to-eyeball shouting competition with a plump, sweaty man in white shorts who seemed sceptical about the gent's musical competence and was using this as a means of vehemently questioning his validity on various other levels. As the ponytail gent became increasingly agitated, some sort of scuffle seemed likely, but the plump man suddenly turned and walked away, calling abuse over his shoulder, leaving the other shaken and trembling with anger as he put away his guitar, unable to continue. I'm not sure if John would have laughed or cried over all this. Actually, I'm pretty sure he'd have either laughed till he cried, or cried till he laughed. Why? Because when asked once if he was a mod or a rocker, he replied, 'I'm a mocker'.

Strawberry Fields wasn't a real place, and then, after the song, it was. Now imagine that the song itself wasn't real either – because it wasn't; not a real song that a group like the Beatles could play and sing in front of an audience. This song, the one that ended up on The Greatest Single, was actually two songs; or, two versions of the same song that were cut up and stuck together to become a strange hybrid that was never performed the way it sounded, and never could be.

It came about because John Lennon listened to all the different takes of the song and decided he liked the start of one and the rest of another, then left the 'Sun Arise' pair of producer George Martin and engineer Geoff Emerick to sort it out. What Lennon chose was the start of Take 7 and the rest of Take 26. Take 7 was a slightly psychedelic version played on rock instruments and a Mellotron. It was more or less in the key of A and was quite slow. Take 26 was more elaborate and included trumpets, cellos, a piano, the sound of backward cymbals, and a swarmandel: an Indian instrument that sounds like a dulcimer. It was more or less in the key of B and was quite fast.

In a miraculous piece of editing, what Martin and Emerick did was speed up Take 7 (the slow one in A), and slow down Take 26 (the fast one in B), matching and combining the two versions almost seamlessly, though you can still hear the join if you listen out for it. About a minute into the song, just after the first verse and before the words 'Strawberry Fields' in the second chorus, there's a slightly woozy bit where the splice was made. If you manage to catch it, rather than detracting from the song, the wooziness adds an extra quality of unreality to an already unreal song about an overwhelming sense of unreality. In fact I can't think of any other song in which the words and music and production complement each other so perfectly.

You probably know the words. They aren't really about anything, apart from maybe sitting alone in a tree and dreaming or hallucinating, feeling disoriented or lethargic; feeling detached from the world, or wanting to withdraw from it. Maybe nothing is real – the song certainly isn't. And the studio recording process isn't real either, not like a proper band singing together and playing songs on musical instruments; nor is the sound of cymbals recorded and then played backwards to give a swooshing sound; nor is the varispeed effect that gives the song its wobbly, meandering sense of detachment as it floats free from any single root note. It's all tricks, electricity and magnetism, strange sounds made by people taking drugs and messing about with microphones and bits of tape in a recording studio.[5]

All of which is strange, and unreal, and absolutely fine, because by the time they recorded 'Strawberry Fields Forever', a strangely unreal song about nothing being real, the Beatles weren't a real band any more. They didn't split up until 1970, but their last live performance in front of an audience took place on 29 August 1966 when they played for just over half an hour in the Candlestick Park Stadium, San Francisco. Between this and 'She Loves You Yeah Yeah Yeah' is only three years, and when they stopped playing live they were still shaving and still wearing suits. It was only after their final performance that they went hairy, at the

---

5 'Strawberry Fields Forever' contains one of the first ever uses of the Mellotron on a pop recording – you can hear it played in a sort of wobbly flute mode in the opening part of the song. It could also sound like trumpets or cellos, or a choir, or almost anything else you cared to make tape recordings of. Not very like the real version of any of these, which is what makes its sound so gorgeous, and so unreal and so right. It's all just magnets, tapes and electricity. Instead of hitting a string like a piano or blowing air through a pipe like an organ, pressing a key on the Mellotron pulls a length of pre-recorded tape across a playback head for a maximum of eight seconds, after which the tape runs out, the sound stops, and the key has to be released, pulling the length of tape back to the start again. The end result, with all its wow and flutter, produces a lovely ethereal sound like a crude sampler or a dodgy tape machine, both of which are what the Mellotron is.

same time becoming a virtual band rather than a flesh-and-blood performing one.

This was something new. Until around that time, the recording of music in the studio tended to be a documentary process, aimed at capturing a reproducible live performance. Records were regarded as little more than demos for the sheet music, sales of which were the measure of commercial success. But with the Beatles, suddenly it was all about the records. And the ones performing the music were also the ones who wrote it; they'd taken over. And strangely, once the Live Beatles disappeared in 1966, the new Virtual Beatles acquired even more of a presence, thanks to the Sheet Music Beatles and the Cover Version Beatles, both of whom made them even more money, because Beatles songs were covered almost endlessly by almost everyone, and still are.[6]

This mutation of the Beatle virus has carried on replicating and evolving, colonising the world, helping to make them the biggest, most covered, most known, most heard band ever, a part of world culture and world consciousness just like Elvis or Jesus, only there were four of them. John, Paul, George and Ringo. Not George, Paul, Ringo and John. Not Ringo, George, John and Paul, or any of the other 21 possibilities – one combination was the right one and the other 23 weren't. It was almost like the way you always said Matthew, Mark, Luke and John but with John first rather than last – because everyone thought of John first, then Paul, then George, then Ringo.

They must have become aware of their superstar household-name status early on, and must have enjoyed it for a while, though learning to live with it subsequently has involved a traumatic journey into dark, tangled and uncharted territory that has lasted more than five times longer than the band itself and still hasn't completely ended. Once a Beatle, always a Beatle. Always a poster, figurine, tea

---

6 'Yesterday' is the most covered song ever, with more than 3,000 versions. On the day after Paul McCartney's 68th birthday a radio station called Resonance FM spent twenty-four hours playing as many of them as it could manage.

towel, ashtray, wig, pair of pyjamas, dinner mat, mug, key ring, record collection, icon, bedroom shrine. They were pop heroes, pop idols, pop gods even, and in an unguarded moment John Lennon once said that the Beatles were more popular than Jesus, which made them even more famous and got them into a lot of trouble, especially in America. More popular then Jesus – quite a claim. What John said may or may not have been true, but since when did trying to talk some kind of truth about the world as you saw it from your strange, privileged, unreal perspective ever get you anywhere?

The statement originally appeared in a feature by Maureen Cleave in the London Evening Standard on March 4, 1966, just five months before their final public performance. The feature was called 'How Does A Beatle Live? John Lennon Lives Like This'. If you read it, what is most significant, and what Maureen Cleave comments on again and again, is the detached, restless nature of Beatle existence. Three of them lived in the Weybridge stockbroker belt with their wives; they didn't see other people very much; they owned lots of TV sets and tape recorders and telephones (and a Mellotron each); they had the TV on all the time (often while listening to records); they travelled about in chauffeur-driven cars fitted with telephones and TVs and bars; they woke and slept and ate out of synch with the rest of the world. They, or some of them, especially John, were taking LSD and smoking a lot of pot. It all sounds dysfunctionally modern, even postmodern, and it is, but this chaotic chemical multimedia experiment in consciousness altering took place over half a century ago: they were among the first people to live like this. For a Beatle or any other super-rich super-celebrity, most of the time it must seem like nothing is real – until something you say or do breaks away, replicates, mutates, spirals out of control, becomes public property then and comes back to haunt you, stalk you and molest you.

What John Lennon said was:

We've never had time before to do anything but just be Beatles.

They keep telling me I'm all right for money but then I think I may have spent it all by the time I'm 40 so I keep going.

There's something else I'm going to do, something I must do – only I don't know what it is. That's why I go round painting and taping and drawing and writing and that, because it may be one of them.

In amongst everything else he said:

Christianity will go, it will vanish and shrink. I needn't argue about that; I'm right and I will be proved right. We're more popular than Jesus now; I don't know which will go first – rock 'n' roll or Christianity.

What did he mean by this? That the Beatle virus or the rock and roll virus or the Fab Four merchandise virus had colonised the world to a greater extent than the Jesus virus or the Bible virus or the Church virus? That the Beatle virus was more successful or worthwhile than the Jesus virus? Probably not. It was really just him shooting from the lip, mouthing off about all kinds of things in the glib, gobby way he often did. Reading the rest of the article puts what he said into some kind of context, but the context didn't do him any good because nobody was interested in it. People never are.

He may have been statistically correct about how popular the Beatles were, he may not. And we still don't know whether rock and roll or Christianity will go first. It didn't matter what he really meant, because after that what he really meant stopped mattering, if it ever did in the first place; and after that events in the outside world burst the Beatles bubble most abruptly and unpleasantly. There followed a disastrous trip to Japan, during which they played to politely quiet Japanese audiences at Budokan and it became apparent how much they had declined as live performers while trapped behind their wall of screams. Declined, but declined from what? It's interesting to compare the Beatles with, say the Who or the Yardbirds or the Rolling Stones or Pink Floyd or anyone else around that time who had what you might call a stage act, something that worked in addition to the music. Smashing up equipment, shaking your butt, turning everything up to eleven, throwing potatoes at a large gong, or bathing everything in coloured lights, strobes and feedback might blow everyone's minds and enhance or distract from the music, but the Beatles had none of that to fall back on, because all they were really doing was playing the records live, performing the sheet music.

Then, four months on from the original feature in the London Evening Standard, an America teen magazine called Datebook reprinted the Jesus quote. After that, there were public bonfires and statements of condemnation by youngsters and oldsters and the Ku Klux Klan. About a month later at the end of August they played at Candlestick Park, and then they retired from live performance.

'Strawberry Fields Forever' / 'Penny Lane' was the first thing to be released after their retirement, a stop-gap containing two tracks that should really have been part of *Sergeant Pepper*.

Sergeant Pepper. The greatest album of all time. Or an uneven assembly of over-complicated pastiches and collages by a bunch of musicians with too many drugs and too much studio time. Or a meandering journey from the ridiculous to the sublime, from 'When I'm Sixty-four' to 'A Day In The Life'. Or a concept album about an imagined northern England that failed because its heart had been cut out and sold as a single. Whatever you think of *Sergeant Pepper*, it wasn't the carefully constructed masterpiece many have assumed it to be and wished it to be. Its disparate, intricate pieces were recorded by George Martin and the Beatles, but were assembled, sequenced and made into an album by Martin alone, because the Beatles took little interest in this process. And everything back then was in mono: the stereo production, the way music is now, the way we expect music to be now, was done later with no input from the band at all. But even so, what an album. Or maybe, what a part of another, greater super-album; what a part of some kind of idea of an album, one which would perhaps known as *The Album*. And if you wanted to know about *The* Album, then you would need to listen to another couple of LPs as well as *Sergeant Pepper*. Because to imagine the music on *The* Album, there are three LPs to hear, and just one psychedelic synergy that allows you to marvel not just at what the Beatles were doing, but also at what other bands were doing on other albums at the same time, however well or however badly, or madly or sadly. Because at the same time in the Abbey Road studios, Pink Floyd were recording *The Piper At The Gates Of Dawn* and the Pretty Things were about to start recording *SF Sorrow*. Both were produced by Norman Smith, who also worked with the Beatles (and went on to have a few forgettable seventies hits under the name Hurricane Smith). So, if you listen to all three LPs, then for a third of that time you must be hearing the *The* Album, though your version of it might well be different from mine.

Whatever your version of *The* Album sounds like, and whatever you think of *Sergeant Pepper*, the Beatles were never just about the music. Way before this, the Beatle virus had spread beyond the music, had been busily reproducing and mutating through into new formats, sheet music and cover versions and new media, movies and newspapers and magazines and merchandise, and over the next few years it would become clear how unprecedented the whole Beatle-virus-media phenomenon was, and quite how strange and out of control things were getting.

Mutations appeared early on in the form of two pop movies, the documentary-esque *A Hard Day's Night* (1964) and the Bond-esque *Help!* (1965). Then, in the short promotional films for songs like 'Rain' and 'Strawberry Fields Forever' and 'I Am The Walrus' the narrative, such as it was, disintegrated, leaving only the music and images, as the Beatles managed to pre-imagine much of MTV's output over the following decades. As the narrative disintegrated, at the same time the band as actual people disappeared from view until they existed only as media images of confused, embattled celebrities rather than performing musicians or real people, if they ever were real people by the time they were famous. As the process continued, over the Christmas period of 1967 a psychedelic coach-trippy made-for-TV road movie called *Magical Mystery Tour* was broadcast to a baffled public who saw it largely in black and white; and along with this there was an LP or double EP that included the acid-soaked 'I Am The Walrus'.

Most spectacularly of all, earlier that year on June 25 the Beatles appeared on TV in *Our World*, the first live international satellite broadcast. They performed a specially-written warm and fuzzy international anthem called 'All You Need Is Love' to a worldwide audience of 400 million people. They were everywhere.

Even when they weren't actually there at all. Between September 1965 and October 1967, a cartoon series called *The Beatles* aired on the American ABC network, produced by Al Brodax. Having previously bought the rights to Popeye and churned out over 200 cheap new episodes in two years, Brodax saw the Beatles on TV and had an idea. The idea was to replicate the Popeye process using the Beatles as the first ever cartoon band, and it worked.[7] Over three years there were three series and 39 episodes, all of which followed the same format: two low-budget cartoon shorts, each loosely based on and incorporating a song being performed by the band; in between the shorts would be a two-song sing-along sequence with even simpler animation and the lyrics displayed onscreen. Although the band disliked the series and Brian Epstein refused to permit its screening in the UK, it

---

7 The second cartoon pop band were probably Hanna-Barbera's Impossibles (1966), a guitar trio of superheroes -- Multi-man, Coil-man and Fluid-man, though the specifications of their instruments are uncertain. They never broke through to this world, unlike the Archies, a cartoon band whose third single, 'Sugar, Sugar' (1969), topped the charts in Britain and America.

was hugely successful in America, along with merchandising that included inflatable plastic cartoon figures from Lux and Nestlé, Ringo Roll bread, and Beatle ice lollies, confectionery and trading cards. Ironically, while the shows were being broadcast, the actual Beatles withdrew from the world, leaving the cartoon Beatles as their default representatives.[8] In 1968 things changed again, yet didn't change at all, as the Beatles cartoons and the movies morphed into the Beatles cartoon movie *Yellow Submarine*. Things changed because this time it looked like art rather than a shoddy and embarrassing piece of exploitation. But it didn't have any real Beatles in it, apart from a few minutes of their heads as they larked about at the end to endorse the project, despite earlier misgivings. Obviously, they sang all the songs, but the spoken voices were those of actors.

'John' was John Clive, an actor and successful thriller writer.

'Paul' was Geoffrey Hughes, later to become binman Eddie Yeats in 'Coronation Street' and chancer Vernon Scrips in 'Heartbeat'.

'George' was Peter Batten, an army deserter who was arrested during the recording of the soundtrack.

'Ringo' was Paul Angelis, an actor who also became 'George' after Peter Batten's arrest.

Like the TV series it was produced by Al Brodax, who clearly knew he was onto a good thing and made it better, managing to produce a great piece of work almost despite

---

8   The idea of cartoon Beatles makes perfect sense, especially when you remember that there were already a bunch of real-life cartoon Beatles called the Monkees. To me they were much more real than the Beatles, because I saw them on TV a lot more. I watched them at other people's houses, without understanding very much, though there wasn't much to understand other than American-style pre-MTV Beatles spoofery, some great songs and some not so great songs. It's strange to think that The Monkees started out as a TV concept then, after the show was cancelled, they became real, went out into the world, played live and did very well, while the Beatles did the opposite, starting out live and disappearing into movies and TV. And the Monkees eventually re-formed, but the Beatles didn't.

himself. Most of the quipping and bantering was provided by Roger McGough, Liverpool poet and member of the briefly famous Scaffold, whose huge hit 'Lily the Pink' took up residence in my young brain and has never really left. The name and the submarine idea came from *Revolver*, and Pepperland was from *Sergeant Pepper*, so the movie helped fill the gap into which the band had tumbled between these two albums, and from which 'Penny Lane / Strawberry Fields Forever' had emerged. Most of the songs were familiar but five were previously-unheard rejects, performed by the real Beatles acting as the cartoon Beatles acting as the real Beatles:

1. All Together Now
2. It's All Too Much
3. Baby You're a Rich Man
4. Only a Northern Song
5. Hey Bulldog.

And the story, well, the story was quite loose, more a way of stitching together a bunch of songs than anything else, with the incidental music and connecting passages written by George Martin, the number one fifth Beatle.

But music, movies, TV, pop cartoons, surreal story lines and psychedelic visuals were only part of the story – other hybrids and mutations were also starting to appear, strange shadowy creatures that arrived unbidden and started congregating outside the great big Beatles tent, creatures that had emerged from dark spaces inside other people's heads. Formed from alternative readings of the multimedia, multilayered text that the Beatles had become, they were generated by people out there, way out there, followers, fans and fanatics. The alternative readings started with the lyrics and then took in the album covers and the movies and everything else, just keeping going, coming up with things that were much more than they were meant to mean, more bizarre or grotesque than anything that could have been imagined by normal people. But the Beatles weren't normal people. They might have been once upon a time, but they weren't any more, and neither were some of their fans.

Even from early on the Beatles were public property, owned by their public as songs in the air, pictures on the wall, and reluctant, bemused spokesmen for their generation. They are probably the most heard and over-interpreted band ever. Bob Dylan is probably the most over-interpreted solo artist for similar reasons – his fragmentary, surreal sixties lyrics weren't obviously 'about' anything in the conventional sense either, and lent themselves to interpretations that he seemed unwilling to either confirm or deny. Much like Dylan's tortuous relationship with self-styled garbologist and Dylanologist AJ Weberman, who stalked and harangued Dylan and went through his bins, anything the Beatles did or said or were thought to have done or said could turn into a story that took on a life of its own and started wandering about causing trouble, another strange creature prowling up and down in the half-light outside the big tent.

One of the best known Beatle stories is the Paul Is Dead story (there was a similar but less heated Dylan tale after he wisely came off his motorbike and went to ground for a while). In 1969 around the time *Abbey Road* was released, rumours began to circulate in US broadcast and print media that Paul McCartney had died in a car crash on 9 November 1966 and been replaced by a lookalike in order not to jeopardise the success of the Beatles, after which the band, especially John, perhaps through a sense of guilt, had taken to leaving cryptic clues about this. The story first emerged as a spoof on a radio show and also ran in a college newspaper, with deliberately ridiculous clues offered as evidence. Some folk took it seriously and went on to find new clues in the album covers, the lyrics, the records and, best of all, in bits of the records played backwards. It couldn't have happened to any other band. Why not? Because the Beatles had always enjoyed playing silly buggers, experimenting, messing about and confusing people for their own amusement, especially when it became clear that some fans had started reading too much into the words and music, which only encouraged them, especially John, because it was easy to go along with it, and take the piss at the same time. Consider 'I Am The Walrus', a song written in response to a letter from a student at Quarry Bank High School, which Lennon had attended. In the letter, the student mentioned that his English teacher was getting the class to analyse Beatles lyrics. Amused, Lennon decided to write a song with deliberately confusing lyrics. Despite or perhaps because of this, the song, released as a single and on the *Magical Mystery Tour* EP, made it to both number 1 and number 2 simultaneously in December 1967.

As their career continued the approach to music and words became more complex, reflecting the range of creative, technical and chemical possibilities they were exploring. Rather than recording music, they were playing about with tapes and electricity; not so much writing songs as assembling fragments of text and speech snatched from anywhere and everywhere. These processes reflected their non-linear lifestyles, non-Western and non-mainstream influences and systematically disoriented states of mind, as well as those of a lot of other people, many of whom happened to be their fans. Less than five years separate 'I Want To Hold Your Hand' and 'I Am The Walrus', but they come from different universes.

They came to call this approach Random: disjointed, chance elements; new meanings or no meanings; things that surprised or amused them; songs assembled by grabbing bits and pieces from the world around them, from radio or TV or magazines and newspapers, or nursery rhymes and playground verses. The band moved beyond what had previously been known as pop or rock or even music, into drones and Indian-sounding guitars, and sitars and swarmandels. They bought Mellotrons, used and abused technology, experimented with slow tapes and looped tapes and backward tapes. They used reversed recordings as early as 'Rain', the B-side of 'Paperback Writer', which contains backwards guitar, so it wasn't just fans making it up; well, not all of it, not all the time.[9]

Ironically, this radically modern and post-modern experimentation with Random was actually part of a tradition, derived from the work of avant-garde artists going back as far as far as World War I. Paul in particular had wide-ranging interests, and was among the first to apply such techniques to pop music, in the process helping turn it into its more serious older-brother upper-case incarnation, Rock. Random borrowed from Dada and Surrealism, whose 'anti-art' relied heavily on arbitrarily selected and reassembled elements. It also borrowed from more recent practitioners such as William Burroughs and John Cage, and from techniques developed using early tape recorders in the late forties in France, known as *musique concrète*.

The first Surrealist manifesto was published in 1924. Because pop didn't exist back then, the manifesto refers to artists, writers and poets but not musicians, though it's obvious that given the chance Surrealism would have embraced pop, then immediately tried to snog it, grope it and get it into bed. In the manifesto, Surrealism defines itself as

> *thought dictated in the absence of all control exerted by reason, and outside all aesthetic or moral preoccupations.*

The manifesto also pays respect to

> *the omnipotence of dream ... the disinterested play of thought*

and claims that

---

9 You can make the run-out groove of *Sergeant Pepper* say, 'we'll fuck you like Superman' if you try hard enough. Apparently, it was never meant to say that, but that doesn't help if you're a Beatle.

it is even permissible to entitle POEM
(or, *it is even permissible to give the name SONG to)*

what we get from the most random assemblage
possible... of headlines and scraps of headlines cut out
of the newspapers.

It was William Burroughs who with Brion Gysin in the late fifties began using 'cut-ups', an initially revolutionary concept that, once understood, seems obvious. Using pages that you have either written yourself or taken from elsewhere (newspapers, books, magazines), simply cut them into pieces of any size or shape, then rearrange them to make new texts in which words are forced together to create new meanings. This is a literary version of the visual collages and montages previously produced by the Dadaists and Surrealists. Burroughs also worked with tape recorders, re-recording over previously made recordings again and again to create sonic cut-ups.

John Cage was responsible for the famous or infamous piece *4'33"*, first performed in 1952 by a pianist who sat down at a piano, opened the lid and then didn't play anything. Instead of the performer, what the audience got to hear were the sounds around them, which they were meant to listen to as though they were music, which in a way they were. Cage also composed pieces for stylus cartridges, turntables and radio sets in the thirties and forties, devised the 'prepared piano' (with objects wedged between its strings), and incorporated Random and nonmusical elements into many of his compositions. He was especially fond of using the I Ching, making aesthetic decisions based on the cryptic statements contained in its 64 chapters and their many possible permutations.

Musique concrète is literally 'concrete music', music that is concrete in the sense of being solid or tangible, existing on spools of tape rather than as sheet music or sounds in the air. Although it might not have been music in the accepted sense (despite being carefully composed), it was definitely tangible, being created from bits and pieces of tape: recordings of trains departing, doors closing and the like. Tapes were cut up and rearranged to produce what was in effect another kind of collage or montage, but of sounds rather than words or images. It was McCartney rather than Lennon who was most interested in this kind of thing, Lennon being fond of the quotable quote, '*avant-garde* is French for bullshit' in the years before he met Yoko Ono.

As well as selfconsciously and un-selfconsciously experimenting with forms and techniques, the Beatles also complicated things by writing self-referential lyrics, amusing themselves by pissing out of their big tent onto some of the pseuds, anoraks and obsessives huddled there, the sort of folk they thought paid them too much attention and read too much into what they did. Not that there weren't a few games to play. An extreme example is the song 'Glass Onion', which contains references to the songs

- 'Strawberry Fields Forever'
- 'I Am The Walrus'
- 'Lady Madonna'
- 'Fool On The Hill'
- 'Fixing A Hole'

and then there are the references within the references, because

- 'Lady Madonna' contains a reference to 'I Am The Walrus'
- 'I Am The Walrus' contains a reference to 'Lucy In The Sky With Diamonds'.

The idea of a glass onion, with its translucent, brittle layers within layers within layers of refracted and reflected light, was just right for these mind games. During the Paul Is Dead episode, it was even claimed that glass onions were transparent balls that were formerly used as coffin handles, and therefore another clue. It was also claimed that it was a slang term for a monocle. The details don't matter: all the muttered and whispered background nonsense added texture and Random, and also perplexed people – it was part of the game. It's hard to know how much of this material to quote, and how much to assume is already familiar. You might be interested, you might know about it already, or you might not care. Me, I'm quite new to all this, I'm interested and I care about it. Does this make me part of the problem as well? I don't know.

What I do know is that one dark and twisting downhill road of Beatle obsession led Mark Chapman to the Dakota Building on 8 December 1980, where he shot John Lennon for being a phony. Another led Michael Abram to Friar Park, where he stabbed George Harrison on 27 December 1999 for being a sorcerer, and in order to save the next generation from drugs and witchcraft. An even darker and more twisting road led to the darkest heart of darkness, darker than anyone could have imagined, except for the man who did imagine it, and who some time later tattooed a swastika between his eyebrows. He was called Charles Manson and he believed, or said he believed, or was said to say he believed, that the Beatles had spoken to him through their music, especially on *The Beatles*, the album popularly known as *The White Album*.

Its plain white cover was designed by the pop artist Richard Hamilton, and even without the darkness of the Manson associations, white is something the music doesn't sound. The album's original title was *A Doll's House*, suggesting, rather than childlike play and innocence, an unsettling miniature environment crammed with strange bits and pieces; fragments that didn't belong but made a weird kind of sense when put together. What the music suggests is the jumble of possessions left behind in the home of a loving but dysfunctional family after things fell apart. Up in the attic, amongst everything else, there's this doll's house, its rooms crammed with tiny lost, found or discarded things, maybe even including a tiny doll's house for the dolls to play with. Maybe in the attic of this tiny doll's house for the dolls there is also another, minuscule doll's house, rooms within rooms within rooms. And the music sounds like the opposite of the plain white cover, the opposite of the film for 'Imagine', where spacious, simple, saccharine nursery-rhyme piano music plays and a white-clad John sings plaintively in a big empty white room while the shutters are opened and everything is flooded with white light. Here, it's dark and airless; the shutters are closing, or have already been nailed shut.

There's an earlier cover for the album, from when it was still going to be called *A Doll's House*, which was before Family released their 1968 LP *Music In A Doll's House*. This other cover is a naïve-style painting of the band by Patrick, a sixties incarnation of Scottish artist and writer John Byrne. It looks a bit like a bleached-out poster of something obscure by the French painter Henri Rousseau. The band are sitting on the ground with their knees drawn up, crammed into the picture along with strange birds, animals and odd bits of greenery. Their glum faces, all staring straight out of the picture, look like the four 8 x 10 portraits that were later given away with *The White Album*. To me, this cover looks and feels like the music sounds.[10]

Charles Manson quoted from the Beatles and from the Bible, in particular the book of Revelation, and he knew his Scientology. He taught his followers, his Family, that they needed to hide in the desert while a race war (the Helter Skelter) raged, with black people killing white people, after which he and the Family would emerge to rule the black survivors. The full story of what occurred is too complex and grotesque to summarise properly here: there are doubts about many aspects of what actually happened; and over everything hangs a disorienting fog of psychosis that obscures and distorts and makes it hard to find your way around and get back to the outside world again. It's a bit like stepping across the threshold into a looking-glass world, an anti-world of distorting mirrors where nothing is

---

10 It was eventually used as the cover for the 1985 compilation *The Beatles Ballads*.

real and everything is permitted. On one side of the mirror are the Beatles, on the other side is Manson, and through all the layers within layers and reflections and refractions and distortions sometimes their faces overlap and morph scarily, especially if you're completely off your head and living on a ranch somewhere out in the desert. Questions and answers become unclear, especially some of the whats, the whos and the whys.

The wheres, the whens and the hows are clear enough, though. In the early morning of August 9 1969, pregnant actress Sharon Tate and three of her friends were murdered at Tate's house on Cielo Drive in Los Angeles, receiving over 100 stab wounds. The word PIG was written on the front door in Tate's blood. Eighteen-year-old Steven Parent was also shot dead because he was in the driveway of the house while the telephone wires were being cut. A few hours later, Leno and Rosemary LaBianca were also murdered, receiving multiple stab wounds with knives and forks. The words WAR, RISE, DEATH TO PIGS and the mis-spelled HEALTER SKELTER were written around the house in blood.

The words were references to the Beatles songs 'Piggies', 'Blackbird' and 'Helter Skelter'. Other songs that came up for discussion during the murder investigations and the subsequent trial included 'Revolution 1', 'Honey Pie', 'I Will', 'Rocky Raccoon', 'Happiness is a Warm Gun' and 'Revolution 9'.

Strangest of all these is 'Revolution 9', which has no lyrics, no tune, no beat and isn't really a song at all but a sound collage. It's the Beatles' most extreme experiment with Random and probably the most widely heard avant-garde piece ever, assuming everyone who bought the album heard this track all the way through. Listening to it is a strange experience. It comes between 'Cry Baby Cry' and 'Good Night', and the latter sounds positively evil as a result, in the same way that Dennis Potter's use of innocuous old popular songs in the TV series 'The Singing Detective' rendered them deeply disturbing ever after (it did for me, anyway).

One particular passage from the Surrealist manifesto says

> *Surrealism does not allow those who devote themselves to it to forsake it whenever they like. There is every reason to believe that it acts on the mind very much as drugs do; like drugs, it creates a certain state of need and can push man to frightful revolts.*

Another passage says

> *The simplest Surrealist act consists of dashing into the street, pistol in hand, and firing blindly as fast as you can into the crowd.*

If this seems a disturbing place to be, just carry on a bit further down the road, because then you can add in the idea of Charles Manson connecting the book of Revelation with 'Revolution 9' and the rest of the album as part of his own manifesto. And then from there, take the shadowy side road that leads down to Nine Inch Nails, whose only permanent member, Trent Reznor, recorded his 1994 album *The Downward Spiral* in the Sharon Tate house, after which it was demolished. Reznor was depressed, alcoholic and drug-addicted at the time of recording, and the album deals with the self-destruction of its central character. He said he had no idea of the house's past when he hired it, though the idea of a 'downward spiral' does parallel that of a helter skelter, and the album includes tracks called 'Piggy' and 'March of the Pigs'. It was also claimed that Reznor took away the front door of the house before its demolition and had it installed in the studio he co-founded, which was called 'nothing'. By doing this, was Trent inside the Tate house pissing out, or outside pissing in? If he owned the front door, he could probably do either (or both) in the gloomy anal seclusion of his private recording studio.

From Trent Reznor, another side road leads to Brian Warner, one of Reznor's first signings, because Brian Warner is none other than the Alice Cooper glam-goth marionette antichrist Marilyn Manson, a tacky, icky collision of Marilyn Monroe and Charles Manson. To think, he could have called himself Charles Monroe instead.

It's a long way from Strawberry Field to Strawberry Fields, and it's a long way from George Harrison's mansion to the Dakota Building back to 10050 Cielo Drive, but through it all we're thinking about the Beatles and maybe still wondering what is real. In part, it's a kind of mind game, a conceit, but it's also a roundabout way of getting to some ideas that don't get thought about often enough. What is 'real', with or without the quotation marks? It has become hard to tell. Our sense of reality is becoming more and more fluid, and in a generation or so, has changed in ways that are deeper than most of us understand. There was a renaissance, there was an industrial revolution, there were a couple of world wars; there was an transistor revolution and an information revolution and lots of other wars and revolutions. And now, somehow, we find ourselves transformed, living in a different world. And this fragmented, instantaneous–simultaneous world, where we live immersed in a womblike infrastructure of technology, media and near-magic, barely existed half a century ago.

Half a century ago, fifty years back, a couple of generations ago, there was Beatlemania. It isn't a long time, though the rate of change makes it seem so. Our sense of history is one based on nostalgia binges that gorge on the ever-more-recent TV and pop past, a past in which black and white TV has become ancient history, and silent films prehistory. To anyone with a short memory or a short attention span 25 years, just one generation, seems like a lifetime. To people with too-short, too-fast-to-live-too-young-to-die lives, 25 years might actually be a lifetime, or more than a lifetime. To me, 25 used be old, but now it's young – that's what happens as time passes, and you get old enough to remember the Beatles on black and white TV.

That's what happens if you live long enough. John made it to 40. George made it to 58.

You could argue that none of this, here, now, is real, not in the long run of centuries and millennia, the long run of us as a species. A lot of what we now call reality is just private dreams and mass hallucinations: stories by JG Ballard and Philip K Dick and William Burroughs; shopping and driving, booze and drugs and ready meals, reality TV, social media and the internet; just electricity and people messing about on phones and computers. What we're living through is actually Deep Change, probably the deepest change ever, and it's all happened so fast. The only time most of us get to see anything really, properly long-term, maybe without even realising it, is in documentaries about hunter-gatherers, people without electricity and houses and roads, being traumatised by contact with us, which is what happened to the aborigines in Australia, which is what Kate Bush made a song about with Rolf Harris. Once upon a time, and for a very long time, for all the time there was, the hunter-gatherer reality was everyone's reality, but it isn't any more, and it's only taken the five hundred years since the Renaissance for it to be swept away.

In a way, I suppose what we're doing now along with everything else is getting over sixties, still getting over that fusion of counterculture and consumerism that changed everything, still getting over The Bloody Beatles. If that's the case, then you can argue that 'Strawberry Fields Forever' is real after all. Maybe it was one of the first pieces of music to take on the new electronic, instantaneous-simultaneous reality, knowingly or unknowingly, and try to deal with it. Maybe the Beatles were among the first people to actively live the dream, and the hallucination, and the nightmare. Maybe 'Strawberry Fields Forever' is one of the most real pieces of music there now is, and the Beatles are one of the most real bands.

The only time I ever listened to any Beatles music was at Radar's, the *Magical Mystery Tour* LP, which I liked a lot. But nothing else really, until the reverential yet touching *Anthology* series that went out 25 years after the band split up, a whole generation on from 1970. Having always wanted to be amazed by music, and never amazed by the Beatles, I had previously ignored them, avoided them and discounted them. It seems harder to be amazed as you grow older because you've heard so much already, and you're afraid of disappointment, but as I watched the TV series I actually found myself starting to like the Beatles.

Then (because you can't rush these things) another ten years or so after the TV series, one Saturday afternoon while I was in Birkenhead visiting my parents, I bought *Revolver* and *Sergeant Pepper* from Skeleton Records. I also got into a conversation with the owner, John Weaver, and that evening I ended up in the pub with him. Almost 40 years earlier in about 1972 I had daringly visited Skeleton for the very first time and bought a David Bowie badge, which I wore after he died. Back then, Skeleton had been down the end of a long dark passageway on Argyle St that led from the sunlit world of Saturday afternoon into another dimension, a tiny, almost impossibly exotic Other Place with loud, strange music, the smell of incense sticks, red light bulbs, and black walls covered with Oz magazines, underground posters and white bootleg LP covers. As it grew and moved to bigger and bigger premises over the years, Skeleton was where I bought hundreds of new and second-hand LPs and singles; spent hundreds of pounds in pocket money and wages and student grant; and also spent hundreds of lovingly drawn-out hours hanging about, shuffling and tugging my way through the thousands of alphabetically crammed covers, gazing at the sleeves on the walls, from the already familiar to the esoteric that became familiar, all the while listening and half-listening to all kinds of music.

So that evening after the shop closed, John Weaver and I went for a few beers, and several hours later found myself in a half-empty black-walled vaguely scummy pub just round the corner, immersed in garish lights and loud music, drunkenly trying to make out what Weaver was yelling into my ear about, which involved Birkenhead being some kind of X-Files experiment organised by whoever really ran the petrochemical industry that sprawled across Merseyside and beyond. At one stage he bought us both a brandy and jabbed a finger across the street at another scummy half-empty pub, lit by sickly green light that made the kids in there look like mutants, and I knew that on some level or other he had to be right.

When I got back from the pub with my portion of chips, my parents were in bed and, flicking through the TV channels I ended up blurrily watching part of something called *It Was 40 Years Ago Today* celebrating the 40th anniversary of *Sergeant Pepper*. In this programme and its follow-up a week later, various bands were invited to play their version of an album track, in The Original Studio, overseen by The Original Engineer Geoff Emerick, who had worked on 'Sun Arise' and 'Strawberry Fields Forever' with George Martin, and whose first recording job with the Beatles had been 'Tomorrow Never Knows'. The point of this exercise was unclear, unless it was to emphasise the vacuousness and mediocrity of much contemporary music, but it did show just how all-pervasive the Beatle virus still is, how it still gets everywhere, how everything still always ends up back with the Beatles.

Two weeks later I got round to playing both Beatles CDs all the way through for the first time. I was driving from Inverness to Glasgow to empty my daughter's student flat, pack all her stuff into the car and drive back home again. Having put off listening to them, when I finally did they made me smile: I knew a lot of the songs; I liked some songs but not others; they didn't sound like two of the greatest albums ever made; I wasn't overwhelmed by joy or disappointment but, really, how could they possibly live up to their reputation, or my prejudices and expectations? What came before and after them was:

The Book Of Dogma	the Black Dog
Autobahn	Kraftwerk
Ladies And Gentlemen, We Are Floating In Space	Spiritualised
I Could Have Been A Contender (Disc 1 of 3)	Jah Wobble
Grand Prix	Teenage Fan Club
The Rough Guide To The Delta Blues	Various Artists
The Mirror Conspiracy	Thievery Corporation
Cannibalism	Can
Daydream Nation	Sonic Youth

Revolver was between Spiritualised and Jah Wobble; *Sergeant Pepper* was between Kraftwerk and Spiritualised. In the car I can play whatever I like, whenever I like. I can create a musical travelogue, compiling a list that is real only on that journey and only for me. Bends in the road combine with instrumental breaks; lochs and mountains and vocals intersect; weather conditions and songs merge seamlessly or are forced into bizarre juxtapositions. It's said that communities of Australian aborigines travel all over their continent using songlines, routes that have their own stories and songs, and that are inseparable from them. The stories and the songs call into being the surrounding landscape as the walkers move through it, mile after mile, song after song, hour after hour, day after day. As they sing and walk and walk and sing, they become the song just as the song becomes the landscape. My musical songlines and everyone else's might be puny by comparison, just lines traced on a map by the experience of driving and listening, but in this case the long black ribbon of A9 was called into existence by music that included the Beatles.

The Beatles weren't real to me. Now they are just as real or unreal as everything else. Like or dislike has nothing to do with it. They make as much sense or as little sense as everything else. They are part of my everything, and of everyone else's everything. Rather than just being irritating young men with suits and silly haircuts, or self-absorbed beardy recluses, they are the Beatles, and nothing else makes sense without them. I've been passively listening to them all my life through the hundreds and thousands of media events that have used their images and music as shorthand for the sixties, for modernity, for change, for nostalgia, for rebellion, for innocence, for loss of innocence, for obsession, for madness, for murder, for whatever you want. The Beatles are whatever you want, you can be a fan or not a fan, you can love them or despise them or be indifferent, but there's no escape from them.

So, how does it end? It ends the way it has to end: with the Beatles. It ends with me getting the remastered CDs for my birthday and loading them onto iTunes. Then, just because I can, it ends with me dragging all their songs across to the iPod, the whole lot with a single, tiny movement, Apple to Apple in one click. And there it is, The Complete Beatles in amongst Everything Else, set adrift, floating free, shuffled, waiting for Random.

Playlist 4 - 46 29 50		
Sun Arise	Rolf Harris	
We're Moving On	The Seekers	*The Four And Only Seekers*
Back To Nature	Fad Gadget	
Shot By Both Sides	Magazine	
The Way I Walk	The Cramps	
We Love You	Psychedelic Furs	
SF Sorrow Is Born	The Pretty Things	*SF Sorrow*
Strawberry Fields Forever	The Beatles	*Sergeant Pepper's Lonely Hearts Club Band*
Astronomy Domine	Pink Floyd	*The Piper At The Gates Of Dawn*
Catfish Blues	Robert Petway	

To listen to the playlists, visit Spotify using the QR links provided.

Links to every playlist are also at www.hungry-ghost.info, along with photographs and archive material to supplement each chapter and enhance the reading/listening experience, just like a great big gatefold album cover.

4

LONG LIVE THE KING

Suddenly, I find myself in two places and two times at once. This kind of thing happens quite often now.

One place is the kitchen of the house in Waterpark Road where I grew up, where it's the evening of Tuesday 16 August, 1977. The other place is the inside of the large badly built fitted wardrobe in the house where my children grew up, where it's late afternoon sometime towards the end of 2002. These two times and places have collided, and in both places and at both times I've been thinking about the King and the Queen.

First the King. On the evening of 16 August he hadn't been dead very long, just a couple of hours. His body was discovered in Memphis at around 2.30 pm, and he was declared dead about an hour later. When I found out, it was sometime after 10.00 pm in Birkenhead. There's a difference of six hours between Memphis time and Birkenhead time, but something else separated the two places as well: where I was, it was John Peel time.

Like in the Beatles song and the teenage girls' magazine, I was Just Seventeen, if you know what I mean: just snotty, skinny, scruffy, spotty, swotty seventeen. Maybe I was a boy, or a youth; maybe I was an adolescent, or a teenager or a kid; I might even have been a young man. It was hard to tell. Whatever else I was, whoever else I was, I was Duncan Marshall. I still am. I was born Duncan Clive Marshall, but at some stage decided I didn't want to be a Clive any more. So, un-Clived, at home I was Duncan; at school I was Marshall and sometimes Marshall, D. with a comma and a full stop, because it was that kind of school.[1] At university I would be Mr Marshall for a term or so until I left, because it was that kind of university, but I hadn't got there yet because Tuesday August 16 was two days before I got my A-level results.

There I was in the kitchen hunched over the radio, army surplus elbows on the wood-effect Formica, head away somewhere or other in the fabulous sprawling soundworld of John Peel, far from home and school and exam results and universities. Round about the time that 'Trod On' by Culture and 'When The Summer's Thru' by the Fabulous Poodles got played, something strange happened. With no preamble and in a very subdued voice John Peel said unconfirmed reports were coming in that Elvis Presley had died, then he went back to playing whatever it was he'd been going to play. Then, a bit later, it was confirmed. Elvis Presley was dead.

Elvis Presley?

Oh yeah, Elvis Presley.

Him. That famous fat old man.

Some people say they can remember where they were when they heard that Elvis

(or Marc Bolan

or Sid Vicious

or John Lennon

or Kurt Cobain

or Michael Jackson

or David Bowie)

died.

I was in the kitchen listening to the radio, and what's more I was annoyed that *my* music was being interrupted because someone like *Elvis Presley* had gone and *died*.

Elvis Presley. He was everywhere; it seemed like he'd always been everywhere, part of the scenery like flock wallpaper, the Beatles, Rolf Harris and pictures of the Queen. It seemed he was on every jukebox in every bar and café,

---

1 For a while, due to some kind of keying error at the bank, I was also Duncan Olive Marshall on my monthly statements. Because this made me laugh so much, it was years before I got it changed.

and even though I wasn't interested in doing anything apart from ridiculing him, I couldn't avoid him. He was on TV, he was on the radio, he was on walls and on jukeboxes. This annoying, boring, old American superstar with his massive appeal, massive gut, bad music, bad hair and bad outfits. I just didn't get it. I'd never liked him, never paid him any attention, except by trying to ignore him. I remember seeing him on TV in a spangled jumpsuit and implausibly black hair, podgy and sweating, wiping his brow on scarf after scarf before tossing each one into the Las Vegas audience, and it bugged the hostile teenage hell out of me. I remember seething with contempt at the sight of him in a different jumpsuit, a white one with fringes, doing karate moves and punching the air in time to 'Polk Salad Annie' on a Top of the Pops film clip, and what the hell was polk salad anyway. I especially remember my indignation on learning that the opening of *2001 – A Space Odyssey* was played at his concerts as he walked onstage. Was nothing sacred?

I didn't hate every single thing he'd ever done, not like I was some kind of bigot. For example, I knew I liked 'Heartbreak Hotel'. It was sparse, melodramatic, anguished, weirdly compelling and compellingly weird. It sounded like it was recorded in the darkest hours before the dawn, in the cavernous echoing ballroom of an empty hotel, by the saddest man in the world and a few of his friends down at the end of a street called Lonely. I heard the song in my bedroom when it was reissued in 1971, on the same radio I would later be listening to in the kitchen in 1977. It sounded so spooked and intense it shocked me, even without knowing the song was supposedly based on a suicide note: a man found dead in a Miami hotel room with nothing to identify him, and a note in his pocket that read *I walk a lonely street*. Mae Boren Axton and Tommy Durden thought that at the end of a lonely street you would maybe find a heartbreak hotel, then they wrote a song about it.[2]

---

2 The line is actually taken from the autobiography of Alvin Krolik, a small-time criminal who turned himself in, worked for a time as a

I also knew I liked 'How Great Thou Art,' a powerful, soaring hymn sung in a powerful, soaring voice that was utterly different from the one in 'Heartbreak Hotel.' 'How Great Thou Art' has become the world's second favourite hymn after 'Amazing Grace.' I knew it from summer afternoons spent on the beach at Hoylake, half-heartedly attending Uncle Stan's sand services at the instigation of my parents, who knew Uncle Stan through Church. Hoylake is a small seaside town on the River Dee/Irish Sea corner of the Wirral peninsula, and unlike Birkenhead was considered a Nice Place. It was there, beneath a red and white striped awning and a banner that said UNCLE STANS SANDS SERVICES, that huge boxer turned evangelist Stan Ford would lead the singing in between quizzes, games, mini-sermons and sausage sizzles, pointing with a huge index finger at the words on the pages of a huge illustrated song book that balanced precariously on a not-so-huge easel. Although he didn't sing like Elvis, Uncle Stan had a massive baritone voice and total conviction, and was accompanied by slight, mild-mannered keyboard wizard Uncle Bert on the accordion.

But these were aberrations, the exceptions that proved the rule, the rule being that I didn't want anything to do with someone like Elvis – he was rich, famous, fat, middle-aged, overdressed, American, unhip, and now he was dead as well. Back then I knew for sure that I wasn't any of those things.

Elvis. He was so popular, it felt like almost everyone apart from me was a fan, almost everyone apart from me was a friend. It felt like the whole world knew him, was on first-name terms with him. In fact it seemed like people were on first-name terms with him in almost the same way they were with Jesus.

Elvis. Jesus. The two Kings. No disrespect, mind, just to point out that Jesus was unique until Elvis came along, whatever John Lennon might have said. Elvis the Pelvis. The

---

mural artist, then died during an unsuccessful robbery. It was quoted extensively in articles following Krolik's death, which is presumably where Axton and Durden came across it.

King. Boring Old Fart, more like. Great Big Dinosaur, more like. God save the King. Not. Just get on with it and play some more music, John. Jeez, he was *Elvis Presley* and he was *forty-two* and he just *died*, what's the big deal? When Elvis died, that's more or less what I would have said if anyone had asked me.

What John Lydon said about Elvis was, 'Elvis represented everything we're trying to react against. He was a fat, rich, reclusive rock star who was dead before he died. His gut was so big it cast a shadow over rock 'n' roll.'

What John Lennon said was, 'Elvis died when he went into the army.'

What John Peel said was, 'Death, for those who live on, is the ending of a chapter rather than the end of the book, and although the dead may have no more part to play as characters, their influence may continue right through the story. Presley's certainly will, for he was the first person we met on page 1, and though his records later became irrelevant to all but the diehard Presley devotees and his private life seems to have plumbed new depths of nightmarishness, nothing can ever take that away from him.' Actually, John Peel wrote this rather than said it, but either way he clearly meant it.

John Lydon was right. Elvis did represent everything they were trying to react against, and he was fat and rich and reclusive, and had been as good as dead for years. That gut was so big it did cast a shadow over rock 'n' roll, and over the lives of those who knew him and loved him. And that shadow is still there, reaching all the way from then to now and beyond, because the ghost of Elvis past is the ghost of Elvis present is the ghost of Elvis yet to come. His ghost music is still playing down at the end of Lonely Street, and in millions of heads and hearts as well.

John Lennon was wrong. Elvis didn't die when he went into the army; he died when his mother Gladys died, at least that's when he gave up on life – that's when he started dying; he just took a long, long time to do it, so long that most people didn't notice it was happening, or didn't want to.

John Peel was right. Death is the ending of a chapter rather than the end of the book for those who live on, and what's more the story that began on page one of what has since become the magical, mythic, golden Book Of Elvis doesn't fill it – there are many unread pages, and many that are yet to be written: this is the way it will always be.

Elvis. John Lennon may have thought the Beatles were more popular than Jesus, but John Lennon was never just *John* the way Jesus was just *Jesus* and Elvis was just *Elvis*. John Lennon was just *John* only in the company of *George*, *Paul* and *Ringo*. He needed the context.

Elvis. First he was larger than life, then he was larger than death. He still is, and as a consequence there has developed a huge market in *Elvis Lives* merchandise. *Elvis Lives* – a phrase and marketing concept which, as well as being demonstrably untrue, shows just how much the cult of Elvis has encroached on territory that was previously only occupied by Jesus.

John. If the proposition was *John Lives* the inevitable question would be, *John who?* Which makes the point that he, John, John Lennon, might have been larger than life and then larger than death too, but despite this *John Lives* doesn't make sense without the context. And *Lennon Lives* is just a baby with a halo on a wall in Mathew Street. Which means he still needs both of his names, and although *John Lennon Lives* might make sense to everyone, it isn't anything apart from perhaps an awful T-shirt that someone, somewhere in the world might be wearing at this very moment.

Elvis Lives. As well as being an unmistakable Christian name followed by a verb in the third person present tense, and as well as being a demonstrably untrue proposition, it's also a concept that became a multimillion dollar industry. You could even argue that Elvis's demise, despite being a tragedy for him and for millions of others who were close to him or felt they were close to him, was a great business move. This is borne out by the fact that today as a consumer, fan or believer you are presented with a wide range of opportunities to buy into Elvis's music and Elvis's legend, with almost every conceivable item of merchandise being made available, and probably a lot you couldn't conceive of. One example (the most obvious one, and you don't need another) is the official shop, ShopElvis®, on the official website, elvis.com.

From the very beginning Elvis's manager, 'Colonel' Tom Parker, kept a jealous and vice-like grip on his boy's merchandising, developing it shrewdly, some might say ruthlessly, starting with things like badges and balloons and going on to boost Elvis The Product into Elvis The Legend into Elvis The Bloated World-Straddling Godzilla Saint, all without seeming to show any interest in the man or his music, both of which became increasingly irrelevant as long as the man was still more or less alive and the music, more or less any music, was still being churned out. And now, all these years later, as well as the usual clocks, car shades, wall hangings, kitchen equipment, watches, T-shirts, baseball caps, belt buckles, key rings, Zippos, sunglasses, teddy bears, umbrellas, beaded curtains, fridge magnets and bathroom accessories, the merchandising pages of ShopElvis®, and therefore the equivalent pages of the ever-expanding, always-being-written Book Of Elvis, are crammed with items like

- an 'Elvis Lives' five-piece luggage set
- a gold lamé tuxedo – for small dog or large dog
- a set of Classic Elvis nesting dolls
- various life-size talking Elvis stand-up cardboard cut-outs
- 'Elvis Lives' fabric for making your own curtains
- a 'Welcome to Heartbreak Hotel' doormat – though surely this is *not* the place you would want to welcome anyone to, unless you didn't like them. When Elvis was there, he felt so lonely he could die; it's probably where he was when he did die that solitary, tragic death. He presumably checked in after his mother died, and never checked out.

There must be pages and pages of the Book Of Elvis given over to Elvisware and Elviswear; chapters on Elvis Media, Elvis Mythology, Elvis Psychology, Elvis Psychiatry, Elvis Interior Design, Elvis Politics, Elvis Food, Elvis Pharmacology and Elvis Literature, as well as the music. Because Elvis isn't just about music, and The Book Of Elvis isn't either. How could it be? Even at the time when I was most awash with the bile of adolescent contempt for Elvis, I realised that it wasn't just about the music, in fact that was the time when this was at its most obvious – it's never just about the music, is it. That's why the hair and the white jumpsuits were so viscerally annoying.

John Lennon wasn't just about the music. John Lydon wasn't just about the music either. It's never just about the music. It's also about the fame or the anti-fame; it's about the attitude, the look, the lifestyle, the moves, the hair. Deep down I knew that, and to me Elvis's attitude, look, lifestyle, moves and hair were so unutterably bad words failed me. Oh yes, and I hated the music as well.

I say it's never just about the music, but it can be sometimes, when your guard is down because you don't know or don't care about context: maybe because you're too young or open minded to consider things like attitude, look, lifestyle, moves or hair. When I was little I didn't hear a lot of pop music, and there was no real context; just songs on the radio and in the air, some of which earwormed their way into my head. Some of which are still there.

1962

Sun Arise – Rolf Harris

1963

She Loves You – the Beatles

1964

Bits And Pieces – Dave Clark Five
Can't Buy Me Love – the Beatles
A Hard Day's night – the Beatles

1965

Help! – the Beatles
I'll Never Find Another You – the Seekers
Walk Tall – Val Doonican

1966

These Boots Were Made For Walking – Nancy Sinatra
Yellow Submarine – the Beatles
Bend It! – Dave Dee, Dozy, Beaky, Mick and Tich
Morningtown Ride – the Seekers

1967

I'm A Believer – the Monkees
Simon Smith And His Amazing Dancing Bear – Alan
    Price
I Was Kaiser Bill's Batman – Whistling Jack Smith
Georgie Girl – The Seekers

1968

Don't Stop The Carnival – Alan Price
Cinderella Rockafella – Esther and Abi Ofarim
Little Arrows – Leapy Lee
Congratulations – Cliff Richard
Those Were The days – Mary Hopkin
Lily The Pink – the Scaffold

1969

(If Paradise Is) Half As Nice – Amen Corner
Two Little Boys – Rolf Harris
Albatross – Fleetwood Mac
Ob-La-Di, Ob-La-Da – Marmalade
The Israelites – Desmond Dekker
Oh Happy Day – The Edwin Hawkins Singers

1970

Come And Get It – Badfinger
Wandrin' Star – Lee Marvin
Bridge Over Troubled Water – Simon and Garfunkel
Yellow River – Christie
In The Summertime – Mungo Jerry
Band Of Gold – Freda Payne
Cracklin' Rosie – Neil Diamond

1971

Resurrection Shuffle – Ashton, Gardner and Dyke
My Sweet Lord – George Harrison
Let's See Action – the Who
Pushbike Song – The Mixtures
Ernie – Benny Hill
Brown Sugar – the Rolling Stones
Banks Of The Ohio – Olivia Newton John
Heartbreak Hotel – Elvis Presley
Get It On – T Rex

The list ends in 1971 because by then I was becoming more aware. I was watching Top Of The Pops with the beginnings of wide-eyed, embarrassing-embarrassed adolescence, cultivating and being consumed by a fascination for the exotic and the strange and the way-out, and wanting to like the right kind of music or the wrong kind, depending on who I wanted to impress or annoy. I had just started at secondary school, and just started to talk about music and think about music and read about music, to listen to it as well as just hear it. Gary Glitter, Slade, the Sweet and David Bowie were still a year away. To put it another way, the list ends in 1971 because there are nine earworms that year and almost forty the year after. Alternatively, 1971 marked the end of a kind of innocence and the start of a kind of awareness, because it was the year I heard 'Get It On', and saw T Rex on Top Of The Pops, which was when I realised just how sexy music could be, and was starting to realise, or trying to imagine, or trying to think about imagining, just how sexy sex could be.

It ends, this list, or if you want to be a bit more sentimental about it, this period of innocence, round about 'Heartbreak Hotel'. Despite a brief fling with the King I don't think my name is going to end up in the still-being-written Book Of Elvis on this basis, not in the section about music, though I might get a sentence or two in the section about Elvis Literature. And if I'm not in there in my own right, I can refer you to a book that's bound to get a mention.

It'll be on the pages dealing with 1993, it's a science fiction novel called *Elvissey* and it's by Jack Womack. In this novel, Dryco, a sinister multinational corporation in a parallel universe, is feeling threatened by a popular religious cult that believes the dead Elvis to be a god-like figure with miraculous powers. As you might expect, Dryco tries to solve the problem by sending a couple of agents back into an alternate past to locate and abduct an alternate Elvis, and this alternate past happens to be ours. The intention is to use the alternative, young, living Elvis to discredit the old, dead Elvis, but things go badly wrong. The ways that they go wrong are too complicated and peculiar to relate here, so you'll need to read the relevant pages of the Book Of Elvis, or the novel.

If you read *Elvissey*, you might want to read Jack Womack's previous novel, *Terraplane*, beforehand. It has some of the same characters in it, and this time there's a brief encounter with the blues guitarist Robert Johnson.[3] I'm sure Robert Johnson appears somewhere in the Book Of Elvis, because he's another king, in this case the King of the Delta Blues Singers. These two kings, Elvis and Robert, Presley and Johnson, are both celebrated and sought out in novels by Jack Womack. What they also have in common is the fact that they both died on August 16, though when I was thinking about Elvis on August 16 1977, I hadn't heard of Robert Johnson and wouldn't get to do so for another nine years. But that's another story.

(That other story, the one about Robert Johnson, begins in 1986 and hasn't yet ended. During a spell of unemployment I spent time working for free in a pottery, learning how to mix clay and throw pots, glaze them and fire them. Music was constantly playing in the workshop, and the heap of dusty cassettes by the creaky tape deck included

---

3 Johnson's first 78 'Terraplane Blues' gives the book its title. The Hudson Terraplane was a powerful, affordable car that was popular in the 1930s.

- a Chris Rea compilation
- *Missa Papae Marcelli* by Giovanni da Palestrina
- the soundtrack album from the TV series *The Singing Detective*
- *Another Green World* by Brian Eno
- the soundtrack album from the David Byrne movie *True Stories*
- Tchaikovsky's Violin Concerto
- the soundtrack album from the movie *Paris, Texas*
- a Robert Johnson album: anguished, scratchy, alien music that completely baffled me. After a while I stopped working at the pottery, got a job and forgot all about it until I bought a CD version in a sale ten years later, after which it really got to me.)

Robert Johnson is King of the Delta Blues Singers, and *King of the Delta Blues Singers* is the title of the album I heard and later bought. It's a compilation of old 78s, originally released in 1961. There are sixteen songs, just guitar and voice, recorded in November 1936 and June 1937 at the only two sessions he ever attended.

Although they are both kings, Robert is in many ways the opposite of Elvis. For a start he was black, which is the opposite of white. Then again, when a lot of people first heard Elvis they thought he was black, which, according to one story, was the whole idea, because this story suggests that the Sun label producer Sam Phillips was in search of a white boy who could sing like a black man, in order to popularise black music and maybe make a fortune.

Robert Johnson is also the opposite of Elvis because Elvis's image is everywhere, and there are only two photographs of Robert Johnson. Both were found in 1972, 34 years after his death in 1938 and 11 years after the release of that faceless LP. On the cover was a striking painting: an overhead view in earthen reds, blacks and whites of a black man sitting on a chair astride his own shadow, head bowed over his guitar. Through the sixties and beyond, that LP became a twelve-inch wide badge of authenticity that was displayed, revered, referenced and borrowed from by countless musicians. If you look at the photograph of Dylan on the front cover of *Bringing It All Back Home*, there's a pile of albums behind him and in the middle is a copy of *King of the Delta Blues Singers*.

Very little is known about Robert Johnson's life or death, which is also the opposite of Elvis. It is widely believed that he died at the age of 27 from drinking poisoned whisky given to him by a bar owner, following some kind of incident involving Johnson and the man's wife. Like Elvis, Johnson probably died alone in agony, some say on his hands and knees barking like a dog, but perhaps that's just a way of describing a man in the throes of uncontrollable retching. Like Elvis, the question is, where did his talent come from? A common story tells of him being laughably incompetent on the guitar, disappearing for a time then reappearing possessed of a style and technique that astonished audiences wherever he played. A related story suggests he might have gone to a crossroads at around midnight and met a big black man who retuned his guitar for him, handed it back and a few years later claimed his soul.

Somewhere in amongst the mythology and the hearsay and the nonsense and the romance and the couple of photos are perhaps fragments of Robert Johnson, though even that isn't definite, as he wasn't always known by that name. Something that made research difficult was the fact that he was also known as Robert Spencer, RL Spencer, Robert Dodds and maybe a couple of other names as well; and the sparseness of official paperwork documenting the lives and deaths of poor itinerant black people in the American south didn't help either. If songs and musicians are all to some extent screens onto which we can project our own fears and desires, Robert Johnson's screen is one of the blankest, allowing the most diverse and vivid projections. The romance of the poor, rootless, sensitive, solitary outsider musician who died young; the eerie, scratchy recordings from another age, another planet almost; the tortured, keening songs of failure, despair and fatalism; the authenticity and directness of a whole race's trauma and suffering condensed into three-minute sides of shellac. It's all there if that's what you're looking for, because Robert Johnson is, or has become, this huge, shadowy, mythic presence in American popular music, a figure constructed from almost no life story, modest record sales and just a couple of photographs, by white blues fans in the years after his death. It's almost as if Elvis had become famous by recording a few obscure sessions for Sam Philips using his mother's maiden name and then disappeared, maybe murdered, maybe kidnapped by Dryco agents, but either way just vanished.

Which he didn't, of course, which is why there was an Elvis, in all his many incarnations, and why there's a Book Of Elvis. It's also why, somewhere in the Book Of Elvis, amongst the anthropology and the mythology and the merchandising and the religion there must be something about the fact that Elvis is a folk hero and an icon and a kind of saint who lived and then died, who had *and still has* a physical presence in this world because there exist, even now, opportunities to buy and own an actual piece of the King. Literally: Elvis hair, strands and tufts and wisps of Elvisness, along with certificates and letters of authenticity to prove their provenance. If you believe in Elvis, you might also believe that these pieces of him are saint-celebrity relics, just like a Jimi Hendrix guitar fragment (or John Lennon's nail clippings or a saint's tooth or a splinter of the True Cross) and, being actual pieces of the King, are charged with a special kind of magic.

Most Elvis hair is offered in tiny quantities, the largest single amount ever sold coming from one of his earliest barbers, Homer 'Gill' Gilleland who, as well as cutting his hair for about twenty years also dyed it black for him. After being replaced by Sal Orifice (his real name) and then Larry Geller, Gilleland retained a wodge of hair clippings in a jar. He kept it for years after Elvis died, the contents eventually being sold at auction for over $100,000. A lock of John Lennon's hair only managed $48,000, though there was a lot less of it, which means that in terms of dollars per gramme it could well be worth a lot more.

Elvis. John. John. Elvis.

Depending on who it once belonged to, hair can be a holy relic, or a historical relic, or a celebrity relic. It can also be a form of currency because, weight for weight, historical and celebrity hair is perhaps the most costly commodity in the world. And like any other commodity it can be bought and sold by people like – oh, I don't know, how about the Michigan collector and dealer Louis Mushro, a man offering hair from persons including

- Abraham Lincoln
- Geronimo
- George Washington
- Napoleon
- John F Kennedy
- Marilyn Monroe
- Ronald Reagan
- Mother Teresa
- Elizabeth Taylor
- Richard Nixon
- John Lennon

and Elvis Presley.

When I looked, a one-inch single hair from the scalp of John Lennon cost $1,500 and so did one of Elvis's, which suggests the two are of equal value, unless one is longer than the other, or both are so over-valued that the price is irrelevant.

John. Elvis. Elvis. John

The other major player in the world of celebrity hair is John Reznikoff. This is a man who says he sold a single Einstein hair for $10,000; a man whose collection, claimed to be the largest in the world, supposedly includes the hair of

- Charles I (before beheading)
- Charles I (after beheading)
- George Washington
- Abraham Lincoln (with fragments of attached brain matter)
- John Wilkes Booth (Lincoln's assassin)
- Napoleon
- Beethoven
- Edgar Allen Poe
- Charles Dickens
- Einstein
- John F Kennedy
- Eva Braun

And Elvis Presley.

Reznikoff is the man who did a deal with Neil Armstrong's barber to buy the astronaut's clippings for $3,000. The barber, when threatened with legal action by Armstrong, was unable to get the hair back but did agree to give his profits to charity. Following this incident, Reznikoff no longer deals in the hair of the living, and went so far as to value all the hair on Britney Spears' head at just $3,500 when her hairdresser put it up for online auction at $1m.

Reznikoff is also the man who provided about ten strands of Beethoven's hair to be incorporated into synthetic diamonds by a company called LifeGem®.[4] Of the three gemstones that were produced, Reznikoff kept one and another was offered for online auction at $1m, eventually selling for £202,000. The third was retained by LifeGem® as the start of an intended 'Chain of Fame.' You can visit the LifeGem® website and vote for celebrities you would

---

4   A LifeGem® is 'a certified, high-quality diamond created from the carbon of your loved one as a memorial to their unique life, or as a symbol of your personal and precious bond with another.' The carbon of a loved one could of course have previously belonged to a pet rather than a person.

most like to have made into diamonds. Because the process involves hair, Elvis diamonds must be a possibility. And it must surely be possible to use DNA from Elvis hair strands to make another Elvis – maybe dozens, hundreds even: Elvis tribute artists with a difference, the difference being that they 'are' Elvis. Dryco never though of this; it would have saved them a lot of trouble. And if that's not bizarre enough, in 2012 Canadian dentist Michael Zuk bought Elvis Presley's porcelain crown for £5,200. Although it doesn't contain any Elvis DNA, Zuk does possess a small quantity of John Lennon DNA: in 2011 he bought a molar (supposedly pulled from Lennon's mouth by the man himself, and then given to his housekeeper) for £19,000. A fragment of the tooth was given to Zuk's sister Kirsten and was embedded in a clay bust she made of Lennon that doesn't look anything like him. Other fragments were incorporated into John Lennon DNA Limited Edition silver pendants by Beverley Hills jewellery designer Ari Soffer. Retailing at around $25,000 each, these humble trinkets mean that 'a very select few will be able to say that they actually wear John Lennon's DNA as inspiration.'

The hair of a living person, although a lot less valuable than diamonds or the hair of certain dead people, nevertheless has at least the possibility of looking good on someone's head. Cut or arranged the right way, it can actually look amazing and can make them feel amazing. The right hair is, and always has been, about fashion, sex, and rock and roll: quiffs, moptops, freak flags, beehives, flat tops, mohicans, dreadlocks, crew cuts, fringes, plaits, ponytails and all the rest. Hair is rock and roll, hair is attitude, hair is power, and hair is a kind of magic – if it wasn't, why would it cost so much to style it, and why would people pay so much money for other people's after death? And why would so many male musicians take to wearing quirky hats or bandannas (and sometimes both) onstage later in life?

John Lennon said Elvis died when he went into the army. Maybe what he meant by this was that Elvis died when he got his hair cut; when he was publicly shorn of his power and his rock-and-roll magic, losing not his hair but his hairstyle. If this is the case, then it's ironic that John Reznikoff's Elvis hair, mounted on blue suede, is accompanied by a photo of the shearing process that represented the symbolic death of Elvis and the symbolic, very public emasculation of rock and roll. When John Lennon said, 'Elvis died when he went into the army,' he went on to add, 'That's when they killed him, that's when they castrated him.'

So hair is rock and roll, hair is power, hair is youth, hair is rebellion, hair is magic. I learned all about it when I was at school between 1971 and 1978, a time when the magic of hair was shown most forcefully to me by the sustained authoritarian campaign to enforce its limitation. It sounds strange now, it sounds ridiculous, but at school hair was not allowed to cover the tops of the ears or the back of the shirt collar. Together with the strict uniform policy, this made it a bit like being in the army or in prison. The rules were policed almost exclusively by the headmaster, a tall, frosty, physically imposing former rugby international referred to as Syph. The deputy headmaster was a tall, ravingly eccentric, handlebar-moustachioed former army officer referred to as Clap, who didn't seem to give a damn about hair. Both men were bald. When I started at secondary school I don't think I knew the informal names of any venereal diseases, and acquiring familiarity by having them personified in this way now seems grotesque. VD wasn't something you talked about in public back then, and I remember being very surprised to read a Radio Times feature in which John Peel openly admitted to having had VD – as though it wasn't something you should be ashamed of. Which of course it was, otherwise why would you give a headmaster a name like Syph.

But this was in the early seventies, in other words just after the sixties, at a time when hair was a big deal. Short-back-and-sides hair tended to mean you were well socialised, and long hair was magical and rebellious and very rock and roll. Actually, long hair was very Rock rather than rock and roll. My first hair idols were Status Quo, their faces outrageously hidden behind mighty curtains on the front cover of *Piledriver*. If I hadn't seen them on Top Of The Pops, I'd have had no idea what their faces looked like. I so wanted hair like Francis Rossi, though nowadays I'm more than happy with my own, because even though it's short I've still got it. Pink Floyd also had cool hair, and Tangerine Dream, at least Christophe Franke and Peter Baumann did, but Edgar Froese's was a bit of a mess. Robert Plant looked too girly and Roger Daltrey's hair looked tough on him but probably not on anyone else. The longest hair was Rick Wakeman's, right down his back, though his sparkly cape was pretty ridiculous. Ted Nugent once did an interview with the NME in which he said he was going to have to get his hair cut because it got in the way when he went to the john. *That's* long hair.

Sometime in the early seventies, one holiday lunchtime I saw a Welsh TV programme on which some local rock band or other appeared. They were good, though singing in Welsh sounded a bit strange. What I remember most clearly, though, is that the singer, who sang while playing his guitar, stood at the microphone with his hair hanging down completely covering his face. This was outrageous like the cover of *Piledriver* was outrageous – imagine having hair so long it covered your face. Then again, what else would a short-back-and-sides adolescent dream of?

A display of hair that made an even deeper impression on me occurred during a TV performance by Jerry Lee Lewis. He started the show sitting down with everything slicked back in place, but as the music wilder and wilder, things started to slip. Then suddenly he stood up and kicked his piano stool across the stage, and for the rest of the time he was on his feet, his hair covering his face as he flailed and quaked and pounded on his piano, eventually climbing on top of it to harangue the audience, yelling incoherently like a man possessed. This loss of control seemed far wilder than starting off looking mad and unkempt – with Jerry Lee you could see the decency and the veneer of civilisation crack and split and fall away to leave this raving animal barely in control of his faculties, or his hair.

Generally, though, there were hairstyles and haircuts, and there was 'just long hair'. Hairstyles and haircuts involved grooming and maintenance: what I wanted was 'just long hair'. It was the final part of my aspirational denim anti-uniform uniform, the part I aspired to but never attained. I got the jacket and I got the jeans (eventually – Mum was fervently anti-jeans for a while), and even a denim shirt. They all faded and fell apart most beautifully, and were then held together with bits of embroidery and studs and patches, all of which I painstakingly did myself. But I never got the hair.

There were barbers, where men went, and there were hairdressers, where women went. Then there were unisex hairdressers, where men or women could go, but not me, not for a long time. I had this idea that if you just grew your hair and let it keep growing it would look fine. Unfortunately, my hair was never very thick and was also quite wavy, so it would often stick up and stick out rather than lying flat like I wanted it to. So, for a number of years I didn't much like going out in the wind or the rain.

If a girl or woman had said this kind of thing I would have laughed, but because this was *my* hair it was serious. Your hair was, I suppose, your freak flag and it was your duty to fly it, if not because of its symbolism in the larger scheme of things, then as a kind of V-sign to Syph. Boys would grow their hair and carefully comb it behind their ears and stuff it under their collars, then walk about stiff-necked in case it sprang out within view of Syph, who could appear from nowhere, poking at your collar until it revealed any hidden luxuriance, and purring menacingly, 'Oooof, your hair's a bit *long*, isn't it... I think you need a *haircut*... why don't you come and see me *tomorrow morning*.' To which you would mutter, 'Yes sir' and at the same time mentally shout obscenities at the top of your lungs right in his face, or think about all the Syph graffiti in secret places around the school, on toilet and changing room walls and inside desks, and imagine copying all this in big red capital letters onto the walls of the school chapel. Or, preferably, getting someone else to do it, rather than taking any chances yourself.

By the time I left school it was 1978 and I didn't want long hair any more, which was probably just as well because it looked horrible and I didn't wash it very often. Boys who actually took a pride in their appearance had their hair styled, something I never went in for, apart from once, during the time I was into ELP, wishing I could have my hair cut like Keith Emerson's even though it was nothing like his. So, with Keith Emerson in mind I daringly made my first appointment at a local unisex hairdresser's called Alan Paul. Sitting in the chair I was completely overcome with embarrassment and didn't ask for anything in particular, because I wasn't sure what to say. They would never have heard of ELP because they were hairdressers. So we, the stylist and myself, sort of agreed on something or other suggested by her, and so it began.

It was a terrifying, humiliating experience, swathes of painstakingly cultivated thatch scythed away in the name of style, a concept that was alien and more than a bit threatening to someone who couldn't remember when he had last used a hairdryer. For the first time ever, my hair was being layered and shaped – and by a hairdresser, a female hairdresser, not a barber. Afterwards I looked shockingly different. Transformed by an actual hairstyle, my head looked unbelievably tiny, and I felt unbelievably self conscious. It was something approximating a feather cut: sort of short on top and longer and wispy at the back and sides – dreadful. It was kind of what I wanted, but because of the way my hair grew it only worked on one side, and the other side looked a mess, or maybe a different kind of mess. To make matters worse, my hair was now so short it didn't cover my ears any more. Nobody else noticed, why would they, but I was mortified. Every car or bus that passed me as I walked home, affecting the kind of nonchalance I imagined Keith Emerson would have displayed emerging from his stylist's, seemed full of people staring, pointing and smirking at my feeble teeny-weeny feather cut. To add insult to injury, during the process itself the loud hairdressery girl who cut my hair kept saying things like 'Oooof, you know what, you're hair's *really greasy*,' and 'Do you work part-time in a garage or anything, because your hair's *really greasy*,' despite which I kept going back there every so often for microtrims when I could no longer get away with it at school. But a properly executed haircut/hairstyle did have an advantage – it meant I could face the wind and rain with a jaunty confidence that bordered on indifference. In fact, one of the first things I did on getting home was put this to the test, standing in front of my bedroom mirror and shaking my head until I saw stars. But no more feather cuts.

The very best hair was just long and straight, nothing fancy or pretentious, though it had to be thick. There were odd exceptions to this orthodoxy. Keith Emerson was one, of course. Closer to home was another, a boy a few years older than us, an impossibly sophisticated sixth former known as Spike, whom we called Dave. He was big Bowie fan, and so was I throughout the seventies, whatever else I was into. For quite a long time Spike kept the same Bowie style, the Ziggy Stardust/Aladdin Sane cut, which looked fantastic. He even dyed it – nothing outrageous, just a slight coppery henna job, though that was enough. He was always getting into trouble for his hair, because to Syph it must have looked freakish and degenerate – otherwise what would have been the point. At some later stage Spike's style changed, he got his hair done like the cover of *David Live* and we didn't like it any more.

'We' were myself and a few other third and fourth form youths who clustered into various loose coalitions depending on our musical preferences; small gangs of intellectually precocious swashbucklers sailing the oceans of rock in search of musical riches, guided by the weekly treasure maps in Sounds, Melody Maker and the NME. We liked various bits of the same kinds of music and would read about it, talk about it, listen to it and swap it endlessly. The music varied, but took in ELP, Pink Floyd, Genesis, Yes, Led Zeppelin, Hawkwind, the Who, Tangerine Dream, Bowie, Dylan, the

Allman Brothers, the Rolling Stones and Eric Clapton – until the mid to late seventies, after which for people like me everything changed and for others nothing changed at all.

Nobody liked Elvis. It wasn't just the music: he clearly took far too much care over his appearance, his clothes, his hair, in ways that we didn't approve of. That hair. That iconic, jet-black sculpture; adored, imitated and parodied ever since. It was too much for me, all that grooming. The words I hated most, that I loathed when applied to clothes or appearance, especially mine, were *neat* and *smart*. Neat people, smart people, they were the ones who went to discos and liked what we sniffily referred to as 'commercial' music. I didn't want to look neat or smart, and I didn't want to look like Elvis, I wanted to look scruffy, a weirdo, a freak. I didn't know anyone who liked Elvis, or dressed like him, or thought he was the King.

The King of what? Rock and roll? Maybe in the fifties, when he and it began, back in the time when he and it must have been something new and strange and wild and amazing, but not afterwards, not after he came out of the army, not in the time when he starred in films and wore jump suits and withdrew from the world into his troubled, tragic bubble of isolation, infantilism and self-destruction. By the sixties the King had become sick, and it was time for change.

The Beatles met Elvis. Just once, on the evening of 27 August, 1965, a year before their final appearance at Candlestick Park. It was set up by Colonel Tom because the Beatles were so famous, and he wanted a bit of easy publicity for his boy. Nothing much happened. Ringo played pool, John and Paul jammed with him a bit, and George smoked a joint with Larry Geller, Elvis's latest hairdresser who also became a confidante in spiritual matters for a while before being ousted by the good old boys of the Memphis Mafia, who were more into booze, pills and Christianity.

Nothing much happened at the meeting, and nothing much needed to, because the very fact of this encounter was immense. On numerous occasions Elvis had expressed his anger at the disrespect shown by people like the Beatles, the

Stones and Dylan. He disapproved of the drugs they took, which weren't the same as his, and he disliked a lot of their music. He went as far as being made an agent of the Bureau Of Narcotics and Dangerous Drugs, receiving his own BNDD badge following a specially arranged meeting with Nixon in 1970 to offer his services. Looking back with all this in mind, the meeting between Elvis and the Beatles becomes a powerful symbol of exchange; the old king and the young kings, the old magic and the new.

Ten years after this strange, symbolically loaded meeting took place, in 1975 I read a book about kings and magic. At the time I didn't know the Beatles had met Elvis and wouldn't have cared if I had known, but it now all falls into place and makes a kind of deep, mythic sense. The book was *The Golden Bough* by the anthropologist JG Frazer. Originally published in 1890, it was an early comparative study of religion, myth and ritual across world culture, and shocked many people because it made no distinction between European Christianity and the beliefs of tribal cultures in places such as Africa and Australia – though Frazer still regarded them as savages. Being an intellectually precocious teenager, I read the whole thing one summer because it had been name-checked in the notes to TS Eliot's strange, dream-like, fragmented poem *The Waste Land*. We studied it at school, and it blew my mind even though I didn't have much idea what it was about. I now know that, amongst other things, it's about fertility, decay, death and renewal; and it's about the myth of the Fisher King, a ruler who was encountered by knights on the quest for the Holy Grail. After being wounded in the thigh or groin, his impotence had made his kingdom barren, a waste land.

I say I read *The Golden Bough*, but the only things I remember clearly about this 700-page work (the single-volume abridged version) were that

- I was sitting on a rock in the late afternoon sun on a beach in Cornwall when I finished it, wearing my favourite navy blue nylon T-shirt, navy blue jeans and ELP BRITISH TOUR 1974 badge. I wore this outfit constantly, sometimes offsetting it with a cheap iron cross on a silver chain that for some reason seemed to bother the lady who ran the B&B we stayed in

- I borrowed the book from Birkenhead Library
- it had a green cover with gold lettering
- the rituals of the cult of Attis involved self-castration.

The first of these facts I now view with a kind of amused embarrassment. The second and third I am neutral about. The fourth still makes me feel queasy.

You might think you haven't come across this rather large, old and esoteric book before, but you could be wrong, especially if you've seen *Apocalypse Now*. Towards the end of the film, as Willard (Martin Sheen) moves in for the kill, we hear the brooding expansive psychodrama that is 'The End' by the Doors, and the camera pans briefly across a table where a few books lie belonging to Colonel Kurtz (Marlon Brando), the kind of books that only a paradoxical, erudite madman who is about to die a symbolically loaded death at the climax of a film directed by Francis Ford Coppola would bother to carry all the way into the jungle and leave lying around in his steamy lair. One of these volumes is a copy of *The Golden Bough*. Another is *From Ritual To Romance* by Jessie L Weston, which is also about the Grail legend and the myth of the Fisher King.

I bet Jim Morrison had read *The Golden Bough*. He might even have read *From Ritual To Romance*. I bet he'd read all kinds of books about stuff like this, if the spoken bit at the end of 'The End' is anything to go by. The Killer awakes before dawn. He puts his boots on, he takes a face from the ancient gallery, and he walks on down the hall. After stopping off to say hi to his siblings, he goes to see his parents. Addressing his father, he says he wants to kill him, then, addressing his mother, he says he wants to BLEUUUUUUUGHO WAAAAAYEEEEEEEEAAAAAHHH.

Jung. Freud. Frazer. Mythology. Psychoanalysis. Anthropology. Deep.

A central thesis of *The Golden Bough* is that many religions, including Christianity, were originally fertility cults centred around the worship of a sacred king who was revered as an incarnation of nature or of a sun god. In the same way that the sun god died with the old year and was reborn every spring in a cycle of death and renewal, his incarnation would have to be challenged and replaced by a younger, more vigorous contender when the incumbent grew old, ill or otherwise unfit to carry on. This new king, chief, or hero would in time be replaced by another, creating a succession of virile young rulers, worshipped as godlike incarnations of divine energy until they too grew old or sick, at which time they were discarded or overthrown.

The Golden Bough was extremely influential, and ideas about myths and archetypes later developed by Jung and his followers can be seen emerging here. Because Frazer died in 1951, he didn't live to experience Elvis, but it feels as though the idea of what Elvis was and what he became is in there somewhere, Elvis's mythology merging with a much older tradition than rock and roll, a lineage of gods, god-kings and heroes as old as stories themselves. The physically, mentally and morally corrupted Colonel Kurtz in *Apocalypse Now* is part of the same tradition, as Francis Ford Coppola goes out of his way to demonstrate.

But it's also possible to connect *Apocalypse Now* with another, quite different idea of mythology. The source of the movie is *Heart of Darkness*, a brilliant, unsettling, 1902 novella by Joseph Conrad set in the Belgian Congo. What the film and book share is a sense of discontinuity that separates modern Romantic or post-Enlightenment myth figures such as Kurtz in the book and the film from earlier heroes and rulers. The more recent god-kings are ultimately overthrown or destroyed not by a challenger, but by themselves. The confrontation, combat and defeat that occurs takes place within, a drama of self-destruction acted out in the mind or psyche or soul of the protagonist.

This is partly a public drama, but is mainly internal, unfolding in a private mental space where social norms and boundaries have fallen away; where deviance and excess are encouraged, and self-expression is highly prized. This is in direct opposition to previous social norms that demanded discipline, conformity and self-sacrifice for the common good. By contrast, this modern myth is that of the talented and doomed individualist, a romantic or Romantic idea that has arisen since the Industrial Revolution and found its most intense expression in the isolated, mediated creative lives of artists, writers, film stars and musicians.

What Elvis and Kurtz have in common is that each man's destruction was brought about by his private journey into himself and the inability to deal with what he found there≈– the often-quoted line from the book that also appears in the film as Kurtz's final utterance is 'the horror, the horror.' The degradation that surrounded them in their respective kingdoms contrasted with their talents and the wealth they had amassed (Kurtz was a successful ivory trader) and reinforced the sense of futility and waste when they died. This external degeneration mirrors the self-destruction systematically carried out in their own psyches after they broke free from their moorings and were swept away by their own delusions, fears and desires. Like Kurtz, who died in obscurity, Elvis had a private death but unlike Kurtz he had a very public funeral, one of the most public ever, and for many people there is still an Elvis-shaped hole in their lives. No-one has really replaced him, even though the Elvis virus has reproduced, mutated and colonised the planet, just like the Beatle virus did.

As well as writing about heroes and kings, Frazer also wrote about magic. According to him there are two kinds: the magic of contact and the magic of similarity, both of which are kinds of 'sympathetic' magic. Magic of contact is based on the idea that items that were once owned by or part of a particular person (such as hair, clothing, teeth, saliva or nail clippings) provide a connection with that person. Possession of these items might allow you to receive protection or blessing from the person, and damaging or destroying them might enable you to do the person harm.

The other kind of magic, magic of similarity, is based on the idea that physical resemblance can connect you with a particular quality, thing or person.[5] The commonest extended examples of this in our culture are visual likenesses such as icons, photographs and figurines: a relationship with the likeness is projected onto the actual person, and can create internal narratives in which imagined events become real. This is the way we think of witchcraft or voodoo working through the use of effigies. The effigies resemble the intended victim, and may also include fragments of their clothing or hair, allowing both magical processes to be brought to bear simultaneously. And the energy flows both ways: you can give, and you can receive. You can curse someone via a likeness, but you can also pray to an image or statue or icon for protection, support or success. Or you can gaze at your Beatles posters, or your authenticated Elvis hair, while you play the records, sing along and daydream.

So much for relics and anthropology, so much for pictures of Elvis and the hair of Elvis. What about the spirit of Elvis, the magic of Elvis the Performer, Elvis the Pelvis? If you want to partake of this you can of course do so through the magic of technology because there are all the terrible movies, the videos, the LPs, the cassettes, the DVDs, the 45s and the MP3s which can bring back the ghost or keep the spirit alive. And you can go to conventions and you can watch impersonators, or you could maybe become one yourself, a shamanic conduit channelling some of the magic directly from its source.

For a while there was something else as well, something much stranger and more wonderful. In 1997, on the twentieth anniversary of his death, before a sell-out crowd in Memphis, Tennessee, Elvis Presley Enterprises and SEG Events put

---

5   For example, tribal beliefs that walnuts are good for the brain; that red fruit juices are good for the blood; that phallus-shaped roots will cure impotence.

on 'Elvis in Concert '97'. Featuring live performances by musicians and vocalists who had worked onstage and in the studio with him, the star/stars of the show was/were a series of concert recordings of Elvis himself, larger than life, larger than death; images on a great big video screen, just like at a stadium concert, which it was, sort of, the only difference being that Elvis was onscreen but not onstage. The lights were on but the King wasn't home, because he'd left the building two decades earlier.

The only concerts Elvis had ever given outside the States during his lifetime were five Canadian shows in 1957. But after the success of 'Elvis in Concert '97' the King went on a world tour with 'Elvis – The Concert,' a scaled down version of the '97 show that toured America and Canada then went to Australia, Europe and Japan. Was it real? Is any of this real? It depends. What is definitely real is the fact that this venture earned 'Elvis – The Concert' a place in the Guinness Book of Records and a certificate acknowledging it as *the first live tour headlined by a performer who is no longer living.* 'Elvis – The Concert.' It just kept on keeping on, like Status Quo without the capital letters, rocking all over the world.

Then a few years after 1997 it was 2002, 25 years on from 1977 and therefore time for The Silver Dead Elvis Anniversary Show, or to give it its proper name, 'Elvis – The 25th Anniversary Concert'. It took place in Memphis on August 16 and included footage from the fifties, the sixties and the seventies, twenty years of his life compressed into a single show, three decades of music performed by a performer who was, and still is, no longer living.[6]

Elvis 1977 to Elvis 2002. Twenty-five years, two and a half decades, gone just like that. A quarter of a century since snotty, skinny, scruffy, spotty, swotty seventeen-year old me listening to John Peel in the kitchen couldn't have given two hoots for bloated lonely forty-two-year-old him lying dead in his bathroom on the other side of the Atlantic,

---

6   This weirdness continues and grows, and now it's all about holograms instead of film projection, but Elvis was the first.

killed by his wealth, his fame, his loneliness and his broken heart. Then I changed my mind about Elvis. It wasn't the silver jubilee Memphysteria, and it wasn't the new number-one single that I couldn't help hearing because Elvis was briefly everywhere again. These things made me notice him, but they didn't change my mind. What changed my mind in 2002 was the realisation that I was now 42, the age Elvis was when he died. Suddenly, it didn't seem very old, especially as an age to die.

Forty-two might suggest middle age, but that wasn't a problem, and even if it was a problem, forty-two was still just fine as a time to still be alive. In fact I was coming to rather like the idea of middle age – a chance to start letting go, stop wearing uncomfortable jeans and accept my modest belly now that I wasn't a youth any more (and hadn't been for some time). As well as ongoing body image realignment, another difference was parenthood. After an intermittently dissolute youth I was now more sedate and had become a father. Twice, on purpose, with the same woman. What I now needed to do was think a bit further ahead; look at the bigger picture, gaze at the horizon rather than my navel. I wanted to stay around for a long time, as long as possible, long enough to enjoy a long second half of my life, long enough to watch my children grow up, and maybe their children too. When you're seventeen, you really are *just* seventeen. When you're forty-two, things are different.

So there I was in 2002, deliberately a double dad, rummaging about inside a large poor-quality fitted wardrobe, accompanied by my children, rooting through boxes of junk and half-heartedly attempting to jettison some of it. As a strategy to keep the children away from the TV, it worked for half an hour or so then they went back downstairs to the Cartoon Network, leaving me covered in dust and sweat to put everything back again.

Then all of a sudden this strange flashbulb goes off inside my head; this is my Personal Silver Dead Elvis Jubilee Moment. Pop. Here's me at forty-two in the wardrobe, and there's Elvis, dead in the foetal position after falling off the toilet 25 years ago. Hang on, 42 isn't the right age to die, I'm 42, and I'm not ready to die. Was Elvis? Probably not; or maybe he'd given up; maybe he didn't care, the way a lot of punks said they didn't care in 1977, only more than they could ever understand. This made him tragic rather than ridiculous, a sad lonely man the same age as me who squandered massive talents he barely seemed to understand, who more than paid the price for his success, who deserved compassion rather than contempt. Same age as me. Wow.

I tried to blink away the lurid afterimage of forty-two-year-old-Elvis-dead-and-forty-two-year-old-me-alive   that had seared itself into my mind's eye in the wardrobe's dusty, capacious semi-darkness, but it sort of stayed there. I might not have been rich or famous in middle age, but I was not fat, drugged up, bored, lonely, overdressed, American or dead either.

Although Elvis's music didn't make much of an impression on me apart from 'Heartbreak Hotel' and 'How Great Thou Art,' the 2002 single must have, because it sneaked up on me and I ended up liking it. What made much more of an impression, though, was something I watched during the TV nostalgia-fest that accompanied the Dead Elvis Silver Jubilee – it was the 'Comeback Special' from 1968. This was his unplugged-before-Unplugged TV show, the one where he appeared in shiny black leather, shiny jet-black coal-black hair (a raven helmet of sculpted, lacquered immobility, the very opposite of Jerry Lee's) and, after a short while, a sheen of sweat. Three years after the Beatles had disappeared, the King briefly returned, looking like an early Beatle, only older with a much higher collar and much stranger hair.

It was a compelling look and a compelling performance, all apart from the fair-haired hippie with no sense of rhythm who sat too close to one of the microphones and banged a tambourine throughout, even though he should have been taken outside and punched senseless. Where are those brutal security guys when you actually need them? Apart from that, which to be fair was nothing to do with Elvis, it was great: he was charismatic, modest and funny, and then I realised: it was okay, I could like Elvis, and feel sorry for him as well. Even if I still didn't want to go out and buy anything by him, I could get closer to seeing what the fuss was about. Behind all the songs, the films, the hair, the clothes and the house was some great music and the first rock and roll superstar. He did it first; there was no road map for him, no instructions to tell him what to do, just 'Colonel' Tom Parker. Poor Elvis.

He was larger than life, and he was larger than death. Nine years before he died, he had already risen from the grave in the 'Comeback Special,' after years spent in Hollywood limbo making mediocre films and shedloads of money. Then, twenty years after his demise, he had done it again with 'Elvis in Concert '97.' Then he did it yet again, made another, even more spectacular Silver Jubilee comeback in 2002, though in some ways I guess he never really went away, never really died, just left his useless, bloated, sclerotic body behind and transmigrated onto record and cassette, film and videotape, then went digital. And he was on the airwaves as well, the TV and the radio, the waves of electromagnetic Elvis travelling out from Earth through space, the earliest Elvis now more distant than the most distant space probe, Elvis ripples on the universal pond, radiating out from our little pebble, ripples that must be a hundred light years wide by now.

Also in 2002 there was 'A Little Less Conversation,' and there he was scaling the charts again, just like old times. The song started out as an obscure 1968 single from the obscure 1968 movie *Live a Little, Love a Little*, his 28th, in which he sings it to a girl by a swimming pool. The movie was a flop, and so was the single. Even so, Elvis liked the song enough to include it in the recording sessions for the 'Comeback Special,' though it wasn't broadcast. Then nothing happened, and carried on happening for another 30 years or so. In the nineties, various versions of it were released on various

CD boxed sets churned out by record companies as part of the ongoing Great Rock and Roll Swindle. Then in 2001 a version of the song was used in *Ocean's Eleven*, one of various remakes being churned out by film companies as part of the Great Film Swindle. Then in 2002 Nike picked up on it and used it in an advertising campaign to promote its part of the Great Sportswear Swindle.

What happened was that a version of 'A Little Less Conversation' was remixed by a Dutch DJ called Tom Holkenborg under the moniker Junkie XL. The name apparently refers to his intensive 'studio junkie' lifestyle, together with the idea of 'e-X-panding L-imits', whatever that means. Unfortunately the Presley estate was unhappy with the name Junkie XL, so it was shortened to JXL for the single, which became a huge Silver Dead Elvis Jubilee Hit, reaching number one in 24 countries. But it wasn't just any old Silver Dead Elvis Jubilee Hit Number One – it was the one that gave Dead Elvis a total of 18 UK number ones, more than anyone else, ever, and one more than even the Beatles (until 'Free as a Bird,' a piece of sleazy electronic necrophilia that ELO's Jeff Lynne produced to sound like ELO, and George Martin had nothing to do with, plumbed new depths and put the Beatles back on top again).

Then, after everyone thought the show was over, that same Elvis song emerged again, in a brief but traumatising episode of ghastly, toe-curling, dad-dancing awfulness. No-one knows what Elvis would have thought of this song being adapted for a soccer commercial; he might have thought it was okay, he might not. I hope it's less likely he would have approved of its use at the 2004 Tory party conference to 'big up' party leader Michael Howard. And although Special Agent Presley had conservative leanings and, like Michael Howard, disapproved of drug taking, hippies and communists, I'd like to think that the muffled squelching sound reported around Memphis in late 2004 was Elvis turning in his grave.

Playlist 5 - Long Live The King		
Heartbreak Hotel	Elvis Presley	
I'm A Believer	The Monkees	
These Boots Are Made For Walkin'	Nancy Sinatra	
Albatross	Fleetwood Mac	
The Resurrection Shuffle	Ashton, Gardner and Dyke	
I'll Come Running	Brian Eno	*Another Green World*
Paris, Texas	Ry Cooder	*Paris, Texas*
Don't Fence Me In	Bing Crosby	
Walkin' Blues	Robert Johnson	
Whole Lotta Shakin' Goin' On	Jerry Lee Lewis	*Live At The Star Club*

To listen to the playlists, visit Spotify using the QR links provided.

Links to every playlist are also at www.hungry-ghost.info, along with photographs and archive material to supplement each chapter and enhance the reading/listening experience, just like a great big gatefold album cover.

5

GOD SAVE THE QUEEN

First the King. Now the Queen.

Before thinking about Elvis in August 1977, I had been thinking about Elizabeth and trying to ignore her and her stupid silver jubilee. It had taken place a few months earlier to celebrate the fact that she had been known as the Queen since 1952, a period of 25 years, two and a half decades, a quarter of a century. To me at seventeen this was a long time, more than a lifetime, in fact it was about 1 ½ lifetimes. Festivities had taken place on 7 June, occupying and preoccupying millions in Britain and around the world. There were street parties, fetes, carnivals and fireworks, with lots of Union Jacks and red-white-and-blue bunting and patriotic festivities. But not for me. I was too busy swotting and sneering.

In 1977 I was taking my A-Levels, taking them very seriously indeed. My free but privileged education was something I worked at, though this was clearly at odds with my vocal support for a new kind of noisy and unpleasant music, which could sometimes give things a bit of an edge.

School was a single-sex Victorian institution with around seven hundred pupils, thirty or so boarders, three fives courts, two rugby fields, a chaplain with fully fitted neo-gothic chapel, and a military cadet force. As well as fanatical restrictions on hair, there was also a quaint authoritarian dress code that included full school uniform – the cap was compulsory in junior school, optional in big school. One member of staff, a morbidly obese maths teacher informally known as Belly, would on occasions send for junior boys and berate them for not wearing their caps after seeing them bare-headed outside school as he drove by in his dangerously overloaded green soft-top Beetle. Because he taught maths its registration number was LCM 1. LCM stands for lowest common multiple, which is the smallest positive integer that... oh, who cares, it's only maths.

Not surprisingly, our school was referred to by boys from other schools, who sometimes stole our caps as we walked home and threw them into people's gardens, as 'the poofs' school', but they were probably just jealous because they couldn't be poofs too.

Every Thursday, boys from the fourth form upwards came to school in army or navy uniform because this was the day the Combined Cadet Force or CCF did its thing, its thing being marching up and down and looking smart. Other activities included carrying rifles, taking them to pieces, putting them back together again and occasionally firing them. Although I planned to refuse to join the CCF for undefined ideological reasons, I was more than a little worried about how this act of defiance might go down, as I didn't like getting into trouble. Fortunately, the CCF became optional at around the time I was due to join, presumably because teachers liked it even less than pupils, so I and a few other scruffs including Radar ended up tidying the school library instead. Tidying consisted of standing around talking about music, book poised in hand, hair behind ears, just in case Syph decided to drop by.

As well as all the other rules about uniforms and appearance, no writing or badges were allowed on rucksacks. Having started off with **ELP** in *Brain Salad Surgery* lettering, I later added **GENESIS** in the lettering from *The Lamb Lies Down on Broadway*, which I never listened to all the way through, though I did experience it live (very peculiar). **ELP** was later replaced by **The Who**, the band's name encircled by a large ♂ symbol.

Then Syph went and ruined my rucksack. It started during divinity – the only subject he ever taught, though he never actually did anything as mundane as teaching, preferring to pass the time recounting stupid anecdotes and making us feel uncomfortable. And occasionally reading aloud from *Pilgrim's Progress* or the works of French

172

mathematician, physicist, inventor, writer and philosopher Blaise Pascal (1623-1662). One afternoon, he was in a particularly bad mood, and spent the entire period pacing up and down between the rows of desks finding fault with attitudes, haircuts and rucksacks more or less at random. And because he assigned someone to note all this down, you knew you would have to turn up at his study with hair cut or rucksack scrubbed clean or socks pulled up.

School rucksacks didn't have the Nike swoosh, Adidas stripes or Puma puma: they were lumpy backpacks bought from places like the Army & Navy Stores in Liverpool. National service had ended about 15 years previously, so there were still mountains of old uniforms and equipment lying about in shops waiting to be bought by scruffy young men. The rucksacks were made from webbing, a tough, knobbly material designed to withstand the rigours of military service, and one bag could in theory last your entire school career. Not mine, though, because Syph took exception to the Who and Genesis, and I was ordered to remove these carefully written logos.

As a quick fix, I hit on the idea of bleach. Unfortunately, I hadn't done much research into what happened when fabrics and strong alkaline solutions were brought together, so I left the offending area of the rucksack soaking for the best part of a weekend. When Sunday evening came and I tried to remove the remaining smears of ink with a scrubbing brush, the top of the rucksack disintegrated into a pathetic, stinking fringe of pale threads. To add insult to injury, when I turned up the following morning, Syph had completely forgotten, being reminded only after noticing the smell. When presented with my acrid, shredded remnants he raised his eyebrows, wrinkled his nose in refined horror and waved me away with some kind of smirky quip. By then I was going off Genesis anyway, though I never went off the Who, as long as you don't count anything after *Quadrophenia*.

The replacement for this rucksack soon had ΤΟ ΜΕΓΑ ΘΗΡΙΟΝ written across it in biro, because that was what occultist Aleister Crowley called himself. It arose from the desire to rebel against my Christian upbringing and at the same time feel esoteric, superior and slightly dangerous. Crowley's parents had been Plymouth Brethren, an obscure, uncompromising and drab Protestant sect whose faith was at the time mine shared by my parents. Crowley was born on 12 October, the day before me and the same day as my friend Fanny, who was also flirting with occultism. Fanny was popular at primary school because he was witty, charming and had a natural talent for sport, all qualities I felt I lacked as abundantly as he possessed them. As Fanny's birthday was the same as Aleister Crowley's and mine was the day after, here too I felt overshadowed, the Neighbour Of The Beast. His parents had a huge stereo system and were hardly ever at home, so from an early age we could drink beer and listen to the likes of Black Sabbath, Deep Purple, Uriah Heep and Wishbone Ash at high volume with impunity. I have no idea why he was called Fanny.

TO ΜΕΓΑ ΘΗΡΙΟΝ is TO MEGA THERION, which means THE GREAT BEAST in Greek. According to the principles of numerology the letters in this name add up to 666, traditionally the number of the Antichrist in the book of Revelation.[1] Either Syph never noticed TO ΜΕΓΑ ΘΗΡΙΟΝ, or he assumed that because it looked Classical it must have been okay. A few years later, the same rucksack accompanied me to university, with Lou Reed's face from *Transformer* painted on it and the word 'Velvets' in red underneath, an eye-catching combination I had seen on the back of someone's jacket at Eric's.

But the Velvets were another layer, and came later. This was 1977, with me in a vague, naïve yet quietly ostentatious way championing Aleister Crowley's strangeness and nastiness in ballpoint pen, and working hard for my A-levels. As well as the swotting, there was the sneering – at Christianity; at school; at my bemused parents; at smartness; at niceness; at anyone who didn't get it, whatever 'it' happened to be. Because I was into

---

1   Recently, following re-examination of the original text a number of scholarly sources have proposed 616 as the true Number of the Beast. For some reason this seems a lot less threatening.

sneering, I was also into the music that encouraged it, rapidly acquiring a feel for how to combine the two in ways that could send me into paroxysms of glee and those around me into ecstasies of outrage. Suddenly there was no such thing as 'it's only rock and roll': everyone had to take a side, because some of the music I'd started listening to was so saturated with bad attitude and so unpopular, it was fantastic. Unlike the Eagles, Fleetwood Mac, Peter Frampton, Wings or Rod Stewart, this wasn't music that adults liked and that far too many young people liked as well, especially smart ones and nice ones and good-looking, long-haired, unobtainable female ones in tight jeans. Unlike all the laid-back jet-set hippie crap, this music seemed raw and confrontational; faster, dirtier and noisier than anything I had heard before; and defiantly inept and/ or dumb, all of which were qualities that suddenly seemed to have been missing from music for far too long.

It was called *punk*. People disapproved instinctively, affording countless opportunities to sneer ostentatiously at them for being old or stupid or bigoted or boring. Instant, effortless controversy. In such volatile times, name-dropping became essential. After all, *punk* covered such a multitude of sins, blasphemies and perversions that you could mention anything even a bit controversial that had become tainted by association, and have an immediate effect. And for a while there was *new wave* as well. Though purists scorned the label, for a short time it lay within the malign shadow cast by the unstable pile of junk, filth and treasure that was *punk*, until it became obvious that *new wave* equalled skinny tie and neat longish hair and leather jeans and red baseball boots, which equalled wanker.

No wonder punk cast such a shadow and was so attractive in so many ways. Tales of spitting, swearing, vomiting, drunkenness, disrespect and nastiness abounded. How much better could it get? And there was amazing music (and terrible music). But even without the music, even without anyone hearing a single note it was possible to provoke and alienate by referring casually to a welter of facetious and/or objectionable names. That was part of the idea, wasn't it?

- the Raped
- the Damned
- the Vibrators
- the Stranglers
- the Sex Pistols
- the Dead Boys
- the Dead Kennedys
- the Moors Murderers
- Johnny and the Self Abusers

These bands are all **The** **Something**, or **Someone And** **The** **Somethings**. Before punk, the definite article was largely absent from band names for a while. It seems like a fifties thing, then an early to mid sixties thing, then it died back in the early seventies before returning with punk. Apart from the likes of

- Eater
- Wire
- Crass
- Suicide
- Kleenex
- Sham 69
- Penetration
- Swell Maps
- X-Ray Spex

but they were exceptions.

Maybe the dropping of the definite article was just an early seventies meme that punk reacted against, consciously or unconsciously. Perhaps, as a reaction against the musical present and recent past, punk bands went back to basics by playing with earlier-sounding fifties names. Bands got to sound like gangs, and band members gave themselves stupid made-up names that allowed them to re-invent themselves and obliterate any irrelevant or embarrassing personal history; with a new name could come instant brand-new dumb-smart trash celebrity status. Names like:

- Johnny Rotten (vocals, the Sex Pistols: another member was Sid Vicious)
- Dee Generate (drummer, Eater: another member was Andy Blade)
- Rat Scabies (drummer, the Damned: other members were Captain Sensible and Dave Vanian)
- Joey Ramone, Johnny Ramone, Dee Dee Ramone and Tommy Ramone (vocals; guitar; bass; drums. They count as a single entity, otherwise it wouldn't make sense. It makes more sense still when you include later members such as Marky Ramone, CJ Ramone, Richie Ramone and Elvis Ramone)
- Poly Styrene (vocals, X-Ray Spex: another member was Laura Logic)
- Jello Biafra (vocals, the Dead Kennedys: other members included Klaus Fluoride, Jeff Penalty)
- Adam Ant (vocals, Adam and the Ants: another member was Lester Square)
- Gaye Advert (bass, the Adverts: another member was TV Smith)
- Steve Ignorant (vocals, Crass: other members included Penny Rimbaud, NA Palmer, Phil Free, Eve Libertine and Joy de Vivre)

The names of singles could be provocative slogans, the kind that you wouldn't have expected to see in the charts:

- Anarchy In The UK (the Sex Pistols)
- Blank Generation (Richard Hell and the Voidoids)
- Now I Wanna Sniff Some Glue (the Ramones)
- California Uber Alles (the Dead Kennedys)
- Borstal Breakout (Sham 69)
- Cranked Up Really High (Slaughter and the Dogs)
- White Riot (the Clash)
- Oh Bondage, Up Yours (X-Ray Spex)

- If You Don't Wanna Fuck Me, Baby, Fuck Off (Wayne – subsequently Jayne – County and the Electric Chairs)
- Fascist Dictator (the Cortinas)
- Orgasm Addict (the Buzzcocks)

It's all games about names. Back then, this kind of thing was shocking; the nearest contemporary equivalents are perhaps black metal or hip-hop, though they're a lot less rough and ready. Back then, you could even pretend you were in a band if you came up with a decent name. At university I was in an imaginary band called 7 Hertz that was sometimes also known as 7 Hurtz, based on the notion that loud noise at this low frequency could supposedly immobilise or kill people by vibrating their insides to mush. I never did form the band but its name appeared on walls from time to time.

After bands, musicians and singles, it's harder to think of album titles, because although a lot of punk singles got made, there were relatively few albums. Here are five that fit in somewhere or other:

1. *Never Mind The Bollocks, Here's The Sex Pistols* (the Sex Pistols)
2. *Damned, Damned, Damned* (the Damned)
3. *Rattus Norvegicus* (the Stranglers)
4. *Do It Dog Style* (Slaughter and the Dogs)
5. *Blank Generation* (Richard Hell and the Voidoids)

The five bands that made these albums – I don't like all of them, I don't even know all of them that well, but they can maybe help to shine some light into the nooks and crannies of the teetering edifice that was thrown together out of various bits and pieces that, for want of anything better, was given the name *punk*.

The name was used by Shakespeare as a term for a prostitute in *The Merry Wives Of Windsor* and *Measure For Measure*. In early 20th century America it referred mainly to the young homosexual partner of an older man, or to a juvenile hooligan or petty criminal, and was used as a term of abuse. In 1970 the poet, activist and member of the Fugs Ed Sanders referred to his own music as 'punk rock, redneck sentimentality', and journalist Lester Bangs referred to Iggy Pop as 'that Stooge punk'. Despite the musical context, neither instance uses the word in the later sense, and when it was used musically it initially referred to sixties American garage bands, like those on the now-classic 1972 *Nuggets* compilation. From these beginnings its meaning and usage evolved until it became the name of a sinister new youth cult. In Britain nobody seemed to know where the word came from, though everybody knew it referred to a horrible teenage movement, and had an opinion about it, with or without hearing any music.

All I know for sure is that, after at first being shocked by punk I was amazed and swept off my feet. It seemed so chaotic, new and exciting, lacking any feeling of organisation, thought or cleverness, the opposite of everything I had assumed I liked. It's only later, on reflection and in the writing of histories, memoirs and commentaries, that any sense of structure and direction either emerges or is imposed on the chaos, newness and excitement that at the time you threw yourself into and let wash over you and carry you along.

As time passes and distance increases, history and structure become more important, but they need reliable evidence to be gathered and processed, rather than just hoovering up the ramblings of liars, lunatics and show-offs. And any sense of structure or direction is based on the assumption that people actually want to 'set the record straight' after almost forty years, what with all the egos and reputations that have been built and lovingly polished during the intervening decades. Consider all the tall stories and selective reminiscence; all the books, documentaries, reissues, anniversaries and retrospectives; all the nostalgia, myth-making and money-making ventures that might be at stake. And is a record that's set straight always better than a bent, twisted and fragmented one anyway?

I've read books and books about British punk and American punk; the alliances and conflicts between musicians and bands and record companies and journalists;

the coincidences and accidents and outrages and cults and schisms. The more I read the less I feel I really know. More and more information is swilling around inside my head, and somewhere in the background I can hear music playing. Some of it, a lot of it, I heard at the time in a state of blissful ignorance, some of it I have heard since in a state of tainted awareness. As a single pixel somewhere near the edge of the bigger picture, all I can really write about, or try to write about, seen through the dim and dimming lens of middle age, heard from long ago and far away, is what I think I remember, things seen and heard incompletely from the perspective of who I was and where I was at the time, stuck between John Peel and the NME and Eric's on one hand and almost everyone and everything else on the other, living a life of modest privilege, intellectual curiosity, musical obsession and vicarious outrage. So, five bands and five albums.

1. *Never Mind The Bollocks, Here's The Sex Pistols* (the Sex Pistols)

As an act of sheer provocation, the name *Never Mind The Bollocks, Here's The Sex Pistols* takes some beating. In its own inimitable way, it exhorts us to ignore the ballyhoo surrounding the band and concentrate instead on their music, at the same time casually lobbing in the hand grenade that was the word 'bollocks' in 1977. This was an LP you couldn't name in polite company: 'Never Mind...', we used to call it. You couldn't name it, and unless you had a plastic bag you couldn't carry it about either, with its fluorescent pink and yellow cover and cut-out lettering that screamed confrontation and controversy at anyone prepared to pay attention, along with something like FUCK OFF WE'RE THE FUCKING SEX PISTOLS at anyone who wasn't paying attention, or who didn't want to know.

And what exactly is a sex pistol, anyway? I know what a Sex Pistol is – a Sex Pistol is one of the Sex Pistols, like a Beatle is one of the Beatles, but what's a sex pistol?

The first two sexy, pistolly, sex-type or pistol-type things that come to mind are a penis and a pistol. So maybe a sex pistol is a pistol that's full of sex – a sperm pistol, perhaps. The fact that the name includes the word 'sex' and nearly includes the word 'piss' as part of 'pistol' gets in the way of the fact that it's perhaps alluding to willies as weapons and/or weapons as willies, which isn't very original but still works. The harshness of the overall sound, all the hissing, all the spikiness and sharpness, make the noise created by the air as it moves through your mouth bristle with sibilance and hostility, irrespective of the semantic content – like sssssssexxxxxxx pissssssstol, only spoken rather than written. And if it was just a question of semantics or phallic allusions, the band could have been called the Love Guns, but it doesn't have quite the same ring to it. And the Fuck Pistols would have been too controversial. According to one story, they might have even been called the Sex Keys after Malcolm McLaren saw a porn mag with a voyeuristic through-the-keyhole cover image, and thought this might be a good name for his band of 'young, sexy assassins'.

Then again, there's a T-shirt called **You're gonna wake up one morning and know what side of the bed you've been lying on!** that was apparently designed by McLaren, perhaps with input from Bernie Rhodes, who later managed the Clash. On sale maybe as early as the end of 1974, this T-shirt was a kind of manifesto for something or other in the form of two lists in small messy type, long enough to cover the whole of the T-shirt front, small enough and messy enough to make you look hard if you wanted to read it. The wearer became the centre of attention, a living text, a mute, ignorant name dropper of heroic or anti-heroic proportions – assuming you could be bothered reading what you glimpsed as the words danced about in front of you, but why wouldn't you want to read a list like that, even if you or the wearer didn't know what it all meant, because that wasn't the point. The point was to attract attention, to confuse, to perplex, to allude, drop the names, spread the words, propagate war as peace, freedom as slavery, ignorance as strength – all in two lists. One list was of hates and one was of loves. One of the loves was **Kutie Jones and his SEX PISTOLS**, right after **Bob Marley Jimi Hendrix Sam Cooke** and right before **This country is run by a group of fascists so said Gene Vincent in a 1955 US radio interview**.

And this is without mentioning 'bollocks,' another allusion to the male member, as well as meaning 'nonsense'. *Bollocks*, previously *ballocks*, is from Middle English *ballock* = testis, before which the Old English *beallucas* was the diminutive form of the word for 'balls'. The trouble was, the bollocks (nonsense) actually did get in the way of the Sex Pistols. Banned from almost everywhere, reported on by almost everyone, they ended up with an unbelievably huge amount of publicity and an all too believably small amount of music.

Like most other people, including a lot of those who claimed they actually had, I never got to see the Sex Pistols. The nearest I got was buying a ticket for a gig at the Hamilton Club in Birkenhead on 20 December 1977. Radar and I were in Skeleton Records one afternoon, when John Weaver sidled over to us and asked in a low voice if we wanted tickets to see the Sex Pistols. I nearly fell over. Wow. The Sex Pistols. In Birkenhead. And he's asking *us*. We hurriedly paid our £1.75 each and left the shop clutching our tickets, beside ourselves with excitement but trying not to show it. Of course, the council found out and the gig was banned, so they never played. I stupidly took my ticket back and got a refund rather than keeping it as a souvenir, but when I met John Weaver again after buying my Beatles CDs we got talking about it, and he told me he still had a wad of tickets. He even gave me one, ticket number 232 for the Sex Pistols non-gig at the Hamilton Club, Henry St, Birkenhead.

I may not have seen the Sex Pistols but I did see local micro-legends Radio Blank at the Old Rockferrians Club a year earlier. Their name at some stage got spray-painted on the railway bridge over Woodchurch Road, RADIO BLANK replacing ROCKERS, which had been there for years. This being Birkenhead, I can't remember whether HENDRIX came before or after RADIO BLANK, because Hendrix was always there somewhere in seventies Birkenhead, in record collections, at parties, in conversations and in the performances of local bands. Hendrix was always there because Birkenhead was a pretty *troggy* place, full of *trogs*, hairy dope smokers in denim or combat jackets and cowboy boots or desert boots who were into Zeppelin and Quo and Sabbath and Skynyrd and Floyd and Purple and Zappa and, of course, Hendrix. None of that *punk shit,* though.

Anyway, one evening in the Old Rockferrians clubhouse, there we were, about half a dozen self-conscious vaguely punky types, with all the rugger buggers quaffing their ale on the other side of the room and looking a bit bemused and a bit hostile. The drummer in Radio Blank, Stephen Brick, had attended Rock Ferry High School and was therefore an Old Rockferrian, which was presumably how they got the gig. At some stage they launched into their set, not much of which I remember apart from when they tore through 'Suffragette City' and did a song called 'Don't Blame Me, It's The GLC'. Sometime during the evening one of the rugger buggers was held down and had his trousers forcibly removed by the others, which seemed to vastly amuse all except the de-trousered one, who looked shaken and upset. At one stage, three or four punky types other than me pogoed and twisted about for a while on the otherwise empty dancefloor while the rugger buggers looked on in contempt. I didn't dance because I wasn't drunk enough, a recurring motif throughout my life.

Radio Blank only ever played about a dozen gigs, at least one of which was at Eric's. Two of the other members were Dave Balfe (bass) and Alan Gill (guitar), both of whom were later in the Teardrop Explodes with Julian Cope before his emergence as shamanic polymath, floored genius and standing stoner. The vocalist was Keith Hartley, who became a fireman. I don't know what happened to Stephen Brick, but that was his real name, and I went to primary school with his brother, Colin. I was always jealous of Colin because he was a great athlete and a great cricketer and, while I was okay at athletics, I was dismal at cricket, so much so that when I was fielding I used to hide behind the only available tree to avoid being hit by the ball. I wasn't much better at football, always among the last to be chosen in the humiliating team selection process. Sport and music are supposed to be the most popular distractions for adolescent males. Guess which one I preferred.

The Sex Pistols.

Do we need to think about what they sounded like? The Stooges playing songs by the Sweet? The New York Dolls playing songs by the Faces? Does anyone not know? All I can say, and all I really need to say, is that their nasty beautiful roar changed my ears forever.

2. *Damned, Damned, Damned* (the Damned)

Damned, Damned, Damned by the Damned – what more is there to say?

How about

- it was the first British punk album, released on 18 February 1977. The band also released the first punk single, 'New Rose,' on October 22, 1976, the B side of which was a cover version of 'Help' by the Beatles. Whatever else anyone has to say about them, they were the first. Also:
    - it's a stupid title for an LP, and probably not by mistake
    - it's got a stupid front cover, a head and shoulders shot of the band smeared with baked beans and cream, and probably not by mistake.
- spot the musician – Dave Vanian (vocals), Rat Scabies (drums), Captain Sensible (bass), Brian James (guitar)
- the last LP track ('I Feel Alright') is a Stooges cover version ('1969'); it's an eight-year old song pushed two years into the future and set in 1979. All other songs are credited to Brian James
- Dave Vanian was played by David Letts, who looked like a vampire, or a Nazi undertaker, or a goth, or all three

- Rat Scabies was played by Chris Miller, who looked like a thug
- Captain Sensible was played by Ray Burns, who looked like a man in a dog collar, a nurse's uniform and Doctor Martens even when he wasn't wearing any of these
- Brian James was played by Brian James, who was the first to leave the band. He was replaced on guitar by Captain Sensible, who was replaced briefly on bass by Lemmy and then by Algy Ward of the Saints, who was still with them when they made their best album, *Machine Gun Etiquette*
- I saw the Damned at Eric's at the very end of 1979 and they were hilarious
- almost forty years on, they played in my town and I didn't go to see them
- not all the original members are still with the band
- they've just made a new album.

3. *Rattus Norvegicus* (the Stranglers)

Rattus Norvegicus might be a bit too clever for punk, like the band. The title of their first LP was the scientific name of the brown rat, a longtime dweller with humans and a serious pest in most parts of the world. I bought it soon enough after it was released to get the free single ('Choosy Susie' / 'Peasant In The Big Shitty'). I also bought their second album *No More Heroes* and their third album *Black and White* (with free white vinyl single 'Walk On By'/ 'Mean To Me'/ 'Tits') before giving up.

The first thing I ever heard by the Stranglers was on John Peel, the ponderously titled single '(Get A) Grip (On Yourself)', released in early 1977. If you like being amazed by music, it's an exhilarating moment when your skin prickles and you go, 'What the hell is *this*?' as you feel another beautiful earworm burrow inside your head. This was what happened as I was gripped by 'Grip.' The first time I heard it, I realised it was far too musical and musicianly for punk, with its plaintive saxophone, oozing synthesiser, rippling electric piano and restless bass; what hooked me was the song's momentum, its pounding melodic rush. I didn't recognise the individual instruments at the time; I was just gripped by 'Grip'.

A lot of bands said they were inspired by seeing or hearing the Sex Pistols or the Ramones, but the Stranglers clearly weren't one of them. They sounded ancient, subterranean and vaguely unpleasant, more pub rock than punk rock; pub rock in a dark and strange pub where you could never be quite sure who you were going to meet. It was maybe a bit naff and not very right-on to like the Stranglers, and the albums haven't all worn well, but a compilation of singles called *Peaches* reminded me of their greatness. The Stranglers were for years a brilliant singles band, which in a strange way makes them just as punk as the Sex Pistols or Buzzcocks, though they lasted a lot longer and were a lot more varied in their approach. A review of the album referred to them as 'an angry psychedelic band' – angry sometimes, psychedelic maybe, hippy definitely not.

In 1977 my friend Bogey, one of the few early punk adopters out of everyone I knew, accompanied me to Liverpool to try and join Eric's on the door and see the Stranglers, but the bouncers told us that we had to be 20 or over to join. Despite being 17 and probably looking younger we tried reasoning with them and arguing with them to convince them we were both the right age, but nothing we said made any difference, not even, 'I am 20' followed by, 'Honest, I am 20' followed by, 'I bloody am 20 you know, honest.' So there we were, humiliated, pissed off, hating Those Bastards and wondering what to do next, when bass player Jean Jacques Burnel came rumbling over the cobbles on his Triumph Bonneville, and we turned and walked away in shame and disgust. They would probably have been crap anyway (They were great, according to Webster, a boy from school who was already a member and who, to make matters worse, was a year younger than we were but needed to shave more often).

The second time I tried to see the Stranglers was on 14 October 1977, when they played at Liverpool University, the day after my 18th birthday. I didn't have a ticket and turned up early, by myself because this time no-one else wanted to go. I assumed there would be tickets on the door. There weren't. Disaster. Oh God, what do I do now? Go home? Get on the guest list? Go to a pub and get drunk on my own, then go home? In quiet desperation, I wandered about for a while, trying to look purposeful and self-contained rather than utterly deflated. Infiltrating the assortment of oddballs milling around outside the Students' Union building, I had no idea what to do next. Along the railings outside the refectory a bunch of punk scallies were arguing about whether it was da Drones or da Ramones who were the support band, and I found myself in the middle of this discussion on the side of da Drones – but tentatively, because although I knew I didn't want to look like a smart-arse. We ended up commiserating with each other about how shit it was not to be able to get tickets, and I probably swore more than usual to show how authentic I was. Then someone caught sight of the Stranglers through the refectory window, after which everyone started yelling and waving to attract their attention, even me in a half-hearted kind of way. Eventually the guitarist Hugh Cornwell came and opened a window, after which there was pandemonium, a brief shouted conversation, and suddenly Hugh Cornwell had got Someone-or-other on the guest list along with a number of friends, one of whom was me.

Suddenly these lads were me best mates. After waiting a while we rushed to the entrance, congratulating one another and laughing hysterically. Pushing through the heaving mass to get to the door, we found that yes, we really were on the guest list, and then we were in. After a brief bit of back-slapping, the others disappeared, and there I was, in, on the guest list.

I walked about in a daze for a while, then made my way into the hall. First were the Drones, who played fast, pogoed about a lot, set off a fire extinguisher and got covered in spit. I still can't think of many more disgusting things than mass spitting, getting covered in a layer of dripping, glistening saliva, whether it's meant as a compliment or not. Hair, face, clothes, guitar, up your nose, in your mouth. According to NME reports, Joe Strummer got hepatitis after someone spat and it went in his mouth.

After the Drones it was the Stranglers. They played

- No More Heroes
- Ugly
- Bring On The Nubiles
- Sometimes
- Dagenham Dave
- Dead Ringer
- Hanging Around
- 5 Minutes
- Something Better Change
- I Feel Like A Wog
- Straighten Out
- Burning Up Time
- London Lady
- Grip
- Down In The Sewer.

I know this because that's what the bootleg of the gig claims to have on it. It's meant to be a great recording of a great gig, about which I remember just four things:

1. To celebrate getting in free! on the guest list! I bought a badge and a T-shirt, both of which had the band's name and rat logo in lime green on a black background. Unfortunately, the T-shirt was too small. Even more unfortunately, it was a cap-sleeve T-shirt. I hated cap-sleeve T-shirts and still do, but I was just eighteen, had got in free! on the guest list! and was feeling a bit reckless, so I bought it anyway. I've still got the badge.
2. As the band came on, Hugh Cornwell walked up to his microphone, glowered at the audience and said something

like, 'Okay, you gotta remember there's no more heroes, right, 'cos they're all dead,' before launching straight into 'No More Heroes' to roars of approval and hundreds of fists punching the air.

3. During the his guitar breaks, Hugh Cornwell scurried about, bent double like a younger more menacing version of Groucho Marx, especially during 'Down In The Sewer'.

4. There were two breaks in the performance. One was when a scuffle broke out because someone had spat at Jean Jacques Burnel and he lashed out with his bass guitar. The other break was when Hugh Cornwell stopped playing to tell everyone to stop spitting because spitting was a fucking drag, but he didn't hit anyone.

A while after this, Bogey I were walking through Birkenhead town centre from one record shop to another on a Saturday afternoon. I was wearing my Stranglers T-shirt (too small, with cap sleeves) and an old green scout shirt (too small, badges removed). The shirt was completely undone, allowing the Stranglers logo to be displayed but covering the cap sleeves. Walking towards was a boy I recognised from school, who I disliked because he was into Uriah Heep and Judas Priest. As he passed he curled his lip and sneered, 'Huh, *the Stranglers*.' Energised by righteous rage, I swung round and shouted after him FOOK-OFF-YOU-YER-BORING-OLD-FART with enough force to ruffle his hair, before remembering I where I was realising everyone was staring at me, which made me wish the ground would open up and swallow me. That's how outrageous I was.

Forty years on, the Stranglers are still touring, with Baz Warne replacing Hugh Cornwell, and Jim Macaulay replacing an 80-year-old Jet Black on drums. It's not the same, whatever anyone may tell you. I know this because I saw the band last year (whenever that was) in front of a large enthusiastic crowd at the Belladrum festival near Inverness. It wasn't the same (how could it be?), but they sounded great, charged with the energy that almost 40 years of familiarity can lend to an energetic performance of favourites and not so favourites: bizarrely (and bravely), they opened with the proggy 'Toiler On The Sea' from *Black And White*. Baz sounded just like Hugh, which is probably why he got the job.

4. *Do It Dog Style* (Slaughter and the Dogs)

Do It Dog Style is a crude promotional pun. The band were awful, apart from their raucous trebly glam chainsaw of a first single, 'Cranked Up Really High' / 'The Bitch,' on Rabid Records. The first night that Bogey and I went to Eric's after we joined in the spring of 1978, we saw Slaughter and the Dogs play midweek to about a dozen people. Either the door staff were having a laugh at our expense last time we tried to join because they knew we went to the poofs' school, or they'd later changed their policy. Either way, we were in, beside ourselves with excitement, and for about fifteen minutes I thought the band were great because it was Eric's, I'd had a few beers and I got a free DO IT DOG STYLE badge and a poster signed by the band, both in a lovely combination of black and fluorescent green with red highlights. They were supported by Blitzkrieg Bop, about which I remember even less than Slaughter and the Dogs, as in nothing at all. For some reason,[2] Slaughter and the Dogs are still touring with two of the original members, Wayne Barrett (vocals) and Mick Rossi (guitar).

The phrase 'do it dog(gie) style/fashion' might be familiar, but was not included in the Shorter Oxford English Dictionary when I checked, so I got in touch and cited the

---

2 The pension plan, which isn't very rock and roll but, if you've survived into middle age, this kind of thing becomes important. Especially if alternative career options are limited or much less attractive.

album title as an example of a hitherto undocumented phrase that they might be interested in. The reply I received read

> *Thank you for your message. I am sorry to report that I have not found the combination DOG(GIE) STYLE in either the full OED or the Shorter OED, so I cannot provide information on citation dates. However, I shall certainly add your contribution to our files.*

5. *Blank Generation* (Richard Hell and the Voidoids)

Blank Generation is a great title, and Voidoids is a great name. As is Hell, of course, though Richard isn't so good. It's better than Donald or Ernest or Martin, but not as good as Billy or Johnny or Frankie or Joey. Impoverished arty New Yorker Richard Hell (disappointingly born with the surname Meyers) was reputedly the first person to adopt the anti-glam ripped clothes and short unkempt spiky hair that became hallmarks of punk rock while in the band Television. Along with others like the Ramones and Blondie and Patti Smith and Talking Heads and Suicide, they were a kind of New York mini-scene, which eventually became a kind of punk mini-scene. The Richard Hell look was perhaps noticed by Malcolm McLaren and perhaps subsequently turned designer by his partner Vivienne Westwood after McLaren spent time in New York trying to manage the New York Dolls as they fell apart. Scruffy degenerate poet Hell's appearance was self-consciously copied from scruffy degenerate French poet Arthur Rimbaud, who looked that way about a hundred years earlier. As well as a picture of Rimbaud on his wall, Hell has said he had photos of two other French unusualists – the playwright and poet Antonin Artaud, and the actor Jean-Pierre Léaud in the 1959 French New Wave film *400 Blows*. Not many British punks would have made that kind of claim.

The 'blank' in *Blank Generation* is meant to be blank as in _____; as in 'this space has been left blank for your personal message', though looking at Hell's appearance and sickly demeanour on the cover of the LP cover it could be 'blank' as in 'doped up, screwed up and barely alive'. Which is less democratic but much more rock and roll. The biggest difference between the early American punk scene and the early British punk scene was that the Americans were older; they were more self-consciously bohemian and musically diverse, having spent years playing their music before anything like a movement 'happened' and got called punk; and they emerged from part of what has since become a tradition or a context, one that includes the Velvet Underground, the Stooges, the MC5 and the New York Dolls. In Britain there was no real equivalent to this, just glam rock, pub rock, fifties revivalism and a seething sense of discontent.

I never heard the album, though the title track is disconcertingly wonderful, full of angular slashed guitar noises, 'ooooooooooh's and anguish. Actually, I did hear it, I must have done, because Radar's brother used to play it all the time, but the title track (also a single) is all I remember. For years I only bought albums, no singles at all, until punk. When you think about how long it might take to record an album, to record, say, 30–40 minutes of music, maybe a dozen or so songs, and how much it might cost to do this, then by comparison a single is almost nothing: minutes, hour or days rather than days, weeks, months or years. Even more so when you realise that to record a dozen songs you have to write them or choose them and have some idea of how to play them and how they might fit all together as an album, assuming they do. And that's without mentioning discipline, practice, competence, consistency, variety, imagination and the like, assuming you think any of that matters. Oh, and maybe someone to produce it, and a design for a sleeve, and all other the other stages without which nothing happens.

But for a single you don't really need a band, just a bunch of people and somewhere to record for a while. If the B-side is no good, it doesn't matter that much because B-sides are often no good, or ignored, or irrelevant. So, all you really need is one song – and even that doesn't have to be very long, in fact, less is often more. This is what the word 'single' means: 'one'. One song. A perfect artefact. Disposable yet around for ever; instantly out of date yet timeless; trivial yet mythic. It might be the only thing that a band ever record, and this can be a good thing, a great thing, a wonderful thing, a distillation of everything they had to say, everything they needed to say, the one and only ingredient in Essence Of (Name Your Band). A band with only one song to offer the world, a great song but just the one, or maybe another one for a great B-side as well, is best remembered as a single. When you hear it, it's great – and that's all you need, like Slaughter and the Dogs or the Cortinas or Eater. If you want more, just play it again. Sometimes there's more than one single to a band, sometimes there are two or three, sometimes there are lots. The Stranglers and Buzzcocks recorded lots. The Sex Pistols recorded four, in just a year and a bit. They didn't need an album, all they needed were those four singles. They were Great *despite* the album rather than because of it.

'Anarchy In The UK.' 'God Save The Queen.' 'Pretty Vacant.' 'Holidays In The Sun.' The music was amazing, it still is, always will be, that beautiful nasty roar that can pin you to the wall even now. But it was never just about the music, and the time it was least about the music, however Great the music happened to be, was at the time of the Jubilee.

I mean, anniversaries and jubilees – who needs them?

In 1977, the Queen did – she was the Queen, and she had been for 25 years,

two and a half decades, a quarter of a century, the kind of duration that people like to celebrate.

Who else needs anniversaries and jubilees? Anyone who's been alive for a long time. So how long is a long time? It depends how long you've been alive. When I was seventeen, a long time was a week or a month or a term. Exams the following year didn't exist. Nowadays, unless I'm waiting for a book or CD I've ordered online, a week disappears almost as quickly as an hour spent messing about on the computer.

Months, invoices, bills and bank statements come and go like the ebb and flow of the tide. The garden changes from season to season time and again. I look out of the window and it's summer. I look again and it's snowing, or at least it used to. My wife, my children and everyone else have their birthdays so often it seems like years have become months. I look at my records and CDs, and it's like decades have collapsed into a few years and then arranged themselves to fill a few shelves.

Even though I don't use my record player very often, I've still got hundreds of albums and singles. I know many of them so well I can play them in my head using a device called a nostalgiaphone. Despite being blessed with this internal serotonin-powered jukebox, it's still not enough, so I invariably find myself looking at row after row of reissued or remastered CDs whenever I wander into a music shop unsure of what to buy, experiencing a combination of curiosity, naked consumer lust and fear of disappointment. Will _____ (insert LP title or titles, continuing on a separate sheet if necessary) still sound as good if I play it now? Will the iridescent silver disc in the slim square plastic box laughingly called a jewel case sound as great as the ungainly cardboard sleeve containing vinyl with its playing and listening history etched into its grooves along with the music? Days, weeks, months, years, decades shrink and dwindle as I hear music from the soundtrack of my life remastered and reproduced on external equipment, out there in the 'real' soundworld, on the radio, on TV, in films, on the internet, in shops, in leisure centres and pubs.

Originally, I only had two Kraftwerk LPs, *Trans Europe Express* and *The Man Machine*. Now I've got both of them on CD, along with pretty well everything else they've ever released, because I can't help it. Kraftwerk have got better and better the more I've listened to them; they've increased in stature, and their shadow has got bigger until they're impossible to avoid. Not because their new material is better – there isn't any, but that's not the point. The point is that the old stuff still sounds new and the more recent stuff sounds classic. Kraftwerk sound like an electronic equivalent of Robert Johnson (or Son House or Skip James or Charley Patton), they are the Teutonic Electronic Delta Blues, part of the source. They will never date because they defined and embodied that style in the first place. White culture took Robert Johnson for blues music, black culture took Kraftwerk for electronic music, and in both cases you can listen to the original, the source, and go, 'Yes, *of course.*'

While it's true that these sources got ideas from other places, and you could maybe keep on looking further and further back to find them, you have to stop somewhere. So because Robert Johnson and Kraftwerk took in ideas and styles and made them their own in some way, and because recordings of them are available, they have become the places to stop and take a look around, because the musical landscapes around them have been eroded and re-shaped over time, leaving them standing high up like monuments, or viewpoints from which to take in everywhere else.

All these CDs, all these reissues. Why buy them? It's not just because I'm a music addict. Well, maybe, it is because I'm a music addict, which means you need to listen to music, and have music. Not want to, need to. And therein lies the problem; therein lies another answer to the question, *who needs anniversaries and jubilees?* The previous answer was, *anyone who's been alive for a long time.* The question then was, *how long is a long time?* to which the answer was, *it depends how long you've been alive.*

It's all about relative time. When I was younger, I would go into town and visit Skeleton Records, buy three or four albums, take them home, sit in my bedroom and listen to them one after the other. Or I would go round to Radar's house, I would drink tea and he would drink coffee and smoke cigarettes, and we would sit there listening to album after album. There was plenty of time to do things like that, hours and days and weeks to sit around and listen to music. It was wonderful. Even if it was a waste of time, it was a wonderful waste of time, a waste of time you could luxuriate in, a waste of time that is no longer available.

I can still sit and listen, but mostly I'm not on a sofa, I'm in a car. So I often hear new music in relatively short bursts driving from place to place. Or while walking, washing up, cooking, hanging up the washing, or doing whatever else needs doing. Not much gets heard in one go, and a static, contemplative, self-contained experience has become a mobile accompaniment to other activities.

An album used to be no more than 45 minutes long, which seemed like the right amount of time to spend listening to one thing – it felt like that was all you needed. Punk albums were shorter. A Ramones album was half an hour long with seven tracks on each side, because that was all you needed, less was more and more would have been less. The first Wire album, *Pink Flag*, was 35 minutes long and had 21 tracks, the shortest of which lasted 28 seconds. Six of the tracks were less than a minute long.

If you only liked half an album you could put something else on after playing the first side, or just put the second side on, something you can't do any more. And do most bands and artists really have a full CD's worth of things to say? You could probably still fit what most of them onto the equivalent of two sides of vinyl. And 75 minutes is a long time if unbroken; it could previously have been a double album, and why expect people to start releasing or listening to double albums just because it's become possible?

Worst of all are reissued or anniversary CDs and LPs that include 'exclusive' unissued material, alternative takes and different mixes, material that was generally unissued for a reason (it wasn't good enough for a 40-minute LP but it'll help fill the CD or the box set). Kraftwerk CDs and Dylan CDs and all the others retain their purity by not including any of this filler, which is why it's a shame that an album like *Who's Next* does; at the end of a great album that climaxes with 'Won't Get Fooled Again,' which was how it was meant to be, you get a couple of half-decent singles and a load of filler tacked on, which means you can't just drift away and enjoy it, instead spending the whole of 'Won't Get Fooled Again' waiting to press the eject button.

Cabaret Voltaire's *Micro Phonies* has an extra track, but this is okay because what you get is the 12-inch single mix of the final track, 'Sensoria,' hard to obtain and one of the best things Cabaret Voltaire ever released. It's highly commercial in a diseased kind of way, a dense, pounding assault, with menacing whispered and gasped vocals, twitchy rhythms, and hooks that are as catchy as typhoid. The mix of 'Sensoria' has the first album track, 'Do Right,' woven into it, and they interweave seamlessly, making this a logical way to end the album. Cabaret Voltaire are like Kraftwerk's mad English bastard cousins, an alternative electronic source, a nightmare instead of a dream, kept locked in a Sheffield cellar after hearing Kraftwerk just once, with only some faulty electronic equipment and a supply of bad drugs for company until they found a way out, or enticed people in. If you stand on the high ground and look in one direction, you see a gleaming metropolis, serene express trains and immaculate autobahns; if you look in the other direction you see urban sprawl, pile-ups and flaming, smoking steel mills. Cabaret Voltaire and Kraftwerk: the yin and yang of electronic retro-futurism.

Trans Europe Express, *Who's Next*, *Micro Phonies*. As well as being themselves, they stand for the rest: all those CDs, all those reissues. Seeing them, buying them, hearing them again, sometimes I want to laugh, sometimes I want to cry; sometimes I flush with elation, sometimes with embarrassment. And it can only get worse. Being half a century on from the sixties, it's fiftieth anniversary time – the TV programmes, the books, the tours, the commemorative reissues with vinyl, CDs and downloads. Forty years on from the seventies, thirty years on from the eighties and twenty years on from the nineties. Things can only get worse.

Anniversaries and jubilees – who needs them?

Record companies with declining sales, and musicians in need of pension plans, obviously. But also us, people who have come to realise that at first time seems to last forever, because life starts off slowly, then gradually begins to speed up as you get older and the seconds, minutes, hours, days, weeks, months, years and decades merge into one another more and more quickly. It's like sitting on a train as it leaves the station and gradually, very gradually, picks up speed. You're in a seat facing backwards and you're looking out of a window at the telegraph poles. One pole slides slowly by, then shortly another one, then another, then another, more and more quickly until what was mainly spaces has become a solid blurred fence of poles, and the sounds that were once separate clicks and clacks have become a non-stop rattle as you hurtle backwards into the future with no idea what's coming until it's passed you and started receding. The longer you've been alive, the faster the train is travelling and the more things there are to watch disappear, the more things there are to do and to be done, to remember and to forget and worry about and make sense of.

Who needs anniversaries and jubilees? People who realise that certain things happened quite a long time ago, things that might be worth being reminded of every so often. Like when they were born, or when they got married, or when Elvis or John Lennon died, or when *Sergeant Pepper* or *Never Mind The Bollocks* was released. Grown-ups, middle-aged people, old people and, now, people like me. People like the Sex Pistols, the Damned, the Stranglers, Slaughter and the Dogs, Kraftwerk, the Who and the Rolling Stones.

Twenty-five years on from the 1952 coronation in 1977, there was a silver jubilee for the Queen, then in 2002 there was a golden jubilee. Whatever you think of the Queen and the monarchy, this is quite a restrained level of celebration: there was no pearl (30th) , coral/jade (35th) , ruby (40th) or sapphire (45th) jubilees in between. And even the most ardent monarchist would have to admit that a paper (1st) jubilee or a wood jubilee (5th) or a tin/aluminium jubilee (10th) would have been stupid, so what we got was silver, then gold, then diamond, which I suppose is something to be grateful for.

On the day of the silver jubilee celebrations I was on a family holiday near Chippenham, and I don't remember seeing any bunting or union jacks anywhere. According to the terse travelogue kept by my dad, in the morning we stayed in to watch the official service at St Paul's Cathedral and see the Queen meeting people in London, and in the afternoon we visited the village of Lacock then went to Avebury to look at the stone circle. Avebury was very quiet, and I found it disappointingly hard to reconcile everything I had read about ley lines and earth magic with all the big grey lumps of rock sticking out of the ground alongside the old houses. At about the time we were getting ready to leave Avebury, the Sex Pistols were setting off on a boat called the Queen Elizabeth to sail up and down the Thames, offend people, promote their single, make a racket and get arrested.

Then it was suddenly 2002, and the Queen's golden jubilee. She was still there, the crowds were smaller and there were now huge TV screens everywhere so people could watch the events on telly without having to go home. 2002 was also the year of the Silver Dead Elvis Jubilee, and it was the year of the Silver Sex Pistols Jubilee – 25 years on from 1977, which had been their year, the only one they got and the only one they really needed.

The Sex Pistols. Born 1976, died 1978. Although they had been gestating for a while before 1976, they burst into the public gaze at the tail end of that year when they appeared in the live TV slot left vacant at the last minute by Queen. The band and a few of their pals were roped in at short notice to be goaded and patronised by grumpy Bill Grundy for a few minutes on Thames Television's 'Today' programme one teatime, and became famous overnight.

Literally. On Wednesday 1 December they were a disreputable cult, on Thursday 2 December they were a national disgrace, and to mark the occasion a series of foaming-at-the-mouth headlines duly appeared in the day's papers, the best probably being THE FILTH AND THE FURY in the Daily Mirror. It was the making of the Sex Pistols, and the unmaking of Bill Grundy. He was suspended for a couple of weeks and, although later reinstated, his contract wasn't renewed and his career more or less ended. Offered less and less work, he hosted 'What the Papers Say' in the early eighties and didn't do much else until 1993, when he died from a heart attack at the age of 69.

I didn't see saw them on the Bill Grundy programme, but I saw them earlier in the year when they played 'Anarchy in the UK' on Granada's 'So It Goes', the show hosted by Tony Wilson in the years before he became Anthony Wilson then Anthony H Wilson. They were strange and wild and amazing, and Jordan (not the Katy Price one) wore a fascistic uniform with a swastika armband that she was not allowed to wear on 'Today', and she threw a plastic chair onto the stage. Apart from her and the band, the studio seemed empty but it resonated with noise and menace. The final close-up shot of Johnny Rotten glaring into the camera with his spiky hair and paper clip earring beamed his hostility and charisma out across the airwaves into every home, energy so powerful that it felt like it could have reached even homes where the TV was off or people were watching another channel. This was something new, dangerous and exciting in 1976, and made my hair stand on end almost like his as I asked myself the question every music lover loves asking themselves, a question that always takes you by surprise and never fails to delight – 'what the hell is *this*?'

Like Status Quo, the Stranglers and Buzzcocks, the Sex Pistols were a brilliant singles band. Their first four singles were

1. Anarchy In The UK / Wanna Be Me (1976)
2. God Save The Queen / Did You No Wrong (1977)
3. Pretty Vacant / No Fun (1977)
4. Holidays In The Sun / Satellite (1977)

Those four singles, the A-sides and the B-sides, which are almost as good as the A-sides, are all you need to hear to really get the idea of the Sex Pistols. If the band had split up after this, their career arc would have been perfect. Hang on, they did. So what happened?

Say, for the sake of argument that, following on from four classic singles, if an album – called something controversial like *Never Mind The Bollocks, Here's The Sex Pistols* – were to be released including all the A-sides, it might perhaps be

a. an overdose
b. gilding the lily
c. over-egging the pudding
d. money for old rope
e. flogging a dead horse.

During the time that the Sex Pistols were still morally and creatively the Sex Pistols, the biggest mistake was releasing the album, because it was a perverse way of proving that they weren't really an album band, or didn't need to be. Having all the A-sides on the album diminished it and for me turned it into volume one of The Great Rock 'N' Roll Swindle.

Before they formed, while they were together and after they split up, they couldn't help but be part of the Swindle, the ongoing story of Malcolm McLaren and his manipulative, incompetent, amoral prankster-wanksterism. So, in 1978 we got Ronnie Biggs bellowing 'A Punk Prayer' over Steve Jones and Paul Cook on one side of a single, and Sid Vicious warbling 'My Way' on the other. You might like to know that the loves on the **you're gonna wake up** T-shirt included *RUBBER Robin Hood Ronnie Biggs BRAZIL* as a possible sign of things to come. Also in 1978, a few months after Sid and Ronnie's offerings, Johnny Rotten had become John Lydon, and Public image Limited had released the 'Public Image' single, putting several light years' worth of distance between himself and his former comrades, who were clearly

f. desperate and/or
g. taking the piss.

In 1979 the Sex Pistols franchise was still churning out product and gave us 'Something Else', 'Frigging In The Rigging', 'Silly Thing', 'C'mon Everybody' and 'The Great Rock 'N' Roll Swindle'. Student disco classics every one. We also got Paul Cook and Steve Jones appearing with Phil

Lynott as the Greedy Bastards (renamed the Greedies for the sake of good taste on Top Of The Pops) singing the medley 'A Merry Jingle' just in time for Xmas.

By the time everyone had taken all this in, John Lydon was way beyond his followers, rivals and disciples; in fact had been somewhere else all along, oblivious to other people's ideas of the right sort of music. Later on in the year the Pistols imploded or exploded, PiL released an album which, although it wasn't brilliant, was different and daring. The following year, they released *Metal Box*, initially three 12" singles in a steel canister. What better way to stake out your new territory, celebrate your record collection and alienate Pistol-fixated fan-punks?

My favourite of the proper Sex Pistols singles is 'Pretty Vacant' because it's so demented and yet at the same time such a perfect pop song, right from the brilliant, stupidly simple opening. The B-side is 'No Fun,' which is the Sex Pistols covering the Stooges, their only official cover version. Unofficially released cover versions or attempts at them include 'Roadrunner' (Jonathan Richman), 'Substitute' (the Who), 'Stepping Stone' (the Monkees), 'Johnny B Goode' (Chuck Berry) and 'Don't Gimme No Lip, Child' (Dave Berry – he's in a footnote earlier about The Solid Silver 60s show). These are on *The Great Rock 'N' Roll Swindle* and reveal, amongst other things, the hollowness of the idea that punk had a year zero.

In terms of effect, though, the killer single has to be 'God Save The Queen', a noisy, stinky firework lobbed into the throng of jubilee well-wishers from somewhere on the fringes, a grotesque publicity stunt by a bunch of naïve deranged hooligans and their smug, clueless prat of a manager – a flash, a bang, lots of loud music and swearing, then the police arrived. It was brilliant – the timing was perfect, the cover was ace, even the music was amazing, another nasty roar, and it pissed off *so many* people. Johnny Rotten got slashed, other people got beaten up and someone I knew got attacked in a pub car park for wearing narrow trousers. How punk was that. Clothes could be dangerous back then.

Best of all, 'God Save The Queen' made it to number one during the week of the silver jubilee, with its cover of the Queen with a safety pin through her face and her eyes and mouth ripped out. Of course it got banned, and everyone pretended that it had only got to number two and that Rod Stewart was number one with 'I Don't Want To Talk About it' / 'First Cut Is The Deepest'.

Then in 2002 there was suddenly another jubilee, and another version of 'God Save the Queen.' There was a 'Party at the Palace' attended by the Queen and a galaxy of stars such as Tom Jones, Ray Davies and Ozzy Osbourne. 'Sex Bomb', 'Lola', 'Paranoid'? Are these tunes Her Majesty knows and loves? Songs about knobbing, cross-dressing and mental disintegration?

Still, there's always Sir Cliff, Sir Elton and Sir Paul. And Sir Rod – him again, symbolically bestriding the two jubilees like a skinny, wrinkly pop colossus. But where were the punks this time? There weren't any, although the Hells Angels somehow managed to get in on the act. A 49 year old Angel called Snob (aka Alan Fisher) led a procession of 50 historic motorcycles past Her Majesty and in the process raised money for Kidscape, a charity set up to help deal with bullying. Surreal. But no punks.

Despite being excluded from the guest list at Buckingham Palace, the Sex Pistols later did their own jubilee show at the Crystal Palace National Sports Centre, called 'Pistols At The Palace', as you might imagine. They also issued a dance remix of 'God Save The Queen' in collaboration with Neil Barnes of Leftfield. So the Sex Pistols bestrode the two jubilees as well, as did their version of 'God Save The Queen', which has, in its own way, become an alternative national anthem.

The original version of 'God Save the Queen' also got a bit of a makeover on the day and, though not a dance remix, it was pretty much the last word in royal rocktabulousness. Because the party opened with Queen's Brian May atop Buckingham Palace, spanking his plank Hendrix-like up there on the roof, blasting out the national anthem, the balmy summer breeze ruffling his ample raven locks. Although the Hendrix connection was probably lost on most people, it's interesting to note that Jimi Hendrix had previously played his own country's national anthem back in 1969, around breakfast time on the morning of August 18 to a field full of bleary-eyed hippies at the Woodstock festival. As improvisations on national anthems go, Jimi's was probably a lot more emotionally charged than Brian's, and certainly a lot more like the sound of a helicopter crashing into an aircraft carrier. On the other hand, Brian's was probably more appropriate for playing at a party to honour a 76 year old lady.

Jimi Hendrix could maybe have done the gig, if he hadn't been dead, because he'd previously played 'God Save The Queen' at the start of the Isle of Wight Festival in 1970, although it degenerated into a drum solo after not very long. And Robert Fripp could maybe have done the gig. He played a wonderful, convoluted version of 'God Save The Queen' on his wonderful, convoluted Frippertronics album *God Save The Queen / Under Heavy Manners*, inspired to do so after someone in the audience called out for the American national anthem on the tenth anniversary of Woodstock.

But Hendrix and Fripp were unavailable, so there was Brian May up on the roof, 26 years after the non-appearance that unleashed the Sex Pistols, and 27 years since he first performed the national anthem on the album *A Night At The Opera*. As you'd imagine, it was the final track; it lasted just over a minute and came after 'Bohemian Rhapsody'.

Brian must have looked very small from the ground, up there among the chimney pots, probably about the size he looked to most people at your average stadium gig – if they weren't watching the screens. The screens meant that as well as looking really tiny and far away, at the same time he looked absolutely huge in close-up. Dressed in white, he was highly visible, and had to be careful in amongst all the chimneys to avoid getting covered in soot and looking like Dick van Dyke in *Mary Poppins*, but with longer hair, a guitar instead of a chimney brush, and no tap dancing.

Remember the T-shirt of loves and hates, and **Kutie Jones and his Sex Pistols**? Brian May probably hadn't heard of it, and he definitely wasn't wearing it, but on this occasion he too became a living text. He too became a mute name dropper – though not ignorant, and of heroic rather than anti-heroic proportions. And yes, I actually could be bothered reading what I glimpsed of the lists he wore as they jumped and twitched about in front of me, lists of names in smallish messy type covering his coat. It looked like a lab coat but I'm sure it wasn't, and the names looked just like they'd been written in felt pen, though I'm sure they hadn't.

As a strange, quite mind-blowing statement about how much things had changed since 1977, all over Brian May's white coat at the Queen's golden jubilee celebration in 2002 were printed words and phrases like

JOHNNY BE GOOD
JAILHOUSE ROCK
GREAT BALLS OF FIRE
YOU REALLY GOT ME
MY GENERATION
PURPLE HAZE
ALL RIGHT NOW
WHOLE LOTTA LOVE
LAYLA
BEAT IT

and

GOD SAVE THE QUEEN.

So, as well as bestriding the roof, Brian was bestriding the generations, from Chuck to Elvis to Jerry Lee to the Kinks to the Who to Hendrix to Free to Zeppelin to Clapton to Van Halen. To the Sex Pistols, maybe, but probably not. As well as being a living page from the Book Of Rock, he also surely got a mention in the Book Of Elvis for the 'Jailhouse Rock' reference. And, amazingly, he wasn't really spanking a plank –

it was in fact a fireplace, or part of one, because Brian's famous guitar, the Red Special, was constructed by him and his dad in the early sixties using wood from an old fireplace along with other bits and pieces, and he plays it to this day using an old sixpence as a plectrum. All of which means that the most impressive things about the whole event were Brian's coat and the Red Special. You can't get a better example of the DIY ethic than writing band names all over your coat and playing a home-made guitar loud while standing on someone else's roof. It was the punkest thing at the party.

Brian played the national anthem, and not the Sex Pistols tune of the same name, which was fine because the Sex Pistols did that for themselves, in tribute to themselves, all apart from Sid, who had never played anything and never could, because he was a tragic cartoon character rather than a musician. Perhaps the band's earliest tribute had come via the pathetic Ronnie Biggs, who had sung 'God Save the Sex Pistols'; I suppose you could call it singing. This was the first line of the single 'No One Is Innocent,' a 'punk prayer' offered up after Lydon had left, Sid had died and Steve and Paul were the only ones left, a ridiculous, pathetic cartoon tribute band backing Ronnie Biggs on this atrocity of a song. I thought calling a band the Moors Murderers was tasteless, but maybe it was the authentically confrontational spirit of punk. And Ronnie Biggs singing about God saving Myra Hindley and Ian Brady (the former horrible, the latter not what you'd call a lady)? That was something other than authentically confrontational. Confrontational, yes, but also cynical, desperate and a bit sad.

Ronnie's voice was even worse than Sid's, which was definitely worse than Johnny's, which was a roaring, snarling, sneering, spluttering, yelling, yodelling force of nature. Despite this, there's a story that Sid, born John Richie, was actually meant to be the original Pistols singer. According to this story, Malcolm McLaren recruited Lydon for the band after watching him mime to Alice Cooper's 'Eighteen' using a shower head as a microphone, and it was only later that his partner Vivienne Westwood told him that when she'd suggested John as the singer she'd meant Richie rather than Lydon.

God Save The Queen.

You probably know some of the words; traditionally it starts

God save our gracious Queen,
Long live our noble Queen,
God save the Queen.

It continues

Send her victorious, happy and glorious

(It's a matter of debate whether any of this has actually been the case. But whatever the victoriousnesses, happinesses and gloriousnesses, there's no doubt about…)

Long to reign over us

(Queen Elizabeth's mother the Queen Mum died on 30 March 2002 at the age of 101. Elizabeth herself was 76 in 2002 and 86 in 2012, though I couldn't be bothered with the diamond jubilee.)

God save the Queen

(Queen Victoria celebrated her diamond jubilee in 1897, and was still ruling when the Queen Mum was born. Victoria's eldest son was 60 when he came to the throne in 1901, and only reigned as Edward VII for ten years, just making it to his aluminium jubilee or tin (10th) jubilee, depending on your metal of choice.)

The earliest version of 'God Save the Queen' was called 'God Save the King', and was originally sung in London in 1745 as a patriotic song. The forces of George II had been defeated in Scotland by Prince Charles Edward Stuart, aka Bonnie Prince Charlie, aka the Young Pretender. After news of the defeat reached London, the band leader at the Theatre Royal in Drury Lane hurriedly combined the words and tune, both of which were already known, for an impromptu public performance in the presence of the King. After the newly created song proved popular, the practice spread to other theatres, and became a tradition. It has now come to seem quaint, old-fashioned or a bit naff, the kind of thing ridiculed in smug TV programmes with mock-posh voiceovers and creaky imitation black-and-white newsreel footage. Nobody sings or plays the national anthem any more, apart from at sporting events. And on occasions when it is played, it sounds pretty grim. Even monarchists would have to accept that it's not a stirring tune, unlike, say, 'Land of Hope and Glory' or 'Rule Britannia' or 'Jerusalem'; or 'Deutschland, Deutschland Uber Alles' or the Marseillaise; or even the Red Flag or the Horst Wessel Song. [3]

I remember seeing an episode of 'Dad's Army' where pompous, plucky, patriotic Captain Mainwaring is in a cinema, and after the film has finished the national anthem starts playing. He stands solemnly to attention, and is knocked off his feet in the rush for the exit, emerging from behind a seat shaken and quivering with indignation, his bowler hat missing and his glasses hanging from his nose. It's a funny but poignant moment, this ridiculously heroic, heroically ridiculous little Englishman's self-regard so rudely

---

3 The Horst Wessel Song was the anthem of the Nazi party from 1930, and the German national anthem between 1933 and 1945. Horst Wessel was a Berlin brownshirt leader who was beaten up by Communists during a dispute with his girlfriend's landlady over unpaid rent, and later died of his injuries. For a time, it was compulsory to perform a Nazi salute whenever the song was played. The tune is a solemn, uplifting folk tune similar in tone to 'How Great Thou Art', and was widely adopted by fascist groups in other countries, including Britain, as a marching song. On one occasion at school, our German teacher was off sick and Belly, who for some reason was sitting in for her, taught us to sing it, handing out typewritten sheets with the German words on and accompanying us on the piano. He was an accomplished musician and played the organ at our church, as well as often playing piano at school assemblies. During one Christmas assembly he stopped abruptly mid-carol, apoplectic with rage on hearing a small minority singing 'while shepherds washed their socks by night', which he considered 'downright irreverent'.

deflated, his dignity trampled underfoot. *Dad's Army* was first broadcast between 1968 and 1977, when deference was in decline. I don't know whether it would have happened like that during the war, or whether people would have stood and sung it heartily, tears in their eyes, united in adversity against a common foe. But I do know that nowadays most people don't care. If it's a grim tune, which it is, then singing all five verses would be hard, and the verse about crushing the Scots wouldn't work north of the border, where 'Flower Of Scotland' is preferred.

The Sex Pistols song is much more stirring, and has itself now become a kind of national anthem, and a kind of anti national anthem as well. As such, it was played at the end of the Reading rock festival back in 1978 by a conspicuously drunk John Peel, the year after it was released, the only year punk made a significant appearance at the festival, and the only year I attended. The very idea of punk rock appearing at the Reading Festival in any capacity was at the time incredible. It was only the previous year, 1977, that the name of the event had been changed from the National Jazz, Blues & Rock Festival to Reading Rock. In that year Ultravox had played and so had Wayne County and the Electric Chairs, perhaps subsequently best known for their transsexual singer Jayne County and their endearingly titled single. The following year Ultravox played again, and so did Radio Stars, Penetration, Sham 69, the Jam, Chelsea, Bethnal, Squeeze, the Tom Robinson Band and Patti Smith.

That was the year that punk and new wave made it to Reading. Kind of. After Patti Smith had finished on the last night, the floodlights came on, 'God Save the Queen' blasted out and everybody made for the exits or stumbled back to their tents. Nobody stood to attention, nobody sang and nobody was trampled underfoot. Even the Lindisfarne fans and the Foreigner fans and the Ian Gillan fans and the Quo fans must have thought it was the perfect way to end the festival.

Playlist 6 - God Save The Queen		
5:15	The Who	*Quadrophenia*
The Musical Box	Genesis	*Genesis Live*
What Goes On	Velvet Underground	*The Complete Matrix Tapes*
Pretty Vacant	Sex Pistols	
New Rose	The Damned	
(Get A) Grip (On Yourself)	The Stranglers	
Cranked Up Really High	Slaughter and the Dogs	
Blank Generation	Richard Hell and the Voidoids	
Neon Lights	Kraftwerk	*The Man Machine*
God Save The Queen / God Save The Queen	Queen / Sex Pistols	

To listen to the playlists, visit Spotify using the QR links provided.

Links to every playlist are also at www.hungry-ghost.info, along with photographs and archive material to supplement each chapter and enhance the reading/listening experience, just like a great big gatefold album cover.

6

THE WRONG TROUSERS

Last year (it doesn't matter which year, because time passes so quickly now) my wife and I went to Granada for a holiday. The apartment we stayed in was on a hillside close to the Alhambra and, it turned out, just up the road from Placeta Joe Strummer. Named in 2013, this small shady square commemorates Joe's relationship with the city of Granada, which blossomed in the mid eighties when the Clash were falling apart.

My wife saw the name on a map – she's good with maps, I'm worse than useless. We found the square and wandered around it, which didn't take long, then I took some photos of the blue and white ceramic name plaque, and also of a large peeling mural of Joe's face, its detached, slightly superior scowl filling a wall next to what looked like a squat when I peered through the open window into a sparse shabby room with mattress and bicycle.

Placeta Joe Strummer. Who'd have thought it. Mind you, who'd have thought the house in Denmark Street where the Sex Pistols once rehearsed would be bought by English Heritage as a listed building and its graffiti preserved for posterity. And who'd have thought Punk London would be a dismal forty-year anniversary of 1976 in 2016, endorsed by the Lord Mayor. Or that the offspring of Malcolm McLaren and Dame Vivienne Westwood would value his accumulated and inherited punk tat at £6 million and burn it in a big stroppy bonfire because it was worth too much money.[1]

---

1 Joseph Corré, head of the Agent Provocateur knicker empire with its £150 thongs, setting fire to his toys and throwing them out of his pram. Just like the KLF burning money, just like rock stars trashing hotel rooms. First-world toddlers, first-world tantrums.

A decade before Joe Strummer went to Spain he was called Woody, as in Woody Guthrie. He was born John Graham Mellor in 1952, the year the Queen became the Queen; he died in 2002, the year of her golden jubilee, from an undiagnosed heart defect after taking his dogs for a walk. It was halfway through his life that he became Joe Strummer and the Clash released their first single, a short, sharp blast of adrenalin called 'White Riot'. It sounded like four angry young men giving cheap musical instruments a damn good thrashing in a garage, which is more or less what it was. It wasn't their best single but it was their first. Lasting less than two minutes, it charted for a couple of weeks and just made the top 40. It wasn't long or sophisticated but then again it wasn't trying to be 'Bohemian Rhapsody'. With 'White Riot', less was more. With 'Bohemian Rhapsody', more was more.

The B-side was called '1977', and had a kind of staccato year zero feel to it. It ended with a countdown (actually a count up) to 1984, which back then made it sound dystopian and threatening, but now just makes it sound dated – rather than timeless like Bowie's '1984'.[2] The song's chorus announces there's no Elvis, Beatles or Rolling Stones in 1977.

In 1977 I hated all three of them, and this song helped me feel good about it. I hated them, their fame and their money, their success and their middle age (they were all over 30). Even so, for Joe and for me there was no Elvis, there were no Beatles, there were no Rolling Stones.

No Elvis
    He was dead.

---

2   Bowie wanted to make a musical based on the novel *Nineteen Eighty-Four* but Orwell's widow refused permission. So instead, in October 1973 he made a futuristic TV special called 'The 1980 Floor Show' which, to make sure you got the pun, opened with the song '1984'. This performance was Bowie's first since retiring Ziggy the previous July, and his final appearance in this persona. The decadent-looking bootleg LP *Dollars In Drag – The 1980 Floor Show* was memorably among those on display in Skeleton Records for some time.

No Beatles
   They had split up, leaving us with

1. John's played-to-death trio of maudlin nursery rhymes 'Give Peace A Chance', 'Happy Xmas (War Is Over)' and 'Imagine'
2. Paul's ongoing adventures with Wings
3. George's 'My Sweet Lord', a big hit which led to his being sued by the Chiffons for copying their song 'He's So Fine', a case that George eventually lost on the grounds of 'unintentional plagiarism'. Then, in 1975 the Chiffons went and released a cover version of 'My Sweet Lord' to capitalise on the publicity. Also in 1975, presumably as a comment on this and the nightmarish proceedings in court as the song was picked apart note by note, George appeared in his white suit on the cultish BBC comedy show 'Rutland Weekend Television'. Introduced by a smarmy Eric Idle in gold lamé jacket, he performed a song that for the first minute or so seemed to be 'My Sweet Lord' then with an abrupt HA-HAAAAR! suddenly became a daft, raucous sea shanty called 'I Wish I Was A Pirate', sung in a Long John Silver voice and accompanied by people in silly costumes. Then after that, to add insult to injury, insanity and inanity, it turned out that George's lawyer Alan Klein had secretly bought the rights to 'He's So Fine', which led by a long and tortuous route to a massive falling out between the pair, and in 1990 copyright of both songs being awarded to Harrison in the UK and North America, and Klein elsewhere. And at some stage talentless, creepy Jonathan King released one of these songs sung to the tune of the other, though I can't be bothered finding out which way round it was. George was also involved in the birthing and sustaining of the Rutles, a surreal satirical mutation of the Beatles that also began on 'Rutland Weekend Television' then escaped into the wider world. At one stage ATV Music, the owners of the Beatles' songs, sued Rutles composer Neil Innes for copyright infringement; Innes settled out

of court, and Lennon/McCartney had to be credited as co-composers on the 1978 album *The Rutles*.

4. Ringo's 'Back Off Boogaloo', which at the sensitive age of 11 hit me like a T-Rex express train and took me all the way to Rock Central splattered across its windscreen. And let's not forget the rather worrying single 'You're 16', released when he was 33. On reflection, maybe we should.

Apart from that and the odd album or two, John, Paul, George and Ringo had probably spent the previous seven years dealing with the anticlimax of being former Beatles, a lifelong project they managed with varying degrees of success.

Then, at the end of 1977, while Elvis was singing 'My Way'; while John, Paul and Steve but not Sid were playing 'Holidays In The Sun' because Sid wasn't a musician; and while John, George and Ringo had gone quiet, who should come striding across the purple heather from his farm and his greenhouses full of dope plants but Paul McCartney, flanked by his wife, by Wings and by a flock of Campbeltown pipers, singing 'Mull Of Kintyre', a song that was so huge it outsold 'She Loves You' which had until then been the UK's best-selling single.

No Rolling Stones

In 1976, the year before '1977', the Stones did a big tour and released the album *Black and Blue*. Included in the review by journalist Lester Bangs were the words 'It's all over, they really don't matter anymore or stand for anything... This is the first meaningless Rolling Stones album, and thank God.'

After 1977 and '1977'; after there was no Elvis any more; after there was no Beatles, and John and George were gone; after 2002 when Joe Strummer died; after all that, what remained, against all the odds, was the wrinkly brontosaurus that was the self-styled greatest rock and roll band in the world (minus Bill Wyman, in case nobody noticed). Now they have their bus passes, Mick has his knighthood and their golden anniversary has come and gone – look on their works, ye mighty, and despair.

In the year of *Black and Blue*, the year before '1977', the NME published a feature by Mick Farren called 'The Titanic Sails At Dawn'. In it he bemoaned how rock had become isolated from its audience – socially, artistically, morally and economically. And also physically: performances had moved from the cheap intimacy of clubs and dance halls to the expensive, impersonal vastness of places where the gap between performer and audience now meant that you needed a pair of binoculars to make out what was happening onstage, because back then there weren't even any monitor screens. Towards the end of the piece, he suggests that

> if rock is not being currently presented in an acceptable manner … it is time for the 70s generation to start producing their own ideas, and ease out the old farts

He ends by saying

> Putting the Beatles back together isn't going to be the salvation of rock and roll. Four kids playing to their contemporaries in a dirty cellar might be. And that, gentle reader, is where you come in.

Despite this sense of impending crisis, the *NME Book of Rock 2*, published around the time of Mick Farren's feature, pays scant attention to icebergs or other hazards, though it does put the deckchairs are in order. The entry for PUNK ROCK:

> …first coined to describe numerous local white rock groups who sprang up all over America between 1965–68… a time when seemingly anybody and everybody could be a Rock 'n' Roll star simply by growing their hair long and picking up a guitar…

> what made punk bands interesting is that they never really had *anything* going for them... gathered all their talent and inspiration into just one record... disappeared as quickly as they'd come.

This seems a fair assessment of the past, though the view of the present is obscured by a thick fog:

> revived as a popular term in the seventies ... to refer to US acts like Bruce Springsteen, Patti Smith and particularly, Nils Lofgren; in UK London bands like Eddie and the Hot Rods helped initiate new punk rock vogue.

> Recommended listening: **Nuggets 1965/68** (Elektra 1972)

Nuggets (full title *Nuggets: Original Artyfacts From The First Psychedelic Era 1965-1968*) provided a sixties model for punk attitudes and approaches in the same way as the Stooges and the Velvet Underground. Its sound has become Classic, timeless in a way that a lot of punk isn't; still contemporary as genres continue to hybridise, mutate, repeat, borrow and steal.

I got it from the bargain bin in Rox Records in Birkenhead for £1.99, though it's now available on CD and I've got that too. When Rhino reissued the Elektra original it was expanded to fill four CDs; there's also a four-CD *Nuggets II* ; and a four-CD *Children of Nuggets: Original Artyfacts from the Second Psychedelic Era, 1976–1995*. I covet the whole lot. Along with the extensive *Pebbles* and *Rubble* sets issued by other labels, of course.

The retrospectoscope is a wonderful instrument, almost as good as the nostalgiaphone (the two are often operated together). It can confer wisdom and insight on the user, but should be operated with caution because along with wisdom and insight there often comes an unbearable smugness. The truth is that very few people knew what was going on back then, not where I lived, and probably not where anyone else lived either, though new and strange things did seem to be popping up on the Old Grey Whistle Test, on the radio and in the NME from time to time: it felt like the old uppercase Bands and Gigs and Albums were no longer enough, for the reasons given by Mick Farren.

Having got punk wrong by being too close to something still unformed, in the 1978 *Book of Rock 2*, the NME set the record straight, or warped it in a new way, with its *Book of Modern Music*. Given away free with successive copies of the paper, this 64-page booklet was, as you might imagine, a fantastically opinionated mixture of wit, erudition, insight, cynicism and whiny smugness. This time around, about a thousand words of closely written bile were written not to define or praise punk but to bury it:

> Originally, Punk was homemade, do-it-yourself (because nobody else will), instant culture ... developed into an entire subculture ... had its young, sharp teeth pulled out by Big Business ... shook up the music industry like nothing else ever did ... fun while it lasted ... the bands who had emerged ... began to evolve distinct individual images ... the Clash were using pop media to perpetuate radical political views, a cross between the Monkees and the Red Brigade ... The Damned were burlesque clowns who owed more to ... Hammer Horror and Carry On movies than to rock and roll ... The Jam were Who-derived Mods ... Siouxsie and the Banshees were ... Nazi poseurs ... Of course, it didn't last long.[3]

---

3   And to show just how on the money certain NME journalists were, Tony Parsons and Julie Burchill wrote *The Boy Looked At Johnny*, a short book described as 'the obituary of Rock And Roll'. Almost the final line is 'compared to the Tom Robinson Band, every other rock musician is wanking into the wind.' The book's combination of superiority, bile, pretension and wrong-headedness is captured in this single sentence.

It might have looked like that from London, where you could maybe argue about beginnings and ends, but what about everywhere else? Well, excuse me for being provincial; for living in Liverpool, or Newcastle, or Glasgow, or Belfast, or Manchester, or Sheffield, or Leeds or anywhere else that wasn't London; anywhere things weren't as up to date or as full of NME journalists. Punk might have been a musical and cultural revolution, but revolutions take time to travel. The agricultural one took millennia, the print one has taken centuries, and so has the industrial one, rippling out around the world. In some places, they're still happening. Those at the epicentre experience 'it' first and might well have moved on by the time the shock waves have travelled further out and caused separate, localised after-shocks. With this in mind, it's clear that David Frost's patronising attitude towards the Beatles a decade earlier was no different from the misguided smugness of the self-appointed London punk elite as they observed, pitied or mocked the ignorance of others.

And we're all guilty. In the Easter and summer holidays of 1976 I took part in a council-sponsored exchange visit to Gennevilliers, a slab of suburban concrete on the northwest edge of Paris that had at some stage for some reason been twinned with Birkenhead. We went over there at Easter and they came over here in the summer. I had already experienced European culture the previous year in Würzburg, Germany, so considered myself quite cosmopolitan. But nothing prepared me for France. The French *didn't wear flares*. They wore *narrow jeans*. I couldn't believe it. Drainpipes. *No-one* wore drainies. They were the wrong trousers. They looked ridiculous.

Those were the days. They still are, kind of, only not really. When I was sixteen I wore a faded T-shirt, combat jacket and faded jeans. Forty years on, it looks like nothing's changed, but things are different. Now you buy your crumpled, faded T-shirt, combat jacket and faded, holey jeans straight off the peg in an already distressed, pre-worn state. And you have to wash everything at 30 degrees because the fabric's so delicate. Jeans? Combat jacket? Really? This isn't just me moaning (though I am), it's more a feeling that there's so little strangeness or surprise left that we have to buy it rather than make it; so few unturned stones, so little opportunity left to find or invent things for yourself. It's about T-shirts, jackets and jeans, but at the same time it's about more than that.

T-shirts

'Like trousers, like brain,' said Joe Strummer. He was good for slogans, though 'like T-shirt, like brain' would have been better. If you are what you wear, then you are probably your T-shirt as much as anything else.

Around 1975 I bought and proudly wore a black T-shirt with a red 'Led Zeppelin' transfer on the chest, obtained via the back pages of NME, one of the few places you could find rock apparel. There were cheesecloth shirts for guys and chicks. Afghan coats ditto. There were T-shirts with band names, but nothing authentically corporate. T-shirts with slogans like WORK IS THE CURSE OF THE DRINKING CLASSES and KEEP DEATH OFF THE ROADS, DRIVE ON THE PAVEMENT, and ENJOY COCAINE, IT'S THE REAL THING. And who can forget one vulture saying to another PATIENCE MY ASS, I'M GONNA KILL SOMETHING. Or a wan-faced, skinny messiah holding a piggy bank, accompanied by JESUS SAVES.

I wore my Led Zeppelin T-shirt until I went off the band, by which time it had shrunk badly, faded from black to dark grey and the lettering was cracked and wrinkly; it looked just like the brand-new faded T-shirts printed with imitation iron-on transfers that you can buy now. When the Clash started out they made their own outfits and looked like they did, stencilling slogans on second-hand clothes, dribbling paint on charity-shop shirts, jackets and trousers because they had no money and it looked like they didn't but it also looked original and visually arresting. This was a simple, dramatic way of shoving slogans in people's faces, drawing attention to themselves and setting themselves apart. Even if it was a posture or became a posture, it cost little, looked different and anyway it was their own posture and not someone else's, unlike the depressing THE CLASH – WHITE RIOTERS T-shirt that I saw on sale in Debenham's for £30. You can say a lot with a £30 T-shirt, more than you might mean to.

How about a T-shirt that says

**You're gonna wake up
one morning and know what side
of the bed you've been lying on!**

It's printed across the front, right at the top. Underneath, down the left-hand side is a list in small print that begins with television (not the group), Mick Jagger, the Liberal Party, John Betjeman, George Melly, Michael Caine, parking tickets and Securicor. Down the right-hand side there's another list that includes Eddie Cochran, Christine Keeler, rubber, the Society For Cutting Up Men, Robin Hood and Ronnie Biggs.

It runs to about 600 words all together.[4] Love it or hate it, this is a T-shirt you can't help looking at, and you can't help wanting to read. It is perhaps the most arty, farty, hip, elitist cultural manifesto you could want – and on a T-shirt, because the clothes, and of course the hair, are at least as rock-and-roll as the music. The Pistols and the Clash wanted to look different, and thought about clothes and haircuts as well as music, though that makes them sound a bit like boy bands. (God, they *were* boy bands – they were *boys*, and they were in *bands*; they were even being advised, managed and manipulated by managers, cannily clueless prankster-wanksters like Malcolm McLaren and Bernie Rhodes.)

---

4 See appendix six.

The things is, if the wearer of this T-shirt was conveniently passed out on a park bench and you had enough time, would you read it? And if you did, would you be able to tell which list to love and which to hate? (Would you even know that's what you're meant to do?) There are no headings to guide you – what you need is the kind of insider awareness that will make you a right person rather than a wrong person. As an idea, it's provocative, arrogant, divisive, pretentious and brilliant. As a self-conscious cultural and political manifesto, it's deeply profound in its superficiality; it's a piece of ridiculous elitist consumerism; and it's playful in the most serious way possible. Kutie Jones and his Sex Pistols are over to the right about halfway down.

The Clash might have been white rioters, or have seen themselves as such, but if they did propose a white riot, they didn't go through Debenham's. They made their own clothes to align themselves with political and cultural issues, though they weren't terribly playful about it. Instead, there were serious big gestures like playing a gig for Rock Against Racism and calling an album *Sandinista*. There was social comment that infused the titles and lyrics of their songs, there was poetic sloganeering, chucking out ideas in bite-size chunks that could or should have appeared on T-shirts and walls as well, or even instead. It was graffiti on cheap clothes when they started out, though later it all turned into a kind of studied, reactionary, rebel chic, a non-ironic Village People mix of guerrilla, biker, cowboy and gangster stereotypes that characterised and caricatured them as serious Serious Rock Stars.

It was a bit much sometimes, the earnestness and the wrongheadedness. In 1978 when the band played in Victoria Park for Rock Against Racism, Joe wore a red BRIGATE ROSSE RAF T-shirt which, through the retrospectoscope, and even at the time, made him look an idiot. You can still buy that T-shirt; you can also buy Che Guevara, Lenin, Stalin, Mao and Hitler T-shirts, but it seems they're worn by people either in ignorance or misguided irony, and Joe didn't do irony – he generally meant it, whatever 'it' might have been and whether or not 'it' made sense. Oh yes, there are also I ♥ JESUS and I ♥ SATAN T-shirts out there as well. Like T-shirt like brain? What's going on?

the Sex Pistols started out they also made their own clothing, or at least adorned it, or at least Johnny did. I remember thinking he looked good in any old rubbish. His first and best T-shirt was the Pink Floyd one with the words I HATE scrawled across it. When I say of the Sex Pistols that 'they' made their own gear, Johnny might have done but everyone else seemed comfortable in bike jackets, jeans and boots. This became the punk uniform – that and clothing from Malcolm and Vivienne's shop: all the bondage gear and the tartan and the splattery T-shirts and mohair jumpers. Bike jackets, jeans and boots were always been fine with me as long as the jeans were the right width, and I dressed that way quite a lot of the time, but I could never have dressed like Johnny with his hand-written T-shirt and baggy trousers and ripped suits held together by safety pins.

Vivienne Westwood, queen of punk fashion: hers has been a long journey, from rebel muse with a shop called SEX to titled international couture icon with her own retrospective at the V&A. The clothing she sold early on changed the emphasis from Do It Yourself to Buy It Yourself. What she and Malcolm did was provocative appropriation and montage, what we now call copying and pasting, and what arty types with continental connections might refer to as *détournement*. Things like Myra Hindley appearing to be modelling Vivienne's clothes alongside her and Malcolm, done in the style of Andy Warhol's Elvis-cowboy prints; or a T-shirt image of a naked young boy with a cigarette; or someone in a gimp mask with CAMBRIDGE RAPIST printed across it, all of which was probably ironic or edgy or something. There was also gay porn, mostly crudely drawn images of naked male punks. Equally tasteless but much funnier, and far more legally risky, were subverted Disney T-shirts showing Mickey Mouse having sex with Minnie, Snow White snorting speed, Mickey Mouse crucified, and Snow White having group sex with various of the seven dwarfs. This kind of provocative appropriation and *détournement* stuck two fingers up at copyright, ownership, decency and good taste, and annoyed or offended more or less everyone. Its spontaneity, technical roughness and confrontational nature complemented the cut-out lettering, photocopied images and badly typed graphics of fanzines, part of an approach that was so distinctive it rapidly became a style and then a cliché.

And, shockingly, it turns out that some of the T-shirts aren't genuine Westwoods. If you look online, it seems that a few disreputable manufacturers have been pirating her clothing, copying her ideas and passing their own products off as hers. The crucified Mickey and the drug-taking Snow White T-shirts are fakes. Rather than authentic Westwood appropriation and *détournement*, this new kind of subversion and provocation involves sticking two fingers up at copyright, ownership, decency and good taste *and* at Dame Vivienne Westwood. Is nothing sacred?

As well as the nasty graphics, Vivienne was also fond of slogans, like the Clash and the Situationists were, only she had the advantage of her own clothing range to display them on – her own textile hoardings that people paid for the privilege of wearing. Slogans like

- ONLY ANARCHISTS ARE PRETTY
- NO FUTURE
- VIVA DURUTTI AND THE BLACK HAND GANG
- BE REASONABLE, DEMAND THE IMPOSSIBLE
- NEVER TRUST A HIPPY
- DESTROY THE ESTABLISHMENT
- VIVE LA REVOLUTION.

Some of them were hard to make sense of, but that was part of the point. It might not be surprising to learn that slogans came from her partner, Malcolm McLaren, who had been involved in the English Situationist scene in the late 60s and seems to have been desperate to be infamous and controversial, a bit like a gauche, clueless Andy Warhol with the Pistols as his Velvet Underground. He had already tried and failed with the New York Dolls, attempting unsuccessfully to manage them, dressing them in red patent leather and adorning them with hammer and sickle imagery, which didn't work and led to them objecting to being told what to do by a haberdasher. He was equally unsuccessful trying to manage Television while Richard Hell was still a member, but seems to have considered Hell's studiously unkempt demeanour worth noting.

So who were the Situationists? They weren't widely talked about, and I'd never heard of them, perhaps because people like Malcolm McLaren and Bernie Rhodes were busy copying them and preferred nobody to know.[5] They were a bunch of bored, dumb-smart, disillusioned urban kids who indulged in provocative and self-consciously absurd behaviour as a way of venting their anger, complaining about society and demanding change (sound familiar?). They were French, they were intense and they intellectualised endlessly about how anti-intellectual or non-intellectual they were. One their most interesting ideas was *détournement* (literally 're-routing' or 'hi-jacking'), taking images from popular culture and giving them alternative meanings, satirising the original context and generating controversy or debate. For example, writing new speech bubbles for comics or applying alternative captions to advertising images. Or writing I HATE on a Pink Floyd T-shirt.

This was still part of a tradition (similar things were done by the Dadaists and Surrealists), one that has become a way of annoying political and media interest groups cheaply and effectively by messing up billboards and infringing copyright law. Such action is cheap and immediate, and the crudeness of its execution, the obviousness of the intervention and

---

5 *Lipstick Traces: A Secret History Of The Twentieth Century* by Greil Marcus is a fascinating, infuriating, illuminating, impenetrable book about the Sex Pistols, Dada and Situationism that you may or may not enjoy. On p35 of my edition is the image for 'God Save The Queen'; on p34 is the 1968 poster that graphic artist Jimmy Reid lifted it from by.

the disrespect it conveys are all part of the attraction. The idea of self-conscious amateurism with a provocative edge spread rapidly thanks to punk, Letraset, typewriters and photocopying, and for a while you could use it for everything including self publishing. After a while, though, it ended up everywhere, co-opted by mainstream media, after which the radicals had to start looking smart and well designed.

The Situationists liked pithy, obtuse slogans that mimicked and mocked advertising. They also liked impenetrably cryptic pseudo-intellectualism: their way of détourning hegemonistic bourgeois thought processes. Or something.

How pseudo-intellectual were they? The first issue of their journal *Internationale Situationniste* (which confusingly translates as 'Situationist International') defined 'Situationist' as

> [adjective:] Having to do with the theory or practical activity of constructing situations.
> [noun:] One who engages in the construction of situations; a member of the Situationist International.

The same journal defined 'Situationism' as

> [noun] A meaningless term improperly derived from the above. There is no such thing as situationism, which would mean a doctrine of interpretation of existing facts. The notion of situationism is obviously devised by antisituationists.

Perhaps the best known of Vivienne Westwood's T-shirts was the DESTROY one, a mindlessly brilliant piece of punk Situationism. The word DESTROY was at the top, in garish, broken lettering. Below the DESTROY were three crude images – a crucifix, a swastika and a postage stamp. The crucifix was upside down, the stamp had the Queen's head on and the swastika was in a circle so it looked Nazi, rather than Buddhist or Hindu. All of which suggested things you might want to DESTROY – Christianity, or maybe religion (or maybe Satanism, as the cross was upside down), and Nazism, and the Post Office, or maybe the Queen or maybe the monarchy. Anyway, DESTROY something, DESTROY anything, be an anarchist, get pissed, destroy.[6] Like in *The Wild Ones*, where a girl says to Marlon Brando, 'What you rebelling against, Johnny?' and he comes back with, 'What you got?'

It was and still is illegal to copy images of the Queen, so the stamp image must have been illegal, though a pound note or a fiver would probably have been more controversial more political, an attack on money and capital rather than the Post Office. A lot of people loved the Queen and would have been upset by this sort of treasonable abuse, which was the whole point.

As for the cross, that would have offended a lot of people as well, especially with it being upside down, though it went well with the opening line 'I am an antichrist' – not *the* antichrist, mind – on 'Anarchy in the UK' (and if you listen to Public Image's first album there's a track called 'Religion' where Lydon goes into a lot more detail about being a lapsed Catholic with unresolved issues).

Then there's the swastika; that would have offended people as well. All the images are superimposed, forced together like they're all as bad as each other, the Queen, Jesus and Nazism, which looks messy and mixed up and it actually is. The ONLY ANARCHISTS ARE PRETTY shirt had an image of Karl Marx on it and no DESTROY; they could have put a hammer and sickle on the DESTROY T-shirt as well as or instead of a swastika but they didn't. (Shoddy attention seeking? Amoral prankster wanksterism? Clever marketing? Sly situationist *détournement*? Probably). Sid Vicious wore a swastika T-shirt, Siouxsie Sioux wore a swastika armband, so did their mate Jordan, not because they were Nazis but

---

6 To be fair, what was being advocated was the destruction of systems of oppression that were all around us: the monarchy, organised religion and totalitarianism. But I don't think Malcolm or Vivienne were really that bothered about the politics.

because they were Rebels, shocking Swastika Rebels. They chose the symbol that they knew would push the most buttons hardest, which was the swastika, and still is. Back then it was only just 30 years after the end of World War II, so anyone in their forties or their fifties (parents, for instance) would have remembered it. In fact, it's strange to realise that more than 40 years now separate us from 1977, and only 32 years separate it from 1945. This means that punk rock is closer in time to World War II than it is to now. History: it's just one damn thing after another.

Sid Vicious and Siouxsie Sioux and all the other Swastika Rebels probably didn't know much about German history apart from Hitler and the Bleeding Obvious. This is a shame, because if they had they might have dressed differently. During the 1930s in Germany a lot of teenagers didn't want to join the Hitler Youth because, even without looking at the bigger picture, they didn't like authoritarianism or uniforms, and just wanted to be left alone. Unfortunately in the 1930s there came a time when that was no longer possible, especially if you were Jewish or communist or black or homosexual or gypsy or disabled or Slavic or in any other way a bit unusual or outspoken or non-Aryan. So a lot of teenagers who didn't want to join the Hitler Youth joined groups like the Edelweiss Pirates, which had their own easygoing communal values, their own ways of dressing, and also organised their own social events. They often mocked or heckled the Hitler Youth; they parodied their songs and on occasions fought with them. During the war some of these groups became involved in the black market, theft and organised crime; a few committed acts of vandalism and sabotage, distributing Allied propaganda and living apart from German society. Although many did not become as overtly criminal or political as this, a number made trouble for the authorities, so much so that in Cologne in 1944 six teenage Pirates were publicly hanged to set an example.

Another group was the *Swingjugend* (Swing Youth), whose name parodied the *Hitlerjugend*. Wearing elaborate, showy English and American clothes, the boys favoured

227

scarves and rolled umbrellas; girls wore short skirts and elaborate make-up. They listened to Jewish and black American swing and jazz music, and their customary greeting was *swing heil!* Because their appearance, behaviour and values upset the authorities, many were arrested and publicly shaved of their long hair (boys and girls), and some of their leaders were sent to concentration camps. There weren't many records in circulation at the time, so the discs that the *Swingjugend* possessed must have been incredibly precious, far more precious than any music we have ever heard or owned. Those Swing Kids must have listened to them over and over again at their record parties and dances, getting to know every vocal nuance and every instrumental flourish along with every crackle and every scratch.

In 1937 the Nazis held an exhibition called *Entartete Kunst* (Degenerate Art) that ridiculed modernism as the work of Jews, Communists, cretins, negroes, the mentally ill, and other purveyors of un-Germanic values. There was a parallel campaign against *Entartete Musik* (Degenerate Music) that attacked, amongst other things, modernism, black music and Jewish music. We think we know what rebel music is, but we have no idea compared to the *Swingjugend*. You'd imagine that the story of these rebels would be widely known, but it isn't. One reason is that the troublemakers had no political motivation; they were just disaffected teenagers like any others. So, when the war ended and their disruption and criminality continued it was lumped together with all the other lawlessness, crime and brutality. What they got up to was never acknowledged or even talked about. So if you thought you had a hard time, punk, just imagine living in Nazi Germany and liking swing records. And if that isn't enough, what about the swastika in the American South, and the role of 'negro music' there. And the Hell's Angels: the most reactionary rebels ever, some of whom actually offered to go and fight in Vietnam. Maybe Malcolm was actually right about the red patent leather and the hammers and sickles as a way of upsetting America, so much so that the whole Commie faggot act might have been just too dangerous

And let's not forget Sid's swastika T-shirt. He did it his way, didn't he. When he was arrested on suspicion of murdering Nancy Spungen, I was at university having a hard time fitting in, living off Smash and baked beans and Vesta curry prepared on the little hotplate at the end of my corridor so I didn't have to meet other students. In response to Sid's predicament and to mask our insecurity Radar and I, already looking badly turned out and unhealthy, considered it amusing to sport SID IS INNOCENT badges. The day after Sid's arrest was my 19th birthday and it being a Friday there was a disco in one of the student halls so, pissed out of my mind, I was permitted a booming, incoherent few seconds at the microphone of a college disco by the 'punk' DJ (long hair, white T-shirt, tie, big badges, flared jeans, white plimsolls) and slurrily introduced 'My Way', to howls of appreciation from the audience.

Fellow student Furb went one better than a Sid badge. He was probably not your typical 1978 Oxford theology student, in spiky hair, leopard-skin leggings and big lace-up boots. One day the pair of us got the train down to London and visited Seditionaries ('Clothes for Heroes' – the follow-up to SEX) so he could buy something, anything. He plumped for a Sid Vicious T-shirt with a picture of Sid's face surrounded by a smeary black wreath-like mess, the obligatory ransom-note lettering reading SHE'S DEAD – I'M ALIVE – I'M YOURS. Having bought this for a ridiculous sum of money in an empty shop from a bored, indifferent assistant, he was keen to put it on as soon as possible, so he got changed while we were on the Tube, and I still have a sequence of photographs taken at the time that proves I am not making this up.

Around this time Furb dyed his hair Elvis black. His mate Sten offered to cut it with a bread knife to make it look more spiky, something Furb agreed to only if he could shave off one side of Sten's beard. Sten consented, so that evening there occurred a bizarre and painful half hour or so of hair modification, after which we went to the pub. Sten was in the TA and wore his camouflaged cap, jacket and trousers to offset Furb's black spikes and Sid T-shirt. Remember, it was the seventies.

Jackets

My first Favourite Jacket was a Wrangler denim jacket bought at the same time as my first pair of Wrangler jeans, maybe in 1974 when I was an adolescent prog monster. At that time denim wasn't pre-washed or pre-faded or pre-anything apart from stiffly and glossily pre-starched, so you had to do all the work yourself. It was a laborious process. Jeans came in one shade, indigo, a deep dark bluey black the colour of the night sky, which took weeks of washing to go even slightly limp and a little bit lighter, fading eventually to, say, dark blue. Every wash produced rivers of deep inky-dark dye but, frustratingly, the denim never seemed to fade, even after soaking in a bucket for days or being scrunched up and dragged about the place. Finally, though, the jacket did start to get lighter, then I tried bleaching it, and it went lighter than I wanted it to, but at least you could tell I'd put the effort in. The finishing touch was the embroidery, something I taught myself in order to be able to add a Jimmy Page *Zoso* symbol, in the middle of the waistband at the back in between the two sets of buttons, in crimson and lime green thread. It looked very professional, though unfortunately within a year or so I had gone off Led Zeppelin and I gave the jacket to my brother.

My second Favourite Jacket was a combat jacket bought from the Army & Navy Stores in Liverpool, the kind of store you never see any more. Nothing in there seemed to have changed for decades. The lower floors were quite well organised and sold old-fashioned school uniforms, overalls, industrial footwear and the like. The top floor was altogether more chaotic and mysterious, and was where I was irresistibly drawn. Because national service had been in operation for so long, there were literally tons of surplus clothing lying about, much of it in places like this, haphazardly hung on racks or sometimes just piled on the floor for people like me to rummage through.

This was where you got your rucksacks, your greatcoats, your combat jackets and later on, as you got a bit more adventurous your RAF shirts, fatigue trousers, British Rail jackets, beige gabardine macs, flying boots, army shirts and woollen British Rail waistcoats. I remember rooting through a pile of US clothing and finding combat jackets that had all kinds of strange, elaborate designs drawn on them in ballpoint or felt pen, presumably by bored, drug-addled American servicemen in places like Germany and Vietnam. What surprised me most was finding on one jacket the equivalent of an illuminated manuscript text based around BABY'S ON FIRE, BETTER THROW HER IN THE WATER, the peculiar first line from a peculiar song on the peculiar first Brian Eno solo album, *Here Come the Warm Jets*, something Brock first played me, and which you wouldn't expect American servicemen to be listening to, let alone writing on their government issue jackets. By the end of the seventies specialist clothing outlets were opening in Liverpool and elsewhere, run by entrepreneurs who had presumably rummaged through huge mounds of surplus clothing and therefore sold items that weren't solely for midgets or the morbidly obese, and might actually fit you. While this new shopping option saved time, to me it also felt a bit like cheating.

My third Favourite Jacket was a leather bike jacket made by Belstaff and it cost £78, which in the late seventies was a lot of money. It was worth it, though, because it was just like the ones the Ramones wore, with epaulettes, and a little pocket at the front, and a belt. It was perfect, though like the denim jacket was disastrously new to start with: smooth, shiny and tending to creak every time I moved. This didn't matter in a vibrant club atmosphere, but when you were sleeping on someone's floor it could get a bit annoying for other people. In my unseemly haste to get a jacket with the remnants of my student grant after leaving Oxford, I bought one that only just fitted, and after a couple of years it was too small, though it's still hanging in the wardrobe next to my suit.

Jeans

My Favourite Jeans were the Wranglers I bought at the same time as the denim jacket. For a number of years my mum refused to buy us jeans, so these flared denims were an indigo milestone. When I got the jacket and jeans from the Army & Navy Stores they were of course deepest blue, shiny and stiff, and must have looked ridiculous, especially when I wore both together, which often did, proudly setting off the ensemble with my large Emerson, Lake and Palmer British Tour 1974 badge and my navy blue nylon T-shirt. As a year or two passed the jeans faded, and I grew. Imagine the dilemma – faded, battered jeans that looked and felt just right but were starting to rise off my feet when I walked and soon would be flapping about my ankles in the most embarrassing manner, rather than dragging along the floor and wearing away at the back like jeans should. So I learned to sew, adding extensions on the bottom, and as holes appeared I patched them – not in matching denim, but in a range of other blue and black fabrics. I embroidered symbols on them – an eye of Horus here, an Egyptian scarab there, a rune or two elsewhere. Sometimes I reinforced patches with metal studs. I was still wearing the same jeans in 1978, but was doing so ironically to annoy off-the-peg punks – at least, that was my excuse. I even wore them when I saw Steve Hillage at Eric's in May 1978, just after I'd seen Slaughter and the Dogs, and just before I saw Sham 69. I wore them not because I didn't have any narrow trousers, but because they were the right thing to wear. If I hadn't been sure whether or not to wear them, one look at the back of the room would have told me YES YES YES, because there in a dark corner sat Pete Burns and his camp gothy pouting entourage, sneering at all the hippies enjoying themselves, him with longest, pointiest, most ridiculously amazing jet black quiff ever. It was truly the sort of hairstyle about which your parents or someone else's parents would have said, 'Careful with that, son, you'll have someone's eye out', followed by something like, 'Er, you *are* a boy aren't you, only it's hard to tell'.

I might not have always looked like a punk on the outside, but I liked to think I was one on the inside. I never saw the Sex Pistols, but I saw the Clash six times, and some of these times they seemed like the greatest rock and roll band in the world. The first time was April 1978 at Victoria Park in London, together with about 80,000 other people, which is ironic after all the bellyaching about Big Rock Bands and Big Concerts, but hey, it was free and it was Rock Against Racism. Bogey and I got tickets from Probe Records for a bus to London that left early in the morning from Liverpool pier head. The folk on board were basically either politicos or punks, and we weren't politicos. We probably didn't look much like punks either.

Rock Against Racism seemed like a no brainer – what kind of rock could be *for* racism? Trying to think of music for a white-only rock soundtrack leads to two main possibilities, hardcore metal or hardcore punk, as both of these were created by and for alienated angry white males and owe nothing to any kind of black culture. Black Flag weren't racist, nor were Napalm Death, nor were Fugazi, nor were Extreme Noise Terror, nor were scores or hundreds of others, but they still succeeded partly by surfing on a wave of alienation, anger, whiteness and maleness that can sometimes take you to unpleasant places. Any music that aspired to be a bit more outward-looking or eclectic, that had even a slight acquaintance with rock 'n' roll or jazz or blues or soul or gospel or rhythm and blues or reggae or ska or doo-wop or ragtime or disco or funk had to acknowledge that something multiracial was going on, and always had and always would in popular music. And the Clash were certainly outward-looking and eclectic (though they could also be inward-looking and reactionary). They even played reggae, which was dead exotic, unless you were the Police.

I got a badge off Joe Strummer the second time I saw the Clash, though he didn't realise it. The band played at Eric's in June 1978 on the 'Out On Parole' tour and it was electric and epic and insane, there was mass hysteria and sweat dripping off the ceiling. They played their best single 'White Man In The Hammersmith Palais' and it probably sounded awful in that sweaty sodden pit, but nobody noticed or cared. I got down the front, squashed against the barriers at the edge of the low stage, wedged in tightly enough to fire off a few shots with my Instamatic, taking advantage of its handy flash-cube facility to capture some shots. Mick Jones all in white with hippily long straggly soaking wet hair. Paul Simonon with no T-shirt but still wearing his leather jacket because he was cool even in the heat. Nothing of Topper Headon because he was at the back and was the drummer. Joe in a black T-shirt with a Clash badge pinned to the upper left arm, flailing about and twitching that leg of his. Then a few minutes after I'd taken the picture the badge wasn't there any more, it was lying on the stage and all I had to do was lean down and pick it up, which I did. It was slightly dented but that didn't matter because it was Joe's Clash badge and now it was mine. No more heroes – yeh, right.

The next two times I saw them were on the 'Sort it Out' tour later the same year, when they were promoting *Give 'Em Enough Rope*. The album was a massive step forward both in terms of songs and production, and seemed to show the band growing into their experience, status and ambition. At the time it felt like they could do no wrong, though now it sounds overblown and leaden. The Pistols had split earlier that year during a disastrous tour of America, so a lot of people were looking to the Clash as the last gang in town, even though it looked like they might be leaving town pretty soon. By then I was at Oxford and Radar and I had started going to the Oranges and Lemons, the pub students didn't go to because it was full of punks and skinheads and such like people. Feeling alienated from academia, into punk and on an inverted snobbery kick, it was perfect – relaxed, pleasantly weird, great jukebox and nice beer.

At some stage Furb and I decided to hitch up from Oxford to his home town, Leeds, to see the Clash there, and Radar and Sten decided to make their way up later. Furb and I got there in about half a Thursday, finally travelling down into Leeds mid-evening, the huge basin of yellow twinkling sodium lights suddenly appearing as we came over the brow of a hill while the guy driving the van was telling us that this (*Bluejeans and Moonbeams*) was Captain Beefheart's best album because all the others were too weird. Then it was a few slabs of hastily fried Spam at Furb's house before we hit the pub. On the Saturday we made it to the University in time for the sound check, and sat about in the hall while the band ran though 'Last Gang in Town' and a few others numbers, Joe stopping to chat to the audience in between songs and note down the names of those who didn't have tickets so they could get in on the guest list. The gig itself was a blast, the band exploding into action with 'Safe European Home', Mick and Paul bounding about the stage, changing places all the time, the band's presence effortlessly projected out to fill the hall and beyond, and Topper Headon drumming like a madman. The backdrop of flags, together with the confidence and energy of the performance, made them seem ready to take on the world. During 'White Riot' in the encore, Joe threw aside his battered guitar and kangaroo-hopped dementedly from one side of the stage to the other with open mouth and bulging eyes until he collapsed from exhaustion and had to be carried off.

Sunday was going home time. In the morning, Radar and I stood on a frosty slip road in the middle of nowhere (somewhere outside Leeds), initially on a high from the night before, but gradually getting colder and less chatty as nobody stopped for us – what did we expect the way we looked? Dishevelled, pale, slouched, lots of black. After a while someone did stop, a man who said he could take us as far as the next service station, about ten miles. It was better than nothing, and a service station would at least be on the motorway, so everyone going south would have to pass us standing there with our hopeful thumbs, best smiles and disreputable demeanour. Fine. We got there, got a cup of tea and sat down in the warmth before venturing out to begin phase two of The Journey South, then realised that a few tables away from us Mick Jones and Paul Simonon were having their breakfast. Wow, the Clash, who's going to believe this. As they left, by coincidence we did too, and I walked up to them and asked them to sign their photo in that week's edition of Melody Maker, which they politely did, then off they went. Next lift, a matter of minutes later, the driver said, 'I can take you as far as Oxford'. He even bought us bacon rolls and tea.

When I saw them again I was at Sheffield University, it was 1980 and *London Calling* was just out. I saw them twice within four days. Having lived up to and surpassed everything expected of them, they went and released a wildly eclectic double album, something unheard of in punk, though that no longer seemed a label you could apply to the Clash. They were turning into more of a punk-ska-rockabilly-dub-rock-disco-rap-type of band, though even this was perhaps too narrow. At more or less the same time the (in name) Sex Pistols were going down the toilet and Malcolm McLaren was trying to make out this was part of a master plan.

Punk was an idea, a state of mind; it was a point of departure rather than a destination. Looking back, it's easy to see now that by the time it had coalesced into a perceived movement it was finished. The two original standard bearers were the Clash and the Sex Pistols. The Damned just got on with not taking themselves too seriously and are still intermittently doing the same. The Pistols exploded/imploded or fizzled out, depending on which incarnation you regard as being the real one. The Clash did something far more interesting but less romantic – they stayed together *and* took what they did seriously, and because of this they had to work out what to do and where to go next, and some of the places they went were really interesting, and some of them weren't. After *Sandinista* it was all over.

They started with 'no Elvis, Beatles, or Rolling Stones', a negation of tradition or influence, then they went and raised their heads, took in the bigger picture, acknowledged tradition, experimented, and sucked up influences like a sponge. In the process they grew and changed and for a while at least were maybe the greatest rock and roll band in the world in a way that they would have despised a few years earlier, but life is full of such surprises and contradictions, as anyone who has lived long enough will confirm. The journey from their brief, terse first album via an over-worked, patchy second album to the textured, disciplined yet loose and expansive double *London Calling* and the sprawling, flawed triple *Sandinista* shows their music evolving, borrowing and transmuting material to create something of their own that is also part of a tradition. After all, the pink and green lettering in the design of the cover for *London Calling* was based on the LP *Elvis Presley*.

I didn't know that John Mellor hadn't become Joe Strummer overnight, though I'd figured out that wasn't his real name. For a while he had been in the 101ers, and I had bought their single, 'Keys To Your Heart/5 Star Rock And Roll Petrol'. Before Mr Mellor became Mr Strummer, for a while he had insisted on being called Woody before deciding to reinvent or re-reinvent himself.[7] The beauty of punk was that it allowed people to do this, adopt new names and new identities, so it became a kind of fresh start and a kind of revolution. But with any revolution there eventually comes a new orthodoxy and with a new orthodoxy come accusations of treachery, and a new crime, that of collaboration. So it was that some people threw out, or said they threw out, their newly unfashionable old LPs, the records that had been

---

7 Woody Guthrie had written THIS MACHINE KILLS FASCISTS on his guitar in 1941, which presumably prompted Joe to write BOSS, NOISE, and IGNORE ALIEN ORDERS on his at various times. In fact, bearing in mind his love of slogans it's surprising he didn't copy Woody's.

dominating the airwaves and earholes of the nation for too long. But not all of it, surely: I mean, I never hated Pink Floyd. I stopped playing them for a while, but not for that long – and John Peel and I both liked *Animals* a lot. I gladly ditched Jethro Tull and ELP and Yes and Genesis, but still liked things like Hawkwind and the Who and Wilco-period Doctor Feelgood and Van der Graaf Generator and Alex Harvey. And Bob Dylan and Neil Young. And I've always loved Abba.

There's a kind of dishonesty in the idea of a year zero, a new start after which all previous music ceased to matter, apart from maybe the Stooges and the New York Dolls, and the MC5 and the Velvet Underground, and some Roxy Music and Bowie. Maybe that was true of some people, or maybe it was a defensive-aggressive way of defining a particular tribe. The Sex Pistols might have been catalysts, they might have motivated a lot of other bands and musicians, but their role as guerrilla leaders wasn't something they wanted, as Johnny Rotten made clear every time anyone took the trouble to ask him. Admitting to being eclectic or liking bands who knew how to play or had long hair or beards or wore flares was in some circles a form of social suicide, which is presumably why Mike Oldfield wasn't heavily promoted by Virgin around this time, nor was Steve Hillage, someone else I liked a lot. I was ridiculed for liking Hawkwind and Abba, even though most bands actually sounded like one or the other of them. Many still do.

Does your record collection or CD collection show how eclectic and broad-minded you are? Can it embarrass you? At least part of it ought to, if you're any kind of well-rounded human being. Joe's influences were pretty broad, as were Mick's, Paul's and Topper's. That's what music is about, or what it should be about, opening things up rather than closing them down, embarrassing you as well as showing how cool you are. If you fail to see that, you disappear up your own backside along with your notions of authenticity.

The artist formerly known as Johnny Rotten was reviled by some for what he did next, but once he got some space to be himself again, or to be a different bit of himself, something amazing happened. Amazing, that is, if all you knew was the Sex Pistol pantomime villain Johnny Rotten. What he did was form PiL, and what they did after a wonderful first single and an uneven first album was *Metal Box*, music from another dimension. But in another way what *Metal Box* sounds like is the same thing that *London Calling* sounds like, music by a band who have raised their heads, taken in the bigger picture and sucked up influences.

The difference is that PiL's influences aren't the American influences that affected the Clash, they're influences from other, stranger, more obscure places, like Germany and Jamaica (of course the Clash played reggae and dub, but not the way PiL did: nobody did that). Original bassist Jah Wobble was a dub enthusiast; guitarist Keith Levine's hero was Steve Howe; and Lydon drew on a range of music that some found perplexing. On 16 July 1977, about a month after 'God Save the Queen', the Sex Pistols juggernaut was hurtling towards a brick wall, and to McLaren's considerable annoyance the artist then known as Johnny Rotten appeared on Capital Radio. The programme was presented by, of all people, Tommy Vance and it was called 'A Punk and his Music'. I remember being taken aback and pleased at the kind of music that someone like Johnny Rotten liked, which is of course why Malcolm McLaren didn't approve – it showed a sense of connection with music way beyond what a recently invented young antichrist was meant to like, and anyway he was supposed to be defined by what he hated rather than what he loved. The way the show ended was with Rotten saying:

> Lets wrap up a really, really tedious interview [laugh], because when it comes to it, that's exactly what it is. Just play the records. They'll speak for themselves.

Here's a list of what was played.

Tim Buckley	Sweet Surrender	*Greetings From LA* (1972)
The Creation	Life Is Just Beginning	Single (1967)
David Bowie	Rebel Rebel	*Diamond Dogs* (1974)
	unknown Irish folk music (jig)	
Augustus Pablo	King Tubby Meets Rockers Uptown	*King Tubby Meets Rockers Uptown* (1976)
Gary Glitter	Doing Alright With The Boys	Single (1975)
Fred Locks	These Walls	*Black Star Liner* (1977)
Culture	I'm Not Ashamed	Single (1977)
Dr Alimantado	Born For A Purpose	*Born For A Purpose* (1977)
Bobby Byrd	Back From The Dead	Single (1974)
Neil Young	Revolution Blues	*On The Beach*
Sex Pistols	Did You No Wrong	B-side, 'God Save The Queen' single (1977)
Lou Reed	Men Of Good Fortune	*Berlin* 1973
Kevin Coyne	Eastbourne Ladies	*Marjory Razorblade* (1973)
Peter Hammill	Institute Of Mental Health (Burning)	*Nadir's Big Chance* (1975)
Peter Hammill	Nobody's Business	*Nadir's Big Chance* 1975)
Makka Bees	Nation Fiddler	Single (1977)
Captain Beefheart	The Blimp	*Trout Mask Replica* (1969)

Continued

Nico	Janitor Of Lunacy	*Desertshore* (1970)
Ken Boothe	Is It Because I'm Black	*Let's Get It On* (1973)
John Cale	Legs Larry At Television Centre	*The Academy In Peril* (1972)
Third Ear Band	Fleance	*Macbeth* (Roman Polanski movie soundtrack) (1972)
Can	Halleluwah	*Tago Mago* (1971)
Peter Tosh	Legalise It	*Legalise It* (1976)

After this, punk, such as it was, could never be the same again. How could it be when it was informed by Nico and Peter Hammill and Captain Beefheart and Culture and Can and John Cale and all these other artists. In other words, after this one radio show it had become part of the bigger picture.

Another aspect of the bigger picture hit me the time I visited Mathew Street, wandering dazed and confused around the Beatle Quarter. Stepping off Mathew Street through a large glass opening along from the boutique emporium that was Cavern Walks, I found myself in the Vivienne Westwood shop. When I entered in my green Berghaus jacket carrying my tourist rucksack, there was no-one else in the shop, which was just as well because the sleek and rather smug-looking staff were far too preoccupied with looking sleek and smug, dissecting one another's social lives in jaded, camp Liverpool accents. Wandering about rather self-consciously, I looked at the clothes and artefacts and noticed there were no price tags: always a bad sign. Displayed reverentially in glass cases were the likes of safety pin pendants (£50), penis-shaped cufflinks (£75), and 'too fast too live too young to die' army-style dog tags (£90).[8] Was this boutique postmodernism, was

---

8   Curious to know the cost of these unpriced items and too timid to ask, I looked online.

it fashion, was it art, was it all three, or was it just taking the piss? It was hard to tell.

What made the biggest impression, though, wasn't the jewellery or the couture, it was the unsettling white unisex 'tits' T-shirt. Printed with a life-sized black and white photo of a pair of tits printed over the area where your tits would be, it cost £75, rather than the £15 or so you would pay for it online. It was the same as the one Steve Jones was wearing the night the Sex Pistols swore their way to infamy back in 1976, only more expensive, and it's a part of pop history. Or a rip-off, or a piece of irony, or a classic. Whatever it was, whatever it is, you can also see it being worn by Charlie Watts on the cover of the Stones 1970 live album *Get Yer Ya-Ya's Out*. Originally designed by Janusz and Laura Gottwald at the end of the sixties for a student project,[9] it was later sold via a company called Jizz, Inc, which was how Charlie Watts got one.

And as well as being a part of pop history, it's also an ironic piece of *détournement*, the irony being that Vivienne Westwood didn't design it; she didn't even have the idea – Malcolm bought one from a New Orleans novelty shop in 1975 and she just copied it, making it her own to the extent that the design has been incorrectly attributed to her. Its shock value even now transcends any connection with Westwood, or the Gottwalds, though it's up against a lot more competition, and if you did buy one from the Westwood shop, you'd need your head examining. Because, like someone almost said, 'like T-shirt, like brain', and it's getting harder to tell which T-shirt and whose brain.

---

9 There was also a man-chest T-shirt, an idea which has for some reason proved less durable.

Playlist 7 - The Wrong Trousers		
My Sweet Lord / He's So Fine	George Harrison / The Chiffons	
I Had Too Much To Dream (Last Night)	The Electric Prunes	
(White Man) In Hammersmith Palais	The Clash	
Rock And Roll	Led Zeppelin	*IV*
Observatory Crest	Captain Beefheart	*Bluejeans & Moonbeams*
Isabel Goudie	The Sensational Alex Harvey Band	*Framed*
A Plague Of Lighthouse Keepers	Van der Graaf Generator	*Pawn Hearts*
Public Image	Public Image	
Did You No Wrong	Sex Pistols	
King Tubby Meets Rockers Uptown	Augustus Pablo	

To listen to the playlists, visit Spotify using the QR links provided.

Links to every playlist are also at www.hungry-ghost.info, along with photographs and archive material to supplement each chapter and enhance the reading/listening experience, just like a great big gatefold album cover.

7

EVERYBODY LOVES ALADDIN STARDUST

A few years ago (it doesn't matter when: time passes so quickly now), my wife and I went to a pub in Inverness to see a band called Tigers On Vaseline. Beneath the head-and-shoulders Aladdin Sane image, the posters bore the strapline *Scotland's No 1 David Bowie Tribute Act*.

The name Tigers On Vaseline comes from 'Hang On To Yourself', the third track on side two of the *Ziggy Stardust* album. It came out in 1972, and although in some ways it feels like Ziggy died over forty years ago, in other ways it seems like this happened only recently. Then again, it also feels like he's still with us, and always will be. Whichever way it is, and it could be all three, we got to know Ziggy more than four decades ago when we heard him on the radio, saw him on TV and bought his LP.

David Bowie was the nearest thing I got to having My Own Beatles, once I'd realised I didn't like Everyone Else's Beatles. After them and before him there were songs like 'Yellow River' by Christie, 'In The Summertime' by Mungo Jerry, 'Resurrection Shuffle' by Ashton, Gardner and Dyke, and of course 'Get It On' by T Rex. These were songs that could rock a ten-year-old's world, shaking it rhythmically to induce disorientation, giddiness and a creeping sense of exhilaration that seemed to trouble my parents.

After Christie's 'Yellow River' came a lacklustre effort called 'San Bernadino'. I don't know at what stage someone decided to turn this record over and decided to play the B-side, but once they did there was no going back to San Bernadino, because I was instantly transported to somewhere much wilder and stranger than the 99th largest city in America. What leapt from the grooves was a rowdy, raucous rock-and-roll beast of a song called 'Here I Am'. It was at warp speed as soon as it started, which was just under five seconds before the vocals kicked in with a 'Weeeeell...', after which the song careered along for a whole two and a half minutes like a runaway train rattling down an echoing tunnel of guitar and vocals, buffeted by frantic piano. Played over and over again at a friend's house on one occasion, its combination of spaced-out echo and hoarse velocity induced a craziness that had us leaping about the living room with the curtains closed and the record player turned up to eleven, so hot we pulled our tops off and kept on rocking right until the moment we were called through to the kitchen for tea, emerging panting into the afternoon sun more than ready for our chips and lemonade.

But the song that changed everything was 'Get It On', which I heard at the end-of-term party in my final year at primary school. There had been discotheques at the local youth club but despite having surrendered to 'Here I Am' I was much too shy to do anything like that in public. And even though I'd watched 'Top Of The Pops', when I heard 'Get It On' I had no idea what T Rex looked like, because I hadn't yet sat through Marc Bolan on TV, me on the floor, my mum behind me on the settee tutting at the antics of this pouting, swanking, satin-and-tat diva. When I did see him on 'Top Of The Pops' with his glittery make-up and feather boa, it made me feel even more uncomfortable than watching Pan's People jiggling about while my mum was sat behind me. I'm not sure if she liked any of this music or was just keeping an eye on me, though it was clear my dad couldn't bear to be in the same room when Marc Bolan was on TV. Maybe I'm exaggerating, but television was very closely monitored in my early years and anything shown on Sundays, or too late in the evening, or deemed otherwise inappropriate was gently but firmly denied.

As you might expect, this policy proved counter-productive and I became attracted to anything forbidden.

Soon I graduated to feverishly scanning the pages of the Birkenhead News every week to see what nasty films I was missing. *House Of Whipcord*. *When Girls Undress*. *Confessions Of A Nymphomaniac*. And *Easy Rider*, of which one reviewer said – and I remember it clearly – 'I loathe drug taking, hate hippies: but I urge you to see *Easy Rider*'. That was good enough for me. At around the same time, I remember the morning-after furore that followed a programme about someone called Andy Warhol, whose name instantly stuck in my mind as a byword for immorality and was therefore hugely intriguing. There was a buzz about it for weeks, everyone talking excitedly yet vaguely about him appearing on TV with a woman who made paintings using her breasts.

It was in this febrile, yearning state of mind that I heard 'Get It On'. What a wonderful song, then and now. I remember sitting in class 4B at the party when it first got played. There was the first low-down chugging riff, a bit of drum and a piano glissando to build the excitement, then a sleazy second riff to build it even more, then that hot breathy voice that oozed dirtiness and sweetness, filth and honey, like he was whispering lasciviously in my ear and everyone else's. I felt shocked, I felt hot and cold, my hair stood on end. 'Get It On' sounded like a girl slapping me in the face to get my attention then snogging me, all inside my head. It was inside my head because it never happened out in the real world, because I was too timid to talk to girls or go to discotheques, so I acted like I didn't want to. When I heard that song on that record player in that classroom, it was a different kind of music to anything else, and a door that hadn't been there before suddenly swung open. Once I stepped through, within a couple of years I had discovered the Parallel Universe of Rock, the Abode of Real Music, where I soon took up residence because that was where Status Quo, the Who, Genesis, Pink Floyd and ELP lived. In fact, they didn't just *live* there, they *dwelled* there. But before that, for a few years before I knew or cared that there was a difference between pop and rock, between singles and albums, I revelled in the charts and glam and 'Top Of The

Pops' and Radio One. And T Rex's brief but intense fling led me to a long-term relationship with David Bowie, legend, musician and artiste, starman.

Although less than a decade separates the Beatles in 1963 from Bowie's first hit single of the seventies, they seem to come from different dimensions – and I saw them both on television. Nine years after witnessing 'She Loves You', in the first year at secondary school I saw 'Starman' on Top Of The Pops at Fanny's house. His TV was much bigger and louder than ours and we always got to watch whatever we wanted. So when David Bowie had to phone someone so he picked on mee-ee-ee, when he looked into the camera and out of the huge screen into my eyes and everyone else's, with his exotic hair, his coy yet knowing smirk and his camp pointy finger, it seemed like a glimpse into a whole other world of artistic and musical possibility, relayed to us by a fabulous being from another planet. I wouldn't have put it like that at the time, but looking back now, I know that's a good way of putting it, because that's how it's turned out – though I can't even remember if I saw it in colour or black and white. I already knew the song because it had entered into my head via Wonderful Radio One, and it contained weirdness and riches that allowed it to lodge deeply and readily.

It was Bowie's first hit since 1969's 'Space Oddity'. It was uniquely strange and it was perfect pop. The seductive come-hither intro, the lazily stoned delivery, the twists and turns of the melody, the hazy cosmic jive, the hooks that dug into you all over, the soaring chorus that yanked you up somewhere over the rainbow. Who could resist? Who would want to? It was a magical song and a magical performance. Bowie's gay provocation when he put his arm round Mick Ronson might now seem pretty tame, but at the time it apparently resonated with all kinds of freaks and outsiders everywhere, as well as making a pair of twelve-year olds snigger, and still we loved the song and couldn't stop singing it in our heads and out loud. But the most overlooked aspect of this television milestone, never mind the gay subtext or the birth of glam, was black-haired bassist Trevor Bolder's ridiculously long, unfeasibly silver sideburns, which lost out to the show-off in the blue jumpsuit. If Boulder had been topless, those silver sideburns would have covered his nipples. Sadly, all the hair attention was on Bowie though, so they went unnoticed.

Through a large part of my teenage years, I attended Bethesda, the church my parents went to. It never occurred to me not to. First I went to Sunday School then I went to a youth group called Covenanters. Being part of the Plymouth Brethren movement, the church was nonconformist and deeply conservative. The interior was light, austere and unadorned. At Sunday morning services there was no musical accompaniment, and no order of service apart from the breaking of bread and a collection. No women ever took a lead role, and they all seemed to wear hats and gloves. There was no priesthood, just a suited, white-shirted, sober-tied board of elders, which eventually included my dad. At some stage Fanny started coming to Sunday School with us, and when the Sunday School teenage boys moved up to Covenanters, and the teenage girls moved up to Girl Covenanters, we just carried on attending – until we were about sixteen, amazingly. As well as being Sunday Worship, Covenanters was also a place to swap LPs. At least, it was for the boys. There was ELP, Genesis, Mountain, Savoy Brown and Yes; and there was David Bowie. There was *Ziggy Stardust* but especially there was *Aladdin Sane*. My dad was one of the Covenanter leaders, and even now I still can't fully bring myself to imagine him or any of the other leaders coming across a copy of *Aladdin Sane*, perhaps resting against the hymn books after being exchanged for something like *Masters Of Reality* by Black Sabbath. And, as if finding it wasn't bad enough, picking it up, inspecting it, that bizarre alien cover; then opening up the gatefold sleeve and being confronted by the shocking Bowie-creature within. And that was without the profanity and oddness, sex, drugs and sci-fi of the lyric sheet, or putting the record on and hearing the eroticism, violence and lilting strangeness of the music itself. I loved it all, and considered myself extremely daring for doing so. Bowie's image was outrageous, seductive and a bit scary, just like he sounded, and quite unlike anything else in my sober, studious life. Despite or perhaps because of this, it fitted perfectly with my quest for the strange, in amongst all the other music, and the science fiction, UFO and occult paperbacks that I flung myself into head first.

In some ways it was hard to get past the drama and shock of Bowie's image, or images, which changed with every album. You had no idea what he was going to do next, or even what he was doing at the time. All of it, the whole Bowie phenomenon, seemed way ahead of anything or anyone else. But if you could get past all that, or alternatively if you allowed yourself to just believe in it, however ridiculous or outrageous it seemed, inside the startling album covers you got to the music and the poetry. Ever since singles like 'Space Oddity' then 'Starman', the songs got under my skin after first hearing them over and over again on the radio. And this was despite the fact that the first LP I bought was by Status Quo, and so was the second. The LPs I bought after that were by ELP, Rick Wakeman, Mike Oldfield, the Who and Pink Floyd: no singles there at all. In fact the first one I bought was 'Anarchy In The UK' because, despite the evidence, I tried to keep on believing there were only albums in the Abode Of Real Music. And I didn't own any Bowie albums until 1978, when I bought *"Heroes"* then seven others – everything apart from *Lodger*, which hadn't been released. So maybe I'm exaggerating the extent of my commitment to Bowie earlier in the decade, but it seems to me now that I was a total fan throughout, and I can't actually bring myself to believe that I wasn't, because I love the music so much, and so much more than ELP or Genesis or Mike Oldfield or Status Quo. Or the Who. Or Pink Floyd.

Acknowledging this nagging sense of uncertainty is hard, because part of me wants to believe that in my gilded adolescence I was mainly a version of me that was both trendy at the time and also uncannily prescient; that managed to like all the right things, which is to say the things that when I look back seem like they're right from the perspective of now (and now, and now), as the then of the seventies and all the other thens recede into the ever more distant past, changing shape as they do so. And maybe I liked some of the wrong things, but only the *right* wrong things – that's to say all the wrong things that for whatever reason seem right now. Having said all that, I'm pretty sure my head was actually a cauldron of seething hormones, voracious intellect, desperate insecurity, overactive imagination and absurd contradictions.

The thread of David Bowie, the various different exotic, brilliant, constantly surprising threads of David Bowie, are woven all through my Seventies, his warp and weft and that of other rock gods, heroes and monsters adding colour and texture to its lurid, bizarrely patterned adolescent fabric, fabric that was bit like an outrageous lining in a sober suit, a suit that I wore with the jacket unbuttoned to show the lining a bit when maybe what I really wanted to do was wear it turned inside out, but didn't have the nerve. From *Space Oddity* to *The Man Who Sold The World* to *Hunky Dory* to *Ziggy Stardust* to *Aladdin Sane*, to *Diamond Dogs* to *Station to Station* to *Low* to *"Heroes"* to *Lodger* to *Scary Monsters*. What a journey, what albums, what a decade, what a career. After that it was all over as far as I was concerned, but what a Seventies. He always seemed to be in the right place at the right time with the right people – Lou Reed, Iggy Pop, Brian Eno, Robert Fripp, Kraftwerk (almost), Neu! (almost). There's a photo of Bowie as Ziggy in the early seventies standing with hand on hip; also present is Lou Reed, also with hand on hip. Bowie has weird eyes and looks like an alien. Lou has shades on indoors and looks like Lou Reed. Draped between them is a diminutive bug-eyed silver-haired Iggy Pop monster with a packet of cigarettes clamped between his teeth. And he's wearing a T Rex T-shirt. That's how happening David Bowie was, or how happening he made himself.

Everyone has their favourite Bowie or Bowies, the one or ones they regard as their own, because, as we all know, he is chameleon, comedian, Corinthian and caricature. Even though it ended with *Scary Monsters*, after which he left me behind and went global with *Let's Dance*, I never left his (and my) seventies behind. The restless protean creativity, genre hopping, genre making and inspired collaborations have come to define the decade, and he more or less owned it, if any one artist can be said to. This makes it entirely right that he is still referenced, appropriated and reinvented now in a time of constant appropriation and reinvention – after all, he got there first, and he's probably the most original appropriator that's ever been.

The tension between originality and appropriation, artifice and authenticity, novelty and tradition, is one that runs through many creative endeavours, but it has been debated especially in music. This is perhaps because music is one of the oldest, most widespread and probably the most human forms of art, and is loaded with political, religious, social, aesthetic, sexual and economic meanings, or has these and other meanings imposed upon it. In addition, music has often involved other art forms such as film, poetry, photography, graphic art and theatre – either to bestow gravitas on content that would otherwise appear trivial, or to further ambitions that might otherwise remain unsatisfied. Bowie can be examined, dissected, compared and contrasted with all of this in mind because his career has been so long and so varied, but I can't help always returning to the idea that My Bowie is Seventies Bowie.

And I don't think I'm alone. In 2013 the Victoria and Albert Museum put on 'David Bowie Is', a career retrospective that rapidly became its best selling show ever. Over 300 items from Bowie's meticulously/obsessively accumulated archives were on display amongst all the graphics, projections and songs. The show highlighted Bowie's massive contribution not just to music but to popular culture as a whole, but it was noticeable the way the show, and its imagery and publicity, focused almost exclusively on a single decade, the seventies, the period when his influence was most wide-ranging and most profound. Since then, he's been an Icon and a Megastar and an A-list Celebrity of course, but largely predicated on that decade. The open-ended title of the show, 'David

Bowie Is…', creates a sense of possibility, allowing anyone to complete it in any way using whatever they bring to it, and almost everyone will have something to bring. The title is also a statement of fact: David Bowie is, and always will be – he exists, and always will: as himself, in his music and through his effect everyone and everything else in mass culture. What I personally bring to the title is what I feel lot of other people bring: *David Bowie is the Seventies*, because the decade defines him and he defines the decade.[1]

Five days after the V&A show opened, a book called *Ziggyology* by Simon Goddard went on sale. A work of archaeologically detailed research and scholarly, almost stalkerly, fixation, it maps out the landscape of planet Ziggy on a minute scale, not just on the surface but digging down deep and ranging through the middens and monuments of the underlying strata. The fact that there is this much to find out and people apart from me want to know about it makes Ziggy a figure resonant with myth; part hero, part alien, part deity. The mythology and the albums it inhabits aren't always internally consistent, but mythology is like that, gods and heroes emerging as composites, mutations, hybrids and tall tales rather than springing into existence fully formed, despite what creation stories (including Ziggy's) might have you believe. Any biography or attempted biography of Odin or Zeus or Venus will bear this out, and what is rock music other than a stage on which modern and not-so-modern myths can be enacted and re-enacted. In its self-conscious assemblage of trash, treasure and trivia, *Ziggyology* the book mirrors Ziggy the myth, the icon, the persona, the marketing

---

1 We never made it to the V&A, so we later went to Bologna instead, using a money-box full of £2 coins saved over the previous few years. It was the best exhibition I've been to, not just because it was about Bowie, but also because of the way it was organised and laid out. Wireless headphones played location-specific commentaries and music, and virtually the only sound from external speakers was the loud music in the massive white cube at the very end, where people gathered to communally enjoy being immersed in the performance footage that was projected around all the walls on a heroic scale.

concept. And interestingly, although the title is an -ology that's about Ziggy, the image on the cover is from *Aladdin Sane*, because the face – not even the face, just the pale skin, the lightning bolt and the hair – is so visually arresting and so familiar; so widely referenced that Ziggy Stardust and Aladdin Sane are now hard to separate, and it would surely be wrong to quibble about details: Ziggy Stardust, Aladdin Sane, Ziggy Sane …[2]

Another book, from 2012, is *The Man Who Sold The World* by Peter Doggett. Anyone who has read *Revolution In The Head* by Ian MacDonald will know what Doggett is attempting – and I say 'attempting' because at the time of his death MacDonald had in fact begun the book that Doggett completed. *Revolution In The Head* is about the work of the Beatles; it's an authoritative, exhaustive musical and cultural examination of every Beatles song, comprehensively cross-referenced and full of stories, comment, musicology and contextual essays. Dogget's book is a worthy attempt at something similar, but it's hard not to compare it with MacDonald's book and find it wanting. For me, what's most telling thing it is its strapline: 'David Bowie and the 1970s'. In other words, *Space Oddity* to *Scary Monsters*.

All of which made it all the more surprising when Bowie released a new album after a gap of ten years: *The Next Day* came out with little advance publicity on 8 March 2013, too late to affect the V&A exhibition, and it took everyone by surprise. I was among the minority who found it brave but

---

2 This image that defines Bowie was improvised on the evening of a 1972 photo shoot for the *Aladdin Sane* album cover. He never wore it again, though on the back of the *David Live* album there's a photo of him holding up in front of his face a white mask bearing the lightning bolt, taken during the 'Diamond Dogs' tour in 1974. Footage also appears in the 1975 BBC documentary 'Cracked Actor'. On the way out of the exhibition was a bank of screens flashing scores of versions of the lightning bolt meme, as it has over the years mutated and evolved from photo session to LP to secular icon, along the way colonising faces that include Kate Moss, Lady Gaga and My Little Pony.

disappointing,[3] with a cover that tried to make some kind of ill-advised statement about obliterating *"Heroes"* and failed – how couldn't it fail; how could *"Heroes"* be obliterated, even by Bowie himself, even ironically? When your back catalogue is that good (there's none better); when it's all but impossible to avoid being defined by it, however frustrating it might be, then there's nothing much to be done.[4]

So I was disappointed with *The Next Day*, and with the fact that it even needed to exist after such a gap. It messed up the nice narrative arc I had constructed, which on reflection was a good thing: despite what I thought, the story hadn't ended, and now that it has it'll still take time to make sense of it. David Bowie is happening even now, whenever now happens to be. Unlike, say, the Rolling Stones, who aren't happening now and haven't been for about forty years, apart from interminable compilations, concert DVDs and box sets of the same old same old.[5] And although hoary old Heritage

---

3 I reserve the right to change my mind about this, and about everything else.

4 Well, I suppose there are two things. One is to become a tribute act, or more accurately an auto-tribute act, a vain pantomime churning out your greatest, oldest hits, like the Rolling Stones. Fifty years on, there they are, still touring songs from the same decade in which Bowie killed off Ziggy, as well as material from the decade before, with no sense of irony: look on their works, ye mighty, and despair. Another thing you can do is carry on doing what you do but in new or different ways, or at least with some integrity, like Neil Young, Leonard Cohen, Bob Dylan, Lou Reed or Van Morrison. The third thing you can do is be Iggy Pop, radio presenter, Sleaford Mods advocate, elder statesman, John Peel lecturer and ferocious Glastonbury 2007 auto-tributeer (but in a good way), who went and recorded again with the Stooges. As in, recording new material. I couldn't imagine Mick Jagger appearing topless in a suicide vest on the cover of an album called *Ready To Die* in 2013, the year the Stones played Glastonbury. And I don't care if *Ready To Die* is any good or not: that's not the point. What Mr Pop had to say was: 'It's just a pig-headed fucking thing I have that a real fucking group, when they're an older group, they also make fucking records. They don't just go and twiddle around on stage to make a bunch of fucking money.'

5 The only thing they have in common with Bowie is the longevity of their logo – their tongue for Bowie's lightning bolt.

Rock is everywhere now that pop and rock have acquired a history to be celebrated, curated and exploited, that didn't happen with Bowie, because the best of his best-ofs still sound so now and so good. David Bowie is happening now because, although all music is happening now, his still sounds contemporary, the past woven into the present and the future. You can pick and mix, you can make your own Bowie, and I know what I'm going to make mine out of: a compilation of compilations.

1 *All Saints*

When I was in Birkenhead visiting my parents, rediscovering Skeleton Records and serendipitously getting to know the Beatles forty years on, an album I bought along with *Sgt Pepper* and *Revolver* was *All Saints*, which I'd never even heard of before. It's a compilation of Bowie's instrumental music, compiled by Bowie himself. Originally an 18-track double CD made for friends in 1993, it was released commercially as a 16-track single CD eight years later in 2001. The first instrumental piece he ever released, 'Speed Of Life', was the first track on *Low* in 1977. It's interesting for two reasons. Firstly, it doesn't appear on either version of the *All Saints* album. Secondly, 1977 was around the time Bowie started working with Brian Eno, absorbing both Eno's influence and his influences. Eno was at the time developing what had come to be known as ambient music, and soaking up the electronic sounds of German bands such as Neu! and Cluster (who he collaborated with). This was new music mostly made on new instruments or in new ways by musicians from a country without a recent cultural history, or, to put it another way, two recent cultural histories, both of which they wanted to obliterate: one was the rock-and-roll culture of the occupying American forces; the other was that of Nazism.

The biggest surprise was hearing the early instrumentals again, especially from *Low* and *"Heroes"*, hearing them out of context and realising how new, strange, compelling and wonderful they were and still are; how they connect with and emerge from German music of the period; a series of extraordinary, evocative mood pieces varying not only in their instrumentation but also the virtual acoustic spaces they inhabit, prefiguring the production work of Martin Hannett on *Unknown Pleasures*.

Another surprise came from hearing this instrumental music by itself: it was originally on the second side of the LPs, and always felt separated from the songs on the first side. You had to pick up the record and turn it over to hear it, a physical act that brought with it a sense of contrast, of drama, and opened up a different soundworld. On this CD, that sense of separation and strangeness is somehow restored.

All Saints surprised me and delighted me: what I knew mingled with the later incidental material I'd never heard before, drifting, meandering moods and atmospheres that aren't really proper songs and aren't meant to be, including some of the music Bowie made for the TV series 'The Buddha Of Suburbia'. It surprised and delighted me, that is, apart from the final track, an orchestral piece called 'Some Are', arranged by Philip Glass for his Symphony No 1, the bombastic three-movement 'Low' Symphony consisting of 'Subterraneans', 'Some Are' and 'Warszawa'. None of it sounds much like Bowie – 'Some Are' least of all. Originally a delicate, three-minute wisp of something that's barely there, 'Some Are' was only ever previously available as an extra track on a CD reissue of *Low* (before becoming available on YouTube like everything else).

It's not that I don't like Philip Glass, it's just that the idea of minimalism being 'less is more' in any way has here overbalanced into a relentless, leaden 'more is more'. Like, three minutes becoming eleven minutes, and a few synthesised textures and breathy vocals becoming a mechanised stadium rally. What was a slight, gossamer creature is transformed into a pumped-up orchestral terminator that squashes its original self out of existence without noticing, like Robocop stepping on Tinkerbell. Or, in Philip Glass's words:

My approach was to treat the themes very much as if they were my own and allow their transformations to follow my own compositional bent when possible... Bowie and Eno's music certainly influenced how I worked, leading me to sometimes surprising musical conclusions. In the end I think I arrived at something of a real collaboration between my music and theirs.

We need 'Speed of Life', we need 'Some Are', we could do with some more from the original double CD, but we don't need this.

2 *iSELECTBOWIE*

I thought I'd never find a copy of 'Some Are' apart from online, because I didn't want to buy another copy of *Low* just for one extra track. I thought I'd never find a copy, but I was wrong. During one of their sales, Inverness Oxfam were selling CDs at ten for 99p, so after finding a drippy Spiritualized single and an unhinged Electric Six 'Danger! High Voltage' remix, I rummaged around for another eight CDs to make up the numbers. One that I scooped up without even looking properly was *iSELECTBOWIE*, twelve Bowie tracks, chosen by him, originally given away with the Mail On Sunday in June 2008 and subsequently released commercially. The full track listing is

1. Life On Mars?   (*Hunky Dory*)
2. Sweet Thing/Candidate   (*Diamond Dogs*)
3. The Bewlay Brothers   (*Hunky Dory*)
4. Lady Grinning Soul   (*Aladdin Sane*)
5. Win   (*Young Americans*)
6. Some Are   (Previously unreleased)
7. Teenage Wildlife   (*Scary Monsters*)
8. Repetition   (*Lodger*)
9. Fantastic Voyage   (*Lodger*)
10. Loving The Alien   (*Tonight*)

11. Time Will Crawl (Remix; originally on *Never Let Me Down*)
12. Hang On To Yourself (*Live At Santa Monica*)

It's revealing that of the twelve tracks, ten are from the My Classic Bowie period; is it also his? Whether or not this is the case, *iSELECTBOWIE* became my second surprise Bowie album, as well as another chance for Bowie to compile Bowie. Track six is 'Some Are'. It's an interesting mixture, and Bowie's notes are also 'interesting' (quote marks are to indicate the word is being deployed in the same way that my art teacher at school would use it: to avoid being disparaging. You could actually hear the quote marks when he said it). You're sometimes left wondering what Bowie was or wasn't on when he wrote these notes. This is what he says about 'Some Are':

> A quiet little piece Brian Eno and I wrote in the Seventies. The cries of wolves in the background are sounds that you might not pick up on immediately. Unless you're a wolf. They're almost human, both beautiful and creepy.

> Images of the failed Napoleonic force stumbling back through Smolensk. Finding the unburied corpses of their comrades left from their original advance on Moscow. Or possibly a snowman with a carrot for a nose; a crumpled Crystal Palace Football Club admission ticket at his feet. A Weltschmerz indeed. Send in your own images, children, and we'll show the best of them next week.

(I looked it up: *Weltschmerz* literally means 'world-pain'. The term was coined by the German Romantic writer Jean Paul and refers to a feeling of pain, sadness or disappointment at the way the world is, and at your inability to cope with it. Does that help?)

3 *The Life Aquatic Studio Sessions Featuring Seu Jorge*

Another album that took me by surprise, one I found in a record store in the middle of a shopping centre in Leeds. In the surreal semi-comedic Wes Anderson movie *The Life Aquatic*, Bill Murray plays an eccentric Jacques Cousteau character with a Jacques Cousteau red woolly hat and a yellow submarine, on a mission of revenge against a large fish: the details are not important here. Throughout the movie, often in the background and for no discernible reason, there are intermittent performances by one of the ship's crew, played by Brazilian musician Seu Jorge, also in a red woolly hat – airy, fragile Portuguese versions of Bowie songs in a tremulous voice accompanied by his Spanish guitar. There are five on the movie soundtrack CD and thirteen on the sessions CD, twelve of which are from *Hunky Dory*, *Ziggy Stardust* or *Diamond Dogs*. Being so familiar with the original versions of these songs, it comes as a shock to hear them reinterpreted in this way. Bowie's endorsement on the cover seems somewhat cautious, perhaps even equivocal:

> Had Seu Jorge not recorded my songs acoustically in Portuguese I would never have heard this new level of beauty which he has imbued them with.

This album represents in spirit all the other tribute albums and cover versions out there, but stands alone by virtue of its difference from the originals. Its plaintive, almost hesitant delivery and understated accompaniment leave nowhere to hide when Jorge's voice occasionally breaks but the sparseness and imperfection of the treatment highlight the songs in a bare, acoustically dry setting where less sounds like more.

4 *Nothing Has Changed*

Who else would compile his own career-spanning triple CD sequenced in reverse chronological order? Who else would record the shocking, dissonant, wonderful 'Sue: Or In A Season Of Crime' as a 7 ½ minute 10-inch single with big band accompaniment, then include it as the opening track? Who else would call such an album *Nothing Has Changed*? Of the 59 tracks, 24 are from My Bowie period, 4 from the sixties, the remaining 31 from the time after we parted company. It's a great overview of those years, in that I like everything here apart from the hideous 'Dancing In The Street' (recorded with Mick Jagger for Live Aid, gamely avoiding the excesses of many charity records, but still hideous). Maybe that means I would like a lot of the later material if I gave it a chance, I don't know.[6] Of course, this is him attempting to curate his work like he still owns it all, even though we know that this isn't the case: at some stage Bowie lost ownership of his songs, apart from in the legal sense: in a larger cultural sense, we all own them now because they're a part of us and of our lives. We're all Bowie, and Bowie is us.

All of which, and more besides, was why my wife and I went to see Tigers On Vaseline that Saturday night. What more can I say? We had some drinks, we had some more drinks, and we had a great night out. You'd have to say that the singer was the only one who looked the part even slightly: green animal print top, tight white trousers, long white lace-up boots. He had red spiky hair and eye make-up, and spent a lot of time with his hands on his hips, which he occasionally wiggled from side to side, though you'd have to say he was a lot older than Bowie had been, nowhere near as skinny, and lacked the bone structure. The earliest song was 'Space Oddity', the latest was 'China Girl' and the next latest was 'Ashes To Ashes'. Apart from that it was wall to wall glamorama: *Hunky Dory*, *Ziggy Stardust*, *Aladdin Sane*, *Diamond Dogs*. What's not to like? We and everyone else there drank more and more and sang along louder and

---

6 I suppose part of me doesn't want to know, having already invested so much in liking what I know and knowing what I like. But maybe that's the point.

louder, waving our arms and punching the air: it was a fantastic evening.

It's that willing suspension of disbelief, leaving your scepticism at the door and just enjoying the music, or your memory of the music, or the communal sharing of different memories of the music and everything that went along with it. And while that was strange enough, what was just as strange was that our son and his friends were there on the other side of the room, eighteen, nineteen years old, shouting along and punching the air just like we were.

Which told me that what we were listening to and watching wasn't just a set of cover versions or tired retroism or pop eating itself or ironic glam, but a new form of folk music. Once there were covers bands, and now there are tribute bands as well, because what has emerged in the decades since the Beatles and Bowie is the idea of Classic Rock and Classic Pop, a musical and cultural canon that, as well as defining the past, is also defining the present and the future. Because nobody can now be free from the The Canon, and all the lists and reference books and rock heritage mags and samples and quotes and reissues and tribute acts and Aladdin Sane merchandising that goes along with it.

And you may ask yourself, is David Bowie *really* happening now? Yes, of course he is, now and for ever, like the Beatles, only the Beatles never got a set of stamps. There were ten, issued in March 2017 – four live images from tours (Ziggy Stardust 1973, Stage 1978, Serious Moonlight 1983, A Reality 2004) and six LP covers: *Hunky Dory*, *Aladdin Sane*, *"Heroes"*, *Let's Dance*, *Earthling*, *Blackstar*. Oh, yes, *Blackstar*. That was when he died, wasn't it. Even his death was a strange, daring kind of performance, or anti-performance, and included the best parting gift – a final album. After being rehearsed and recorded in secret, this oddly profound, profoundly odd album was released on 8 January 2016, his 69th birthday; two days later he was dead, cremated within a matter of days and gone with no public rituals, services or ceremonies other than the ones people arranged themselves in memory of their shared and personal Bowie or Bowies.

A career like this, a life like this, a death like this, a song like 'Blackstar', and an album like *Blackstar* – if any such things exist – can't be summed up by people like me in places like this. Paul Morley's love letter to his personal Bowie, *The Age Of Bowie*, shows one way to do it and also a way not to do it: passionate, rambling, smart, pretentious, annoying, moving – as you might expect, the adjectives just keep on coming. One thing Morley suggests is that with the death of Bowie, rock and pop and music as we once knew it have also died, and in a way he's right: Bowie often addressed us from other times, mostly in the future, but sometimes the past (like *Pin Ups*, or all the other compilations which, although they came from the past, also sang of the future), effortlessly anticipating and becoming part of our sense of the messed-up everything-now tidal surge we find ourselves adrift in. His death, the death of the Rock Star, the death of record labels, of analogue, of recorded formats, of the musicians of his generation whose physical presences are gradually decaying, dying, digitising and transmigrating online, is the end of some kind of era, and at the same time the continuation of the Age Of Bowie.

Playlist 8 - Everybody Loves Aladdin Stardust		
Here I Am	Christie	
Get It On	T Rex	
Starman	David Bowie	
Children Of The Grave	Black Sabbath	*Master Of Reality*
Search And Destroy	Iggy and the Stooges	*Raw Power*
Walk On The Wild Side	Lou Reed	
Where Are We Now?	David Bowie	
Some Are	David Bowie / Philip Glass	
Life On Mars?	Seu Jorge	*The Life Aquatic With Steve Zissou* (soundtrack
Blackstar	David Bowie	

To listen to the playlists, visit Spotify using the QR links provided.

Links to every playlist are also at www.hungry-ghost.info, along with photographs and archive material to supplement each chapter and enhance the reading/listening experience, just like a great big gatefold album cover.

8

AN ANATOMY OF LISTS

1973

It wasn't much of a list to start with; just two LPs, both by
Status Quo.

1974

I bought all five Emerson, Lake and Palmer LPs. And I saw
them live, so now there were two lists.

I bought both of Rick Wakeman's LPs, *The Six Wives Of
Henry VIII* and *Journey To The Centre Of The Earth*. It was
about the keyboards, and the big ideas. The other albums I
bought were *Dark Side Of The Moon*, *Tommy* and *Tubular
Bells*. More big ideas.

I bought my copy of *Tubular Bells* from the tiny record
section in a local department store called Beatties, using
money from my paper round. It cost £1.99. Before buying it
I remember gazing in awe at its strange, surrealist cover – a
huge bent chrome tube the size of a space station hanging
in a blue sky dappled with white clouds. Beneath, along the
bottom of the image, a frothing wave-top tumbled messily
onto an unseen beach. On the back of the cover was a blue-
tinted image of sky, waves and beach, though what got my
attention was the small print, which told me Mike Oldfield
played fifteen instruments on side one and thirteen on side
two. Clearly, a Real Musician. And he had a sense of humour
that chimed with my own, based on two rather smug notes
that said

In Glorious Stereophonic Sound. Can also be played on mono-equipment at a pinch

and

This stereo record cannot be played on old tin boxes no matter what they are fitted with. If you are in possession of such equipment please hand it into the nearest police station.

This was fine by me, because proper albums of proper music by proper musicians needed proper equipment, rather than a clunky old mono radiogram with a speaker on the underside and a flip-over LP/78 stylus, like the one we had in the front room. Fortunately, shortly after that my parents bought some proper stereophonic equipment, and so did I. Theirs was quite sophisticated and went in the lounge. You knew it was sophisticated because it had separate speakers, which you positioned carefully for optimum effect. The turntable was so sophisticated the playing arm needed balancing with a tiny dial and a highly sensitive counterweight, a process that caused my dad considerable difficulty, after which nobody was allowed to adjust it ever again. To play a record, you set the turntable in motion, then guided the feather-light arm across to the edge of the record and respectfully placed it in position. Pushing gently on a silver lever allowed the arm to descend sedately onto the record's surface, something you did at eye level because the turntable sat on a shelf above the TV, in full view rather than hidden away in a wooden cabinet. Their stereo sounded great. Mine sounded pretty terrible, but I thought it was fantastic because it went in my bedroom and, like theirs, it had separate speakers and a smoked plastic lid.

Tubular Bells was the seventh LP I bought. It was the first album to be released on the Virgin label and for some reason that word, *virgin*, sounded a bit rude, a bit threatening; a bit like *sex*; a bit like something you might say in private but not in public. I mean, I was a virgin but it wasn't something I wanted to talk about. Sometimes when I got the bus into town to buy books and records, on the top deck at the back the words EMERGENCY EXIT had been partly scratched away to read V I RGI N EXIT instead, and that looked rude, though I wasn't sure why. Even though I was a virgin, it wasn't the kind of exit I would want to use. And anyway, how could you tell who the virgins were? And if you weren't a virgin, which exit were you meant to use?

Similarly rude was the Virgin record shop in Liverpool, halfway up Bold Street. When it opened in 1971 it was one of the first in the country. Above the door was a logo designed by Roger Dean which included that word, VIRGIN, in big letters. When I first walked past it with my dad, the door was open, rock music was blaring out and I could see longhaired youths sitting cross-legged on the floor inside. My dad said it looked like 'a most objectionable place' and despite or maybe because of this it definitely looked like my kind of shop.

Tubular Bells has of course become a Contemporary Classic, so much so that its opening accompanied the National Health Service segment in the opening ceremony of the 2012 Olympic Games. It's now hard to appreciate how strange this kind of minimalism once sounded, though its use as incidental music in *The Exorcist* at the time of its release might give you some idea. From this sparse, rather eerie beginning, the music rises and falls over a whole side of vinyl for 25 minutes, culminating in the final third with Viv Stanshall as master of ceremonies, calmly introducing the instruments one by one as they build, layer upon layer, towards the orgasmic finale, climaxing with the triumphant 'plus... *tubular bells!*' that provided the idea for the album title. It seems self evident: what else could it be called? Well, its working title was *Opus One*. And at some stage Richard Branson wanted to call it *Breakfast In Bed*: on the cover, a boiled egg in an egg cup with blood running down the side. However, Viv Stanshall happened to be around with the Bonzo Dog Doo-Dah Band during the recording, which was why he did the honours, which was why there was a space-station-sized tubular bell with dappled clouds on the cover, and why it was called *Tubular Bells*. It was a huge success:

because it was so unusual, so compelling and so seductive; and because the teenage Mike Oldfield composed and played so much of it; and because Richard Branson believed in it; and because Viv Stanshall was master of ceremonies; and because John Peel played it on the radio.[1]

Two years after its release, *Tubular Bells* was orchestrated by David Bedford to become a Contemporary Classical Classic, and has since spawned *Tubular Bells II* (1992; MC Alan Rickman) and *Tubular Bells III* (1998; numerous singers, no MC), both of which featured the tubular bell all by itself on the cover, and I had to confess that without the clouds and the wave-top it looked a bit empty. There was even *The Millennium Bell* in 1999, its cover a horrendous montage of new-agey Cultural Icons (melting watch, spaceman, dolphin, electric guitar, sunflower, sword, self-referential tubular bell, blah blah blah), all of which made it look like the backdrop of a middle-brow TV quiz, or perhaps the lid of the accompanying board game.

Then, 30 years on, finally, there was the entirely re-recorded *Tubular Bells 2003*. The music and the bell were given a new digital sheen by Trevor Horn, the MC was John Cleese, and there was a shiny new sky and sea on the cover. It looked great, apart from a few seabirds that had somehow got into the sky at the side, though on something the size of a CD cover they were little more than specks, so why bother. Other mutations followed. In 2012 I ended up buying a blue kazoo with the bell logo on it at 'Tubular Bells For Two', an athletic, good-humoured rendition by two barefoot Australian musicians, Daniel Holdsworth and Aidan Roberts, and a large number of musical instruments. And in 2017, *Tubular Brass* was released – David Bedford's orchestration re-imagined for 28-piece brass band, the ends of the tubular bell flaring out to resemble the bells of two

---

1 Fittingly, John Peel later got to MC a truncated version on Radio 1: his 'plus a computer approximation of tubular bells' was rather downbeat, lacking Viv Stanshall's pregnant pause or indeed any sense of orgasmic release. Which, with John Peel, was entirely as it should have been.

silver trumpets, with TV chef and Yorkshireman Brian Turner as MC.

I have no idea what any of these other versions of *Tubular Bells* sounded like, and I don't feel the need to find out, but the great big tubular bell has stuck with me over the years, its serene, dream-like chromium immensity hovering somewhere at the back of my mind, waiting to be struck, waiting to reverberate again. And eventually it did, when a CD version of the original album was given away free with The Mail On Sunday in April 2007. I didn't know about it at the time, but a few years later when I was on holiday I found a copy in the house where we were staying, so I got to listen again. Side one was still great and side two still wasn't, though they were now both on the same side because it was a CD, and somehow this seemed wrong.

The idea of an album being given away with a newspaper might have seemed strange once, when music was LP-sized, and was a much rarer, more precious thing; but not any more. Newspapers do it quite often, and music magazines offer compilation, tribute or 're-interpretation' CDs with every issue. Charity shops are full of them, and so presumably are landfill sites. So, if the idea of a newspaper giving away *Tubular Bells now* fails to surprise, what about the idea of it being issued as a stamp, which is what happened in January 2010 as part of Royal Mail's Classic Album Covers commemorative issue.[2]

It might seem a bit picky, but with 'Classic Album Covers' are we talking about the covers of ten 'classic albums', or about ten 'album covers' that are classics whatever the music sounds like? Neither, as it happens. I mean, what would you have in your top ten of either category? Surely it wouldn't be (British artists only, in alphabetical order):

A Rush Of Blood To The Head – Coldplay
Led Zeppelin IV – Led Zeppelin
Let It Bleed – the Rolling Stones

---

2   Issued as stamps, and also as postcards of stamps. I have both.

London Calling – the Clash
Parklife – Blur
Power, Corruption And Lies – New Order
The Division Bell – Pink Floyd
Tubular Bells – Mike Oldfield
Screamadelica – Primal Scream
Ziggy Stardust – David Bowie.

Even if some of them really are classic albums or classic covers or even both, they're not classic stamps, apart from *London* Calling, *Screamadelica* and *Tubular Bells*, all of which work at this scale. And it really is a question of scale: what might work as 144 square inches of LP, or even 144 square centimetres of CD, is lost on a square inch of gummed paper. *The Division Bell*? Nice image, but it should have been *Dark Side of the Moon*: the perfect stamp LP (as shown in July 2016's commemorative Pink Floyd issue[3]).

Ziggy Stardust? You can't see anything. It should have been *Aladdin Sane, "Heroes"* or *Hunky Dory*, all three of which were included in the Bowie issue of March 2017 as proof.

And *Led Zeppelin IV*? It was a gatefold cover, the point being that the cover was two square feet in size, big enough to make out the details, and it only made sense when opened out, when you see the bigger picture: the old man with the sticks on his back, in the picture, on the wall, which was, it turned out, part of a semi-demolished house on waste ground, with a block of flats looming in the background. A dramatic, strange, multi-layered image whose meanings literally unfolded in real time, like a poem or a short story. Even with a gatefold stamp or a double stamp, this would just look tiny and insignificant, impossible to make out. When I was into Led Zeppelin, when I embroidered the *Zoso* on the waistband of my denim jacket, I thought that

---

3   *The Piper At The Gates Of Dawn, Atom Heart Mother, Dark Side Of The Moon, Wish You Were Here, Animals, Endless River*. Plus stamps of live performances, which seemed a bit unnecessary. Available in both stamp and postcard form; I have both.

the sleeve image was tawdry and mundane, unworthy of the mighty sounds etched into the grooves of this mysterious artefact. Now, it's almost completely the other way round. I think the cover is amazing: the dramatic contrast (and paradoxical connection) between the inside and the outside, stylistically and symbolically, the photograph and the drawing, the light and the dark, the urban and the rural, the ancient and modern, the two old men with staffs. One is a countryman bent double with his burden, looking out at the viewer. The other is the Hermit from the ninth trump card in the traditional tarot deck, lantern held aloft, looking down at a tiny supplicant kneeling far below. His lantern is the lamp of truth, used to light the way; his staff supports him along the rocky path to enlightenment; his robe represents discretion and introspection. It's all there, and it's meant to be – cryptic, esoteric, my kind of thing. So cryptic, it was an album without a name; like *Unknown Pleasures* an LP without text, apart from the inner sleeve and the label. So esoteric, it communicated its identity using four symbols, one for each band member. I wore my *Zoso* with pride, it being Jimmy Page's, him being a guitar virtuoso and a weird, eldritch Crowleyan warlock, rather than a prancing, preening Robert Plant (feather), or a bass player (a circle intersecting three overlapping arcs) or a drummer (three intersecting circles).

As well as the contrasting yet complementary outside and inside of the gatefold cover, there was another dimension – the inner sleeve. There, along with the four symbols, track listing and credits are the famous lyrics for that famous song, one of the most famous and best loved songs ever, 'Stairway to Heaven'. These feeble, pretentious meanderings are best not dwelt on: why make a feature of something that bad? And they are bad, New Order bad. The only thing worth considering about these words is that if you play some of them backwards and you know what you're meant to be listening out for, it might sound like they're about Satan. The right way round it's:

If there's a bustle in your hedgerow, don't be alarmed now, it's just a spring-clean for the May-queen. Yes there are two paths you can go by, but in the long run, there's still time to change the road you're on.

What's it all about? Goodness knows. If you play it backwards, something that was hard to do with a record player but is now easy, it's been suggested that what you hear is:

So here's to my sweet Satan, the one whose little path would make me sad; whose power is Satan; he'll give you 666. There was a little tool shed, where he made us suffer, sad Satan.

So that's what practitioners of dark magick do when they're not kissing goats' arses, drinking the blood of infants or desecrating churches: laboriously playing music backwards and listening out for nonsense messages. Version the first seems to suggest that too much Tolkien-inspired reading material leads to terminal tweeness, and version the second seems to imply that Satanism damages the language centres of the brain – and makes you a bit twee as well: 'sweet Satan'? 'little path'? 'little tool shed'? Sounds a bit like Evil and a bit like Enid Blyton. Backmasking, as the deliberate use of reversed sound is called, was a technique originally developed as part of *musique concrète*, but although Led Zeppelin were regarded as degenerate and demonic, enticing young people into sweet Satan's tool shed to give them 666 by playing records backwards was probably a too far out, even for them.

One evening while listening to Led Zeppelin via a music streaming site, I accidentally selected an instrumental version of 'Stairway to Heaven' and ended up listening to it all the way through, because I realised for the first time (this time around) that it was a masterpiece, because I got past the words and the vocals, and heard the music. Mind you, I was quite drunk. But I think that if you ditch all the tweeness and pomp, on this album you've still got 'Black Dog', 'Rock and Roll' and the music for 'Stairway to Heaven' which, for an album that I revered and then despised, is pretty good forty years on. I also like 'When the Levee Breaks' (7:07), but having heard the original by Kansas Joe McCoy and Memphis Minnie (3:11), it could be argued that on some occasions less might be more.

It's not just about philately, though. These stamps are commemorations of rock/pop albums as mainstream culture, National Treasures, Secular Icons. Rather than visual artefacts in their own right, these small rectangles operate as reminders of the original LPs; if the albums themselves are uppercase Icons, then the stamps are lowercase icons, just like the little rectangles you click on your desktop. They activate links to full-sized images on the screens in our memories; to auditory, visual, tactile and maybe even olfactory and gustatory stimuli; to emotions, ideas and associations; and they have a PLAY ▶ function as well. They're as much for the benefit of the storytelling homunculus in his bone-house as they are for you, here, now, sticking them on the corner of an envelope. Music is everywhere, even in places where it's not playing, places where the cues are so tiny you hardly notice them. These stamps are the buttons on an imaginary jukebox, piping nostalgia into our heads.

But if you really want a square inch that works visually, as well as a different cover by Pink Floyd and a different one by Bowie, and as well as keeping *Tubular Bells*, *London Calling*, and *Screamadelica*, you could pick another five stamps from the likes of

> *Before And After Science* (or *Music For Airports* or *The Plateau Of Mirror* or *On Land*) – Brian Eno
> *Brain Salad Surgery* – Emerson, Lake and Palmer (even though it's kind of a gatefold)
> *Damned, Damned, Damned* – the Damned
> *In The Court Of The Crimson King* – King Crimson (even though it's a gatefold)
> *The Magic Whip* – Blur (no idea what it sounds like)
> *Motörhead* – Motörhead
> *Music Complete* – New Order

Never Mind The Bollocks, Here's The Sex Pistols – Sex Pistols

Peter Gabriel III – (the 'pizza' photo) Peter Gabriel

154 – Wire

Selected Ambient Works, 85-92 – Aphex Twin

The Slider – T Rex

Sticky Fingers – the Rolling Stones

The White Album (or *Abbey Road*) – the Beatles

Leaving aside the debatable visual impact of tiny squares, and their undoubted pressability as buttons on your nostalgiaphone, perhaps the most telling thing about these stamps is the poignant, tacit suggestion that LPs are somehow 'better' than CDs: all the album covers reveal a tantalising edge of black vinyl peeping out, just to make the point. And this was before the recent re-fetishisation of vinyl as desirable artefact, retro plaything and, largely, waste of money.

1975

Seven LPs. Some of them were by Genesis and Tangerine Dream, both of whom I also went to see that year. By myself. I saw a lot of bands by myself. Didn't everyone? I think I know the answer to that question.

I saw Genesis a day or so after returning from a trip to Germany. This was the band's last hurrah as an extension of Peter Gabriel's peculiar imagination and love of dressing up. There were the songs and there was the impenetrable text (I've still got the concert programme); there was a succession of bizarre costumes; there were slide projections; and there was Gabriel himself as Rael, anti-hero of *The Lamb Lies Down on Broadway* rock-opera multimedia *Gesamtkunstwerk*. It was ambitious, incomprehensible, overblown, and therefore profound. At the end of the evening I emerged numbed and confused. What struck me then and now was Peter Gabriel's appearance – short hair, narrow jeans, white T-shirt and black leather jacket. This New York street punk (still in the old sense) was at the time an exotic look, and pointed to a future that no-one there, including, Peter Gabriel, could have anticipated.

Tangerine Dream also pointed to the future in unexpected ways. On Thursday 16 October they played in Liverpool Cathedral, the perfect venue for a trio of experimental cosmic rock musicians from Germany, back when what they were doing still was experimental and cosmic. The sound of their music was in between the harsh electronic noise they started out with and the new-age elevator music that followed once they had been caught up and copied by everyone else.

The fact that there was an everyone else catching them up and copying them shows how far ahead and far out Tangerine Dream were for a while. Julian Cope even included their first four albums among his top fifty LPs in the mini-masterpiece *Krautrocksampler*,[4] but nothing from the time after they left the German Ohr label and signed to Virgin after Mike Oldfield and Faust, just before Gong. That was when they became more well known; when they started acquiring roomfuls of state-of-the-art equipment that you could now fit in your pocket; when they began their inexorable slide down the slippery slope into cheesiness, and became a big, gooey Edgar Froese fondue. Their music certainly became more accessible after signing to Virgin, but electronic music that failed to rock was still widely regarded as inauthentic and unmusicianly. The first two Virgin LPs, *Phaedra* (1974) and *Rubycon* (1975), now sound like early masterpieces of chilly ambience. The third, *Ricochet* (also 1975), was what I experienced in Liverpool Cathedral, at ridiculously high volume, immersed in throbbing bass and lit by cold blue light.

There are actually two cathedrals in Liverpool. One is a massive, neo-gothic, red sandstone Anglican edifice officially known as the Cathedral Church of Christ. The other is a modernist conical concrete Catholic structure,

---

4   *Electronic Meditation* (1970, no. 43), *Alpha Centauri* (1971, no. 44), *Atem* (1973, no. 45), *Zeit* (1972, no. 46) .

officially known as Liverpool Metropolitan Cathedral. In true Liverpool fashion (part ironic, part heroic, part sentimental) the Protestant and Catholic cathedrals are connected by a road called Hope Street.

From the laying of the first stone in 1904, the Cathedral Church of Christ took 74 years to build, so when Tangerine Dream played there it still wasn't finished. It's a vast space, the largest cathedral in Britain. It has the highest and heaviest peal of church bells in the world, and probably the largest operational organ – more than 10,000 pipes, though Tangerine Dream never got to play it, which was a shame. On the same tour, they also played in Coventry Cathedral. Both cities were badly bombed during World War II – Liverpool's cathedral was damaged and Coventry's was completely destroyed – so the temporary occupation of these two buildings by Germans for an evening of cosmic experimental music was a strange and wonderful thing. You might wonder why Tangerine Dream didn't play in the more modern Metropolitan Cathedral, and the reason relates to what happened the previous year at Reims in France. Unfortunately, about five thousand people turned up at the 13th century cathedral for an event that had been organised with a thousand or two in mind, and as a consequence there were some crowd management and public hygiene issues, after which Tangerine Dream were formally banned from all Catholic places of worship. Which is why in 1975 they played at Coventry Cathedral, Liverpool Cathedral and York Minster.

Three days after my sixteenth birthday, my dad dropped me off by the huge doors of the Cathedral Church of Christ, and I joined all the freaks milling about outside, me in my blue woollen polo neck, indigo jeans and parka. As we, the freaks (I included myself), entered the cavernous interior we were handed leaflets headed A WELCOME FROM THE DEAN, and a bit later we were asked from the pulpit to enjoy ourselves in a way that would benefit the music, the surroundings and the greater glory of God. As far as I remember, everyone did, though I could be wrong.

If you have ever listened to *Ricochet*, imagine hearing it for the first time, unbelievably loud, in a huge vaulted, chilly, reverberant stone space more than 180m long, 60m wide and 50m high. Imagine you're only just sixteen, and sometimes you're lying on your back, staring up into the darkness, and sometimes you're sitting cross-legged, watching the three German longhairs in front of you, seated in their pools of blue light, making continuous tiny movements with their hands, and all the while you're trying to connect these tiny movements with the massive pulsing booming sound you're sitting inside, sometimes closing your eyes and seeing shifting patterns on the insides of your eyelids, patterns that vibrate with the cool vibrating air, the cool vibrating floor and your warm vibrating guts.

Imagine you're quite close to the band. Then imagine that every so often you stand up, feeling horribly conspicuous because everyone else is sitting or lying down, and all the time you're standing up you're an annoying silhouette of a sixteen-year-old in a polo neck and a parka fumbling with a camera, hurriedly firing off a flashcube on your Instamatic then dropping to the floor again, face burning with embarrassment even in the dark. Then imagine that, after sending off the film and getting back the carton of slides, the images look great, even though what they show are banks of scuffed, knobby, buttony, switchy surfaces almost obscuring three separate, static, seated musicians in denim and long hair, frozen flat in flashlight and a perhaps even a bit like the cover of *Piledriver*, only sitting down with keyboards and a single white guitar – showing all of this rather than, say, luminous blue mermen in the sapphire depths of a dark cathedral ocean, conjuring a pulsing vortex of crystalline sound that rises from the depths to ascend and spiral out across the solar system.

Now imagine that it's after the concert, you've met some school friends who were also there, and you're getting a lift home from a compliant dad. Travelling through the Mersey Tunnel, you're all talking loudly (being temporarily deafened and very excited), earnestly (being sixteen and taking your music seriously), and all at once about how the keyboard is now *The Instrument*, the Future Of Music. At the time you're partly right, then a bit later you're terribly wrong, yet you end up being completely right in ways you could never have imagined.

1976

Thirty-six LPs – things were expanding in all directions. It was a time of transition. Van der Graaf Generator, Doctor Feelgood, Faust, Alex Harvey. Camel, Genesis, Yes, Jethro Tull.

Assuming, perhaps unkindly, that the names of the support acts are irrelevant, the nine bands I saw included Doctor Feelgood (insane), Camel (gently likeable), Rick Wakeman (turgid in sparkly cape; and one of the band played a guitar with *three necks*), Eddie and the Hot Rods (insane) and Steve Hillage (as cosmic and engaging as you could be in a venue like the Liverpool Empire Theatre).

At the end of the year I bought my first single, 'Anarchy In The UK'. Some people claim to have thrown all their old records away when they heard punk. Not me, though I did sell some of them in Skeleton.

1977

Twenty-two LPs; not that many, but they included the debut albums by the Stranglers, the Clash, the Jam, Television, the Damned, the Sex Pistols and the Boomtown Rats. My identity crisis, or eclectic tastes, also took in Gong and Blue Oyster Cult; the Stooges and Pink Floyd; Van der Graaf Generator and Tangerine Dream, which is the way it should be. Never trust a purist.

The only bands I got to see were the Jam, the Stranglers and Steve Hillage again, along with their respective support acts. I also bought a lot of singles, took my A-levels and, by the way, Elvis died, and the Queen had her silver jubilee.

1978

Seventy-six LPs, sixty-four bands, about half of which I saw at the Reading festival.

This was the year I left school, signed on and then got a job at a petrol station. It was my second job, the first being the paper round I had during various school holidays to buy LPs like *Tommy*, *Dark Side of the Moon* and *Tubular Bells*. At the petrol station, some of the time I worked with a man called Phil who had served in Northern Ireland. When I rather inanely asked him what it was like, he shrugged and didn't say very much. Phil had shaggy hair and long sideburns, and his huge forearms were covered with tattoos, which I tried not to look at but couldn't help myself because I hadn't been that close to such a large area of tattoos before.

Apart from the Spiderman one. Every year, the Sunday School organised a summer outing to somewhere in Wales, we always went by bus, and I was always sick. One year the outing was to somewhere with an outdoor swimming pool. Although it was a sunny day, the water was cold and covered with a slimy skin of stalks and leaves from nearby trees. Trying to avoid this mess and prevent it sticking to my face and shoulders, I noticed a man sitting at the edge of the pool with his back to me. There were two reasons I noticed him. One was because his back was burned red by the sun. The other was because, on his red back, lit by a shaft of late afternoon sun, was a Spiderman tattoo. It covered the entire surface, from his glowing shoulder blades all the way down to the base of his spine, a huge image of Spidey in suitably athletic pose accompanied by POW, IT'S YOUR FRIENDLY NEIGHBOURHOOD SPIDERMAN! set off with a large expanse of web. I can't remember whether the spelling of NEIGHBOURHOOD was British or American, but I assume it was British otherwise I would have thought that it wasn't spelled right,[5] because I always noticed things like that, which is perhaps why I later spent many years working as a proofreader.

Dick and Mac both had ancient, inept tattoos. I met them after I got fed up working at the petrol station and got a job in a factory. This was my first proper full-time job with proper disposable income, so I made sure I disposed of it – on LPs, gigs and beer. I also saved enough to go to the Reading festival, and to buy a decent stereo – a silver Pioneer amp, a grey Pioneer turntable that felt like it was made of concrete, and a pair of big speakers. I kept this setup for years because it was nice and big, it was nice and heavy and it was nice and loud. When my mum drove me down to Oxford at the end of that summer, the car contained me, a suitcase of clothes, my heavy stereo boxes and my heavy record boxes. And, heaviest of all, a deep sense of foreboding.

Working in a factory was a strange experience. As well as money, I felt it gave me some much-needed authenticity because it was noisy and hot and was full of tough, confident, sweary people who hadn't been to a school like mine. I tried to talk like them, but I don't think I fooled anyone into believing I was tough or confident, though I was quite sweary. I don't think anyone else there liked the same music as me, which surprised and disappointed me – weren't working class people meant to like punk?

Mac was an ancient, hunched, toothless, bleary-eyed, wild-looking, foul-mouthed old fucker who did something or other, though I never worked out what, apart from the fact that it involved a foccchen gondola, and that the foccchen gondola was always focked. I couldn't make out a word he said apart from 'foccchen... foccchen... foccchen...', each 'foccchen' sounding like he was about to bring up a lump of phlegm the size and colour of a Werther's Original. Dick was about the same age as Mac, plumper and better preserved, with more teeth, and he said fookin rather than

---

5   Ironically, if the British spelling had been used, this would have been incorrect, as the original was of course American

foccchen. He was easier to understand, in fact compared to Mac he sounded like Alec Guinness. Dick had been in the navy, and had a limited repertoire of stories that he recycled tirelessly whoever he was working with, wheezing helplessly at the funny bits so we knew when to laugh. For me, after having listened endlessly to Peter Cook and Dudley Moore's ramblings on *Derek and Clive Live* at Radar's house and learned the filthiest bits off by heart, Dick's best story was one he didn't even know he was telling. It was the one where him and his mates were in fookin Egypt they went to look for some fookin women and they found this fookin place where there was this room with a hole in the fookin wall and you could fookin look through it and fookin watch a man and woman, like, you know… *together*.

The factory produced cereals, cake mixes and ice cream mixes. Where I worked it was cornflakes. I got to wear overalls and work boots and work jeans for real, and wore my boots and jeans when I wasn't at work, especially at Eric's and ultimately at Oxford as well: set off with my British Rail guard's jacket, it must have looked a bit odd. The factory was old, dirty and leaky, and, being a cornflake factory, what it leaked was cornflakes, so much so that there were trolleys and bins all around the place to catch all the flakes that fell in showers from leaky ducts and pipes like the sun god's eczema.

I worked for Hygiene, who did all the dirty jobs like emptying the bins, cleaning the toilets and clearing up cornflakes. Hygiene wore brown overalls, Process wore white, and the reclusive fitters wore oily dark blue. The factory was unbelievably hot and noisy. While I was sweeping up around the huge machines with my ear defenders on, in amongst the relentless roaring noise I could often make out industrial-sounding music like 'Mass Production', the dark dissonant track at the end of Iggy Pop's album *The Idiot*. Cornflakes constantly fell like autumn leaves into large strategically placed bins, and were constantly needing to be swept off the floor around the machines. When the bins were full they were wheeled away and their contents tipped into a room already adrift with cornflakes with a large metal funnel at its centre: the Grinder. When I was assigned to feed the Grinder, the cornflakes often came past my knees as I shovelled them down the funnel, and all the time more bins arrived and more cornflakes were tipped out. If you shovelled too slow you started to disappear; if you shovelled too fast the Grinder ground to a halt you had to go and get a fitter, which gave you a break but meant that when you re-started you found yourself half-buried in a slowly shifting dune of cornflakes. I once found a screwdriver buried there, and I've still got it. I've also still got a piece of a drive chain from one of the big machines that steamed the corn kernels and rolled them flat before they were dried into flakes. It's like a bike chain, but off a very big bike: fifteen links, each about three inches long and two inches wide, and the whole thing weighs about fifteen pounds. It was lying in the yard where the fitters would sit smoking fags and drinking tea. I asked one of them if I could have it; he looked a bit puzzled, but said he didn't see me take it. I got it to my locker, but it was hard getting it out of the factory in an empty cornflake packet, pretending I was carrying a box of cereal. For a while I used to dream about cornflakes, and before I went to sleep that was were all I could see when I closed my eyes.

Before the cornflakes there was the elation of leaving school, there was Eric's, there was the Clash in Victoria Park, there was working in a petrol station. After cornflakes there was still Eric's, and there was hitch-hiking to and from the Reading festival. I travelled with Des, who I knew from Covenanters. My dad was one of those who ran the group; his dad was a missionary who had spent years in India. That year we decided to go on the Covies' summer outing to Southport and do it semi-ironically. Over lunch, as I photographed the sparrows eating our sandwich crumbs next to my work boots with their cornflake encrustations that I couldn't be bothered scraping off and didn't completely want to, I evangelised about punk rock and he seemed interested, so I told him that Magazine were playing at Eric's that night and he seemed interested in that as well, so I took him along to Eric's and we saw Magazine, who were amazing. Two weeks after that he came along again and saw the Clash, who were amazing as well, so a couple of months after that we hitch-hiked to Reading and back together, and that was also amazing, and the only festival I went to until about 30 years later in 2007, when I started camping in the grounds of the Belladrum estate outside Inverness.

1978 was a year of contrasts. I went from a quite posh quasi-public school to the novelty of signing on, to petrol pumps and cornflakes, to a preoccupation with punk rock, and a rock festival. After this came the profound disillusion that was a term at Oxford – a miserable, intense twelve-week blur spent immersed in archaic beauty and impossible privilege, Victorian literature, beer, punk rock, beer, street burgers, beer, chips and ketchup, beer, Smash, beer, and Vesta curries. And beer. By Christmas I looked pale, thin and unhealthy, which upset my mum almost as much as it had upset her to drive away and leave me in Oxford with my clothes, stereo, record boxes and sense of foreboding.

1979

Twenty LPs, sixty-three bands.

After Christmas and my Big Decision, I had to go back down to Oxford to break the news to my tutor, who seemed pretty relaxed about the whole thing, though he did look askance at my studded wrist band as he shook me by the hand and wished me well. He must have meant it, though, because on the strength of his reference I got a place at Sheffield University without even attending an interview. Before that, I spent the best part of a year at home on the dole as a rather self-satisfied drop-out, much to the concern of my parents, and I saw a lot of Radar, who had adopted a similar attitude and lifestyle. I also saw a lot of a rather troublesome girlfriend I had somehow acquired (she acquired me, that's how). Then, in the autumn I found myself in Sheffield, where

I settled in straight away, had a blast and spent enough time studying to be awarded a degree.

Sixty-three bands. Three of them were mod bands – the Purple Hearts, the Merton Parkas and the Mods. I didn't like any of them.

Not only were the Purple Hearts terrible when we saw them in London at the Marquee, but in the preceding hours Radar and I in our bike jackets and black jeans spent what may or may not have been a long time attempting to evade a boisterous bunch of mods and skinheads who followed us wherever we went (just for a laugh, it turned out when, in desperation, I decided to go and speak to them).

The Purple Hearts at the Marquee came about because one night someone I knew in Eric's asked me if I knew of anywhere that three punk girls from London could stay for the night and I, being drunk and quite fancying one of them, suggested my house, yeah, what the hell, why not. So that's what happened. I got these girls into the house, then stumbled and blundered about in the dark for a while, whispering at the top of my voice, finding blankets and sleeping bags and making mugs of tea, then my mum appeared to see what all the noise was. Despite being more than a little bit taken aback to see these exotic black-eyed creatures in leathers and leopardskin dossing down in the lounge, she made sure they had everything they needed, said good night and went back to bed. Next day she made them breakfast and my dad drove them over to Lime Street Station. Before leaving the girls gave me a phone number and address in London, and that's why Radar and I decided to go to London, dropped off by his mum, who was driving to France, leaving us to be stalked by mods and skinheads before seeing the Purple Hearts, because that was who was playing at the Marquee. They weren't very good and the girls weren't interested in us, though they did let us sleep on their floor before we grumpily hitched home.

The Merton Parkas weren't very good either. I saw them in Liverpool immediately afterwards, and to add insult to injury a French boy called Jean-Pierre spent the entire gig trying to feel me up. I'd been introduced to him by Davey

Jones, my former English teacher who was widely recognised as an all-round Good Bloke. Jean-Pierre was staying with Jonesy and his wife, who seemed to always have bohemian and/or foreign people staying with them, *and* they knew Roger McGough, something Jonesy never tired of telling us in English lessons. Jonesy's hair was quite long – it fell over the back of his collar, long enough for him to talk semi-jokingly about the Headmaster telling him to get it cut. He was sufficiently hip for us to semi-believe him, and it seemed like the kind of thing Syph would do: we knew he referred to staff by their surnames, so it seemed logical he would tell them if he thought they needed a haircut.

Anyway, Jonesy phoned me up and asked me in a matey kind of way to take Jean-Pierre to Eric's and 'show him a good time', which I did, only not in the way Jean-Pierre was expecting. It meant that while we were standing in the small crowd watching the Merton Parkas I had to sort-of-nearly-dance every so often to keep away from his hands and thighs, the kind of thing girls have to put up with all the time. I sort-of-nearly-danced, even though it was the Merton Parkas and I didn't like them, apart from their version of 'Tears of a Clown' which I liked (because it was 'Tears Of A Clown') but Jean-Pierre didn't.

The Mods were terrible when I saw them in Sheffield, and I can't remember anything else about them.

1980

Seventeen LPs, seventy-six bands.

I saw another three mod bands. There was a mod revival of kinds happening at the tail end of the seventies and into the eighties, and there was two-tone as well. I tried to like it, and was reasonably successful. I saw Madness and the Specials and the Selecter at the Top Rank in Sheffield and ran on the spot a bit because that was what you did. Two-tone sounded like ska, until Madness and the Specials outgrew it and the Selecter more or less disappeared. Ska was so itchy and catchy you couldn't not like it, and for a while chicka-chicka-chicka songs were everywhere, with ska songs on Top of the Pops and at all the university discos because even students could dance to ska: all you had to do was run on the spot. Unless you were in Madness, and especially if you were called Chas Smash, in which case you moved like a Gerry Anderson puppet on elastic strings. When I first heard Madness's single 'The Prince' on John Peel it sounded like psychedelic reggae quirking out on too many caffeine tablets in a bouncy castle. And when I saw them on 'Top of the Pops' that's how they looked as well, in suits.

The Specials supported the Clash in 1978 as the Coventry Specials when Des and I saw them at Eric's, and they were miserable as anything, especially Terry Hall. A few years later, just as the early sun was rising on the Saturday morning after the Friday night before, in June 1981 I found myself wandering about in the almost deserted Moss Side Centre, shopping for cartons of milk and grapefruit juice, and the ingredients for a stew (liver, potatoes, carrots, swede, onions, Oxo). The psychedelically creepy 'Ghost Town' was playing wherever I went, and as it followed me around, reverberating off the glass, concrete, metal and plastic surfaces, it made me aware that hardly ever had a song and a time and a place been so perfectly made for each other.

I tried to like some mod music, but apart from 'Time for Action' by Secret Affair's hookiness I pretty much failed, and was quite relieved, despite John Peel's enthusiasm. A mod revival. Talk about desperate. Two-tone was ska, a choppy poppy progenitor of reggae that could quite plausibly be gobbled up by the Clash and all the other bands. Mod, on the other hand, was more like poppy soul, which to me was slicker and far more threatening, associated with discotheques, smart clothes, natty dancing, and scooters. I mean, who wanted to look *smart*? Mods did. At primary school ten years earlier I had desperately wanted a parka, not because parkas were either smart or scruffy, and not because mods wore them, but because everyone else had one. And it seemed everyone else apart from me had a Ben Sherman shirt; and everyone else wore long trousers and then zip-up ankle boots or slip-ons to school before I did. I eventually got long trousers and zip-up ankle boots and slip-ons, but I never got a Ben Sherman shirt.[6] But I did get finally get a parka: it was a fish-tail with quilted red lining and a grey fur trim round the hood. Despite this I was more of a rocker than a mod on the inside, and scruffy rather than smart on the outside, ever since I was able to understand the difference and do anything about it.

I never wished I had a suit or a scooter. I was always in awe of faded jeans, leather jackets, and big noisy motorbikes. To pre-adolescent and early adolescent me, motorcyclists and rockers (they weren't called bikers back then) were wild, exotic and cool; they were barbarian superheroes. Triumphs and Nortons and, when I saw pictures of them, choppers, were mighty fuck-off space ships from a distant, dangerous dimension. These beings and their machines seemed both magnificent and terrible to behold, they were awesome to hear, they were the horrible antithesis of everything I had been brought up to be and to believe in. Consequently, the shock and awe of them, for a while at least, made me weak at the knees.

The equation was: Hair + Leather + Denim + Bikes = Power x Noise x Rebellion = Rock. I had no Hair to speak of, no Leather, and no Bike, though I did have Denim. And thusly I felt I possessed the Power of Rock and the Noise of Rock and the Rebellion of Rock, which in turn meant I had the Rock of Rock. And every parental tut, every disapproving comment, every outraged news report made me go yeah-yeah-yeah and want more-more-more, even early on, even

---

6 Though a few years ago I did buy a Ben Sherman T-shirt, from Debenham's in Stirling. We were going on holiday and I realised I had forgotten to bring any T-shirts, so my birthday that year was spent trawling humiliatingly through clothes shops. The Ben Sherman was grey and had a guitar on it: what's not to like? The other T-shirts were Fruit of the Loom, bought from a factory seconds shop and much cheaper.

in my parka, which had a quilted red lining, just like it was a secret bike jacket.

This fascination persisted for a number of years until during my brief term at Oxford 1978 I got to attend a question-and-answer session and book signing with the fantasy author Michael Moorcock, who was for a while my teenage literary hero. It was laid on by some college literary society or other in some dark panelled room or other, and there was free wine. Michael Moorcock had been my literary hero on account of two things. *Secondly*, his connection with Hawkwind, which meant a lot to me because it connected literature and poetry with rock. Michael Moorcock was therefore an alchemist, an incarnation of the almost mystical process by which the base metal of ordinary words were transmuted into LPs of golden lyrics, golden music and golden artwork. I loved the fact that Michael Moorcock worked with Hawkwind, and the fact that the band had songs called 'Damnation Alley' and 'Lord Of Light' (sci-fi novels by Roger Zelazny); and a song called 'The Iron Dream' (a sci-fi novel by Norman Spinrad). And Bowie had obviously read books like *The Man Who Sold The Moon* and *Starman Jones* by Robert Heinlein; and Yes had a song called 'Starship Trooper', which was also a Heinlein book. I loved liking Literature and Art and Music, and I loved the idea of connecting these things, weaving a web of knowledge and association and allusion that included more or less everything I was interested in or thought I ought to be interested in. So I loved the fact that 'Supper's Ready' off the Genesis album *Foxtrot* was full of references to the book of Revelation; and that 'Watcher Of The Skies' off the same album was based on the sci-fi novel *Childhood's End* by Arthur C Clarke, and the title of the song was from a line in a sonnet by John Keats called 'On First looking into Chapman's Homer.'

Really:

> *Then felt I like some watcher of the skies*
> *When a new planet swims into his ken*

Or like stout Cortez, when with eagle eyes
He stared at the Pacific—and his men
Look'd at each other with a wild surmise

This was part of John Keats's response on reading George Chapman's translation of *The Odyssey*. And if you looked carefully at the opening credits of 'University Challenge' a few years ago, you might actually have seen these lines swirling about for a few seconds as they wove themselves in amongst all the other quotations and equations and diagrams that formed, and still form, the rich and varied tapestry of our higher education TV quiz heritage. I've no idea how I noticed this, but I did. That's what my mind was like and still is. So I liked the fact that 'The Cinema Show' off *Selling England By The Pound* by Genesis was a rewriting of lines 215–56 from the 'Fire Sermon' section of TS Eliot's *The Waste Land*. But as much as liking the fact that that's where the songs come from, I liked the fact that I knew about or could find out about all these connections, could see in my mind the golden threads stretching from node to node, joining songs to poems to novels to pictures to films in one vast gleaming web of interconnected knowledge. So of course I liked the idea of ELP's *Pictures At An Exhibition*; I probably liked the idea more than the music itself. I looked for novelistic, poetic, musical, painterly and occult allusions everywhere, and, being quite well read for my age, I found them, and I treasured them. It all helped to validate the ambition and complexity of the clever, serious music I loved so much, connecting it with an older, larger and more profound tradition of European culture that I was discovering at school, and it all made me feel like I was part of a powerful secret society.

But even without the Hawkwind connection, I liked Michael Moorcock *firstly* because I had devoured dozens of his books about Dorian Hawkmoon and other characters with names like Corum Jhaelen Irsei, Erekosë, Jherek Carnelian, Jerry Cornelius and Elric of Melniboné. These characters, about 20 of them, were all incarnations of the

Eternal Champion, a being who was a warrior forever, sometimes fighting the forces of Chaos and sometimes the forces of Law, keeping the multiverse in balance and at the same time trying to come to terms with his own nature. I became absorbed in, no, I hurled myself headlong into, this sweeping panorama of anguished heroism, mythic struggle, febrile imagination and ripping yarns for a number of years along with all the other mainly Klaw-derived books that I hoovered up.

Anyway, there we were, students quaffing wine with a clearly uncomfortable Michael Moorcock, and after several glasses and a bit of Q&A hero worship, someone finally asked him about Hawkwind. He was quite evasive at first, being at an Oxford college and wanting to promote his new Jerry Cornelius book, *The Condition Of Muzak*, but he did eventually get round to talking about the band, and about the bikers who had hung about with them. He remembered them as rather unpleasant individuals, with poor impulse control and prone to violent outbursts. Even worse, they were really boring. You had to look interested when they talked about their bikes, or told their drinking, fighting, riding and shagging tales, in case they took offence and turned nasty. On hearing his diffident but emphatic rejection, I was disappointed but not surprised. For some time one of my brothers had been working as a motorcycle mechanic, and I had via him got to know a number of barbarian superheroes. And guess what, most of them turned out to be racist, sexist, xenophobic, homophobic bike bores. Even worse, they wore flares and they liked really shit music.

Even so, I still wanted a bike jacket. I had no intention of buying a bike – all I wanted was the jacket. When I finally got it I loved it, and I liked to think it made Radar jealous, though he never admitted it. He never admitted it – he just went out later and bought a cheaper imitation. And then he bought a pair of black vinyl trousers, something I wanted to wear but never had the nerve. And he dyed his hair ginger, something else I would never have dared to do. And every so often he painted his thumbnails black. Ditto.

And by the time I did buy a bike (blue Honda CG 125, from the shop where my brother worked) I had outgrown the jacket, and bought an inferior Lewis Leathers replacement, which was accompanied by another bike (white Honda CX 500, bought off my brother and subsequently sold back to him). And although I gave this jacket away to a friend's son when it was too small to wear, after all these years I'm still a closet rocker, because the Belstaff is still there in the closet next to my suit.

Playlist 9 - An Anatomy Of Lists		
Tubular Bells (Part One)	Mike Oldfield	*Tubular Bells*
When The Levee Breaks	Kansas Joe McCoy and Memphis Minnie	
I Wanna Be Me	Sex Pistols	
A Sprinkling Of Clouds	Gong	*You*
Look Into The Sun	Jethro Tull	*Stand Up*
Get Out Of Denver	Eddie and the Hot Rods	
The Tears Of A Clown	Smokey Robinson	
The Prince	Madness	
Watcher Of The Skies	Genesis	*Genesis Live*
Ghost Town	The Specials	

To listen to the playlists, visit Spotify using the QR links provided.

Links to every playlist are also at www.hungry-ghost.info, along with photographs and archive material to supplement each chapter and enhance the reading/listening experience, just like a great big gatefold album cover.

9

DISCREET MACHINE MUSIC

Suddenly, the seventies ended and so did my careful lists; glam-rock, prog-rock, pub-rock and punk-rock all mutated, shrivelled or died, and along came post-punk, industrial, indie, New Romantics, electro, hip-hop, the eighties, the nineties, post-rock, the twenty-first century, the third millennium and the rest of my life. When 1980 arrived I found myself conga-ing precariously down a friend's icy front path yelling happy new year and happy new decade, part of a long intoxicated line of revellers: she was having a party, her mum was out, and it seemed she knew everyone from Eric's.

It all just sort of happened: for seven years I kept these careful lists of LPs and gigs, because that's that sort of person I was, and then something changed. By the time I realised something had changed, I couldn't remember everything I'd bought or where I'd been any more, and it was too late to write it all down. Seven years of lists. That was more than a third of my life, so at first the feeling that there was something missing made me a bit anxious, like I hadn't done my homework or brushed my teeth. I got over it, though I didn't stop spending money on records and I didn't stop going to gigs – I couldn't. What changed was that the lists were becoming a chore at a time when I considered myself far too crazy for anything regular and systematic – apart from disordering my senses, reading books and writing essays. I have since realised that I am not crazy at all, not in the way I thought I was.

Like any other old decade that became a new decade, some things were changing and some things weren't, and although ten years is a convenient period for measuring change, it's not necessarily an accurate one. The new decade felt different for me, though, and it felt right, for three reasons – I was in the north of England, I wasn't in Oxford, and I wasn't miserable.

Having wrapped myself in a tribal late-seventies security blanket of bike jacket, narrow jeans and boots, I was still blissfully swaddled in it as the eighties got underway. It removed any worry about what to wear – the same things all the time, often without even washing them. But although bike jackets were still fashionable and always had been because, let's face it, a lot of punks looked like rockers with novelty hairstyles or bikers with narrow trousers, I couldn't help noticing that there were more and more other, differently dressed people on the streets of Sheffield, Leeds, Liverpool and Manchester. Many of the ones who weren't mods or skinheads had floppy fringes and some of them, boys and girls, were wearing eyeliner. And there were long grey macs as well. I never had a long grey mac, though predictably I had wanted an army greatcoat for years. Unfortunately, by the time I bought one I realised it was too late to wear it, which didn't stop me for a while, until I sold it to a student in Oxford who must have been even more unfashionable than I was. I did briefly wear a belted beige mac, with white jeans, white rugby shirt, black waistcoat, black studded belt and black flying boots. I was working on my own, unique look.

The first band I saw in Sheffield were a power-poppy good-timey punk band from Ireland called the Starjets. They played at one of the halls of residence during freshers' week, and I was far too aloof to like them. Bogey was also at Sheffield, and was a lot more open and straightforward than I was, didn't have a bike jacket and thought the band were great, which they probably were. But having been to university already *and* been a drop-out, I considered myself more sophisticated and jaded than other first-years: eager, slightly hysterical fresh-faced freshers a year younger than me and therefore just as naive and unformed as I had been, and in many ways still was. During the gig, I slouched about at the front of the stage, still in my jacket even though it was boiling hot, watching as the band grinned at everyone and everything and leapt about enthusiastically. While leaning on the edge of the stage, conspicuously not dancing, I occasionally made eye contact with a short-haired girl in a bike jacket and dark eye make-up on the other side of the hall. She was dancing in an understated robotic way, just the top half of her body swinging from side to side, one hand pressed to the side of her head. My kind of dancing, I decided, though the fact that she seemed to be looking at me whenever I was looking at her freaked me out a bit. At the end of the gig I felt I needed more beer before deciding what to do next, so overwhelming was this potential opportunity. By the time I had bought a pint she had disappeared.

The weekend after that I went home and saw Crass at Eric's. Crass were a strange mixture of angry, dumb, smart, hardcore, and experimental. It made perfect sense that they were originally formed by angry older middle-class 'drummer' Penny Rimbaud and angry younger working class 'vocalist' Steve Ignorant. The lyrics were for the most part angry-dumb-hardcore, and the music was as well, a tinny rattling band-saw sound that complemented the vocals and didn't do the band any favours. Despite the shouty Cockney vocal style and sweary lyrics, they weren't what you might have expected if all you'd read was sneering reviews by the likes of Tony Parsons and Garry Bushell.[1] They were anarchist hippies with short hair and dissenting attitudes, a perverse, eccentric, unsettling, mixture of throwback and anticipation. They handed out leaflets with strange poems and collages on them; they had their own dour but compelling dyed-black military surplus look that avoided any rock star or

---

1 The band's name came from a description of fans in the song 'Ziggy Stardust'. Like many seventies misfits, Steve Ignorant was a Bowie fan, a Ziggy fan and therefore, according to Bowie as Ziggy, writing about him(self) in the third person along with Weird and Gilly, 'just crass'. Weren't we all.

personality issues; they had an eye-catching logo that looked like a cross, a swastika, a union jack, and a snake eating its own tail, which got stencilled everywhere; they included amazing photorealist montages by artist Gee Vaucher with their records; they had brilliantly stupid punk names like Steve Ignorant, Gem Stone, Phil Free, Virginia Creeper, Joy de Vivre and, best of all, NA Palmer, assuming that wasn't his real name; and they had strong, uncompromising views that encompassed pacifism, vegetarianism, feminism and anarchism (as opposed to anarchy). And they split up in 1984 after counting down to it with each release.[2]

Crass's contradictions were made more apparent and easier to appreciate when I learned that the band had been formed by Rimbaud in grief and rage following the unexplained death of a man called Wally Hope, previously Philip Russell, a gentle, naïve, eccentric individual who had been involved in the original Stonehenge free festival movement. Russell had emerged as Wally Hope from a self-identifying 'tribe of Wallies' who, when later prosecuted, ridiculed a legal system that was powerless to make them respect its rulings, and thereby claimed moral victory whatever the outcome. This was the dumb-smart power of names to challenge, reinvent and redefine and, in the case of the Wallies, avoid legal costs. Penny Rimbaud himself was born Jeremy Ratter and apparently changed his name by deed poll in 1977: 'Rimbaud' from the French poet; 'Penny' after being called a toilet-seat philosopher by his brother at a time when a penny was the required price for such a pastime.

My favourite Crass pieces (you couldn't really call them songs) came on cheap, imaginative experimental singles like 'Nagasaki Nightmare' and 'Bloody Revolutions'. When their 18-track 12" EP *The Feeding Of The 5,000* was first released, workers at the pressing plant refused to handle it because they considered the track 'Reality Asylum' blasphemous, so Crass replaced it with an empty track called 'The Sound

---

2   There have been intermittent re-formations, re-interpretations and
    reissues.

Of Free Speech' and on the lyric sheet included negative reviews written by Tony Parsons and Garry Bushell. Then they went and released 'Reality Asylum' by themselves. This was among their most intense, brilliant, experimental and political pieces, a deeply unsettling sound collage and feminist/anti-religion statement that was backed with a savage avant-feminist poetic rant (but in a good way) called 'Shaved Women'. Much of the time, though, listening to early Crass albums sounded a lot like being beaten up, then thrown downstairs, savaged by dogs and run over by a truck in order to make a point about how unfair life can be. And it was sometimes hard to get past the hysteria and the doggerel: 'Coronation Street' as grey puke, fucking shit; not giving a toss about the fucker who died on the cross, that kind of thing.

'Shaved Women' is about misogyny; it's an image that combines the punishment of women collaborators after World War II with the cosmetic shaving of female legs, armpits and genitals. It disarmingly simple, just tape loops, repetition and shouted fragments, ending with repeated screaming of the words 'in all your decadence, people die'. In this terse statement, rage and eloquence combine: alliteration, directness and repetition distil an idea down to six words, critiquing globalised consumer culture decades before we started watching reality shows about traumatised British softies being flown around the world to be filmed scrabbling about down sapphire mines and weeping over sewing machines in clothing factories.

I saw Crass because I was curious: they were despised in the music press and were politically, musically and artistically extreme at a time when this was still quite startling. As Radar and I arrived to get the train to Liverpool in our black security blankets, we were approached by two youths who asked us if we knew where Eric's was. Hey, do we look like punks or something? They were both Crass fans, both quietly-spoken Londoners and both extremely polite, but there the similarity ended. One was a grungy-looking punk with leather jacket, bondage trousers, kilt and spiked hair;

the other was a lean, dapper skinhead in narrow Levis, check shirt, two-tone jacket and shiny ox-blood DMs. We got them to Eric's, though it was a bit uncomfortable at times, some of the looks we got from other folk on their way to nights out that didn't involve Crass. Later I briefly caught sight of the kilt-boy standing on the edge of the packed stage doing a kind of slo-mo robo-dance like the one the Starjets girl had done, while Crass yelled and thrashed and sweated their way through their set. I couldn't make out a word, all the songs sounded the same, and the singer's face was bright red, the veins standing out like his head was going to burst. I knew his face was bright red because Crass only used white lights that stayed on all the time, there were no fancy pyrotechnics or strobes or dry ice or colours or entertainment or anything like that.

Not long after Crass I saw Artery, a quirky, angular Sheffield band; there were a lot of them. Like Manchester, Liverpool, Leeds and other places, Sheffield had its own music scene that included the Human League, They Must Be Russians, Cabaret Voltaire, Clock Dva, B Troop, Vendino Pact, Stunt Kites, De tian, Vice Versa, Disease, Veiled Threat, the Process, Repulsive Alien, Comsat Angels, I'm So Hollow, Shy Tots, Heaven 17, and Artery. Artery recorded a live album and I was there, but got nasty looks that I was too drunk to notice for remarking loudly between songs to whoever was next to me, 'Huh, the Psychedelic Furs are better'. They probably weren't, apart from on their first album, which I played to death.

A lot of these bands were post-punk even before punk, or would have been if the name had been around, but it was too early. A lot of them seemed to be using keyboards and tape recorders and electronic noise, or slide and film projections, or would dance around video monitors at a time when such behaviour was adventurous and futuristic. Strange as it may seem, in addition to being angry arty shouty spartan hippies, Crass were also adventurous and futuristic – when I saw them at Eric's there were video monitors standing on the stage showing I can't remember what, while they stood rooted to the spot and barked and slashed and bashed their way through their set.

An alternative history of the seventies, rather than being about rock, about different kinds of guitar band, from glam to prog to pub to punk and all the rest, would be about electronics. Not the big flashy banks of keyboards played by the likes of Keith Emerson and Rick Wakeman, but their cheap, mass produced bastard offspring, the kinds of instruments that the Human League used, affordable instruments for the masses. If Keith and Rick were in Jags, the Human League and their knob-twiddling chums were driving Ford Escorts.

The Human League seemed adventurous and futuristic and, like punk, the fact that they were barely competent didn't matter, or it did matter and was part of the point. Their singer Phil Oakey had the biggest, floppiest, most ridiculous fringe ever, and an ear-catchingly odd baritone voice. I heard their first single 'Being Boiled / Circus Of Death' on the radio in 1978, before I knew I was going to live in Sheffield, and it sounded alien, electronic and keyboardy in a way that was both pop and strange. 'Being Boiled' is still the only song I know of that takes a standpoint on the harvesting/killing of silkworms.[3] 'Circus Of Death' is of course about a circus of death, Steve McGarrett from 'Hawaii Five-O' and a drug called Dominion.

The Human League made me frown and made me smile. They also made me whoop with joy to see Captain Scarlet and Captain Kirk slide-projected on the walls of the venues they played. At the time, this sort of media appropriation was exhilarating and funny; it was something new because people hadn't been taking slide pictures off the TV for very long – I mean, why would they? It was thrillingly strange, enjoyably incompetent and low-budget, a recipe for perfect avant-garde pop. Synthesisers had been reclaimed from proggy musicians and expert soloists, and become

---

3   The first lines are is 'Listen to the voice of Buddha/saying stop your sericulture'.

amateurish, intuitive and exciting, as *Gesamtkunstwerk* became cheap multimedia. Here comes the future: it's the past now, of course, but the idea of more and more people playing this kind of music was, once, the future. Synthesisers were a new idea of what was to come, pointing the way to a different, almost guitar-free, futuristic new future populated by Kraftwerk, Suicide, the Human League, Devo, Ultravox, the Normal, Fad Gadget, Tubeway Army, Killing Joke, Throbbing Gristle, then Depeche Mode, the Pet Shop Boys, Yazoo, the Art of Noise, Soft Cell and everything else that followed on from them and made them the present and then the past, by which time I realised I had started losing interest.

They Must Be Russians used slides of World War II for some of their songs, the ones that were serious. One called 'Nagasaki's Children' was about the first atomic bomb; one called 'Circus' was about the Holocaust, and both were on their first EP. The band got their name from a foaming-at-the-mouth tabloid headline about the Sex Pistols, but they didn't sound like them: one of them played an acoustic guitar. He played it on 'Circus', a spooky ballad that was a question-and-answer exchange between a mother and her uncomprehending child in a concentration camp. 'Nagasaki's Children' was weirder and more electronic, with soft, slow, distorted drum machine, treated guitar and vocals, and heavily warped clarinet. One summer evening I was back in Birkenhead during the summer holidays, sitting in the Queen's Arms with various chums for yet another evening of beer, laughter, exaggeration and competitive abuse. Eager to impress with my eclectic tastes at a time when punk was still considered edgy, I had brought along some singles for the resident DJ. After a terse discussion I handed over my They Must Be Russians EP, requesting *this* track on *this* side, which he duly played. I glowed quietly with inner pride at this minor triumph for underground obscurism, especially when other drinkers seemed bemused by 'Nagasaki's Children'.

Unfortunately, the track that followed 'Nagasaki's Children' was a short, up-tempo number which the DJ played, ignoring my instructions. The extent to which the mood previously established by this eerie masterpiece was undercut became tragically apparent with the onset of 'Nellie The Elephant'. The second it began I started to sweat profusely, coolness evaporated like a snowball in hell and I was consumed by a firestorm of humiliation (invisible to everyone but me). I had no option but to sit it out, feigning amusement at this hilarious juxtaposition, though 'Nellie The Elephant' seemed even longer than *Welcome Back My Friends To The Show That Never Ends... Ladies And Gentlemen, Emerson, Lake And Palmer*.

I took music very seriously. 'Nellie The Elephant' was flippant, light-hearted and exuberant, and although I valued anti-technique and anti-cleverness over their opposites, there were limits. I still preferred music that would overwhelm, impress or confront, which made noise, ugliness or ineptitude cool, and their opposites uncool. Paradoxically, I prided myself on the breadth of my tastes, on how adventurous and broad-minded I was, unlike all the narrow-minded, boring and ordinary people who just didn't get it, whatever 'it' was at any given time. If they had got 'it', of course 'it' wouldn't have been 'it' any more: 'it' was always something they didn't get and never would. As Howard Devoto memorably put it, assuming you know the B-side of 'Shot By Both Sides', 'My mind / ain't so open / that anything / could crawl right in'. That was me. In my mind there was no room for mods. There was no room for the amiable, good-natured, unpretentious fun of the Starjets. There was no room for 'Nellie the Elephant' following 'Nagasaki's Children'. There was no room for new wave or power pop. There was however room for controversy, obscurity and wearing black.

It got perverse sometimes, what you liked and what you didn't like. I'd always thought Throbbing Gristle were a good idea, if only because they seemed to upset so many people. Then, ever since the night I experienced them in the Students' Union I've thought that even if they were a good idea, which they weren't, I didn't want to have to listen to them or see them again. Dressed in camouflage gear, with all the lights on, they unleashed a murky, relentless barrage of ugliness that assaulted and then dispersed the audience like a power hose filled with slurry. Hilariously-named front man Genesis P Orridge jerked about and shrieked into a microphone while the other three stood motionless and made horrible grinding noises on electronic equipment. Sometimes Gen also hacked in a jagged, nonmusicianly way at a violin, his bow trailing streamers of pale, fine horsehair that floated about behind his shoulder, picked out in a spotlight along with the beads of sweat that flew from his head as he sawed at the strings. There was no applause. After this, Cabaret Voltaire's snarling, crunching, thudding sounded like the Starjets.

Later we met up in the bar, and my pal Brummy Dave, tight-lipped and ashen-faced after this ordeal, said deliberately, one word at a time, 'That. Was. Shit.' Because I was studying philosophy during my first year, things seemed more nuanced, so my reply was, 'Er, no, actually, you *think* it was shit,' to which he replied, 'No. It. Was. Shit.' I countered gamely with, 'No, that's your *opinion*, it's just a *value judgment*', to which his response through clenched teeth was, 'No: *It – Was – Shit. Really. Shit*'. On reflection, he had a point, and I think if I'd carried on flaunting my newly acquired smart-arsery in such a provocative manner he might have hit me.

I worked hard at music, because I thought anything was better than normal; better than bland, ordinary, acceptable, conventional or popular. To prove the point, Radar and I would make a point of listening to things like 'Frankie Teardrop' on the first Suicide LP, *Suicide*. It came out in 1977 and could well have been the first synth-pop album ever, as long as you didn't include Kraftwerk. I originally heard Suicide on the punk/new wave show that Phil Ross used to do on Radio Merseyside. At that time, any such programme was wonderful, even Stuart Henry broadcasting 'Heat From The Street' on Radio Luxembourg from behind a wall of static. When Phil Ross played the Suicide single 'Ghost Rider', it stood out like a festering sore thumb with a skull ring and chipped black nail varnish because it was so haunted, haunting, rough, groovy and, well, electronic at a time when you just didn't hear that kind of thing. Suicide were primitive poppy anti-pop, they were the inhuman league, they were the ones to like if you wanted to confuse people. There were only two of them, Martin Rev (drum machine, toytown keyboards, absurdly large shades) and Alan Vega (moans, grunts, gasps, shrieks, intermittent headband) and, although nobody knew it at the time, they were the future.[4] They made a trashy, twisted, doomy, sparse, pulsing, melodramatic pop music saturated in reverb, echo and distortion that sounded great but alienated the casual listener with its twitchy aura of menace. Playing in basements and lofts since the early seventies, Suicide eventually ended up supporting Elvis Costello, of all people, in Brussels, of all places, in 1978 and this brief performance, captured on a cassette recorder, is available with the CD reissue of the first album as *23 Minutes Over Brussels*. By their second number, 'Rocket USA' the crowd are booing and jeering enthusiastically in a way that you just know will only encourage Martin and Alan to try harder. Six songs and nineteen minutes in, 'Frankie Teardrop' never really gets going, the microphone has been stolen, the audience is roaring and it's all over.

If that's the kind of effect Suicide had, now imagine 'Frankie Teardrop', a drum machine thudding like a migraine only faster, and a droning pulse of fuzzy organ. Over this, a swooning unhinged voice close, very close to the microphone, slowly moaning things right inside your head, interspersed with abrupt, terrifyingly loud screams, Frankie looking at his wife, shooting her, AAAAAAAAAAAAAA AAAAARGH AAAAAAAAAAAAAAAAAAAAAAAAAA AAAAAAAAARGH, Frankie putting the gun to his head, AAAAAAAAAAAAAAAAAAAAAAAAAAAAAAAAAAAAAA

---

4 Think of all the duos that came after them: Soft Cell, Erasure, Yazoo, Pet Shop Boys, Sparks, Goldfrapp, Yello, DAF, right down the line to Sleaford Mods.

RGH, Frankie dead, AAAAAAAAAAAAAAAARGH AAAAAAAAAAAAARGH AAAAAAAAAARGH.

The song is almost 10 ½ minutes long and by half way through Frankie's already dead. It's horrible yet strangely compelling, a drawn-out, brutal assault of a song, far more disturbing than anything else then on offer, maybe even 'Reality Asylum' / 'Shaved Women'. To create a similar but less intense ambience, we also used to enjoy things like

- 'Beautiful Gardens', 'Surfin' Bird' and numerous others by the Cramps
- 'Careful With That Axe, Eugene' by Pink Floyd
- 'European Son', 'I Heard Her Call My Name', 'Sister Ray' and 'Heroin' by the Velvet Underground
- anything off Iggy Pop's *TV Eye Live* or *The Idiot*
- anything by the Stooges.

The first Suicide album was the first industrial pop music; in fact it was the first industrial surf music; in fact it was a mouthful of bubblegum and blood from a girl who kissed you while slipping in her Hubba Bubba then punched you in the face. I still listen to it, but now I skip 'Frankie Teardrop'.[5] In fact I only listen to side one, just like *Tubular Bells*.

Nick Hornby wrote a book called *31 Songs*,[6] and one of them was 'Frankie Teardrop', which he hates but thinks that everyone ought to hear once. He doesn't say anything about how great the rest of the album is, and I don't suppose that should come as a surprise, as the book is about songs rather than albums. But he should have said. What troubled me most, though, wasn't his dismissal of Suicide: it was the fact that out of the thirty-one songs he writes about I only knew seven, including 'Frankie Teardrop'. It troubled me that I wasn't familiar with so many songs he knew so well

---

5   The second album, produced for free by Rik Ocasek of the Cars, was meant to have been produced by Georgio Moroder. It would have been stunning; as it is, it's just really good. There's no equivalent of 'Frankie Teardrop', and in places it sounds like Kraftwerk.

6   See appendix seven.

and had so much to say about. Then I thought, well, maybe we just have different tastes, and perhaps he's being a bit self-satisfied, a bit smug about all his favourites, assuming that everyone else wants to know them as well as he does; that everyone else wants be part a some cosy pop community that's he's reaching out to and bonding with. Unlike me, who's just rambling on about cults and obscurities and perverse oddities to what remains of what was once the awkward squad. It also annoyed me that he said the Sex Pistols were just the Stooges with bad teeth, which is lazy and untrue (even though they covered 'No Fun' on the B-side of 'Pretty Vacant'). Then again, maybe his Suicide is just my Throbbing Gristle.

I was reminded of that Frankie Teardrop feeling after a package arrived at our house. I didn't know who it was from, but I knew a man who did know. The man who did know had said a friend was replacing/upgrading a lot of his music, and would I like some of the tapes this chap was getting rid of. The package that arrived contained about 40 home-recorded cassettes.

Brilliant. More music, nearly all C90s, which meant about 80 albums. You can't have too much music, I thought, as I stacked them carefully in the kitchen next to the tape player. That end of the kitchen was already full of cassettes; the worktop was getting narrower, and other things you did in the kitchen apart from listen to music, like preparing food, were becoming increasingly difficult in such a small, cluttered space. Ignoring my wife's disquiet and running my eyes down the spines of the cases, I nodded approvingly. Mostly *never-heards*, with some *never-heard-ofs*. P16 D4, My Life With The Thrill Kill Kult, Legendary Pink Dots, Trans Am, O Rang, Tortoise, Clock Dva, Laibach, Skinny Puppy, Throbbing Gristle, Einsturzende Neubauten, FM Einheit, Naked City, Psychic TV, Coil. And for some reason, Joni Mitchell and Pink Floyd. I didn't make a list, though I should have.

Much of it turned out to be the grinding, depressing, atonal kind of music I wanted to immerse myself in years before on my quest to hear everything, especially the kinds of everything that other people didn't like. For a while my solo car journeys around Glasgow took place to sounds of destruction, rage, despair and Pink Floyd (but not Joni Mitchell), which for the most part proved deeply unsettling, but I persevered. Some of the best music was by Naked City, who played headlong bursts of precision rock noise in a dizzying rush of styles and timings that made me laugh out loud at the stunning, ridiculous nature of their achievement as I crawled along the M9. It reminded me of music for a particularly savage cartoon, like Quentin Tarrantino had taken illegal stimulants then made 'Itchy and Scratchy'. At the time, our house had a satellite dish and decoder left by the previous occupants, so we spent a lot of family time watching free satellite TV. What we watched most was the Cartoon Network. There were recent cartoons, but there were also hours and hours of old cinema shorts featuring the likes of Bugs Bunny, Daffy Duck, Tom and Jerry, Popeye and Roadrunner, along with others whose laugh-out-loud violence and profound strangeness made a deep impression on me. I'm not sure what it did to the children. The music for these cartoons isn't something you usually notice, because it's just one element of a furious sensory assault, but when you hear it by itself it's a revelation. One of the greatest composers for cartoons was Carl Stalling, credited with over 600 scores for Warner Brothers – the likes of Looney Tunes and Merrie Melodies. At the time I was watching these cartoons, I also heard a radio programme about Carl Stalling and for the first time got to hear the music by itself, and it was a revelation This was also around the time I got to hear Naked City. It tuned out the group were led by John Zorn, a composer, arranger and musician who was a great admirer of Carl Stalling. Suddenly it all made sense.

What really made me wonder at this cassette collection of oddness and darkness and ugliness, though, was not just what it sounded like, but the way it was organised. On the spine of each cassette case was a label with a hand-written number. The highest number I found was 550, which meant the chap who sent it to me could have had 1,100 albums on cassette, all labelled. I felt humbled by this attention to detail.

When I say I persevered with the cassettes, I mean I persevered for a while rather than a long time – definitely not as long I would previously have done. Things have changed, and so have I. In middle age, with two grown-up children, I realise I'm three times older than I was when I first heard 'Frankie Teardrop'. I've got a much better idea of what life can do to people, and what people can do to each other. I've not had a bad life or a hard life, but I no longer feel I want to go where this kind of music takes me – I'm there every time I turn on the TV or worry about the world my children are living in. When you have a family, things change, including your music. So eventually the cassettes went in the bin, apart from number 540 (*Millions Now Living Will Never Die* by Tortoise), which I still have. And one by P16 D4 called *Kühe In ½ Trauer*, which I unspooled and used along with a Bach cassette, an Action Man and a piece of plywood to make a cassette collage that hangs on the wall behind me.

Following Neil Young's fourth LP *Harvest*, in the early seventies he found himself overwhelmed by its success, later memorably commenting that this experience put him 'in the middle of the road. Travelling there soon became a bore, so I headed for the ditch.' I once felt myself drawn away from the sunny mainstream to the murky edges of darkness, where the emotions and aesthetics were more extreme. In the middle of the road I felt awkward socially, emotionally and sexually. I didn't, or couldn't, fit in; I felt excluded, so I excluded myself, and headed for the ditch. Being sensitive, intellectual and perpetually anxious about things like clothes, girls and dancing, I put distance between myself and everyone else in the way I dressed, thought and acted, and in the kind of music I listened to – rather than seeking out trouble in more direct ways. It's partly a question of stamina, just like partying: how far, how much or how long till you've had enough? When you're young, you can do this if you want to, testing yourself and even taking a pride in it. You feel invulnerable, indestructible, and you don't know very much about life, so you can watch harrowing or 'unflinching' films and read troubling or 'brave' books and listen to traumatic or 'uncompromising' music to see what it's like. You can explore your limitations safely by watching things, reading things and listening to things rather than living them. You can even impress or outrage or intrigue other people whose tolerances are less elastic than yours, and all of this leaves no scars.

Having spent a lot of time avoiding the middle of the road, I've come to realise there are considerable gaps in my listening experience, as Nick Hornby has reminded me. Nevertheless, things have changed. I'm hopeless when it comes to dancing, but I've fallen in love with Brazilian and Latin music, and with sunny African sounds, along with country, bluegrass and exotic easy listening. I've always liked Abba, and now realise I actually liked a lot of the pop music I used to sneer at. When people talk of 'guilty pleasures', is this is the kind of thing they're referring to? There should be no such things as guilty pleasures: just like what you like, without shame, without embarrassment – but maybe across a confusingly wide range. You don't have to share other people's tastes, just be aware you can wrongfoot them. At the time of writing, or at one of the times of writing, the in-car CDs on constant rotation in our Ford Focus and Vauxhall Corsa[7] were:

in the Focus

A gorgeous budget compilation called *Pure Brazil: Instrumental Bossa Nova: 20 Lounge Brazilian Tracks*.

In the Corsa

Hex, Or Printing In The Infernal Method by Earth. *Hex* is also an instrumental album, a massive metallic windswept

---

7   That time of writing was so long ago that we no longer own either of these cars.

poem about America's heart of darkness; mountain ranges and deserts of music about the West. Although there are no words, the album was inspired by a book: Cormac McCarthy's relentless, bleak, primal, poetic *Blood Meridian*. To get a visual analogue of this, look through the booklet of photographs that comes with *Hex*, or imagine any other collection of images of the American West. What you see is a sequence of fragmented, ghostly, grainy and often puzzling monochrome images saturated in such sadness, death, vastness and desecration that it numbs the brain. There's a lot in there, and the music, although sparse, feels like it's loaded to bursting point with qualities and meanings that only emerge after repeated listening. It's like entering another time zone, where things unfold at an almost geological pace. It's like a country song slowed down from 45 rpm to single figures: your ears and brain need a while to adjust. I was playing it very loud in the dark one night while waiting to pick my son up. When he got in the car he was just as embarrassed and exasperated as my dad used to be about my music. Result.

Earth are a kind of metal. They're on the Southern Lord label that they share with another, even slower, louder and more astonishing band called Sunn 0))) that includes label owner Greg Anderson. This is not metal as most people know it, and that's not really surprising: metal is probably the most enduring and in some ways the most elastic of all musical genres. Although ridiculed as dumb, nasty or reactionary, its range of genres and subgenres suggest it's still vital, still evolving and mutating, re-inventing itself in ways that can make some more 'serious' or 'proper' music look a bit pathetic. And for sheer strangeness as one of metal's myriad bastard offspring, there's something called black metal – dark, intense, profane, neo-pagan, pro-Norse, anti-Christian, quasi-crypto-Nazi.

I became interested in black metal because it seemed so transgressive – sonically, politically, aesthetically, racially, sexually, spiritually, culturally. Am I easily shocked? Is this ultimate rebel music? Is black metal 'worse' than gangsta rap? Than punk? Than 'Rock around the Clock'? If you pick your own folk devils and compare them with black metal, just by way of a diversion and to remind you that you can perhaps still be shocked, consider the story of Per Yngve Ohlin, aka Dead, black metallist and one of the strangest, but not in a good way: as we know, bad ways are sometimes preferred to good, especially in rock and roll, especially in metal, especially in black metal. Dead's life and death as vocalist in the Norwegian band Mayhem are so tortuous and tortured that there isn't room here to describe them adequately, but if you're curious you can look him up. For a sample song, try 'Mayhem – Necrolust (Live) [vocals: Dead]' on YouTube. A lyric search is also recommended to get the full effect, because the intensity of the vocal interpretation makes it impossible to follow the lyrics about necrophilia, blasphemy, death and self-loathing.

There's a photo I found of Dead, dead, after cutting his wrists and then shooting himself in the head with a shotgun in 1991. This garish, washed-out, unreal-looking image became the cover of the Mayhem album *Dawn Of The Black Hearts*,[8] and bits of the dead Dead's skull were supposedly made into a necklace by Euronymous and/or Hellhammer, the Mayhem guitarist and drummer, who supposedly went out and bought a disposable camera to take photos of the dead Dead before phoning the police to tell them that Dead was dead. Euronymous was later murdered by the black metal musician Varg Vikernes (aka Count Grishnackh, aka Burzum), who served a sentence for this and the arson of medieval Norwegian churches.

Significantly, the names Count Grishnackh and Burzum are from *Lord Of The Rings*. Grishnákh is the name of an orc leader. *Burzum* is the word for darkness in Black Speech, the language devised by Sauron for the servants of Mordor.

---

8 Track listing: Deathcrush; Necrolust; Funeral Fog; Freezing Moon; Carnage; Buried By Time And Dust; Chainsaw Gutsfuck; Pure Fucking Armageddon.

Black Speech appears in the inscription on the One Ring,[9] which is the only full example of its use because Tolkien, having created the language to sound unpleasant, didn't much like using it. The reason for all the nerdy Tolkien detail is that Varg Vikernes is a bit like that. As well as writing extensively about paganism and mythology he has also devised and written about his own fantasy role-playing game and recorded dozens of highly articulate short video talks about racial, historical, political and cultural matters from a 'Thulean' perspective that, shall we say, challenges the Western liberal democratic consensus. He also proposes that what we call autism would seem like a natural way to be in a tribal society, and it's those who seem to thrive in over-stimulated over-populated technological societies who are the freaks. Some of his ideas are interesting and others lead to some pretty dark places.

Black metal is nothing if not nerdy and transgressive, and therefore a magnet for polarising the iron filings of disaffection lodged in the brains of certain young white males. Whether you think it's just noise and a lot of posturing or something more sinister is up to you, though is there ever such a thing as 'just noise'? Noise is part of rock and roll, part of the attitude and part of the aesthetic, and you only have to listen to the Velvet Underground or the Stooges and all their imitators to enjoy the tension between noise/atonality/ugliness and music/sweetness/beauty.

But even by itself, torn free of its musical moorings and just left to drift in its own perfect storm, noise fascinates at the same time as it repels, so much so that it has become Noise, with its own capital letter.[10] I don't think I like it, but I keep going back, just to make sure. With its uppercase N,

---

9 Ash nazg durbatulûk, ash nazg gimbatul,
   ash nazg thrakatulûk agh **burzum**-ishi krimpatul.
   (One Ring to rule them all, One Ring to find them,
   One Ring to bring them all and in the darkness bind them)
10 While I was in a position to do such a thing, I successfully proposed
   that 'Noise' with this meaning be included in forthcoming dictionaries by my employers.

Noise becomes a type of music, or of unmusic or antimusic. Maybe it sits outside music altogether, but I don't think so because it has to be defined by music, if only as its opposite. Music has qualities like rhythm, harmony and melody. Noise has rhythm (sometimes), harmony (or its opposite), and no melody but lots of texture or timbre. That's not to say music doesn't have texture – sometimes that's almost all it has. When I first heard Tangerine Dream and the other knob twiddlers one of the things that amazed me about them was that there was almost nothing there – apart from texture or timbre. It still amazes me when I listen to electronic music. There's almost nothing there, and if you played it on a piano, there would be even less. What you are hearing and luxuriating in is the throbbing, burbling, swelling, squelching, droning texture of the sound, something that constantly changes while the notes themselves (as written on a page) change little, if at all. So what is noise, or Noise, apart from an extreme form of texture?

If you listen to the extremes of music and noise, it becomes apparent that pure, smooth, pleasing, melodic, harmonic music isn't always the most interesting or satisfying thing to listen to because you can end up with a type of sloppy gloop, the kind that accumulates in the lofts of charity shops. Pure grating shrieking roaring atonal noise isn't very interesting either; but when it's a certain kind of music and it's a certain kind of texture or a certain kind of noise; when there's a tension between the music and the noise, and sometimes you can't tell whether it's music or noise, and it keeps changing between the two, then things can become a lot more interesting and much more satisfying. While rooting around looking for something else online, I came across an essay by TS Eliot about free verse, in which he says:

> '... the most interesting verse ... has been done either by taking a very simple form ... and constantly withdrawing from it, or taking no form at all, and constantly approximating a very simple one. It is this

> contrast between fixity and flux, this unperceived
> evasion of monotony, which is the very life of verse.'

And the very life of music. Pure noise is one kind of monotony and pure musicality is another; or pure nastiness and pure niceness; or pure dumbness and pure smartness; or pure directness and pure obliqueness. Whichever extremes you choose to start from, it's about *the unperceived evasion of monotony*.

Eliot's essay was called 'Reflections on *Vers Libre*', which, appropriately enough, I found while looking for information relating to John Cage and his use of chance. Cage called himself a composer, but claimed that everything was or could be music. Cage's most famous piece, *4'33"*, is composed for any instrument or combination of instruments, and the performer(s) are instructed to sit and not play their instrument(s) for the duration of the performance. This is not four minutes thirty-three seconds of silence – the piece actually consists of otherwise unnoticed sounds from the audience, the concert hall and the outside world, so you could actually argue that Cage wasn't composing music, he wasn't even composing sounds; what he was composing was a new way of listening. Another piece, *Imaginary Landscape No 4* (1951), is written for twelve radios, and although the instructions for the changes in volume and frequency are very precise, performances vary hugely depending on what is being broadcast. And when people complained about radio noise on the beach or on the street or anywhere else, Cage's response was apparently, 'Ah, they're playing my piece again.'

It seems as though it's getting harder and harder to be sonically extreme, because sonic extremeness, like everything else, has become a genre, acquired a history and a tradition and become a valid part of art or music or pop or rock, part of Dada or Futurism or Situationism or Punk or Hardcore or Whatever. After a half century of rock and roll it seems like everything has turned from rebellion, anger, craziness, lust and youthful exuberance into middle-aged cultural history, with its own nerdy, self-congratulatory halls of fame and anniversaries and museums and classics and top tens and top hundreds and top thousands. It's all somewhere on pop and rock's family tree now, though there are still things down in the ditch that have been there for a long time and show no sign of being excavated any time soon. Uncle Merzbow's *Merzbox* and Grandpa Lou's *Metal Machine Music* are still not played much, nor is the output of their myriad bastard offspring. But given time, who knows.

So, Merzbow, Schmerzbow. Merzbow happy, Merzbow sad. Merzbow in a good mood, Merzbow in a bad mood: how would you know the difference? He is Masami Akita, Japanese vegan Noise/noise god, bondage connoisseur and King Crimson fan, maker of around 200 albums since 1979. *Merzbox*, a box set of his CDs, was released in 2000 by Extreme Records and consisted of 50 discs spanning his career from 1979 to 1997.[11] Thirty were reissues from LP, CD, or cassette and the remaining twenty consisted of previously unreleased material. *Merzbox* also contained a T-shirt, posters, a book, a medallion, stickers, postcards and two CD-ROMs. It came in a custom designed 'fetish box' limited to 1,000 copies. Merzbow's first official studio album, disc two in *Merzbox*, was *Metal Acoustic Music*, a nod to Lou Reed: it gets a bit self-referential sometimes, doesn't it.

Merzbow the noise god: I saw him, I heard him, I felt him at the Instal mini-festival that I went to most years while I lived in Glasgow. The name comes from the meaningless German word *merzbau*, a title given to various constructions assembled between the early 1920s and the early 1940s out of scavenged materials by the eccentric German artist Kurt Schwitters. The second part of the word *merzbau*, the -*bau* bit, literally means 'building' or 'construction'. The first part,

---

11 In December 2002, Georgia Tech student radio station WREK 91.1 FM (paradoxical slogan: 'music you don't hear on the radio') broadcast the *Merzbox* in its entirety from December 17 to December 19. *Creative Loafing* magazine rightly described this heroic piece of programming as 'the most counterintuitive move in the history of radio'.

merz-, has no meaning and was supposedly taken from the name *Commerz Bank*, part of which appeared on a piece of torn paper in one of Schwitters' early collages.

I became familiar with Kurt Schwitters because he'd composed and performed meaningless, wordless sound poetry, a refined form of gibberish that appeared briefly in the track 'Kurt's Rejoinder' on the 1977 Eno album *Before And After Science*. Talking Heads did something similar after Eno played David Byrne a Dadaist sound poem by Hugo Ball, refined gibberish which became the basis for the track 'I Zimbra,' on *Fear Of Music*.[12] Byrne was lost for words at the time, and the words of most songs are often just sounds anyway, though they need to be the right sounds otherwise you end up sounding like New Order or Crass.

The right sounds are what I settled for after trying to find the lyrics for Bowie's elusive song 'Some Are'. There were no definitive words to be found, and this it didn't matter, because evocative meaninglessness is fine. Just listen to the B-side of *Low*. There's a line between sense and nonsense, just as there's a line between poetry or lyrics and nonsense. Nonsense is fine, it's pretentious or banal nonsense that I don't like, just as I don't like pretentious/banal art or pretentious/banal anything else (most of the time: always give yourself a bit of wriggle room).

But back to Merzbow. I had some idea of what he was like, but wasn't prepared for the actual event. It was amazing, it was brutal, it was intense, it was so loud it was quiet, so harsh it was relaxing. Unable to move, almost unable to think, I just stood still and let wave after wave of abrasive

---

12 The first four lines of 'I Zimbra' by Talking Heads are:
Gadji beri bimba clandridi
Lauli lonni cadori gadjam
A bim beri glassala glandride
E glassala tuffm I zimbra
The first four lines of 'Gadji Beri Bimba' by Hugo Ball are:
gadji beri bimba glandridi laula lonni cadori
gadjama gramma berida bimbala glandri galassassa laulitalomini
gadji beri bin blassa glassala laula lonni cadorsu sassala bim
gadjama tuffm i zimzalla binban gligla wowolimai bin beri ban

digital noise wash over me as my sandblasted brain somehow tricked me into believing I was hearing a kind of ambient music, which I possibly, very possibly, could have been if it wasn't for the volume. Under a few magenta spotlights the Noise God sat at a table on a stage in front of a wall of Marshall amps, dressed in black with long black hair and steel-rimmed glasses, gazing intently at a couple of laptops, both hands mousing and clicking, dragging and scrolling intently, understatedly geeking out like some kind of Zen multi-keyboard player without keyboards. What's the sound of one hand clicking? Merzbow. What's the sound of two hands clicking? Merzbow. I wasn't sure whether I wanted to like him or hate him, and by the end I wasn't sure what I felt at all about anything, because I remember virtually nothing about any of it. But for some bizarre reason, in some strange way, I found it quite soothing, where I have generally found other noise confrontational and atonal, or annoying and monotonous, rather than, for example, hypnotic and immersive. I have no idea whether the unperceived evasion of monotony was what happened with Merzbow, though I do know that by the end of it I felt numb, yet curiously refreshed.

Somewhere between Earth and Merzbow, between music and noise, between monotony and its unperceived evasion, I found 'More Light', which turned out to be the title track of an album by J Mascis + the Fog. I was browsing in Monorail, an independent music store in Glasgow where it's impossible to leave without a small square brown paper bag of CDs or a large one of LPs, partly because it carries such a range of music, and partly because it's situated inside a bar, so you can drink and browse at the same time. Amongst other things, that evening in Monorail I bought a Rough Trade double compilation CD called *Rock And Roll 1* that was going cheap. On it was music ranging from five tracks I knew

1. 'I Got A Right' – the Stooges
2. 'Human Fly' – the Cramps

3. 'Rocket USA' – Suicide
4. 'Know Your Product' – the Saints
5. 'Nonalignment Pact' – Pere Ubu

to forty-one I didn't know. After it had lain about for a while in a pile of other CDs, I played it loud in the car on a long drive, and my ears were shredded, in a good way. The first track on the first CD was 'I Got A Right'. The last track on the second CD was 'More Light' by J Mascis + the Fog, about which I knew nothing. 'More Light' is a Truly Great Song, and from the very start of its howling, roaring electronic squall like the start of 'Silver Machine' heard over a telephone line and amplified a thousand times, I knew it was Truly Great. After a full minute's blissful jagged, swirling static, a distant nasal voice comes in, moaning a simple, aching tune into a blizzard of white noise, just about held in place by the bass and the drums, and every so often an ethereal female voice drifts in and out as well, so fragile it has no right to be there and perfect for that very reason. It builds and builds and sort of stays the same, like howling into a storm, then for the last minute an extra wave of guitar noise comes crashing in, making the sound almost impossibly dense, with screams of minimal high-pitched guitar in amongst it. Like early Hawkwind remixed by Merzbow when he was in a good mood not a bad mood, and you knew the difference. For some reason, the drums gradually speed up throughout and you almost don't notice the increasing sense of urgency. As I drove, it made me grin and then it made me laugh out loud into the noise, because it was the kind of exhilaration I don't get often enough from music nowadays. Music, but only just; noise, but only just; an ecstatic blend of the two, like a lot of the best rock and roll music.

I found myself playing 'More Light' over and over again and sort of moaning along with it, wondering what the lyrics were. Sometimes, maybe quite often, when you look up lyrics they're a disappointment, but living with that disappointment is the chance you take. Lyrics don't have to be anything in particular, they just need to fit the music. I reckoned the lyrics to 'More Light' would be downbeat and fragmented and a bit poetically odd, or even a bit oddly poetic, but I never got the chance to confirm or refute any of this because I couldn't find them anywhere, which is fine, just catching the occasional fragment through the interference.

I tried searching different combinations of MASCIS, FOG and LIGHT, but found no lyrics and ended up watching a tuneless video which, more important than any lyrics or tunefulness, showed how Mascis had produced the electronic squall that dominates the song, and it was wonderful to behold. The video clip starts with whoops and clapping from the small audience as the previous number finishes, then Mascis adjusts his guitar and his centre-parted curtains of hair. A roadie hands him a small but bulky keyboard that he puts on. Hangs it round his neck along with his guitar, like the biggest, most stupid piece of chunky plastic jewellery you could imagine. He presses a couple of the keys, pushes a few buttons and an immediately recognisable squall starts to build.

I recognised it immediately, and so did the audience. The bass player and the drummer look at each other and Mascis looks at them, and they're off. For a while Mascis fiddles with the buttons, then he's playing the guitar, then he's playing both at once while he wails into the mike, barely audible. And it's not done in a spirit of virtuosity, because there is no virtuosity, no ego; there's nothing to show off about when all you're doing is twiddling knobs, because it's not done in a spirit of music, it's done in a spirit of noise, and Mascis is doing it because he can make twice as much noise with a keyboard and a guitar as he can with just a keyboard or just a guitar. It's a Truly Great Song, an example of how music can still sometimes surprise you. After that I bought the album, and apart from the title track it all sounded like whiny crunchy indie guitar music. This is an example of how music can often disappoint you.

The spirit of music and the spirit of noise are complementary: yin and yang, or maybe yang and yin. Either way, *Discreet Music* is one of the two, a 1975 Brian

Eno album, his first ambient piece, the first ever to be called 'ambient' and the one that's always there to go back to and lose yourself in. The story of how it came about is an example of how chance can create interesting possibilities; how an attuned mind can recognise these possibilities; and how the right circumstances can let them develop.[13]

Part one of the story has Eno in bed at home following a hit and run accident, medicated and immobile, listening to or just about hearing an album of harp music turned down so low he can hardly make it out over the sound of the rain through an open window. This gives him ideas about a new way of listening to music, and perhaps a new kind of music.

Part two has Eno making a backing tape as part of a collaboration with the guitarist Robert Fripp. On the tape, things are left sufficiently loose and open for Fripp to improvise: a simple melodic synth fragment that Eno played into a home-made twin-tape delay system[14] before going out to answer the phone.

Part three has Eno playing the tape back to Fripp at half speed by mistake and, most importantly, realising what he's accidentally created, or what the machine has created. This beautiful, melancholy, minimal work became the title track and first side of the album *Discreet Music*. As much as a long tune, it's an environment in which to be, or a serene low-key accompaniment to whatever you choose to do while it's playing. The second side consists of repeated extracts from Pachelbel's 'Canon in D', which gradually warp and mutate into increasingly strange shapes. Both are examples of generative music, another Eno term, coined while working

---

13 Eno has used and subsequently made available a pack of a hundred or so cards, Oblique Strategies, designed to provide creative assistance when working. Some are simple instructions: 'discover the recipes you are using and abandon them'. Some are bizarre: 'Short circuit (example: a man eating peas with the idea that they will improve his virility shovels them straight into his lap)'. The most telling, and perhaps the most profound is 'honour thy error as a hidden intention'.

14 An idea first used by minimalist composer Terry Riley and referred to by him as a 'time lag accumulator'.

on the 1995 *Koan* music software and referring to music made by following simple instructions that sooner or later create surprise and complexity. A simple pre-Eno example of this process would be the sound made by a set of wind chimes.

The yin to Eno's yang, or the yang to his yin, is *Metal Machine Music*, a Lou Reed album that a lot of people know about of but almost nobody has actually heard. Is it art, is it music, is it noise, is it Lou Reed taking the piss or having a laugh at the record company's expense in order to fulfil a contract? It was released in 1975 in the same week as Discreet Music, a coincidence that has a mythic, yin-yang perfection to it because both pieces were created by machines rather than musicians and both are open-ended, their duration constrained only by the limitations of vinyl. (In fact, Eno went on to make longer, more expansive pieces on CD, such as *Thursday Afternoon* and *Neroli*, before *Koan* and other generative software, which can run indefinitely.)

Whenever I went to buy LPs after school *Metal Machine Music* was there in the bargain bin, but I never bought it. Everyone who had bought it (Radar said his brother knew someone who had) said it was shit, just a load of noise, and had taken it back to the shop for a refund. I was intrigued – how could something be that extreme, that controversial? – but I never followed up, until I was reminded of it a few years ago. First, I read a rambling review of it called 'The Greatest Album Ever Made' in a Lester Bangs anthology, and it made me curious. Then I heard an overly respectful radio interview with Lou Reed on the occasion of a CD reissue, in which he made all kinds of extravagant claims about it. Then I heard some of an orchestral version by an avant-garde chamber ensemble called Zeitkratzer, which sounded so weird, or so awful and annoying, I realised I had to find out more. At some stage I saw the CD advertised online for £4.22, so I bought a copy. It lay around in its shrink-wrap for almost 18 months because I couldn't decide when to play it, because I already knew it would be too awful or annoying to be worth the emotional energy. Then one morning I was driving from Inverness to the Highland Theological College in Dingwall to take an adult education class, and I put it on.

The front cover is a photo that looks like it's been taken at a concert. Lit by a single spotlight, Lou Reed is standing against a black background. He has short bleached blond hair. He's wearing sunglasses and a studded black leather jacket that's too small for him. He's standing with his hands by his sides, as though they're jammed into the pockets of his jeans, only they aren't. He looks unbelievably cool and weird and exotic for the mid seventies, even at a time when all I wanted was long hair and a greatcoat. Impossibly cool, that is, apart from the stupid silver riveted capital letters of the album title across the top of the cover on either side of Lou's head, like if he moves slightly he might bang his head on the E at the end of MACHINE or the M at the start of MUSIC. On the back cover he's wearing a different leather jacket without studs, different sunglasses, and dark (probably black) nail varnish. Also on the back cover is 40 lines of nonsense about the technical specifications of the instruments and recording techniques, like

5 Piggyback Marshall Tube Amps in series
and
Sennheiser Headphones
and
Drone cognizance and harmonic possibilities vis a vis Lamont Young's[15] *Dream Music*
and
Combinations and Permutations built upon constant harmonic Density Increase and Melodic Distractions.

---

15 **La Monte Young** is the name of the musician Lou Reed is referring to, someone he spent a lot of time with early on. Musically, and also perhaps sexually: Lou occasionally claimed to have been 'the first Mrs La Monte Young'. **Lamont Young**, on the other hand, was a surveyor employed by the New South Wales Mines Department who disappeared in mysterious circumstances in 1880. He was also an Italian architect and urban planner based in Naples who died in 1929.

Originally released as a double album with one track on each side, it's now a four-track CD. Each track starts and ends abruptly, is sixteen minutes long and consists of four simultaneous layers of noise made by guitars feeding back through amplifiers, recorded at various speeds, and mixed so that two layers' worth play back through the left speaker and another two through the right speaker. Originally the fourth side of the album ended in a closed groove, so it would have carried on playing until you got up and lifted the stylus off the record, assuming you lasted that long. Logically, there should have been a closed groove at the end of each side so that unless you intervened whichever side you had put on would play for ever, making the album of virtually infinite duration and eventually turning it into music, as the last few instants made themselves familiar by looping over and over and over and over and over and over and over and over and over until you went mad, or deaf, or died, or the vinyl wore out.

It was an unsettling experience at first. As I left home I felt quite uncomfortable, but by the time I had got to the Kessock roundabout a few miles along the A9 it had become quite relaxing, and I turned it up almost to maximum. The relentless, almost painful barrage of noise started breaking down into varying abrasive textures, I started to perceive howling metallic resonances and intermittently rhythmic screeches, and every so often demented little tunes would shriek out at me briefly. I found myself driving more slowly than I should have along the ten miles or so of dual carriageway up the A9 to the Tore roundabout. When I arrived in Dingwall, the College wasn't where I though it was, so I made my way in a leisurely fashion around the streets for a few minutes until I found it, parked then sat in the car park for a few minutes, listening to this indescribable vortex of noise, bathing in it like a frog bathing in a liquidiser. Then I went in and took the class, came out and drove home, borne along by a curious sense of elated detachment that may or may not have been conducive to driving a motor vehicle. It finished as I approached the last roundabout before home, and I was disappointed to note that although the final closed groove repeated a few dozen times, it stopped well before filling whatever remained of the seventy-odd minutes afforded by the CD format. After it had finished I left it in the CD player and it started again. It stayed there for almost a week. What eventually happened was that I, or my brain, or a part of my brain, turned it into music.

Playlist 10 - Discreet Machine Music	
Shaved Women	Crass
Nag, Nag, Nag	Cabaret Voltaire
Penthouse And Pavement	Heaven 17
Being Boiled	The Human League
Jocko Homo	Devo
Warm Leatherette	The Normal
Are 'Friends' Electric?	Tubeway Army
Follow The Leaders	Killing Joke
Know Your Product	The Saints
Discreet Music	Brian Eno

To listen to the playlists, visit Spotify using the QR links provided.

Links to every playlist are also at www.hungry-ghost.info, along with photographs and archive material to supplement each chapter and enhance the reading/listening experience, just like a great big gatefold album cover.

10

EVERYTHING IS REAL

When I think about Tangerine Dream, I find myself in several places and times at once. Part of me is in Liverpool Cathedral in October 1975, and another part of me is in a bedroom in a tower block in Paris, six months later. There's also a part of me here, now, thinking about *Quantum Gate*, a disappointing recent album by a band that no longer exists, yet still does.

(It's the paradox of Theseus's ship. After the hero's return, the Athenians kept his ship in the harbour as a monument. As it rotted and was replaced piece by piece, it became increasingly uncertain whether or not the original ship still existed. With Edgar Froese's death in 2015, the only continuous member of Tangerine Dream is gone; during the band's 50-year history he was accompanied by 25 others. As bands outlive their original members, this kind of thing has become increasingly common, as have disputes between estranged survivors about whose version of Pink Floyd, Yes, UB40 or Boney M is the real one.)

In April 1976 in a bedroom in France, I heard the Tangerine Dream album *Ricochet*. I had experienced the band's thrillingly loud, immersive music in Liverpool Cathedral six months previously, so when I saw the sleeve as the record was being taken out there was a jolt of excitement that stayed with me as the long, deep opening note materialised out of the air, serenely expanding to fill the space it occupied, any space anywhere, from cathedral to bedroom.

The jolt of excitement was accompanied by surprise that the LP had been put on by a girl, because until then I hadn't met any who liked Tangerine Dream. Mind you,

I hadn't met that many girls, and even fewer French girls. Most exciting of all, though, was the fact that this girl, who had put on a Tangerine Dream LP, wanted to snog me while it was playing. So, pretty much the first time I ever snogged a girl, it was to *Ricochet* by Tangerine Dream. She was called Evelyn, and she was small, lean, dark haired, dark skinned and unbelievably exotic. This Anglo-French mingling of limbs, music and saliva occurred during a more formalised cultural exchange involving thirty or so students from secondary schools in Birkenhead and the same number from Gennevilliers, a district on the northwest edge of Paris.

Evelyn's exchange partner was called Judy and mine was called Jean-Michel. Evelyn didn't get on too well with Judy, or with her own parents, or with anyone else, it seemed, apart from a few disreputable longhairs, which automatically impressed me. Whenever Judy and I and all the others went on our coach trips to Places Of Interest such as Versailles, Evelyn would follow the coach on the back of a hairy friend's scuzzy Japanese motorbike, which got her into trouble and also impressed me, as did the glamorous but completely unselfconscious way she shook out her long black hair every time she took her crash helmet off.

I'd got to know Judy on the long train-ferry-train journey from Birkenhead. She was friendly, kind and open, never sneered or used sarcasm, and told me I was 'quite troggy'. She seemed slightly confused and perhaps mildly disapproving about this, which I took as a compliment. She also said my music was quite troggy. She knew this because I talked about it a lot, and had recorded a cassette specially for playing on the coach. It would have been the Who, Genesis, Pink Floyd, Doctor Feelgood, that kind of thing.

After we'd been in France for a few days, Judy told me that she was struggling with the language, and with Evelyn. We didn't live that far apart, so I went round to see her a few times with my uncommunicative partner Jean-Michel in tow. We would all sit in Evelyn's cramped bedroom and attempt to chat, although Judy didn't speak much French, Evelyn didn't speak much English, and Jean-Michel said little in either language. By that time I had been speaking French for about six years, having begun in primary school and so, delighted with the fact that this gave me a social advantage, I did most of the talking and all of the translating.

One evening, after we had all been conversing awkwardly for a while, out of the blue Judy announced that Evelyn wanted to *flirt* with me. It seemed such a strange word to use. At first I wasn't sure what to make of this proposition: the idea of any kind of intimacy with a girl, especially a girl I didn't know, especially a foreign one, left me astonished and confused. However, I duly gave my consent, like this kind of thing happened all the time. There followed a brief muttered conversation during which Judy reminded me that I should make sure to use my tongue because that's what they did in France, and this was why it was called French kissing. Then she and Jean-Michel went out onto the tiny balcony for a breath of fresh air and some stilted conversation, leaving me in a dimly-lit bedroom with a French girl I'd hardly spoken to and a Tangerine Dream album.

What can I say? It was amazing and it was intense, and I didn't make any mistakes. Because she wore a leather jacket and smoked Camel cigarettes, she creaked and tasted of tobacco. We rolled about on her bed for all of side one, and probably side two as well. For the remaining week of the visit I was in a daze. We subsequently snogged in her room to *Ricochet* again; to *Obscured by Clouds* and *More* by Pink Floyd; to *Harvest* by Neil Young. I can't even remember if Judy and Jean-Michel were in the room or not. Later, in the corner of a cellar disco somewhere or other we snogged in the dark to just about everything, which was great, because as well as all the kissing it meant I didn't have to worry about dancing. We snogged a lot, we hardly said anything, and I was besotted. Before we went home, via Judy she gave me a brown leather bracelet which I wore all the time, even at school, which I considered extremely daring and allowed me to tell people that my French girlfriend had given it to me. When the return visit to Birkenhead came in the summer I hurriedly sought her out, but was too late: it was over. I was of course devastated, but not all that surprised. I still had my bracelet, and my own copy of *Ricochet*.

So what is *Ricochet*?

It's a live LP: 'Part One' (17:02) and 'Part Two' (21:03).

It's the classic line-up of Tangerine Dream:

> **Edgar Froese** (Mellotron 400, Mellotron Mark 5 with double tape set and double keyboard, Farfisa 400 double keyboard organ, Farfisa electric piano, VCS3 synthesiser with EMS sequencer and EMS keyboard, Moog sequencer)[1]

> **Peter Baumann** (Farfisa double keyboard organ, Farfisa Professional organ, Fender Rhodes electric piano, Mellotron 400, Elka electric string organ, two AKS synthesisers with EMS touch keyboards, ARP 2600 synthesiser with keyboard, Moog sequencer)

> **Cristoph Franke** (modified AKS synthesiser, Elka electronic string organ, two Moog 300 P synthesisers with two modified 4-Moog synthesisers, ARP 3600, Farfisa Professional organ, Mellotron 400, custom-built computerised rhythm controller).

It's a recording mostly made at Fairfield Halls in Croydon a week after Liverpool Cathedral, and partly in Bordeaux the previous month. Before deciding which material to use for the LP, the band had apparently listened to around 40 hours of improvised live recordings.

It's a video game that was played a lot during the European tour and gave the album its name.

It's two vivid memories of how I experienced it lying down: first, the transcendent isolation and immersion of live

---

1   He also played a Fender Stratocaster.

electronic music at high volume in the chilly blue darkness, alone but surrounded by other people; second, propulsive cosmic music on a small record player in the fumbling intimacy of a tiny bedroom, only I wasn't really listening.

It's the intersection and layering of these two experiences, and others. Its artistic absence permeates *Quantum Gate*'s limp melodies and lush, overworked arpeggios. In fact when I first listened to *Quantum Gate* in the car, it was dark and I thought I'd put something else on. As a consequence, my first impression of the lo-fi electronic music of Swedish musician Callenberg was that it sounded like not-very-good Tangerine Dream.

It's a source of confusion: if the music on the tour was improvised, could I have recognised it on an LP six months later? Edgar Froese's memory of the tour was apparently: 'We went up on stage and called out the key to one another, and we said "Ok, tonight it's E"... and one of us started with a soundscape maybe, or sometimes with a flute, or someone surprised us by kicking in with the rhythm right at the beginning, and then things started to converge and everything ran together – or it didn't converge at all; it was a total adventure.' So maybe I recognised the sounds on the LP, or maybe I didn't. Maybe I saw the cover when Evelyn put it on. What's for certain is that when I found a recording of the Liverpool gig online, it wasn't *Ricochet*: musically, it was the same band, but on an evening when things didn't quite converge; sonically, it suggested that someone had recorded the event on a dictaphone.

Ricochet is part of my headful of music: a strange, wonderful, intoxicating, fascinating, baffling, overwhelming, evocative, seductive, addictive mix of sounds, thoughts and feelings that I can't live without but is sometimes hard to make sense of. And out of all those adjectives, it's difficult to tell from moment to moment which ones apply to any of the music in my head and in my life, because they all do, at different times in different places. And that's without including things that are banal, cynical, derivative, self-satisfied, ridiculous, grim, disappointing, tedious, pretentious or just plain shite.

The lived experience of music is part of the lived experience of life – for performers, audiences, critics, collectors and listeners. And the older you get, and the older music-as-we-know-it gets, and the more of it becomes available, the more it all seems to collide, intersect and overlap. Memories, feelings, meanings, music: everything connects. What was once an album (or just an album) when released might now have been around long enough and become important enough to have made the transition from 'just an album' to an uppercase canonical Classic Album. Patti Smith released *Horses* in 1975. Whether or not you liked it at the time, the remarkable (or once remarkable, but not any more) fact is that in 2005 on its 30th anniversary, she performed the album in its entirety at the Meltdown festival in London, which she also curated. Her performance of the record was itself recorded and released as an album – a double album that as well as this live performance also included a remastered version of the original, and was sold as *Horses/Horses*.

Patti Smith was inducted into the Rock and Roll Hall of Fame in 2007. Along with Grandmaster Flash and the Furious Five, REM, the Ronettes and Van Halen. According to the Hall of Fame website, artists become eligible 25 years after the release of their first commercial recording. Besides demonstrating unquestionable musical excellence and talent, inductees will have had a significant impact on the development, evolution and preservation of rock and roll.

This kind of thing happens all the time. David Bowie was inducted in 1996, along with Gladys Knight and the Pips, Jefferson Airplane, Pink Floyd, Pete Seeger and the Velvet Underground. When he curated Meltdown in 2002, he performed the whole of *Low* as well as a new album, *Heathen*. Although he's no longer with us, this year (and it doesn't really matter which year any more), you could have joined his former pianist Mike Garson on 'Aladdin Sane: The Tour' as he performed 'Bowie's masterpiece album in its entirety in addition to a second set of Bowie favourites'. And earlier in the year, Tony Visconti and Woody Woodmansey performed *Ziggy Stardust* along with an all-star line-up at Friar's Aylesbury because the album's performance debut had been at the same venue in 1972. Forty-five years previously. And Rick Wakeman, who played piano on 'Life On Mars', has been performing it as part of a 'Piano Portraits In Concert' tour, also taking in the likes of 'Stairway To Heaven', 'Wondrous Stories' (Yes), 'I'm Not In Love' (10 CC), and 'Space Oddity'.

And then there's Bootleg Bowie UK; Pop Up Bowie; The Bowie Experience; The Sound of Bowie; Ziggy: The Ultimate David Bowie; The Thin White Duke Band; David Live; The Sensational David Bowie Tribute Band; Absolute Bowie; Rebel Heroes; Spiders on Mars...

Now that so much music has acquired such an unwieldy sense of importance and self-importance and everything is preserved online steeped in the brine of history, a kind of osmotic pressure has built up, a subliminally absorbed and cumulative knowingness that didn't exist when the music was fresh and everything was happening for the first time. Once experienced, it can't be un-experienced; freshly picked is different from carefully (or carelessly) preserved. And after marinating for so long in my life, music has changed, and so have I: we've both grown older. The ways I've changed are there in the mirror and the size of my trousers, as well as in the fact that I have two adult children: one of them is older than I was when I met my wife; the other is past the age that I myself was when she was born. As for music, it's changed in ways that are obvious, and some that are less so.

It's common for older people, old people, or people like me to remark on the rate of change in the world, and over my lifetime and my listening time, I have experienced 78s, 45s, LPs, cassettes, CDs and downloads, and now I have over 46,000 disembodied songs on my computer. More than 129 days of continuous music.

Allowing an average of ten songs per album, that's more than 4,500 LPs.

At 140 g per LP, that's about 630 kg of vinyl without album covers.

Allowing 250 LPs per metre, that's around 18m of shelving

Which is about 1.6 cubic metres of vinyl, cardboard and paper. Stored on something not much bigger than a cassette.

In 1969 the Canadian composer, writer and environmentalist R Murray Schafer coined the word *schizophonia* to refer to the splitting of sound from its source.[2] This began with the telephone, then the radio, phonograph, and tape recorder. In essence, they're different permutations of the microphone and speaker/earphone system used to capture, transmit, store and reproduce sound. Whether it's phone conversations, radio broadcasts or albums, we live immersed in schizophonia like fish in an ocean of sound. Just as language was captured and fixed in writing and then print, sound has been plucked from the air and preserved in discs, tapes and hard drives. This process of reification, of turning sound into things, into *stuff*, prompts new ways of thinking that were unimaginable when speech vanished after you had spoken; when your voice travelled only as far as you could shout; when listening to music meant sitting in a room with musicians.

We all now listen to music from elsewhere or elsewhen, and this changes everything. Once sound has become *stuff*, it can be chopped up, slowed down, reversed, copied and recombined with other sounds. The medium itself becomes musical material, and its characteristics come to inform what music actually is. The Beatles realised this; and so did those whose influences they absorbed via multi-tracking, *musique concrete*, sound effects, cut-ups and all the rest. The medium is a message; the studio is an instrument; the producer is an artist.

---

2 Using historical records, his 1977 book *The Tuning Of The World* documents changes in the acoustic environment over the centuries, and proposes terms such as 'soundscape' and 'soundmark' (from 'landscape' and 'landmark') as part of a new discipline, acoustic ecology.

In 1964 the brilliant, eccentric Canadian pianist and Golden Record contributor Glenn Gould gave his last public performance at the age of 31. Between then and his death in 1982, he concentrated on studio work, recording different versions of pieces and assembling them to create idealised composite recordings. At one stage in an ongoing argument about the authenticity of live versus studio recordings, he apparently challenged listeners, musicians and sound engineers to identify the points in his recordings where splices occurred: all identified splices in different places, and none were correct. Gould likened what he did to the work of a film editor: nobody would think a two-hour film had been shot in two hours, so why expect this of recorded music? In fact, you could argue that in the schizophonic age the most authentic approach is to acknowledge the microphone and the recorder, and celebrate the possibilities they offer. To deny or discount this new kind of artificiality as inauthentic, would itself be inauthentic. With this in mind, consider the words of Lord Henry Wotton in Oscar Wilde's novel *The Picture Of Dorian Gray*: 'Being natural is simply a pose, and the most irritating pose I know.'

In 1977, something amazing happened twice: an LP called *The Sounds Of Earth* was issued to the cosmos via the Voyagers. Was the music it contained a pose, an irritating pose, and therefore a betrayal of some kind? All of it, the field recordings and studio recordings, from folk to classical to blues to jazz, was captured and reproduced 'naturally' rather than naturally, contained within sonic quote marks. These signify that the journey of the sounds from the air, via microphones, tapes and records, to their eventual incarnation in spiral scratches on discs of gilded copper, was highly mediated, but went unnoticed or unacknowledged. Swimming in the ocean of schizophonia, there was no separation from the vast, immersive infrastructure of energy and technology that made recording possible.[3]

---

3 Ironically, Alan Lomax went on to develop the hugely ambitious Cantometrics and Choreometrics projects to document and preserve

In fact, there is an electronic composition on the LP, but it's not with the music. Following on from Kurt Waldheim's opening message, the greetings in 55 languages, the UN greetings and the whale song, it can be heard at the beginning of the second part, the audio collage of Earth sounds. The sounds are ordered from the distant geological past (volcanoes, earthquakes and thunder) through to the technological present (EEG recording, pulsar recording). The electronic music isn't included as music, nor as a sound from Earth. Called 'Music of the Spheres', it's actually a representation of the sounds of planetary motion as proposed by the German astronomer, mathematician and astrologer Johannes Kepler in his 1619 book *Harmonices Mundi* (The Harmonies Of The World). The piece acts as a cosmic introduction to the collage section, with the imagined music of the spheres setting the scene for the sounds of our own sphere, Earth.

What you hear is a slowly changing set of electronic tones. On one level, it's a piece of music that's not especially pleasant to listen to. On another level, it's potential made manifest: Kepler described the ratios of the planetary orbits but was unable to generate the sounds. 'Music of the Spheres' came about in 1977 when the American composer and computer musician Laurie Spiegel ran a programme to 'play' Kepler's analyses of planetary motion. Carl Sagan liked the idea, and so an extract of the piece was included on the LP, making Laurie Spiegel and Chuck Berry the only living composers on the record and the only explicit examples of the schizophonic, electronic culture that brought into being the Voyager LP and launched it into space. Implicitly however, schizophonia is everywhere, if you know where to listen. It's in the recording and editing together of speeches

---

the diversity of pre-radio, pre-phonograph folk music and dance around the world before it was swept away. These projects were only possible once the film and tape technology required for the under-taking had become good enough and cheap enough for widespread use, a process which was itself accelerating the decline in localised indigenous cultures.

and greetings, which suggests an illusory crowd of people addressing an imagined listener one by one: there was no such gathering. It's also in the collecting of sounds and music from around the world, and in their sequencing/juxtaposition. It's even in a detail like the way the greetings fade out, as though each speaker has moved rapidly away from the microphone/listener until inaudible, either because they're too far away or have lowered the volume of their voice until it becomes too quiet to hear.

It's hard to think yourself into the kind of acoustic literal-mindedness that preceded schizophonia.[4] For example, contrast something simple like an edited fade-out, the kind of thing we don't even notice, with a physically enacted fade-out, or diminuendo, like the one in 'Neptune, the Mystic' from Gustav Holst's 'The Planets' (1914-16). In performance, the chorus sings from a separate room offstage while the door is slowly closed, the chorus repeating the final bar until the sound has disappeared. Using a mixer to generate the same effect, you just move a fader.

The first technologically produced fade-outs were used for practical reasons when music stretched across two sides of a 78, in order to soften the transition between the two sides and give a feeling of continuity. One of the earliest creative uses to end a piece of music was as early as 1933, on 'Old Man Harlem' by the Dorsey Brothers. Since then, such artificial techniques have come to seem natural and familiar, and no longer sound odd. Which in a small way is why, in a big way, it's ironic that the Voyager LP is schizophonic in its format but not its content. Apart from Chuck Berry and Laurie Spiegel.

You could argue that none of this really matters, because the Voyagers are too slow and too late – by the time they've covered a fraction of a fraction of a fraction of the distance to the nearest star at their ant-like 35,000 kmph; in fact, before

---

4 I remember hearing songs on the radio when I was very small, and thinking that the room the broadcast was coming from must have been enormous if it was able to hold so many singers and musicians, all gathered there to play their songs.

they even begin their journey in earnest, they will have been outstripped by electromagnetic waves billowing out from our speck of dust at the speed of light: all the radio and TV signals powerful enough to make it into space; popular music, popular culture, humanity with no filters; a surging tide of junk rather than a single, dignified artefact; an electromagnetic tale of sound and fury, signifying nothing – or maybe revealing everything about what we are.

These are two contrasting ideas of culture: midden versus monument. In the movie *2001*, at various stages of development representatives of humanity encounter a featureless, pristine, black monument signifying a powerful and enigmatic Other that, it is suggested, is purposeful and maybe benign. By contrast, in the Russian novel *Roadside Picnic* by Arkady and Boris Stugatsky (1971), the human race is traumatised by a series of unexplained 'Visitations' in various locations that are now cordoned off because alien artefacts with highly unpredictable, almost supernatural properties have been found there. This was the book on which Andrei Tarkovsky's film *Stalker* (1979) was loosely based. The title of the novel provides a suggested explanation for what has happened: imagine us as timid forest creatures rooting about in a trashed, polluted, garbage-strewn human campsite that has been abandoned after a wild party. *The Sounds Of Earth* is the rational monument; radio and TV signals are the roadside picnic.

There was a proposal to include country music on *Sounds Of Earth* to represent the culture of the people who made Voyager and sent it into space. It didn't happen, but what did happen was everything else we've ever broadcast: there's plenty of country music in there, and so there'll be plenty out there as well. This is at least in part down to NASA itself, and its system of 'wakeup calls': music played by Mission Control for the personnel in space. Explanations of the practice vary. According to material compiled by Colin Fries of the NASA History Office, music was originally played to 'promote a sense of camaraderie and esprit de corps among the astronauts and ground support personnel'; alternatively, 'astronauts... were serenaded by their colleagues in mission control with lyrics from popular songs that seemed appropriate to the occasion'. Another explanation by journalist Steve Knopper is slightly looser: 'think of the space shuttle as a high-tech road trip with a difference: you can't get out until the trip is over, pot and beer are forbidden, and 125 miles straight down, somebody who isn't even travelling with you gets to pick what's on the tape deck'.

The first documented wakeup call was in 1965, when 'Hello Dolly' sung by Jack Jones was played to the crew of Gemini 6 on or around December 15, and the idea continued through the Gemini, Apollo, Skylab and Space Shuttle missions. As you might expect, 'Also Sprach Zarathustra' from *2001* got a few plays, and so did 'The Ride of the Valkyries'.[5] 'A Walk in the Black Forest' by Herb Alpert and the Tijuana Brass was played because it was 'symbolic of the fact that the crew of Skylab 4 will be taking a walk in the blackness of space to repair the control system for an Earth-scanning antenna'. 'Stardust' by Willie Nelson got a few plays, as did 'Paralyzed' by the Legendary Stardust Cowboy. Another stardust cowboy, David Bowie, was represented by 'Changes' and 'Space Oddity'.

However, Bowie's greatest triumph surely came when the song 'Space Oddity' was *played in space* by astronaut Chris Hadfield. In some ways it's not a great rendition: musically a bit saccharine, and lyrically tweaked to avoid the original's downbeat ending. But visually it's stunning. And it's *in space*. About 65 seconds in, instead of the countdown to lift-off, there's a some pleasant piano music, and accompanying it a mesmerising but all-too-short ten-second shot of a gently spinning guitar floating off down a cluttered passageway. Then at 4:25 the shot repeats, but this time we see Hadfield

---

5　On one occasion this was because two astronauts had been students at the California Institute of Technology, and 'at 7:00 am it was traditional for students with hi-fi systems to tie them together and wake up everybody in the undergraduate dorms by playing "The Ride" at full volume'.

glide after the guitar, grab it, then when he reaches the end of the corridor he pauses before propelling himself 'upwards' and out of sight. Magical.[6]

Messing with Major Tom despite the warnings heard during the fade-out of 'Ashes to Ashes', the altered lyrics in Hadfield's 'Space Oddity' ensure a successful outcome and satisfy the requirements of life rather than art. It couldn't be otherwise, though it's hard to overlook the irony of this flawed homage to a successful song about a failed space mission: unlike the beautiful, unsettling, downbeat original, there's no eerie orchestration at the end as Major Tom drifts away: we see Chris Hadfield's capsule land and he is lifted out safe and well after six months. The shrieking of nothing isn't killing him, and we know he's not a junkie. Which is a good thing.

Hadfield had previously worked for a number of years as CAPCOM, or capsule communicator, at Mission Control, broadcasting wake-up calls to his fellow astronauts. When 'Details' magazine asked Bowie what he would choose to play to the astronauts, he chose 'Music For 18 Musicians' by Steve Reich. DJ Armand Van Helden chose 'Fly Like An Eagle' by Steve Miller and 'Space Oddity'. Back in 1977 there was a proposal to include 'Here Comes the Sun' by the Beatles on *Sounds Of Earth*, and it was turned down. Then in November 2005 the wake-up call for astronaut Bill McArthur and cosmonaut Valery Tokarev was 'Good Day Sunshine' – performed live by Paul McCartney during his US tour, 220 miles below the International Space Station.

The symbolism of Bowie and Beatle moments like these is inescapable in a world where we've been immersed in popular

---

6   Another, even stranger triumph for the song came with its use as the music playing along with 'Life On Mars' on the music system of a red Tesla Roadster launched into space by Elon Musk's SpaceX corporation in early 2018. The vehicle is the first privately funded payload to escape Earth's gravity. At the wheel is a dummy in a space suit, known as Starman. The Tesla's progress can be followed online, though it is predicted that it will eventually be consumed in the atmosphere of either Earth or Venus.

music for so long it unites generations as well as dividing them. The transmission and accrual of cultural meaning down the years has an apparently irrefutable logic now that everything is stored somewhere to be searched, repeated, shared, re-appraised, covered, referenced, sampled, revived and re-issued. As well as soundtracking our lives, music is the sonic ocean in which we swim, preserving memories and associations, and at the same time defining them. It's programmed into each and every person's nostalgiaphone, that internal serotonin-powered jukebox, that ultimate personal stereo. And, like the students in the dorms at the California Institute of Technology, we can link them up and, enjoying a sense of camaraderie and esprit de corps, play the heck out of them. It's not just the omnipresence of music: there's also that sense of inevitability, of comfort, naturalness and normality in what we for convenience call pop or rock, a quality which allows, almost expects, that it be everywhere all the time, taken for granted and at the same time revered and celebrated and referenced and appropriated, 'our' folk music, 'our' classical music, 'our' cultural heritage.

From the beginning of pop, from the beginning of my life, and from the beginning of this book to now and beyond stretches the magic golden thread of the Beatles. Not just Liverpool's Beatles Quarter around Mathew Street, with the Rubber Soul Oyster Bar and Lennon's Bar and the Cavern Pub; not just the Magical Mystery Tour bus trips around the city; not just the Beatle-themed Hard Day's Night Hotel round the corner from Mathew Street; not just Strawberry Fields in Central Park. There's also **The Beatles Story**, a multimedia exhibition and self-styled 'New Magical Experience' that's 'Getting Better All The Time.' One day when I was down in Birkenhead, I took the ferry 'cross the Mersey and visited it, having until then avoided this *Gesamtkunstwerk* of what could be the greatest story in pop and rock whether or not you like the Beatles, if you don't include Elvis, or maybe even if you do, I don't know.

(Actually, I do know. The Beatles story has to be greater than the Elvis story, because although Elvis came first, the

Beatles did more in their eight years of fame than Elvis ever did in his twenty-odd years of fame, decline and fall. And anyway, John Lennon said Elvis died when he went into the army (though he also said that without Elvis there would be no Beatles); and even though I can imagine there's no Elvis, I can't imagine there's no Beatles, however hard I try. And to show how easy it is for me to imagine there's no Elvis: in the year that the King wore his white jumpsuit in *Aloha from Hawaii*, a live concert beamed by satellite to over 40 countries, and the first live global music event of its kind, in that year, when the technology was sophisticated and powerful enough to allow it to happen, Elvis was still being the same old Elvis, and his music was still the same old music.[7] That was in 1973, the year Pink Floyd released *Dark Side Of The Moon*, which was a kind of *Sergeant Pepper* for the seventies. So I can imagine there's no Elvis, but I can't imagine there's no Beatles, and I now realise I can't imagine there's no Pink Floyd either.)

Anyway, **The Beatles Story** is the Beatles' story, or one version of it, as well as apparently being *the world's only Beatles-themed visitor attraction*. Appropriately, it's a Living History audio guide – produced by Antenna Audio, who are also responsible for Graceland. And why wouldn't you want to experience the Beatles story in audio, as without audio they're nothing but landfill.

So, down the steps and into the bowels of the earth, or the bowels of Albert Dock, which means the bowels of the Mersey. Then along a dark-on-a-sunny-day corridor past grainy Beatles faces much bigger than I am, paying at the till, picking up a headset, turning a corner and stepping into the Beatles labyrinth.

This was going to be

---

7 *Aloha From Hawaii* was one of the three main performances that featured in Dead Elvis's *Elvis: The Concert*. The other two were *Elvis: That's The Way It Is* and *Elvis On Tour*.

A labyrinth isn't the same as a maze. A maze is a puzzle: you constantly have to decide which way to go, remembering every twist and turn otherwise you get lost and can't find your way back. A labyrinth doesn't branch; it's just a path you follow, and although it takes you backwards and forwards and round and round, you never get lost: all you have to do is keep going.

Walking a labyrinth can be a form of meditation. It can be a microcosmic pilgrimage, walked or even crawled over a cathedral floor, like the one at Chartres, by all those who never travelled but wanted to go on a journey. Enacting such a ritual of contemplation and worship, you lose all sense of where you are and who you are, remaining mindful only that wherever you are, whoever you are, whichever direction you are facing from moment to moment, you began at the beginning and will end at the end, and in between you surrender to the journey and follow the path, walking the line, living your life, travelling your story, in the moment now, and now, and now.

Strawberry Fields

So, where did I go? Well, it was a labyrinth, so I went everywhere, and nowhere. Like the other pilgrims, I surrendered to the journey and followed the path. I walked the songline down a replica street, through a replica café, newspaper office, record store and Cavern club; a replica yellow submarine and a replica airliner; a replica music shop, pub, recording studio and Octopus's garden, and ended up looking through a pair of John Lennon's glasses.

quoted a few lines at a time

On the way I saw a Beatles writing pad, dinner plate, stockings, tie pin, tea tray, wig, record cabinet and handkerchief, although none of this was music. I could have stopped 43 times at any of the listening stations, the Stations Of the Beatles on this subterranean or submarine labyrinthine Beatles Cathedral floor. There was no music on the headphones: I heard mainly John's sister Julia Baird intoning platitudes (not necessarily her own) from the Beatles story, along with other people such as Gerry Pacemaker, Brian Epstein, Peter Blake and George Martin. Every time I stopped to listen, although I could hear the voice of Julia, Gerry or Brian, I could also hear at least two Beatles songs playing nearby, and I could hear none of these things clearly. Rather than poor design, this could have been a clever way of evoking the sensory overload that the Beatles themselves experienced when they watched TV with the sound turned down and the radio turned up while glancing through magazines and newspapers, taking drugs and opening themselves up to Random. After all, everybody does this kind of thing now.

alluding to the words of the song

Here and there a mannequin posed woodenly or plasticly in a dusty replica Merseybeat office, or outside a replica Casbah Club, or, most bizarrely, in a small boxy white room that was meant to be the Abbey Road studio. Four Beatles dummies stood stiff, dusty and angular in their matching suits and wigs, maybe inspired by Kraftwerk.[8] I waited to see if Johndummy, Pauldummy, Georgedummy and Ringodummy would start moving, break the glass, and start to dance, like Ralfdummy, Floriandummy and the other two – perhaps just a little bit at first, then more and more until eventually, twitching and flailing, overloaded by so many songs, they overheated and fell apart in a smoking, acrid jumble of melted limbs, singed hair and sparking chest cavities, because there was just *too much music*. But they didn't.

and the cut-up techniques

---

8   Although the Beatles had stopped wearing matching clothes by then. And Kraftwerk wouldn't dress this way for a number of years.

It was hard to separate what was meant to be real from what wasn't. The Beatles were meant to be real, even though they were dummies; and some kind of Beatles' story was real, as related by the labels, notices and listening stations; but so was the health and safety signage, which meant that near the replica studio and next to the fire exit was a jumble of notices that said

Abbey Road Studios

No Admittance

PUSH BAR TO OPEN

This famous photograph showing the Beatles walking across the pedestrian crossing was taken outside EMI's studios in London

WARNING STROBE LIGHTS are in limited use in the Abbey Road Studio set

Rolf Harris creating a sound effect while recording 'Tie Me Kangaroo Down Sport' in studio two at Abbey Road, 1960.

used to create the music

Further on in the display but further back in time was a video showing the Maharishi Mahesh Yogi chapter of the story, and under the screen a notice said

PLEASE REMOVE YOUR HEADPHONES TO LISTEN TO THE PROGRAMME OR LOWER THE VOLUME ON YOUR HEADSET.

I removed my headphones and was able to make out some of the video commentary, but what I could mainly hear was 'Magical Mystery Tour' and 'Sergeant Pepper's Lonely Hearts

Club Band' playing to my left and right, and screaming, lots of screaming from behind me – four different things at once.

from pieces of magnetic tape

The screaming was the strangest thing of all. It drew me towards it and, hypnotised, I entered a long narrow corridor with seven TV screens set into one wall, all of which showed the same black and white slow-motion footage of hysterical writhing girls, mainly in close-up, endlessly repeated. The opposite wall was mirrored, showing multiple reflections of the screens and of me looking at the screens. At the same time I was immersed in a sea of metallic screaming from a row of speakers, an endlessly self-referential, endlessly cycling, endlessly reflecting shrine, not to the Beatles, but to the fans, mainly the girls but really all the fans, and the tidal wave of abandon and desire they generated, a collective tsunami that swept the Beatles and everyone else along until it all went wrong, collapsed, and washed them up on their four desert islands, leaving us scattered everywhere else in their detritus: writing pads, dinner plates, stockings and all the rest.

and set it free

For several minutes I stood transfixed, partly there and partly back when I heard that screaming for the first time, perhaps on October 13, 1963, my fourth birthday, the night the Beatles played at the London Palladium, the night before the word *Beatlemania* first appeared in headlines and then later on in dictionaries. What a strange, overwhelming noise and what a strange, overwhelming exhibit; what a perfect, inspired thing amongst all the tat and noise and gratuitous information; what a perfect surreal hyperreal shrine to the impersonal, screaming jet-engine sonic universe of hysteria, greed, money, fame and desperation that was the Beatles on tour and in real life, and in unreal and hyperreal life. A shrine as well to the people who lived through it with them – as fans and friends and spouses and siblings and parents and children and lovers and gurus and rivals and groupies and managers and dealers and writers and photographers and stalkers and killers.

Because who needs all the usual stuff about the Beatles? It's all out there already, and the kind of people who visit **The Beatles Story** probably know it. Instead of that, what I wanted were bizarre-*in-a-good-way* tableaux; art and artefacts that revealed the power of Random; jokery that was deliberately rather than unintentionally funny, and at the same time deadly serious, the type of humour that the exhibition organisers obviously didn't get. Like they probably didn't get Edward Lear, Lewis Carroll, Dada, The Goons or listening to records while watching TV, reading magazines and taking drugs.

Like they didn't get the *Sgt Pepper* LP cover, where the Beatles, dressed as the Lonely Hearts Club Band, stand next to waxworks of their earlier selves, and in front of a crowd of their heroes, fifty-odd cut-out figures of stars, artists, eccentrics and weirdos crammed together in a collaged crowd that's as packed with meaning as it is with familiar and not-so-familiar faces. You can tell the organisers didn't get the LP cover, because in this display the waxwork Beatles and the real Beatles were just cut-outs like all the rest, the depth and playfulness gone, layers of allusion flattened to an assemblage of grainy cardboard flatness.

to drift through history

As part of my research for this book, I visited a hypnotherapist to find out what musical memories I might be able to recover. I was excited at the prospect of all kinds of vivid, surprising flashes of recall and insight flickering across a screen somewhere inside my head, with my little homunculus sitting there watching and making notes. But throughout the session, down behind the chocolate darkness of my closed eyes, the detached feeling of relaxation in a comfy armchair and my occasional desire to giggle, all that really came back was an image of me standing in my cousin's living room hearing screaming. All I could see was flashes of him, small, the same height as me, rosy-cheeked and excited; the arms of some brown or grey furniture, and a TV set; and all I could hear was Beatlemania.

and through our minds

In the labyrinth I saw the Cavern. As we know, the Cavern in Mathew Street is a replica on the other side of the street from the actual Cavern, and here in the Beatles Story there's another replica, a stage set, surrounded by signage:

NO SMOKING

NO PHOTOGRAPHY

CARBON DIOXIDE

The Original Cavern Club opened in 1957 and closed in 1971. In 1995 this actual set was used in the making of the Beatles video 'Free as a Bird' in which original Beatles footage was superimposed onto this stage.

It was used for about five seconds, almost a minute into the video, as the camera veers about, like it's flying, and like it's a bird, and it's free.[9] There were rows of wooden chairs to sit while you gazed at the stage and took surreptitious photos, though there was a red rope drawn across to stop you getting too close or touching anything.

something that still sounds

I saw the gravestone of Eleanor Rigby, died in the church and buried along with her name – only she didn't die and she

---

9   And by the way, in the video you get to see things like a 'paperback writer', and a birthday cake with '64' on it, and some 'piggies' and an 'eggman' and a 'helter skelter' and a 'long and winding road'.

wasn't buried because it was just a song but, weirdly, she still has a headstone, and a sign that says:

> *This 'Film Prop' Eleanor Rigby Gravestone was used by 'The Beatles' in their 1995 comeback video 'Free as a Bird'. The Beatles Story 'replica Cavern' was also used in the same film. When the filming was complete 'The Beatles' contributed this gravestone to be exhibited in 'The Beatles Story'. It weighs 50 stone and is made of solid granite.*

It appears for about three seconds as the free-as-a-bird-cam swoops round it, then round the churchyard, before moving on. The gravestone didn't need to be made of granite: it could and should have been made of polystyrene or cardboard, like a TV or theatre prop, which is a much less literal and more authentically Beatle approach.

strange, wonderful and new

The Yellow Submarine was nearby, or the interior was. The exterior was parked a few miles away outside John Lennon Airport (motto: 'Above Us Only Sky'). The interior had port holes you could look out of to see actual fish in fish tanks. Which was a great idea, because we were underwater in the Albert Dock at the time, and the jokey artificiality of fish tanks was perfect. But unfortunately there were no big long levers to pull or big shiny buttons you could press to make daft Yellow Submarine noises like those in the song, because this was something else the organisers didn't get: 'Yellow Submarine' is a crazy tune full of noises and sound effects, none of which were here.

after all these years

By keeping going I reached the end, where a hasty summary got us through the last four decades, along with four little shriney booths and a great big **THE STORY**

CONTINUES... Along the final corridor were photographs of faces, and the word *imagine* in different languages. Then, around the corner was a white piano with a pair of glasses resting on it, and you could hear 'Imagine' playing while peering through the glasses.

Imagine 'Imagine', a song written and performed by a secular saint with an airport named after him, above which there's only sky. For me, it's actually Phil Spector's production that makes this song. That and the piano. And John Lennon's voice. And there's the tune as well, which locates the song in a curious musical space somewhere between a maudlin nursery rhyme and a God-free hymn written and sung specially for atheists.

Now imagine 'Imagine' being so popular and iconic that it's played by bellringers on the massive bells of Liverpool's Anglican Cathedral, ringing out across Merseyside. If you can't imagine this, check online, because that's what happened on 16 May 2009 as part of the Futuresonic festival. And if that isn't enough, imagine that just by playing 'Imagine' to a glass of water you can transform it into a special kind of holy water that's better for you than ordinary water, and forms beautiful ice crystals when you freeze it. And imagine that, by contrast, playing heavy metal to a similar glass of water produces distorted and fragmented crystals, because of the way that the *hado* or subatomic vibrations from these different kinds of holy and unholy music affect the structure of the water.[10] Now imagine there's no 'Imagine'. You can't, and neither can I.

of being played

I handed back my headset and came out through the Costa coffee franchise, up the stairs and into the souvenir shop that squatted over the exit. I bought a commemorative box of postcards and a pack of playing cards and then, deaf with music and platitudes, blind with images, stupid with

---

10 See appendix eight.

information, I emerged blinking and exhausted into the glare of the afternoon sunlight.

I think what happened in **The Beatles Story** was that I went down into a kind of Beatles netherworld and came out knowing that I'd been, but unsure of anything else. I took away souvenirs, a scrambled brain and a sense of disappointment. Like the meaning of a dream, only later did the realisation emerge that although the Beatles are just as real or unreal as everything else, and although they make as much or as little sense as everything else, sometimes, when you turn and face the strange, that's not enough.

over and over and over and over again

After listening to them all my life through hundreds of media events that used them as shorthand for the sixties, for modernity, for nostalgia, for rebellion, for innocence, for loss of innocence, for obsession, for madness, what I eventually realised was that in that trip to the underworld, in a place haunted by their absence, I found My Beatles.

but then I discovered how expensive it could be to obtain permission, how long it could take, and how costly it might turn out to be if permission wasn't obtained, and decided not to bother.

So, to draw attention to this (and question the need for such a paranoid regime of copyright protection around words and music that have become part of everyone and everything), here, cut up and rearranged in alphabetical order, are all 69 of the words used in the song, allowing you to imagine it or create something else:

a, about, all, always, and, bad, be, but, can't, 'cause, closed, disagree, doesn't, down, dream, easy, eyes, fields, forever, get, getting, going, harder, high, hung, I, I'm, in, is (29), it, it's, know, let, living, low, matter, me, mean, misunderstanding, much, must, my, no, no-one, not, nothing (46), one, or, out, real (50), right, see, someone, sometimes, strawberry, take, that, think, to, too, tree, tune, when, will, with, works, wrong, yes, you.

Playlist 11 - Everything Is Real		
Baba O'Riley	The Who	*Who's Next*
Ricochet (Part One)	Tangerine Dream	*Ricochet*
Old Man	Neil Young	*Harvest*
Warszawa	David Bowie	*Low*
Space Oddity	David Bowie	
Life On Mars?	David Bowie	
Ashes To Ashes	Davis Bowie	
Breathe	Pink Floyd	*Dark Side Of The Moon*
Showroom Dummies	Kraftwerk	*Trans Europe Express*
A Day In The Life	The Beatles	*Sergeant Pepper*

To listen to the playlists, visit Spotify using the QR links provided.

Links to every playlist are also at www.hungry-ghost.info, along with photographs and archive material to supplement each chapter and enhance the reading/listening experience, just like a great big gatefold album cover.

11

THE EAR IS A HUNGRY GHOST

As 1984 came and went, along with the music of Crass, Bowie, the Clash, Van Halen, Yusuf Lateef, Hugh Hopper, Anthony Phillips, Rick Wakeman, Spirit, Oingo Boingo and Nash the Slash that namechecked it, I found myself living in Birmingham.

In many ways things felt even more strange and fragmented than now, because at that time we were still between worlds, still crossing the bridge from Analogue to Digital. This is what really, truly separates the seventies from the eighties, rather than anything you can measure using diaries or calendars; this is what separates the seventies from everything that followed; separates our sense of Then from our sense of Now. Then was Analogue, Now is Digital. And back in 1984, at that stage of transition, somewhere on the bridge between the approaching Now and the receding Then, I got to do two things that gave me some idea of me how the future was leaching into the present.

First of all, I saw a job in the Guardian, applied for it, got it, and ended up working as a lexicographer on a research project at the University of Birmingham. This was computational linguistics – an early chance to work with what's now referred to as big data. Despite this description, the work itself was rather prosaic, and all the more fascinating for it – if you're someone like me. It involved reading single lines of text extracted from a six-million word corpus of

English[1] to analyse and define words for a new dictionary. This computerised, evidence-based language project was among the first of its kind, and at the time six million words seemed unbelievably vast, almost infinite. Computers were big, new, expensive mainframes, and access to them was limited – so much so that we worked on A4 printouts using coloured felt pens to mark the different senses of each word, then wrote our conclusions on paper slips (pink for definitions, white for examples), and this information was keyed in by clerical staff. When I used the same database almost twenty years later, I would sit at a terminal in Bishopbriggs just outside Glasgow and the corpus had increased to around five hundred million words; and it was still growing.

As part of one early batch of work, I was given 'fuck' and other associated words to investigate – 'fucking', 'fucker', 'fucked', 'fuck off', 'fuckable' etc. This pleased me for all kinds of reasons, some childish, some academic. Amongst the former was the fact that when the project manager asked me what I was doing I was able to look his way and say, 'I'm doing fuck all at the moment, Patrick'. Another, both childish and academic, was that in the course of my investigations I managed to find a single Derek-and-Clive of a sentence in which 'fuck' was used as verb, adjective and noun:

'Fuck me, George fucking Farr, what the fuck are you doing here?'[2]

Not many people can say they put 'fuck' in a dictionary. It was a bit childish, a lot interesting, and all about pragmatics. As we all know at some level or other, fuck-words rarely refer to any kind of sex act. Most of the time they have almost no semantic content, though their use carries considerable force. Pragmatics is the study of this kind of thing, including the contexts in which language is used, and the choices that are made when expressing yourself: for example, decisions

---

1   Novels, newspapers, magazines, leaflets, transcribed conversations, nonfiction: an attempt at a representative sample of the English language.
2   I think it came from *The Punch Book Of Short Stories*.

about whether or not to swear, which swearwords to choose, which words to emphasise with your swearing, how often to do it, and whether you are doing it to fit in or to stand out. Back when the Sex Pistols were briefly on TV, saying 'fuck' to someone like Bill Grundy in a TV studio was something revolutionary and shocking, the poetics of Quentin Tarantino were yet to come, and Peter Cook (Clive) and Dudley Moore (Derek) were folk heroes. So why wouldn't I be pleased with myself to be doing 'fuck'? It later led to 'bloody', a word which, although also used pragmatically, has much more of a semantic presence.[3]

Now that large amounts of language can be gathered, stored and analysed in new ways, new ideas emerge about how it all works. This was an early example of how big data changes things. Looking at large amounts of language makes it possible to amass evidence about how words are actually used, the previous prescriptive idea about what words mean being replaced by one that is descriptive: rather than being solid, language can be considered as a viscous fluid, everything in flux.

With big data and computational linguistics, we have an overload of the present – it's all about the liquid now. New words, different ways of saying things, new things to talk about; word of the week, word of the month, word of the year.[4] In some ways, this is the opposite of what has happened to music: with music, it's the past that has expanded exponentially, the online archives of all previous music overwhelming the present and maybe the future as well.

---

3 What about the likes of 'cunt' and 'prick' and 'dick' and 'twat'? Another member of the team, Emily, characterised as 'a feminist' (ie assertive, political and for both these reasons a bit scary) had previously bagged them: no idea how she failed to get 'fuck'.

4 Oxford University Press words of the year (others are available): 2017 'youthquake'; 2016 'post-truth'; 2015 the emoji 'face with tears of joy/laughter'; 2014 'vape'; 2013 'selfie'; 2012 'omnishambles'; 2011 'squeezed middle'; 2010 'big society'.

Second of all, I went to some evening classes. As a university staff member, I had the right to attend extramural courses for free which, being in a new place and at a loose end, was what I did: two evening courses on experimental music. They were run by Jonty Harrison, Professor of Electroacoustic Composition, and they changed my ears and my life. The first course was by that time turning out to be quite old-school – *musique concrète*, reel to reel tapes, creative messing about in the Department of Music's studio, recording dropping marbles into a bottle, scrunching up and tearing aluminium foil, banging things and shaking things, splicing and editing magnetic tape. What happened on the course was that my sense of hearing changed so that afterwards any interesting sound I encountered became invested with musical possibility. I learned that once tape-recorded or 'sampled', a sound could be cut up and rearranged, slowed down, speeded up, reversed, looped or manipulated using all kinds of effects. We also worked for a time on a huge Emersonesque, Wakemanly synthesiser with a patch field like an old telephone exchange and banks of knobs and dials that we could twiddle to produce gorgeous, ugly, exotic and bizarre sounds. Between them, these approaches to sound characterised two early schools of 20th century experimental music: tapes versus synthesis; French taped *musique concrète* versus German synthesised *elektronische Musik*.

The first music course was analogue; the second was digital, and involved a Fairlight, something that looked like it had been wrenched from the bridge of the *Enterprise*. There was a QWERTY keyboard and a floppy-disc drive; there was a cream-coloured box the size of a suitcase; a cathode-ray monitor screen displaying green waveforms, a light pen and, oh yes, a music keyboard. Its full name was the Fairlight Computer Musical Instrument, and it had been beamed in from the future. We take digital sampling for granted now, the fact that music is just movable ones and zeros; the idea that it might contain or be made entirely from other music, or perhaps sound sources such as car doors slamming and engines revving,[5] or breaking glass,[6] or dogs barking[7].

None of this is now surprising, but the first time I heard someone say the phrase 'do right' into a microphone then play it up and down a keyboard, it stunned me: doo **doo**-doo doo-doo-**doo**, doo **doo**-doo doo-doo-**doo**. Later, when I found out that 'Do Right' was a track off the Cabaret Voltaire album *Micro-Phonies*, that was stunning too, as was the way it was mixed into another album track, 'Sensoria' to produce a thudding, cavernous 12" single, also confusingly called 'Sensoria'. Just a few years later, I bought myself a small Yamaha VSS-30 Portasound sampling keyboard. At a time when the Fairlight would have cost about £20,000 I got the Yamaha for £60. Now I can do similar things on my phone.

I used the Yamaha to make the only piece of recorded music I have so far released. The instruments used were my Yamaha sampler, a radio cassette recorder and the Voyager spacecraft. I recorded the end of a news item about Voyager[8] using the radio cassette recorder, sampled it one phrase at a time along with fragments of music from another news item, then laboriously recorded it back onto the radio cassette recorder using the built-in microphone, phrase by phrase, fragment by fragment, sample by sample. At some stage after this Martin Archer, musician and owner of the independent label Discus, advertised for pieces of music less than two

---

5 'Close (To The Edit)' (1984) by The Art of Noise which, as well as A VW Golf, also sampled 'Owner Of A Lonely Heart' and 'Leave It' by Yes. The title of the single is itself a kind of sample, referencing the Yes LP *Close To The Edge*.

6 'Babooshka' (1980), a single by Kate Bush from the album *Never For Ever*, and one of the earliest songs to feature Fairlight samples.

7 German electronic musician and producer Harry Thumann released a series of 'dog records' under the name Wonder Dog, derived from recordings of his dog Calypso. One of these, 'Ruff Mix', was acquired by Simon Cowell and charted at number 31 in August 1982. Cowell promoted the single with a series of visits to TV studios in which he danced to the song and gave interviews wearing a blue dog costume.

8 'What we hear is the sound from Voyager, as it swept safely past the five rings of Neptune, never to return.'

minutes long to be compiled on a CD, *Network: Volume Two: 54 Music Miniatures* (1995).[9] So I sent him an edited version of 'The Sound from Voyager', in which what we hear, just about, is the sound from Voyager as it sweeps safely past the five rings of Neptune, never to return. Fittingly, it was the last track on the CD.

Other appropriations of Voyager sounds include *Scrambles Of Earth: The Voyager Interstellar Record, Remixed By Extraterrestrials*, formerly available via the website of sonic activists and copyright troublemakers Negativland. It's currently out of print, though the website[10] provides more than enough information to make you really want a copy. A couple of other reworkings, perhaps less *Alien* and more *ET*, are tracks by John Lomberg's daughter DJ Merav, and by Tonio Sagan, Carl's eldest grandchild.

From new devices and new ideas, from cheapness and availability, all kinds of strange, fragmented, wonderful new music has emerged, because the sound of Voyager can be music, and so can the sound of anything, just like John Cage said. And the sound of music can be music as well, because one of the things we've ended up with is the fragmentedness and mutant strangeness of 'do right', which I heard in a recording studio in Birmingham, then later in a record shop where I was pummelled by a 12" single and then compelled to buy it, only to realise later again that it was two album tracks being played at the same time. Which is nothing compared with what's happened since – like *As Heard on Radio Soulwax Pt. 2* by 2 many dj's, a mix album in which two Belgian chaps from Ghent (David and Stephen Dewaele)

---

9 There was previously *Network: Volume One: 55 Music Miniatures* (1994). Prior to this, musician and artist Morgan Fisher released *miniatures - a sequence of 51 tiny masterpieces* (1980) , featuring the likes of the Residents, Roger McGough, John Otway, David Bedford, Robert Wyatt, George Melly, Robert Fripp, Andy Partridge, Quentin Crisp, Ralph Steadman, Ivor Cutler, Dave Vanian, Mark Perry, Michael Nyman, Kevin Coyne, RD Laing and Pete Seeger. A second volume followed in 2000, but failed to live up to its predecessor. How could it?

10 earthscramble.com; see also negativland.com

smash, clash and trash more mashes than you'd get doing the mashed potato on a great big mashed potato mountain.[11] As well as sounding unbelievable, it's a stunning piece of conceptual art – you don't have to hear it to get it, though you do need to hear it to realise how funny, clever and bonkers it is, and how well it works. And even if you never hear that album, every live set they do or that or anyone like them does will be a different variation of the same thing. If I had to choose a favourite, it might be the hard and horny one where 'Push It' by Salt 'n' Pepa meets 'No Fun' by the Stooges, which turned out to be one of the small number of Nick Hornby's 31 songs that I actually knew.[12]

Once the sampler was out of its box, once the tapes and the turntables were turning, it was getting too late to be modern any more, because we were getting to be post-modern, and then post-everything. In a way, it felt like the end of history. Linear history was short, it lasted about five thousand years, from the clay tablet to the tablet computer, from linear and hierarchical record keeping to random access. It feels like we are now living in a different world. I think the first time I heard this was back towards the end of the Analogue Age on *My Life In The Bush Of Ghosts*. I now have only two things to say about that album:

1. I had never heard anything like it before
2. It came out in 1980, about forty years ago; how did that happen?

And sampling not only begat *My Life in the Bush of Ghosts*; not just hip-hop and house and trance and techno and grime and footwork and all the rest I can't be bothered to name-check or don't know anything about. It has also cosmically begotten the ultimate version of the Grateful Dead. Yes, the

---

11 See appendix nine.
12 Apart from this and 'Frankie Teardrop' by Suicide, the others I knew were 'I'm Like A Bird' (Nelly Furtado); 'Heartbreaker' (Led Zeppelin); 'Samba Pa Ti' (Santana); 'Reasons To Be Cheerful, Part 3' (Ian Dury & The Blockheads); 'Röyskopp's Night Out' (Röyskopp).

Grateful Dead, in collaboration with a Canadian called John Oswald. Over the years Oswald has produced a series of 'plunderphonic' sample works of sonic anarchism/terrorism, the densest of which, *Plexure*,[13] claimed to be a condensed history of the CD, plundering and combining the work of over a thousand pop stars including

Aretha Vanilli
Bing Stingspreen
Bolton Chili Overdire
Moody Crue
Superloaf
Jon Bon Elton
Little Keith Richard
Debbie Idol
U-52s
Halen Oates
Marianne Faith No Morrisey
Cheap Pixie Peppers
Doobie Osmond.

Much of the end result is more or less unlistenable, which is a shame because we need music as well as concept art. Where we do get music from Oswald, though, is in *Grayfolded*, which is where the Grateful Dead come in. Via bassist Phil Lesh, Oswald was commissioned to make a piece using material from the Dead vaults, because they, or Lesh, got the *Plexure* joke. What Oswald came up with was a CD, *Transitive Axis*, and then another CD, *Mirror Ashes*, in which he did a similar thing to *Plexure*, using only performances of the Dead live favourite 'Dark Star', a hundred or so versions stretched out, chopped up and overlaid to form a cosmic conceptual concept double album that must be at

---

13 For this and a range of related material, visit negativland.com. You can for example buy CDs and books relating to Negativland's lengthy, absurd and arduous copyright battles with representatives of a well-known rock group whose name includes the letter U and the number 2.

least as cosmic and conceptual as *Murmurs of Earth*. And to make the conceptual point visually as well, mapped out on the sleeve are the sections of the performances Oswald used. In this strange and beautiful monument, *Grayfolded* has become studio-distilled essence of 'Dark Star' in the way that 'Strawberry Fields' became a distillation of 'Strawberry Fields'.

This type of work uses the computer like a microscope, operating within songs almost at the cellular level, taking things apart and reassembling them to create new forms that can be so abstract they don't sound like songs, sometimes because they aren't songs, just ideas. Above the cellular, it's more like vivisection, reconfiguring heads, limbs and torsos, creating fantastic Franken-sounds that might be recognisably still songs and recognisably, viscerally, enjoyable, with the shock of recognition and juxtaposition being part of the process. Once disc jockeys worked *between* songs; now DJs can work *within* songs as well.

Either way, what we're listening to is what we've always listened to for as long as there have been DJs – the choosing, ordering and juxtaposition of music by someone else; another person's tastes applied to their choice of music for our entertainment and enlightenment. And the more highly developed or broad or just plain eccentric those tastes are, the greater the potential for surprise and enjoyment. That's what the greatest DJs are about; that's why we need them, and that's why for me there has to be something about John Peel here. The man who more or less ran a pirate radio station from within Radio One for 37 years and who, instead of adhering to a playlist, adopted a policy he described as childish, arbitrary and unfair. He was the first to give out titles and record labels on air; to play tracks complete without talking over them; to play the same record twice in a row ('Teenage Kicks'). Two years before he died, in 2002, the year of the Queen's Golden Jubilee and my Silver Dead Elvis Jubilee Moment, John Peel was responsible for *Fabriclive07*. This was the seventh in an ongoing series of Fabric mix CDs that I had never heard of until I read a review of *Fabriclive07*, after which I bought it. It's basically a John Peel mixtape made in a particular place at a particular time, in the same way that all his radio programmes were, only this one was a distillation of all the others, essence of music, essence of Peel.[14] If you want a summary of John Peel, all the music he played and loved throughout his life, what's so great about music and why I thought a book like this one was a good idea, raise a few glasses to the old fart and put on *Fabriclive07*.[15]

This CD is the sort of thing that should go with the next Voyager probe if there is one, assuming NASA doesn't just super-glue a nuclear-powered iPod to the side. It's all there, or most of it is; as much music and ideas about music as you're going to get on one CD, all bookended by excited football commentary from a Liverpool game at one end, and the Kop singing 'You'll Never Walk Alone' over 'Love Will Tear Us Apart' before it crashes into 'Teenage Kicks' at the other end. And because Peel tended to overlook bands he felt were getting enough attention elsewhere, he acknowledges the Sex Pistols and Iggy Pop by playing bluegrass cover versions ('Purty Vacant' by the Kingswoods and 'Lust For Life' by the Bad Livers). Songs he wanted to use but couldn't included something by the Ramones – too costly – and something by Status Quo – too unfashionable, and therefore surely perfect.

What John Peel and 2 many dj's and all the others represent is a way of managing or making sense of All The Music All The Time. Enthusiasts, DJs, critics, journalists, nerds, bloggers, compilers, collectors, curators, gatekeepers – they're the ones who filter out the rubbish and feed you decent or interesting stuff to save you listening to everything or worrying about what you've missed. Life's too short to listen to everything (it's mostly shite anyway), so let others do the filtering. We need this kind of mediation, especially when there's too much media.

---

14 From an interview on the BBC website: 'Nobody had asked me to do it before, and it's nice to have, it'd be nice for my children to have when I'm dead – you know, "Dad chose these".'
15 See appendix ten.

To some extent it's about breadth versus depth. You might want breadth (you might not), but much of the time that's the way we experience music: as covers, tributes, pastiches, mixes, compilations, playlists. You might want depth, riches in scarcity, listening to the same music all the time because less is more. This what I often do in the car. In-car CD players have a simple, magical and often overlooked feature, *resume* – every time you turn on the ignition, the CD continues from where you left off, so you (eventually) get to listen to any album from start to finish, maybe over a period of several days, in a way that doesn't happen anywhere else. Listening time is expanded and yet at the same time compressed, with all the bits between the listening edited out, and all the occasions of hearing the same thing blurred together or superimposed. It's a peculiar feeling. There's no real beginning or end, just a timeless cycle. And because we have two cars, I can listen to two endless CDs at once, a bit at a time, enjoying them over and over again, like *Pure Brazil* and *Hex*, savouring their fragmented entirety and, when I've had enough, moving on.

For a long time in one car I listened to just one disc of a two-CD set compiled by the DJ Erol Alkan. The two discs were *A Bugged Out Mix* and *A Bugged In Selection*. Because it was a lot more relaxing to drive to, I found myself bugging in.[16] The CD cost a pound in a second-hand shop. It's an eclectic, panoramic selection of tunes beginning with 'Passing Through' by Rare Bird and ending with 'Big City' by Spacemen 3, with birdsong at the beginning and the end so continuous play is truly continuous, and also really rather lovely, as Laurence Llewellyn-Bowen once said of what he'd done to someone's living room. In the other car at the time was a wallet of 20 or so CDs sent to me by a friend, ranging from gamelan to *musique concrète* to field recordings to musical sculptures to experimental piano music to bizarre vocalisations by La Monte Young. You'd have to call that some kind of breadth.

---

16 See appendix eleven.

For another kind of breadth, there's always Random. Back when they were still something new, my wife won an iPod in a raffle. Won it. In a raffle. A 30 Gb iPod Classic. Although I was impressed with its smallness and smoothness and shininess, at first I couldn't be bothered with what seemed like yet another new-fangled smart-alec toy with its own sales stands in music shops, its own website and its own shopping-mall shrines of tasteful, overpriced accessories. Then everything changed. Someone I knew got an iPod and didn't have a computer, so I offered to help by putting a pile of my CDs and his CDs onto our computer to fill his iPod. It was a 4 Gb iPod nano and I got 868 songs on it. It was quite easy and it was quite fun, unlike my previous fumblings with MP3 technology that had left me exasperated and contemptuous after loading just 'Sex Machine' by James Brown and 'The Man Machine' by Kraftwerk.

During this introduction to iPodding, I became enthralled by the idea of so much music being crammed into something so tiny, and offered to start putting music onto my wife's iPod, which in the process became *our* iPod. It was claimed *our* iPod could hold about 7,000 songs and I'm a person who likes this kind of challenge. So I went though the CD shelves, at first quite selectively, then less so, and loaded a few piles, then a few more, and still there was room. By the time I had loaded almost 7,000 songs onto it, grudgingly leaving my wife a bit of space for podcasts of 'The Archers', I realised that I wanted – I needed – more storage space. I needed my own 160 Gb iPod (around 40,000 songs, supposedly), so I could visit everyone I knew, borrow all their CDs that I liked, or that I quite liked, or that I might want to hear, and upload them. So, apart from the fact that the iPod is such a small, smooth, shiny artefact and it's so easy to use, as if that wasn't enough, what changed my mind?

Partly the idea of acquiring so much music; acquiring it and having it and wondering at it and looking at it and comparing it and contrasting it and sharing it and loving it and listening to it. When I told my wife I was thinking of getting a 160 Gb iPod, she said, 'but you don't really need one', to which there are two possible answers, which may really be just one answer:

1. I've already filled 30 Gb; there's no space left, so of course I need one

and anyway

2. Who said anything about *need*? It's much deeper and more important than that.

Partly the fact that it's the same size as an audio cassette.

Partly because you can take this cassette-sized device anywhere and plug it into almost anything to enjoy a wide range of private and communal listening experiences.

Partly the realisation that loading music doesn't need a lot of agonising and decision making. When I was younger, I used to compile tapes. You got a cassette and you filled it with songs. You had to choose the right tunes and you had to make the right decisions, because you could only get a limited amount of music onto a cassette, so every tune counted and the wrong one could spoil everything, like the first track on *It's All Too Beautiful*. But all that has changed. A while ago I read *iPod, Therefore I Am* by Dylan Jones, in which he described spending hours and hours listening to the music he owned in order to decide whether or not to put it on his iPod. No, no. You don't need to do that. You don't need to agonise any more, because what do you put on an iPod? Everything – just throw it all in, shuffle it, *then* make your decisions by clicking 'next'.

Selecting, choosing, making all those decisions: it seems so pointless now. It's still the cassette paradigm, based on finity and limitation. I still do that when I'm compiling mix CDs, but the iPod is different, a new paradigm. What you do is put more or less *everything* on it as long as you don't actually hate it, then let the machine do the work – that's what machines are for.[17]

I can still choose an album and do a bit of linear listening, but the rest of the time I'm shuffling myself free of decision making, setting myself adrift in an ocean of music, within and without and between artists and genres and albums: turn off your mind, relax and float downstream. With 160 Gb it's no longer just a load of CDs – at some stage it acquired the critical mass that makes it more like a radio station – Radio Random. In the house, on the train, in the car, wherever I go, what I'm listening to is Radio Random. And although I originally chose everything myself, there's so much music on it that I can't remember what's there, and I never know what's coming next, which means most of the time I'm

- *delighted* – to hear again what I know and love, when it takes me by surprise
- *baffled* or *intrigued* – to hear what I don't know or don't remember, including all the bonus tracks, and the different versions of the same song, which are now okay. In shuffle mode you've got to think differently, be a bit perverse, a bit more eclectic: the more perverse and the more eclectic the merrier, the stranger and the better. So load all those freebies you keep meaning to listen to. Buy a few cheap 50s, 60s, 70s, or 80s compilations or greatest hits albums from charity shops and chuck them in as well because it all enriches the mulch, and stops it getting too serious or earnest or purist or exclusive or samey.
- *irritated* – to hear what I don't like, but never mind, it'll be over soon, and anyway it's all part of the mix, and maybe I'll end up liking it, though there are limits (whatever you might pretend, there are always limits)

---

17 Actually, there's still the work of loading everything into iTunes CD by CD, and of entering the album, track and artist information if it's wrong or not available online – am I doing something wrong, or is there really music that's too obscure to be listed?

- *amazed* – at the weird juxtapositions and connections that crop up when this many tunes are shaken and stirred together.

This is the joy, the tyranny, the adrenalin rush of music – new music, old music, more music, any music. It's music now and, it seems, music forever, a strange, wonderful, intoxicating, fascinating, baffling, overwhelming, evocative, seductive, addictive mix of ideas and sensations that's sometimes hard to make sense of.

But there are ways. A few years ago, someone told my wife about a music quiz, then she told me about it, and I got a team together. Because I work in a library our team was called Conan The Librarian, and that night we won. The quiz was to raise money for a local charity, and by the end of the evening I had volunteered for the charity: Inverness Hospital Radio.

After a period of shadowing and training I got my own 60-minute show, *Ten Items Or Less*.[18] It involved a weekly trip to the Digital Supermarket Of Song, leaving via the express checkout with no more than ten tunes in my basket, with any songs chosen from the 'Theme Of The Week' aisle subject to a generous discount. Being a bargain kind of person, it wasn't long before all the items in my basket were themed. Theming makes things easier and, I think, more interesting. It can generate complexity and surprise by jumping across genres and time periods in pursuit of subject matter, bringing together songs so disparate they would never otherwise appear on the same playlist. Although this is a convenient way to enrich the familiar by juxtaposing it with the novel and the strange, it's often ignored because most themed shows are based around a single decade or genre: what we really need is any music from any decade and any or no genre – as long as it somehow refers to clothes,

---

18 I know that strictly speaking it should be 'ten items or fewer', but some battles aren't worth fighting.

or colours of the rainbow, or the moon, or the sense of smell, or geometry, or the sea, or trains...

After a few more years and a broadcasting course, I heard about a local online community station that was looking for volunteers, and made the move to North Highland Radio. The Digital Supermarket Of Song closed its doors, and I became a driver and tour guide, leaving the ring-road and heading out onto *A Road Less Travelled* for two hours a week.[19] Of course the trip is themed: space, children, the colour red, the sense of touch, fire, history, metals, the weather, the sun, wildlife...[20]

I used to wonder what to do with this headful of music, and now I know: share it through broadcasting. Music is older than radio, older than recording, older than sheet music, and it's older than writing. So is broadcasting: the word goes right back to the dawn of history, when hunter-gatherers stopped their wandering and started living settled lives, which was when agriculture began. Originally, *broadcasting* referred to one of the earliest and simplest agricultural techniques, the sowing of seeds by casting them over broad areas of ground: effective, although not very efficient.

Although the familiarity of this idea from much earlier times gave the word a new meaning in the age of radio, its use as an image for spreading ideas can be seen much earlier – in the New Testament (Matthew 13), where Jesus tells a story about broadcasting, one that would be readily understood by people who lived in a region where agriculture began:

> A farmer went out to sow. As he scattered the seed, some fell along the path and the birds ate it. Some fell on stony ground without much soil. It grew quickly, but when the sun shone, it withered because the new plants had no roots. Other seeds fell among thorns, which grew up around the plants and choked them.

19 It used to be *The* Road Less Travelled – the change to *A* was made because there are many roads less travelled, not just one, and they all lead to different places.
20 See appendix twelve.

> Still other seed fell on good soil, where it produced a crop fifty or a hundred times what was sown. Whoever has ears, let them listen and hear.

So that's what I do: once a week I go out and sow music, scattering it across the airwaves and hoping for the best. You may ask yourself what kind of person would do this. The book you have just read is meant as an answer to that question: *an* answer, rather than *the* answer, because there are more answers than there are questions. Or are there more questions than answers? Sometimes it's hard to tell. What I do know it that there are at least as many roads as there are travellers. Some roads might seem hard to find, but they're not that hard; just get a different map, or draw your own, or throw away the one you're using and head for the horizon, the next motel, or the full moon. After all, it's about the journey, not the destination.

I've got a headful of music, and I am where I am on a road to somewhere or other. I'm also on the radio, and I've written a book. For the moment, this is where the story ends. Keep your ears peeled, thanks for listening, and good night.

Playlist 12 – The Ear Is A Hungry Ghost		
1984	David Bowie	*Diamond Dogs*
Sensoria (12")	Cabaret Voltaire	
Help Me Somebody	David Byrne and Brian Eno	*My Life In The Bush Of Ghosts*
Dark Star	Grateful Dead	*Live At Fillmore East, February 13-14, 1970*
Mr Pharmacist	The Fall	
Down Down	Status Quo	
Willow's Song	Magnet	*The Wicker Man (soundtrack)*
Your Hidden Dreams	White Noise	*An Electric Storm*
Rainbow Chaser	Nirvana	
The Man Machine	Kraftwerk	*The Man Machine*

To listen to the playlists, visit Spotify using the QR links provided.

Links to every playlist are also at www.hungry-ghost.info, along with photographs and archive material to supplement each chapter and enhance the reading/listening experience, just like a great big gatefold album cover.

APPENDIX ONE

OZYMANDIAS

I met a traveller from an antique land,
Who said: 'Two vast and trunkless legs of stone
Stand in the desert; near them, on the sand,
Half sunk, a shattered visage lies, whose frown,
And wrinkled lip, and sneer of cold command,
Tell that its sculptor well those passions read
Which yet survive, stamped on these lifeless things,
The hand that mocked[1] them, and the heart that fed;

And on the pedestal, these words appear:
"My name is Ozymandias, King of Kings;
Look on my works, ye mighty, and despair!"
Nothing beside remains. Round the decay
Of that colossal wreck, boundless and bare
The lone and level sands stretch far away.'

Percy Shelley, 1818

---

1 I learned this poem off by heart in a college library one lunchtime
to distract me from the apprehension I felt before teaching a class
of A-Level students. After puzzling for a long time over the word
mocked, I read in a commentary that it's being used here in the same
sense as in a *mock-up*, or model. So the sculptor's hand has carved or
modelled the passions of Ozymandias in stone, rather than ridiculing
them.

APPENDIX TWO
THE GOLDEN RECORD

1 Brandenburg Concerto No 2 in F, first   4:40
movement (1967)
Composer JS Bach
Performed by the Munich Bach Orchestra
Conductor Karl Richter

2 'Puspawarna' (Kinds Of Flowers) (1971)   4:43
Composer Mangkunegara IV
Performed by the Javanese court gamelan of
Pura Paku Alaman
Director KRT Wasitodipuro
Recorded by Robert E Brown

3 'Cengunmé' (1963)   2:08
Percussion and flute music
Performed by Mahi musicians of Benin
Recorded by Charles Duvelle

4 Alima initiation song (c 1951)   0:56
Performed by Mbuti ('pygmy') people of the
Ituri Rainforest, Democratic Republic of Congo
Recorded by Colin Turnbull

5 'Barnumbirr' (Morning Star) and 'Moikoi   1:26
Song' (previous title 'Devil Bird') (1962)
Aboriginal songs from Arnhem Land, Australia
Performed by Tom Djawa, Mudpo and
Waliparu
Recorded by Sandra Le Brun Holmes

6 'El Cascabel' (The Rattlesnake) (1957)   3:14
Composer Lorenzo Barcelata
Performed by Antonio Maciel and Los
Aguilillas with El Mariachi México de Pepe
Villa

7	'Johnny B Goode' (1958)	2:38
	Written and performed by Chuck Berry	
8	'Mariuamangi' (1964)	1:20
	Men's house song, Nyaura clan, Papua New Guinea	
	Performed by Pranis Padang and Kumbui	
	Recorded by Robert MacLennan	
9	'Sokaku-Reibo' (Cranes In Their Nest) (c 1967)	4:51
	Japanese shakuhachi (flute) music	
	Performed by Goro Yamaguchi	
10	'Gavotte En Rondeaux', Partita No 3 in E Major for Violin (1960)	2:55
	Composer JS Bach	
	Performed by Arthur Grumiaux	
11	'Queen Of The Night' aria from 'The Magic Flute' (1972)	2:55
	Composer WA Mozart	
	Performed by the Bavarian State Opera	
	Soprano Edda Moser	
	Conductor Wolfgang Sawallisch	
12	'Chakrulo' (date unknown)	2:18
	Georgian polyphonic folk song	
	Performed by Georgian State Ensemble	
	Soloists Ilia Zakaidze, Rostom Saginashvili	
	Director Anzor Kavsadze	
	Collected by Radio Moscow	
13	Roncadora music (previous title 'El Condor Pasa') (1964)	0:52
	Roncadora (flute and drum) music from Ancash region, Peru	
	Recorded by Jose Maria Arguedas	
14	'Melancholy Blues' (1927)	3:05
	Composers Marty Bloom and Walter Melrose	
	Performed by Louis Armstrong and his Hot Seven	
15	'Mugam' (c 1950)	2:30

Azerbaijan bagpipe music
Performed by Kamil Jalilov
Recorded by Radio Moscow

16   'Sacrificial Dance' from 'The Rite Of Spring'   4:35
     (1960)
     Composer and conductor Igor Stravinsky
     Performed by the Columbia Symphony
     Orchestra

17   'The Well-tempered Clavier', Book 2, Prelude   4:48
     and Fugue No 1 in C Major (1966)
     Composer JS Bach
     Pianist Glenn Gould

18   Symphony No 5 in C Minor, first movement   7:20
     (1955)
     Composer L van Beethoven
     Performed by the Philharmonia Orchestra
     Conductor Otto Klemperer

19   'Izlel Je Delyo Haydutin' (1968)   4:59
     Bulgarian bagpipe and vocal music
     Performed by Valya Balkanska, Lazar Kanevski
     and Stephan Zahmanov
     Recorded by Ethel Rain and Martin Koenig

20   Yeibichai dance and night chant (1942)   0:57
     Performed by Ambrose Roan Horse, Chester
     Roan and Tom Roan of the Navajo nation,
     Arizona
     Recorded by Willard Rhodes

21   'The Fairie Round' (1973)   1:17
     Composer Anthony Holborne
     Performed by Early Music Consort of London
     Director David Munrow

22   'Naranaratana Kookokoo' (The Cry Of The   1:12
     Incubator Bird) (date unknown)
     Panpipe music from Small Malaita, Solomon
     Islands
     Collected by the Solomon Islands Broadcasting
     Service

23   Wedding song (1964)   0:38

Performed by a young girl from Huancavelica
region, Peru
Recorded by John and Penny Cohen

24 ' Liu Shui' (Flowing Streams) (date unknown) 7:37
Chinese guqin (zither) music
Composer Bo Ya
Performed by Kuan Ping-hu

25 'Jaat Kahan Ho' (1953) 3:30
Vocal interpretation of Raag Bhairavi
Sung by Kesarbai Kerkar with tabla and
harmonium accompaniment

26 'Dark Was The Night, Cold Was The Ground' 3:15
(1927)
Written and performed by Blind Willie
Johnson

27 Cavatina from String Quartet No 13 in B Flat 6:37
(1960)
Composer L van Beethoven
Performed by the Budapest String Quartet

APPENDIX THREE
OCEAN OF SOUND

CD1

1	Dub Fi Gwan	King Tubby
2	Rain Dance	Herbie Hancock
3	Analogue Bubblebath 1	Aphex Twin
4	Empire III	John Hassell
5	Sorban Palid	Ujang Suryana
6	Prélude À L'Après-Midi D'un Faune	Claude Debussy
7	Sunken City	Les Baxter
8	Loomer	My Bloody Valentine
9	Lizard Point	Brian Eno
10	Shunie Omizutori Buddhist Ceremony	
11	The Music Of Horns And Whistles	Vancouver Sound Project
12	Howler Monkeys	
13	Machine Gun	Peter Brötzmann Quartet
14	Yanomami Rain Song	
15	Bismillah Rrahmani Rrahim	Harold Budd

CD2

1	Black Satin	Miles Davis
2	Poppy Nogood 'All Night Flight' (excerpt)	Terry Riley
3	Coyor Panon	Detty Kurnia
4	Virgin Beauty	Ornette Coleman
5	Chen Pe'i Pe'i	John Zorn and David Toop
6	Rivers Of Mercury	Paul Schütze

7	I Heard Her Call My Name	Velvet Underground
8	Bearded Seals	
9	Boat-Woman-Song	Holger Czukay and Rolf Dammers
10	Fall Breaks And Back Into Winter	Beach Boys
11	Faraway Chant	African Headcharge
12	Cosmo Enticement	Sun Ra
13	Untitled	Music Improvisation Company
14	Seven-Up	Deep Listening Band
15	In A Landscape	John Cage
16	Suikinkutsu Water Chime	

APPENDIX FOUR
LPS AND GIGS

Italic LPs have been sold; the rest I still have.

1973

Piledriver	*Status Quo*
Hello	*Status Quo*

1974

Brain Salad Surgery	*Emerson, Lake and Palmer*
Pictures At An Exhibition	Emerson, Lake and Palmer
Journey To The Centre Of The Earth	*Rick Wakeman*
Trilogy	*Emerson, Lake and Palmer*
Tubular Bells	Mike Oldfield
Emerson, Lake And Palmer	*Emerson, Lake and Palmer*
The Six Wives Of Henry VIII	Rick Wakeman
Tommy	The Who
Dark Side Of The Moon	Pink Floyd
Tarkus	*Emerson, Lake and Palmer*

Back Door / Emerson, Lake and Palmer

1975

Relics	Pink Floyd
Nursery Cryme	*Genesis*
Quadrophenia	The Who

Genesis Live	*Genesis*
Close To The Edge	Yes
Phaedra	Tangerine Dream
The Yes Album	Yes
Genesis	
Tangerine Dream	

1976

Foxtrot	Genesis
Live At Leeds	The Who
Selling England By The Pound	*Genesis*
Who's Next	The Who
Malpractice	Doctor Feelgood
Presence	Led Zeppelin
Odds And Sods	The Who
Ricochet	Tangerine Dream
The Snow Goose	*Camel*
Meddle	Pink Floyd
Down By The Jetty	*Doctor Feelgood*
Mirage	Camel
Led Zeppelin II	*Led Zeppelin*
Led Zeppelin IV	Led Zeppelin
Argus	Wishbone Ash
Relayer	*Yes*
Hello	Status Quo
Benefit	*Jethro Tull*
Trespass	*Genesis*
Blue For You	*Status Quo*
Still Life	Van der Graaf Generator
Stupidity	Doctor Feelgood
H To He Who Am The Only One	Van der Graaf Generator
Back Street Crawler	*Paul Kossoff*
Hergest Ridge	*Mike Oldfield*

Pawn Hearts — Van der Graaf Generator

Stand Up — *Jethro Tull*
The Faust Tapes — Faust
You — Gong
Flowers Of Evil — *Mountain*
L — Steve Hillage
Next — The Sensational Alex Harvey Band

Fish Rising — Steve Hillage
Tomorrow Belongs To Me — *The Sensational Alex Harvey Band*

Get Yer Ya-Yas Out — The Rolling Stones
The Impossible Dream — The Sensational Alex Harvey Band

Roogalator / Doctor Feelgood
Hazzard and Barnes / Camel
Rick Wakeman

Vice Versa / Eddie and the Hot Rods

Nova / Steve Hillage

1977
Camembert Electrique — Gong
Framed — The Sensational Alex Harvey Band

Godbluff — Van der Graaf Generator

In The Court Of The Crimson King — *King Crimson*
Agents Of Fortune — Blue Oyster Cult
Rattus Norvegicus — The Stranglers
Meaty, Beaty, Big And Bouncy — The Who
Lone Star — *Lone Star*
The Clash — The Clash
Rubycon — *Tangerine Dream*
In The City — The Jam

Marquee Moon	*Television*
Motivation Radio	Steve Hillage
Raw Power	Iggy and the Stooges
No More Heroes	*The Stranglers*
Damned, Damned, Damned	The Damned
Radio Gnome	*Gong*
Angel's Egg	*Gong*
Never Mind The Bollocks	The Sex Pistols
Rubycon	Tangerine Dream
Wish You Were Here	Pink Floyd
Boomtown Rats	Boomtown Rats

the Mutants / the Jam
the Drones / the Stranglers
Glenn Phillips / Steve Hillage

1978

Ramones	Ramones
Quark, Strangeness And Charm	Hawkwind
Heroes	David Bowie
Low	David Bowie
In the Court Of The Crimson King	King Crimson
Leave Home	Ramones
The Idiot	Iggy Pop
Lust For Life	Iggy Pop
Aqualung	*Jethro Tull*
Space Oddity	David Bowie
Burning Spear Live	Burning Spear
Green	*Steve Hillage*
Another Music In A Different Kitchen	Buzzcocks
Do It Dog Style	Slaughter and the Dogs
New Boots And Panties	*Ian Dury*
Tell Us The Truth	*Sham 69*
Black And White	The Stranglers
The Only Ones	The Only Ones
Power In The Darkness	*Tom Robinson Band*

Rocket To Russia	Ramones
Roadhawks	Hawkwind
The Stooges	The Stooges
High Tides And Green Grass	The Rolling Stones
Real Life	Magazine
Hunky Dory	David Bowie
Afrorock	Assagai
Pink Flag	Wire
Fulham Fallout	*The Lurkers*
Eternally Yours	*The Saints*
Clear Spot	Captain Beefheart
Bullinamingvase	*Roy Harper*
The Modern Dance	Pere Ubu
Ziggy Stardust	David Bowie
Plastic Letters	Blondie
Astounding Sounds, Amazing Music	*Hawkwind*
Lick My Decals Off, Baby	Captain Beefheart
It's About Time	*Tonto*
Kill City	Iggy Pop and James Williamson
Ultravox!	Ultravox!
The Man Machine	Kraftwerk
Zuma	Neil Young
Doremi Fasol Latido	Hawkwind
Aladdin Sane	David Bowie
Handsworth Revolution	Steel Pulse
TV Eye Live	Iggy Pop
The Man Who Sold The World	David Bowie
Suicide	Suicide
Harvest	Neil Young
No Future UK	Sex Pistols
Funhouse	The Stooges
The Image Has Cracked	Alternative TV
More Bob Dylan Greatest Hits	Bob Dylan
What You See Is What You Are	*Here and Now / Alternative TV*
Velvet Underground and Nico	*Velvet Underground*

Bob Marley And The Wailers Live	Bob Marley and the Wailers
Velvet Underground (double LP)	Velvet Underground
John Otway and Wild Willy Barrett	John Otway and Wild Willy Barrett
Chairs Missing	Wire
Diamond Dogs	David Bowie
Station To Station	David Bowie
Stiff's Live Stiffs	Stiff
Wilko Johnson	Wilko Johnson
So Alone	Johnny Thunders
Crossing The Red Sea	The Adverts
My Aim Is True	*Elvis Costello*
New York Dolls	New York Dolls
Give 'Em Enough Rope	the Clash
The Scream	Siouxsie and the Banshees
Love Bites	Buzzcocks
T Rex	T Rex
The Spotlight Kid	Captain Beefheart
Gary Glitter	*Gary Glitter*
Paranoid	*Black Sabbath*
Moving Targets	Penetration
All Mod Cons	The Jam
Two Sevens Clash	Culture

The Clash / Tom Robinson Band / Steel Pulse
Big in Japan / Penetration / Buzzcocks
Blitzkrieg Bop / Slaughter and the Dogs
National Health / Steve Hillage
Sham 69
The Germs / Penetration
Wire
Magazine
The Specials / The Clash
The Fall / Here and Now
The Automatics / The New Hearts / Radio Stars /
Penetration / Sham 69 / The Pirates / Ultravox! / The Jam

/// The Speedometers / The Business / Jenny Darren /
Next / Greg Kihn / Nutz / Gruppo Sportivo / Lindisfarne /
Spirit / The Motors / Status Quo /// After the Fire / Pacific
Eardrum / Chelsea / Bethnal / Squeeze / The Albion
Band / John Otway / Paul Inder / Ian Gillan Band / Tom
Robinson Band / Foreigner / Patti Smith
Tanz Der Youth
Elvis Costello
John Otway / NW10 / The No
Patrik Fitzgerald
The Innocents / The Slits / The Clash
Random Hold
The Innocents / The Slits / The Clash
Cygnus / Tapper Zukie

1979

Deep And Meaningless	*John Otway and Wild Willy Barrett*
Please Please Me	*The Beatles*
This Year's Model	*Elvis Costello*
Armed Forces	*Elvis Costello*
Metallic KO	Iggy and the Stooges
Ha!-Ha!-Ha!	Ultravox!
Inflammable Material	*Stiff Little Fingers*
Systems Of Romance	Ultravox
1969	Velvet Underground
Replicas	Tubeway Army
New Values	Iggy Pop
Unknown Pleasures	Joy Division
154	Wire
Public Image	PiL
Lodger	David Bowie
Transformer	Lou Reed
Undertones	The Undertones
Metal Box	PiL
Exposure	Robert Fripp
London Calling	The Clash

Gang of Four
Stiff Little Fingers / Essential Logic
Wire / Prag Vec
the Undertones
Those Naughty Lumps / SPG
The Skids
Patrik Fitzgerald
The Pretenders
The Fall
Girlschool / Motörhead
Jean Jacques Burnel
Iggy Pop / The Zones
Penetration
The Undertones
Elvis Costello / The Yachts
Bobby Henry / The Cramps / The Police
The Pop Group
The Human League
China Street / Wilko Johnson
The Teardrop Explodes
The Mekons
The Cramps / Pink Military
The Fall / Echo and the Bunnymen
Wire / Nightmare in Wax
Activity Minimal
The Purple Hearts
The Merton Parkas
Joy Division / Swell Maps
The Not Sensibles
Echo and the Bunnyrnen / The Teardrop Explodes / The
Expelaires
The Starjets
The Mods
Crass / Poison Girls
The Curves / The Stranglers
Artery / The Leyton Buzzards
Joy Division / Buzzcocks
The Selecter / Madness / The Specials

Gang of Four / The Au Pairs
Wilko Johnson
The Damned
Orchestral Manoeuvres in the Dark

1980

End Of The Century	Ramones
Nuggets	Psychedelic compilation
The 13th Floor Elevators	The 13th Floor Elevators
Horses	Patti Smith
A Nice Pair	Pink Floyd
Psychedelic Furs	Psychedelic Furs
Songs The Lord Taught Us	The Cramps
Machine Gun Etiquette	The Damned
The Doors	The Doors
God Save The Queen	Robert Fripp
Soldier	Iggy Pop
No Pussyfooting	Fripp and Eno
Betrayal	Jah Wobble
Bouquet Of Steel	Sheffield compilation
Live At The YMCA	Cabaret Voltaire
It's Alive	Ramones
Closer	Joy Division

The Clash
The Clash
The Boys / Ramones
Ramones
The Spiderz / Psychedelic Furs / lggy Pop
Joy Division
Disease / They Must Be Russians
Artery
Vendino Pact
Stunt Kites
The Cramps
Psychedelic Furs

Joy Division
Sexual Lotion / Vendino Pact
Veiled Threat / The Process
Reality / UB40
The Electric Tent Pegs / The Expelaires
The Teardrop Explodes
The Corridor / They Must Be Russians
Vice Versa
The Scarborough Antelopes / Disease / Artery / The
Process
Throbbing Gristle / Cabaret Voltaire
Deemus Mint / Pink Military
Echo and the Bunnymen
Veiled Threat
Artery / Grace Poole 5 / Nine Below Zero
The Naughtiest Girl Was A Monitor / De Tian / Vendino
Pact / Artery
The Stranglers
I'm So Hollow / Altered Images / Acrobats Of Desire /
Modern English / Clock Dva / Blah Blah Blah / Wasted
Youth / U2 / Echo and the Bunnymen / Siouxsie and the
Banshees /// Household Name / Naked Lunch / Vice Versa
/ Artery / The Frantic Elevators / Boots For Dancing /
The Flowers / Brian Brain / The Not Sensibles / Classix
Nouveaux / Tribesman / Blurt / The Soft Boys / Durutti
Column / Young Marble Giants / 4 Be 2 / Hazel O'Connor
/ Psychedelic Furs / Gary Glitter

APPENDIX FIVE
THE ROCK MACHINE

The Rock Machine Turns You On (1968)

Side 1

1	I'll Be Your Baby Tonight	Bob Dylan
2	Can't Be So Bad	Moby Grape
3	Fresh Garbage	Spirit
4	I Won't Leave My Wooden Wife For You, Sugar	The United States of America
5	Time Of The Season	The Zombies
6	Turn On A Friend	The Peanut Butter Conspiracy
7	Sisters Of Mercy	Leonard Cohen

Side 2

1	My Days Are Numbered	Blood, Sweat and Tears
2	Dolphins Smile	The Byrds
3	Scarborough Fair / Canticle	Simon and Garfunkel
4	Statesboro Blues	Taj Mahal
5	Killing Floor	The Electric Flag
6	Nobody's Got Any Money In The Summer	Roy Harper
7	Come Away Melinda	Tim Rose
8	Flames	Elmer Gantry's Velvet Opera

The MOJO Machine Turns You On 2018

1	Need A Little Time	Courtney Barnett
2	Cracker Drool	Goat Girl
3	Talking Straight	Rolling Blackouts Coastal Fever
4	Maraschino-Red Dress $8.99 At Goodwill	Ezra Furman
5	Curse Of The Contemporary	Lump
6	Telluride Speed	Ryley Walker
7	There's A Light	Jonathan Wilson
8	A Lifeboat	Kacy and Clayton
9	I'm Grateful	Brigid Mae Power
10	Ehad Wa Dagh	Imarhan
11	Evan Finds The Third Room	Khruangbin
12	Smile	Durand Jones and the Indications
13	Short Court Style	Natalie Prass
14	Not In Love We're Just High	Unknown Mortal Orchestra
15	Slow Fade	Daniel Avery

APPENDIX SIX
T-SHIRT

**you're gonna wake up
one morning and <u>know</u> what side
of the bed you've been lying on!**

Television (not the group)/Mick Jagger/The Liberal Party/
John Betjeman/George Melly/Kenny & Cash/Michael Caine/
Charles Forte/Sat nights in Oxford Street/SECURICOR –
impotence or complacency (slogan + Robert Carr)/Parking
tickets/19, Honey, Harpers, Vogue in fact all magazines
that treat their readers as idiots/Bryan Ferry/Salvador
Dali/A Touch of Class/BRUT for - who cares?/Peregrine
Worsthorne/Monty Modlyn/John Braine/Hughie Green/
The Presidents Men/Lord Carrington/The Playboy Club/
Alan Brien. Anthony Haden-Guest, Vic Lownes, to be
avoided first thing in the morning/ANTIQUARIUS and all
it stands for/Michael Roberts/POP STARS who are thick and
useless/YES/Leo Sayer/David Essex/Top Of The Pops/Rod
Stewart oh for money and an audience/Elton John - quote in
NME 25th Sept re Birthday spending/West End shopping/
Stirling Cooper, Jean Junction, BROWNS. Take Six, C&A/
Mars bars/Good Fun Entertainment when its really not
good or funny Bernard Delfont a passive audience/Arse
lickers/John Osborne Harry Pinter Max Bygraves Melvyn
Bragg Philip Jenkinson The ICA and its symposiums John
Schlesinger Andre Previn David Frost Peter Bogdanovich/
Capital Radio/The Village Trousershop (sorry bookshop)/
The narrow monopoly of media causing harmless creativity
to appear subversive/THE ARTS COUNCIL/Head of the
Metropolitan Police/Synthetic foods/Tate & Lyle/Corrupt
councillors/

G.K.N./Grey skies/Dirty books that aren't all that
dirty/Andy Warhol/Nigel Waymouth David Hockney and
 Victorianism/The Stock Exchange/Ossie Clark/The Rag
Trade/E.L.P./Antiques of any sort/Housing Trusts who
profit by bad housing/Bianca Jagger/Fellini/John
Dunbar/J. Arthur's/Tramps/Dingwalls without H/
Busby Berkeley MOVIES/Sir Keith Joseph and his
sensational speeches/National Front/ W. H. Smith
Censorship/Chris Welch and his lost Melody
Makers/Clockwork soul routines/Bob Harris (or
the Sniffling Whistler as we know him)/
The job you hate but are too scared to
pack in/Interview magazine - Peter
Lester/rich boys dressed as poor boys/
Chelita Secunda, Nicky Weymouth, June
Bolan, Pauline Fordham halitosis/Rose
& Anne Lambton Chinless people/
Antonia Frazer/Derek Marlow/Anne
Scott-James/Sydney Edwards/
Christopher Logue/Osbert
Lancaster/Shaw Taylor - whispering
grass/The Archers/BIBAS/Old
 clothes old ideas and all this
 just resting in the
 country business/The
suburbs/The Divine
Light Mission/All those
fucking saints.

Eddie
Cochran/
Christine Keeler/Susan
602 2509/My
monster in black
tights/Raw Power
Society For
Cutting Up Men/

RUBBER Robin Hood Ronnie Biggs BRAZIL
/Jamaican Rude Boys/Bamboo
Records/Coffee bars that
sell whiskey under the
counter/THE SCENE - Ham
Yard/Point Blank/Monica
the girl who stole those
paintings/Legal Aid - when
you can get it/Pat Arrowsmith
/Valerie Solanis/The Price
Sisters/Mervin Jones article The
Challenge To Capitalism in New
Statesman 4th Oct 74/Buenoventura
Durutti The Black Hand Gang/Archie
Shepp Muhammed Ali Bob Marley Jimi
Hendrix Sam Cooke/Kutie Jones and his
SEX PISTOLS/This country is run by a
group of fascists so said Gene Vincent in
a 1955 US radio interview/Seven Days
with Alexander Cockburn/Olympia Press
/Strange Death of Liberal England –
Dangerfield/Mrs Scully love goddess from
Shepherds Bush her house slaves and Search
magazine/Labour Exchanges as your local/FREE
RADIO stations/A chance to do it for more than a
month without being ripped off/The Anarchist Spray
Ballet/Lenny Bruce/Joe Orton/Ed Albee/Paustovsky/Iggy
Pop/John Coltrane/Spunky James Brown/Dewey Redman/
KING TUBBY'S sound system/Zoot suits and dreadlocks/
Kilburn & the High Roads/Four Aces Dalston/Limbo 90
- Wolfe/Tiger Tiger - Bester/Bizarre Humphries/Woolf -
Waves/Walt Whitman poet/Exupery, Simone de Beauvoir,
Dashiell Hammett, Dave Cooper, Nick Kent, Carl Gayle
writers/Mel Ramos painter/David Holmes the newsman/
Mal Dean cartoonist/Guy Stevens records/Mal Huff funny
stories/D.H./Valveamps/Art Prince/Marianne Faithfull/Jim
Morrison/Alex Trocchi - Young Adam/Patrick Heron v.

The Tate Gallery and all those American businesslike painters/Lady Sinthia 908 5569/ Experiment with Time - Dunne/John Lacey and his boiled book v. St Martin's Art School experiment to be seen in New York. Imagination............

APPENDIX SEVEN
31 SONGS

1	Your Love Is the Place Where I Come From	Teenage Fanclub
2	Thunder Road	Bruce Springsteen
3	I'm Like A Bird	Nelly Furtado
4	Heartbreaker	Led Zeppelin
5	One Man Guy	Rufus Wainwright
6	Samba Pa Ti	Santana
7	Mama, You Been On My Mind	Rod Stewart
8	Can You Please Crawl Out Your Window	Bob Dylan
9	Rain	The Beatles
10	You Had Time	Ani DiFranco
11	I've Had It	Aimee Mann
12	Born For Me	Paul Westerberg
13	Frankie Teardrop	Suicide
14	Ain't That Enough	Teenage Fanclub
15	First I Look At The Purse	J Geils Band
16	Smoke	Ben Folds Five
17	A Minor Incident	Badly Drawn Boy
18	Glorybound	The Bible
19	Caravan	Van Morrison
20	So I'll Run	Butch Hancock and Marce LaCouture
21	Puff The Magic Dragon	Gregory Isaacs
22	Reasons To Be Cheerful, Part 3	Ian Dury and the Blockheads
23	Calvary Cross	Richard and Linda Thompson

24	Late For The Sky	Jackson Browne
25	Hey Self-Defeater	Mark Mulcahy
26	Needle In A Haystack	The Velvelettes
27	Let's Straighten It Out	OV Wright
28	Röyskopp's Night Out	Röyskopp
29	Frontier Psychiatrist	The Avalanches
30	No Fun / Push It	Soulwax (Salt 'n' Pepa / the Stooges)
31	Pissing In A River	Patti Smith Group

APPENDIX EIGHT
HADO WATER

http://www.hado-energy.com/about_hado.php

Researcher Dr Masaru Emoto, chief of the Hado institute in Tokyo… has discovered an effect on water that was given the name the 'Hado' effect. He describes it as follows, quote: 'Hado is the intrinsic vibration pattern at the atomic level in all matter, the smallest unit of energy. Its basis is the energy of human consciousness'…

… Water was his subject of study and he started out studying the shape of water ice crystals… He noticed that water from heavy polluted rivers doesn't crystallize at all and that clean mineral spring water produces beautiful ice crystals when frozen.

So far so good, it is a result that may be expected. However to his amazement he discovered that the crystallization of the water molecules was somehow related to his mood…

Next he experimented with all kinds of music to test the effect. Music is a natural expressing of vibrations and it was no longer a surprise that the vibrations of lovely classical music versus aggressive angry hard rock music were also reflected in the ice crystals.

http://hado.com/ihm/water-crystals/

We played music to water and observed water crystals. Perhaps it is not a human who listen to music but it is water in the human listen to music.

John Lennon 'Imagine'
Prelude a l'apres-midi d'un faune by Debussy
'La Mer' by Debussy
Mendelssohn's 'The wedding march'
The Sound of Music 'Edelweiss'
'Amazing Grace'
Schubert's 'Ave Maria'
Tchaikovsky's 'Swan Lake'
Vivaldi's 'The Four Seasons'
'The Blue Danube' by Johann Strauss II
Pachelbel's 'Canon'

https://www.quantumbalancing.com/hado_water.htm

Here are some steps you can take to prepare and drink the HADO water.

1. Buy some mineral water. If you can find some in a glass container, that's best. The plastic containers leach plasticizers into the water that pollute it. Tap water is hard to purify because the chlorine seems to affect the structure even after the chlorine evaporates according to Dr Emoto's research.
2. Keep a gallon or two of mineral water in front of a music source where you can play purifying water music. In Dr Emoto's two books, you can find out the names of various symphonies and songs that produce great crystals. Some of these musical sources of HADO include Beethoven's Ninth, John Lennon's 'Imagine', and 'Amazing Grace'…
3. Prepare a HADO bottle of water… Cut out small pieces of paper (about 3" by 5"). Write messages on the pieces of paper. One message should be 'Love and Gratitude' … Tape these messages onto the outside of the container so that they face inward towards the water … Keep this HADO jar full of mineral water that has been in front of your speakers that have been vibrating with high HADO music …

4. Drink as often as possible from the HADO jar and refill it. Drink the amount of water that's healthy for you. But try to get as much of that water as possible from this jar. You can carry some of the water with you when you are away from your source.
5. Be thankful as you drink the water.

APPENDIX NINE
RADIO SOULWAX

1	Peter Gunn / Where's Your Head At	Emerson, Lake and Palmer / Basement Jaxx
2	Fuck The Pain Away	Peaches
3	I'm Waiting For The Man	Velvet Underground
4	J'Aime Regarder Les Mecs	Polyester
5	I Wanna Be Your Dog	Dakar and Grinser
6	Disko Kings	Ural 13 Diktators
7	The 'O' Medley / Silver Screen (Shower Scene)	Bobby Orlando / Felix Da Housecat
8	No Fun / Push It	Stooges / Salt 'n' Pepa
9	Joe Le Taxi / Crush On You (A Capella)	Hanayo with Jürgen Paape / The Jets
10	Funkacise / Motocross Madness / French Kiss	Funkacise Gang / Soul Grabber / Lil' Louis and the World
11	Serious Trouble	Zongamin
12	Androgyny 'Thee Glitz Mix' by Felix Da Housecat	Garbage
13	Disc Jockey's Delight Vol 2 / Kaw-Liga (Prairie Mix)	Frank Delour / The Residents
14	Shake Your Body	Carlos Morgan

15	Into The Stars (Firebirds Remix)	Alphawezen
16	Concepts/ 99 Luftballons	Insterstellar / Nena
17	Independent Woman Part 1 (A Capella) / Dreadlock Holiday	Destiny's Child / 10cc
18	9 to 5 / Epie	Dolly Parton / Roysköpp
19	Death Disco	Arbeid Adelt
20	Keine Melodien	Jeans Team Featuring DJ Lan
21	I Wish (A Capella) / My Gigolo / Cannonball	Skee-Lo / Maurice Fulton presents Stress / The Breeders
22	Human Fly	The Cramps
23	Danger! High Voltage	Electric Six
24	Don't Bring Me Down	Op:l Bastards
25	Hand To Phone	Adult
26	La Rock 01	Vitalic
27	I Was Made For Loving You	Queens Of Japan
28	The Beach / Sandwiches (A Capella)	New Order / Detroit Grand Pubahs
29	I Sit On Acid (Soulwax Remix)	Lords of Acid
30	Start Button	Streamer featuring Private Thoughts in Public Places

APPENDIX TEN
FABRICLIVE 07

'This CD isn't supposed to be mood-establishing. If anything, it's mood-demolishing. These are some of my favourite songs... there's a real risk I'll listen to nothing else ever again.' (John Peel)

1	Hana (excerpt) BBC commentary, 1981 European Cup Final, Liverpool vs Real Madrid (excerpt)	Asa-Chang and Junray Peter Jones
2	Break 'Em On Down	The Soledad Brothers
3	Late Night Blues	Don Carlos
4	Hipsteppin'	MC Det
5	Needle In A Haystack	The Velvelettes
6	Lust For Life	The Bad Livers
7	Let's Get Small	Trouble Funk
8	There's A Moon Out Tonight	The Capris
9	Mr Pharmacist	The Fall
10	15.5 Remake	Smith and Selway
11	Too Much	Jimmy Reed
12	In The Midnight Hour	Maloko
13	Moon Hop	Derrick Morgan
14	In Love	The Datsuns
15	Purty Vacant	The Kingswoods
16	Liar	Sinthetix
17	Lion Rock (John Peel Session)	Culture
18	Tom The Peeper	Act 1

19	Love Will Tear Us Apart	Joy Division
	BBC commentary, 1978 European Cup Final, Liverpool vs FC Bruges (excerpt)	Alan Parry
20	Clock	Elementz Of Noise
21	Corn Rigs Tunes	The Cheviot Ranters
22	Identify The Beat	Marc Smith vs Safe 'n' Sound
23	You'll Never Walk Alone	The Kop Choir
24	Teenage Kicks	The Undertones

APPENDIX ELEVEN
BUGGED IN SELECTION

1	Passing Through	Rare Bird
2	Love Me Now	And The Lefhanded
3	Miss You	The Concretes
4	Willow's Song	Magnet featuring Paul Giovanni
5	Your Hidden Dreams	White Noise
6	End Of A Love Affair	Julie London
7	Overnight	Gonzales
8	Obsessed With Gloom	Campag Velocet
9	Vapour Trail	Trespassers William
10	Lollipop Minds	Wimple Winch
11	Rainbow Chaser	Nirvana
12	Birds	M83
13	Kuschelrock	DJ Koze
14	Love Movement (Ulrich Schnauss Remix)	Justin Robertson Presents Revtone
15	Just An Illusion	Imagination
16	Holland Tunnel Dive	impLOG
17	Come Into Our Room	Clinic
18	Big City (Remix)	Spacemen 3

APPENDIX TWELVE
PLAYLIST: WILDLIFE

	Song	Artist	Album
1	Stone Fox Chase	Area Code 615	Delta Swamp Rock – Sounds From The South
2	Ride A White Swan	T Rex	The Ultimate Collection
3	Bewick's Swan	British Library	British Bird Sounds
4	Twentieth Century Fox	The Doors	The Doors
5	Moanin' At Midnight	Howlin' Wolf	The Devil's Music
6	Download Sofist	Mouse On Mars	Niun Niggung
7	Nyimbo Nakawasu	The New Black Eagles	Zimbabwe Frontline
8	Big Ten Inch Record	Bullmoose Jackson	Rhythm & Blues II (1942-52)
9	Red Deer Stag Roar	Chris Watson	Outside The Circle Of Fire
10	The Fox Has Gone To Ground	Bamboo Shot	Nightmares In Wonderland (Rubble 3)
11	Male Capercaillie Display	Chris Watson	Outside The Circle Of Fire
12	Pallin' With Al	Squirrel Nut Zippers	Swing Around The World
13	Your Protector	Fleet Foxes	Fleet Foxes
14	Wolf Kidult Man	The Fall	Imperial Wax Solvent

	Song	Artist	Album
15	The Galaxist	Deefhoof	Wake Up! New North American Indie
16	New Moon At Red Deer Wallow	Rain Tree Crow	Ambient 2: Imaginary Landscapes
17	Wolf In The Breast	Cocteau Twins	Heaven Or Las Vegas
18	Beetle	Paul Giovanni	The Wicker Man (Soundtrack)
19	Death-watch Beetles	Chris Watson	Outside The Circle Of Fire
20	Dire Wolf	Grateful Dead	Workingman's Dead
21	(Get A) Grip (On Yourself)	The Stranglers	Rattus Norvegicus
22	Moondog's Symphony 1 (Timberwolf)	Moondog	The Viking Of Sixth Avenue
23	Wildlife Analysis	Boards Of Canada	Music Has The Right To Children
24	A Public Execution	Mouse	Nuggets: Original Artyfacts...
25	Viva Super Eagles	Super Eagles	African Funk
26	Crow Jane	Carl Martin	Good Morning Blues
27	Dirty Horse	Gram Rabbit	Strange Country
28	Trouble In My Way	The Swan Silvertones	The Roots Of Drone
29	White Belly Rat	Jah Lloyd	Build The Ark: With Lee Perry & Friends

	Song	Artist	Album
30	Reynardine	Fairport Convention	Liege & Lief
31	White Belly Rat	Lee Perry	Build The Ark: With Lee Perry & Friends
31	Reynardine	Archie Fisher	Electric Eden: Unearthing Britain's Visionary Music
32	The Salmon Song	Steve Hillage	Fish Rising

Printed in Poland
by Amazon Fulfillment
Poland Sp. z o.o., Wrocław